Hopping for Unconsciousness

by

Dave Hodson

**Warning: contains punctuation.
Not for persons under 36 years of age.**

**This book is best read within three days of
opening.**

Published by Dave Hodson (dave@mweffle.co.uk)

Editing: Dave Hodson.
Cover design: Dave Hodson.
Cover photography: Dave Hodson.
Typesetting: Dave Hodson.
Proffreading: Dave Hoddson.

A Mweffle enterprise.

Set in Georgia 10/12.5.

Cover set in Belligerent Madness
(Font Monkey, courtesy of pmagnus@fecundity.com)
and **Nobile Bold** (Vernon Adams).
Cover fonts obtained from www.fontsquirrel.com.

Printed by CreateSpace, an Amazon.com company.

Available from Amazon.com, CreateSpace.com, and other
retail outlets.

www.CreateSpace.com/6020372

Preface

This is a work of fiction. No resemblance is intended to any persons or animals alive or dead[1], companies or corporations solvent or insolvent, products, processes, institutions, organisations, societies, football clubs, religions, cults or other belief systems. In fact, even quite a lot of the words don't bear much resemblance to anything in the dictionary.

It's dedicated to Jill and Nix, to Oreo our cat, to the nice people who keep the shelves of the Co-op topped-up with bottles of Merlot, and to the high wild places of the north. (So many dedications promised, so little time...)

I would also like to thank the following for help, inspiration and encouragement: Paul & Sue Armstrong, Adriana Baber, Sue Baker, Zoe Barber, Mark Blamire, Rich Brewer, Andrew Bryant, Chris Carter, Mike Chappelle, Paul Charnock, Elizabeth & Mark Chivers, Pete Cork, David & Trish Courtman, Tony Davis, Howard Dawson, Sarah Dexter, Mavis & Nev Fowles, George Fradley, Danny Gaunt, Mike Gibbs, Lindsay Greer, Ted Hayes, Stephen Helm, Julie Hibbert, Geoff Hicks, Steve Howgill, Karen Hunt, Ruth & Simon Love, Simon Mason, Lesley McKenzie, Dave Naegeli, Fay Parker, Gail Pritchett, Graham Purkins, Dave Robbins, Zoe Rogers, Peter Scholes, Adam Stuart, Kerry Tilley, Richard Toon, Bob Wallis, Fiona Watson, Julia Wherrell, Betty Whitchurch, Sarah Whyld, Matt Wilby, Lesley Williams, Grae Woollett, and of course Nix and Jill. (There, that should be at least fifty copies sold!)

I would like to state categorically, incidentally, that any errors or flaws in this book are entirely the fault of the people named above. Any genius it modestly possesses was down to me alone. Thank you.

DH, UK, 2016.

---

[1] Apart from the Duke of Wellington and one or two others, who are or were well known and instantly recognisable nationally famous British figures, but who are used here entirely fictionally.

Although the rotation of the earth is cunningly arranged so that every point on the planet gets an equal amount of daylight over the course of a year, Wormhouses was one of the places that didn't. This was because it was located in a hole, or to be more precise at the bottom of a deep and dank gorge cut into the surrounding limestone plateau by the River Wurum. Some properties in Wormhouses were so badly sited that they never saw direct sunlight, and indeed got precious little light at all for most of the year. One such building was a rather battered pub, adrift in the middle of a large car park in which a solitary car was self-consciously parked.

Crunching their way across the rough gravel towards the hostelry were two men. Ian, the younger and taller of the two, led the way. Strong from all the sporting activities at which he excelled, with a healthy suntan from weekends spent taking a variety of friends and girlfriends to sea on his boat on the south coast, he looked the very image of relaxed self-assurance. His broad face and chiselled features exuded a mix of calm competence and friendliness. Indeed he was both in generous measure. He was debonair, charming, witty, intelligent and popular. In short, he was Mr Perfect. Or he would have been, had his Ph.D. from Cambridge not made him Dr Perfect.

How I hate people like that. Luckily, though, the hero of this book is actually the slightly flustered chap at his side. Steve was not so perfect, not by quite a long way. His story is one of weaknesses and hang-ups; of awkward moments and pained anguish. It might be a tale of great adventure – it *might* – but it's also a tale of real life, with its problems, disappointments and miseries; all part of the rocky path we trudge through this vale of tears, until overtaken by sweet, sweet death.

Anyway, back to the plot, as it's a little soon for me to lose it just yet. Two men. One pub. Two hundred million pieces of gravel. Such a gentle peaceful scene, poetically completed by the last remnants of daylight turning to gloom and by the soft hooting of an owl flying off with the discarded cheeseburger that it had just caught.

Pausing only to trip over his own feet and to step into a small September puddle, Steve hurried after Ian. He couldn't help being clumsy, he always told himself: it was in his blood. It might have got there on the occasion when his father managed to lift him from his cot in the nursery and drop him straight onto a carelessly discarded set of chisels. Or it might have been related to the fact that he happened to come from a long succession of ancestors whose last words had been 'Damn' or 'Oops'. It was a wonder his gene line hadn't died out back around the time the dinosaurs were being hounded to extinction by the first small shrew-like mammals. (Hey, everyone's entitled to their own crazy theory.)

Although Steve was not as good looking or socially polished as Ian, and although his engagement diary was never as full, that's not to say that he was the complete opposite of Ian. It's just that Steve was rather more average. With his slightly thinning just-past-forty hairline and with a slightly lined father-of-two face that could best be described as functional, he was not the sort of person anyone would much notice in most circumstances. For two strangers to walk into the public bar of the Infected Follicle was not entirely most circumstances however. For one thing, not many people ever visited the backwater in which it squatted, and for a second thing not many of those who did were ever tempted into its one hostelry with its all too graphic sign.

The journey to get there hadn't exactly been Steve's finest hour, especially considering that Ian's satnav had been only three days old when Steve had spilt coffee on it, but at least they were there now, and Steve was determined to put the traumas of the day behind him and to have a relaxing drink or three. Of course, getting a drink did rely on the place still being in business, and even when they pushed against the door and discovered that it was, there was something about the Infected Follicle and its clientele that made Steve wonder whether strangers were truly madly deeply welcome. The slow stares from the locals and their mid-sentence silence didn't exactly bode well. Neither did the solid middle aged man with an open shirt and several serpenty sorts of tattoos who stood behind the bar. He appeared to be the only person serving, and as the two men wound their way past the obstacle course of tables, chairs and squashed chips that guarded his lair, his narrowed eyes never left them.

'Yes?' he enquired gruffly. It was more of a threat than a question.

'We've booked two rooms for the night,' said Steve, trying to sound self-assured, respectable, friendly, down-to-earth, and a thoroughly good bloke. And if only he'd remembered to clear his throat before he started, the first two words wouldn't have come out as a strangulated squeak.

'Oh, and I, we, er, wondered whether it would be possible to get, eat, have, er, some food here? Er, please?' he added, trying to cover his embarrassment at sounding like a mid-pubertal schoolboy.

'You can. And do you and your friend and that frog you're gargling want some drinks?' The man seemed to have a cruelty to his unfriendliness, Steve noted with a sinking feeling as he felt his cheeks redden. The landlord winked at the other clientele. They both grinned back, in a curiously uncurious kind of a way. It wasn't often much happened in the Follicle, and this was as entertaining as it ever usually got. They always enjoyed trying to follow bits of Terry's exchanges with strangers.

Steve managed to corral his vocal cords into ordering a couple of pints of lager, a chicken curry and a beef and ale pie, and went over to the table that Ian had chosen in the corner by the bar. Ian flashed him an empathetic, and of course perfect, smile, causing his colleague to shrivel inwardly. It was bad enough feeling like a clown with two left feet, but Ian's sympathy made him feel like he used to feel every time that he had yet again disappointed his parents with some missed achievement or other. Nothing had ever been said, and their looks had always been kind beyond depth, which of course had made the hurt all the deeper. It bothered him still; he could almost feel the tears welling up again now as he sank into the tatty leather chair.

Steve Oscroft. Twenty-six years old, dynamic, decisive, almost brilliant. Unfortunately, that was fifteen years ago and now he was forty-one (in case you can't do maths). How quickly those years had gone by: how rapidly his career had progressed from Bright Young Thing to Oldest Fool On The Block. He'd given SLSL what would have been the best years of his life if he hadn't spent them working at SLSL.

Actually, considering it a little more carefully, he hadn't been dynamic or decisive or the teensiest bit brilliant even back when he was twenty-six. He was getting himself mixed up with someone else, now that he thought about it. Another Ian, by one name or another.

He looked around and took stock of the room. By the looks of the place, it didn't appear that it either got or expected much custom. The landlord did seem to be doing a special offer of a free cobweb with every drink, but even that hadn't exactly pulled the crowds in. The jukebox was clearly in a state of disrepair, and the framed clippings from the local newspaper that adorned the walls dated back nearly twenty years. The one closest to Steve was a story about an elderly local woman who carved oranges into animal shapes using her teeth. This wasn't really the kind of place he had been expecting. Alex Deese had made it sound like the sort of establishment that got featured in lifestyle magazines, not the sort of place with a fascination for stories about mad old women with citrus obsessions. Why hadn't Steve checked it out a bit more carefully before he booked the rooms? What on earth was Ian thinking now? Senior Sales Managers were used to five stars, not five inches of dust, for goodness sake. Why oh why had Steve relied on someone from Accounts to recommend somewhere to stay? What a classic, fundamental schoolboy error. He glanced over, but his colleague was diplomatically studying a cutting about weasel trekking, with a good humoured and tolerant smile on his face.

'Is this project going the way of the last three?' asked Ian suddenly, interrupting the death spiral of depression that was starting somewhere inside Steve's head. 'If this meeting tomorrow doesn't show a bit more customer interest, then I really think we should consider pulling the plug.'

Steve most definitely didn't want this project to go the way of the last three. Only twelve months ago he'd been working on four separate development projects, each of them rated as Alpha by his boss, Barry, who had taken a particular interest in them. Well, he'd been interested enough to contribute the project names – during the period when he'd been going through a bird and animal phase – and had also occasionally proffered what he called advice and the team members called unhelpful interference. But unfortunately Projects Albatross, Possom and Dodo had all died in turn, and now only one project was left. None of that had been Steve's direct fault, of course, but he knew that he could have done more to achieve success, if only he'd had the time to focus on things a bit. Technology development was never easy, of course, but he felt that he would be letting everyone down if Project Lemming also failed.

'I think we can make it work,' said Steve, knowing that neither he nor Ian would really believe him.

'Even with that problem with the sealing lacquer?'

'Well...' Steve pulled out a bundle of papers from his briefcase. On the top sheet was a list of things that needed doing if Lemming was to be saved. Somewhere on the list was something about lacquer testing experiments, but Steve was rather sensitive to the possibility that more than half his time got frittered away making lists, and lists of lists, and lists of lists of lists, and that perhaps that was somehow related to the fact that he never seemed to get anything done and to the fact, or at least the very strong suspicion, that Ian's career was going to go further than his own was. He stuffed the sheaf of papers away and closed his mouth.

'I don't know,' he admitted, remembering to open his mouth again for vocal convenience. 'We have a few things that we need to work on.'

The food arrived at that moment, so Steve earned a reprieve and time to collect his thoughts. Principal amongst them was the thought that his chicken curry looked distinctly unappetising. Certainly, the odd protruding downy feather offered reassurance that it was indeed chicken, but the accompanying vegetables looked as if they had long since passed their prime, and the whole creation wore a decidedly deadpan expression. Ian's pie looked rather nicer, and for some reason came with a much fresher looking selection of veg. Steve wondered whether he would say something to the proprietor, but one glance in his direction persuaded him that it might not be a positive experience, so instead he took a first reluctant mouthful of the curry. That brought a fresh discovery of some unpleasantness, but Steve didn't send it back, because he preferred his food cold rather than spat in.

They ate in silence for some minutes, Ian complimented the chef and ordered another round of drinks, Steve chewed his way through his dinner, and the two locals across the room played dominoes, very slowly. Ian told a few amusing anecdotes about past customer meetings, usually in grand hotels in exotic locations, Steve told a couple of long stories that each ended with the line 'You had to be there', and the locals sat and scratched themselves. Eventually, midway through Steve's account of the failure of Project Glory a few years earlier, Ian stood up and said that he had to go and get some money out and also telephone a couple of important contacts, if Steve didn't mind?

'Is there a cashpoint machine anywhere around here?' Ian asked the landlord.

'You could try the one over in Barton-in-the-Roadworks,' suggested one of the domino players, 'It's the next village along the road.' He took a sip of something that looked like pond. 'Mind you, it can be difficult to reach when the cones are in full bloom.'

'OK, we'll call there in the morning, before the meeting,' said Ian, and with a brief 'Goodnight' went to fetch the bags from the car and then retired to his room. Steve was left alone with the dregs of his second drink, and the bill, and his thoughts.

He was going to raise his game. He was going to start hitting winners. He was going to seize the day.

He was going to stop thinking in clichés.

***

Morning came early to Steve, who had spent a rather disturbed night mentally struggling with what he was going to do differently for his new beginning. Most of his resolutions had been along the lines of things he was already trying to do, and all of them probably required reserves of time and energy that he didn't really have. In the cold light of dawn his plans seemed about as well thought-out as a dead-end one-way street. He lay there for a while, staring thoughtfully at the ceiling with its covering of those expanded polystyrene tiles that were popular in the seventies until someone worked out what they did in a fire. For now, his immediate priority was making the day's meeting a success. After that, he could go back and sort out Lemming's technical problems.

He joined Ian for breakfast at the same table at which they'd eaten the evening before. In what passed for daylight, the bar looked somewhat more welcoming than it had done. Even the arrangement of trampled food on the carpet had quite a cheerful familiarity now. They discussed tactics for the meeting, checked through their presentation materials, and then went to get their things and check out. The landlord hadn't improved in affability with the dawn of the new day, but with the magic that is money even he managed a slight smile as Steve settled his bill.

To save acquaintance with the roadworks, Ian decided to postpone his diversion to the cash machine, borrowing sixty pounds from Steve instead, and they drove straight to the head-quarters of Abbotang Industries, a few miles further east. The meeting was not the success that Steve had needed and for which they had both hoped. They had arrived in good time, despite a minor navigational disturbance, and had been led into a lavish waiting area furnished with deep soft armchairs and studded with immense glossy plants. The room was hung with pictures of clearly great expense but rather limited artistic merit. The wall facing Steve was dominated by an enormous watercolour of two people, painted by someone who had obviously never seen one. If Natalie had brought something like that home from school, Steve would probably have ripped it up and asked Miss Blatherspit to confiscate her paints.

As they had arrived rather early, the receptionist had offered them coffees, and a combination of that and the fast-flowing water-feature in the middle of the room sent Steve off on a search for the toilets. Unfortunately that had turned a surplus of time into a significant deficit as it took him something like ten minutes to find his way back through the maze of stairs and doors. He arrived to find that Ian had already gone into the meeting, via a quick visit to the gents that had been right behind them. He entered just as Ian was making a promise he knew they would struggle to keep. Technically, it would be a challenge. Commercially, it would be marginal. Doing it in the six months that Ian was suggesting, it would be a near impossibility. But he couldn't correct Ian in front of potential customers, and in any case he could hardly blame the sales manager for portraying things in such a positive light when he himself had kept quiet about some of the key technical problems that Project Lemming still needed to overcome. Not that they gave Abbotang their internal code name, of course. To customers, it was known as the 1Sr14B Sensor project. Barry's code names were only ever for internal use. Barry was the only one who ever forgot that rule.

Steve's presentation went reasonably smoothly – he certainly knew his technical stuff well enough, having wrestled with Lemming for so long now – but it was clear by the end of the meeting that Abbotang weren't going to wait for resolution of the remaining issues and weren't going to pay the price that it was likely to cost. After all, they needed to save their money for expensive paintings, potted rainforest, and splashy water fea-tures. It looked like another contract that either Senssertive or Sensandetect Ltd. would win. It was disappointing, and in the light of some of Ian's comments of the previous evening it seemed likely that he would be questioning the project's future at the next management meeting. If major potential customers weren't showing much interest, Management was unlikely to allow them yet another six months to sort out the manufacturing difficulties.

They steered clear of discussion of work on the long drive home, however. Ian chatted amiably about some of his sailing trips and about some of the great times he had had with his large circle of friends. Steve didn't have a circle of friends. He had a triangle of friends. If he included himself. And his next holiday wouldn't be spent exploring the coast of Brittany but investigating the reason his drains kept smelling so bad. His one consolation was that his next door neighbour was in the business and might be willing to help him.

His thoughts were interrupted by Ian's suggestion that they find a radio station to listen to, but Steve's button-pushing and knob-twiddling efforts only provided some teenage band trying to sing a song about the emotional poignancy of human experience. From the few lyrics that Steve could make out for sure, it appeared that their experience was limited to problems sending text messages to one another. He managed to find one other channel, where someone called Prod was singing something called '*Wossit and Why?*', which was, frankly, no better.

They gave up on entertainment and sat in silence for most of the rest of the way back to Steve's house, where Ian dropped him off. Steve did invite him in, but he made an excuse and drove off, with a cheerful reminder to finish development of Lemming before the year three thousand.

Chloe was asleep in bed, Natalie was at a friend's house for a sleepover, and Jackie was watching Part Eighty-One of some gripping costume drama on the television when Steve got in, so he went to the kitchen, boiled the kettle, dropped and broke one of the mugs that had come free with some breakfast cereal, and made himself a cup of coffee. He sorted out the papers in his briefcase, unpacked his overnight bag, and went upstairs for an early night and some much needed sleep, calling in to the lounge briefly to tell Jackie how it had gone.

'Shh, I need to follow this next bit.'

'Sorry,' said Steve, and retreated upstairs. Another day was over; tomorrow could only be better.

***

SLSL developed and made state-of-the-art sensors, and sold them for premium prices to blue-chip companies. Whatever blue-chip companies were: Steve wasn't quite sure and had meant for some years to look it up, but never quite did. The sensors they made were of all types: temperature probes for demanding applications; strain gauges for extreme environments; accelerometers for, er, measuring acceleration; you name it, SLSL did it. What they all had in common was that they all pushed the bounds of sensitivity, and that they were all pigs to develop. The industries that used them were willing to pay good prices, and often bought them in quantities of hundreds of thousands, but their specifications got ever more demanding and SLSL's competition got ever sharper at beating them to contracts. And somewhere in the middle of all this, trying to coordinate impossible deadlines, inadequate resources, undeliverable deliverables, unhelpful suppliers, and un-cooperative laws of science, was Steve. Aided and abetted of course by the small team of highly skilled colleagues of which he was proud to be part.

'Where's Simon?' he asked, as he entered the shared open-plan office area the next morning.

'He's at the doctor's. He got a nasty splinter in his eye when he was playing with his shatter-proof ruler yesterday,' reported Darren, with a possible hint of relish.

'Oh. Oh dear. Is Lisa in yet, then?'

'No. She's coming in after she's been de-wormed.'

Steve was pretty sure that that was a reference to Lisa's cat, but it didn't do to dwell too much on the subject of Lisa Hemsley when Darren was around. He hadn't forgiven her yet for ending their relationship some three months earlier, and from what Steve knew of him, he suspected that he never would.

'Well, can *you* help me then?' Steve asked, 'I need someone to recheck when those lacquer experiments are going to be finished. Has the oven been sorted out yet?'

'I don't know why you're bothering,' grumbled Darren. 'That oven's never worked properly since Simon used it to melt that plastic packaging all over my best Albatross prototype, and there's no way that your stupid lacquer is ever going to be a proper seal on something that flexes as much as that probe head does.'

'By lunchtime, please,' Steve requested wearily. 'I've promised Ian Firth that we'll have it sorted within two weeks.'

'Pah!' exclaimed Darren, which seemed to mean 'Yes'. He wasn't a bad worker, by any means, but he always had to be so negative about everything. Some people see the great glass of life as half full, some as half empty. Darren definitely saw it as half full. But half full with poison, and with shards of broken glass in it.

Steve sat down at his desk and switched his laptop computer on. His nerve-centre, as he'd called it until Darren had starting making references in the canteen to it being his nerd-centre. To his complete lack of surprise, a total of twenty-nine of his colleagues had managed to fill his electronic in-tray with a total of sixty-one e-mails during his trip to Abbotang Industries. And to his even less surprise, sixty of the e-mails were asking for his assistance or involvement in one way or another. The other e-mail had been sent to him in error. None of them supplied answers to the various questions that he'd sent out before his trip, nor provided any help with Project Lemming or with anything else.

He worked his way through them, trying to provide responses where he could, but mostly filing them away for another day. He broke off only once, to take a brief stroll round the office in an attempt to restore the blood supply to his left leg. These days he seemed to struggle with the simplest of tasks: he couldn't even manage to sit in a chair without giving himself pins and needles.

He picked up the telephone to try to talk to one of the manufacturing engineers about the possibility of trials on the pilot plant over in the assembly department, but all the phones in the office appeared to be connected through to the great exchange in the sky. He had the number somewhere of the person that you were meant to ring to get them fixed – great system – but his previous experience of such people was similar to everybody else's experience of such people, so it hardly seemed worth the effort.

He went to get himself a hot drink, but he was so busy thinking about the problems with the phones that he typed his phone number into the vending machine and ended up, not with coffee, black, no sugar, but with orange squash, extra white, double sugar. He had just got back to his desk and sat down, when the phone rang - apparently it was still accepting incoming calls. This one was from Barry, and was in the form of a summons to his office on the next floor of the building. Steve went upstairs with a notebook, a pen and some concern. He was pretty much resigned to Project Lemming being stopped, bearing in mind the way things had been going recently, so it came as rather a surprise to discover that his boss wanted to discuss the possibility of Steve getting involved in a completely new project that he was thinking of starting. In fact, he wanted Steve to consider leading it. In fact, Steve was going to have to lead it, because he had no-one better available at the moment. Barry was good at making you feel good about yourself like that.

Ten minutes later, Steve was back at his own desk, trying to remember some of the things that he had just been told but had omitted to write down. He had to sort a team as soon as possible, and then work out plans for the project. Somebody in Marketing – he'd already forgotten who – would supply the full list of user requirements, and Chris Tomkinson would need to be the Manufacturing representative. To Steve's considerable surprise, there was to be a budget of around half a million pounds, and he was to be allowed a core team of up to four people to help him. Even more surprisingly, the team was going to be allowed to choose its own project name. There was just one tiny little snag, apart from the fact that Steve's time was already completely taken up by Project Lemming and a variety of other responsibilities ranging from competitive awareness to managing the database of approved suppliers and all manner of similarly worthy causes: the project had to be finished in time for the big industry conference in Germany in January. He had less than four months to develop a completely new sensor, and he had to get it right. Drum roll, please.

2

For a minute, when he had first woken up, Steve hadn't remembered that he had agreed to a Saturday trip to the zoo. Oh happy golden minute. But it was not to last, and a boisterous early morning visit from Chloe, which involved her springing at Steve's recumbent form from a distance of six feet and landing with her knee in his groin, was enough to cut short any hopes he had for a leisurely day or personal space. Or further children.

For her previous birthday, they'd agreed to pay to let Natalie 'adopt' one of the zoo's cheetahs, which allowed them to visit it free of charge whenever they liked, all year. 'Frenzy' didn't do a lot – he seemed to spend twenty-four hours a day asleep – but at least there was the reassurance that an animal at the top of the food chain wasn't likely to be mysteriously missing when they called in to see him. Unlike the wallaby that Steve had befriended when he was Natalie's age[1].

The journey there wasn't particularly fun – it was evidently National Drive Like An Idiot Day – and the long walk from the car park was only of interest to lovers of concrete, but children's excitement is always infectious, and even Steve felt his pace quickening as they approached the first enclosure. Unfortunately, the giraffe wasn't on show, a small sign pointed out, as he was suffering from glandular mange, so they had to content themselves with peering at a gemsbok (Mr Pitchfork Head, as Jackie christened him) instead. Then it was on to the lion (five minutes), gibbons (three minutes), camels (thirty seconds), and macaws (straight past without looking), before they reached Frenzy (over an hour, during which time he snored a lot and his eyes twitched twice).

Steve was beginning to feel hungry by this time, so he was relieved when Jackie managed to tear the girls away from their cage-side vigil with a promise of seeing the elephants and then having lunch. Steve never understood why the things held so much fascination for anyone. To him, they just looked like giant jacket potatoes with a leg surplus (he was definitely getting

---

[1] Please note that no animals were harmed in the making of this book, nor in the research for it. Nor were their basic human rights infringed.

hungry), and what was particularly inexplicable was why so many daft people go all the way to the zoo to see the world's biggest land animal, and then spend all the time going 'aah' or 'coo' over the smallest one in the herd.

'Aah, there's a baby one over there – isn't it sweet?' said Jackie.

'What if they escape, and try to squash us?' asked Natalie, a trifle apprehensively. She was old enough, at seven going on eight, to get nervous about things.

'We'd run away, of course,' said Steve, who wanted food and a sit down, not a discussion about stampeding elephants. He'd had a long hard week and he wasn't sure which was worse, a mid-life crisis involving project deadlines, or an end-of-life crisis involving large escaped animals with pointy tusks, but he was sure that if he didn't get some food soon he might have to break into the lion's enclosure and try to eat *it*.

Unfortunately, lunchtime in the zoo's café gave Chloe and Natalie a perfect opportunity to put the case for owning a pet. Chloe, at four going on fifteen, started the bidding by wanting 'a turtoise'. Now, pets are of course an excellent way of getting across the message about responsibility and looking after others. And lo and behold, within a few days of buying Natalie and Chloe a hamster some months before, Jackie had clearly got the message that children don't like to be responsible for feeding a pet, cleaning a pet, or looking after a pet in any way whatsoever. So a few weeks later their parents had told the girls, so as not to upset them, that Gnosher had died suddenly of a terrible disease, but in reality he was now living under the assumed name of Xerxes Agamemnon III with somebody else. He had never been replaced, even though his apparent death had led to an instant determination to have a new pet and to many subsequent heartfelt vows of future responsibility and reliable devotion. They had all fallen on deaf parental ears, and since then the only 'pet' that either of them had owned was Natalie's small airplant, Tiddles. But neither girl had since missed an opportunity for persuasive lobbying.

'We could call her Shelley,' suggested Natalie helpfully.

'No,' said Jackie. 'Tortoises belong in the wild.'

'Well, what about a dog?' asked Chloe.

'Furball,' suggested her sister.

'We wouldn't be able to go on holiday,' said Steve, 'unless we left it in a doggery. We don't know anyone who would look after something as big as a dog.'

'...a gerbil?'

'No. they're vicious little brutes, you know. They're armed to the teeth with, er, teeth.'

'A guinea pig then?'

'They've got incisors that can chop through a man's finger.'

'A rabbit?'

'Natural born killers.'

'Oh for goodness sake Steve,' interjected Jackie, 'isn't there anything she can have?'

'Oh I'll get them a balloon. They can call it Poppy.' He returned clutching a large blue helium balloon with a picture of a leering chipmunk on it. Being a man of foresight, he had very securely tied the end of its string to his belt, so that they wouldn't lose it.

'Thanks Dad!' yelled Natalie, tugging at the string to pull it down for inspection as they left the café. As she did so, the chipmunk dived towards her with a wicked grin, bounced back up, and parted from the other end of its tether. Steve grabbed upwards for the balloon, but it slipped from his grip and drifted away in slow motion over the cheetah enclosure. The tip of Frenzy's tail moved quarter of an inch as it passed over his favourite sleeping spot.

For nearly five minutes they watched the balloon as it made its leisurely way over the treetops of a distant wood, before disappearing from sight. As soon as it had vanished, the girls both burst into tears and were only consoled with ice-creams and bags of sweets. Steve wouldn't have cared so much, but it took him nearly ten minutes to untie the string from his belt.

***

Steve actually felt more relaxed than he usually did as he arrived at work on Monday. The previous week now seemed so long ago that he could hardly remember what he did for a living, never mind remember the details of any problems that he'd put off until this week. He furrowed his brow as he walked across the car park: he didn't recall having left anything particularly awful to today. There was the little matter of the impossible new project to sort out, of course, but he was going to maintain his new philosophy of being positive, and it would all work itself out somehow. There was even an upside to having too much work, he reminded himself. After all, blessèd be the person who has three times as many things to do as they can possibly manage, for theirs is the choice of which bits to do. As they're going to be leaving two thirds of it undone, they might as well decide to do the bits they like and not the bits they don't. And why bother with the things that are for people they hate? Pity the poor souls whose workloads just match their hours, for they can't pick and choose. Steve had a choice, and he was going to choose to concentrate on his new assignment and leave the difficult bits of Lemming to someone else. It was about time that Simon pulled his weight a bit more. For once Steve was so resolved to be determined and upbeat that he could almost have whistled, if he hadn't got his teeth clenched.

There was only one envelope waiting in his pigeon hole behind the reception desk, and that was recognisable enough to go straight into the bin, unopened. He was too busy to go on courses on efficient time management. He passed Darren on the stairs ('Morning', 'Morning'), and then reached the office, where Lisa and Simon were already sitting.

'Morning', 'Morning', 'Morning', 'Morning'. It was very hard to sound particularly original when you'd worked with the same people for a long time.

He switched on his computer, and went off to get himself a cup of coffee while it booted up. Back in the old days before the arrival of the drinks machine, they'd just had a kettle and had made their own drinks. As happens in every place of work, though, there were people who routinely borrowed other people's milk and routinely forgot ever to unborrow it again. And as happens sooner or later everywhere, the kettle system eventually got abandoned and the vending machine got installed instead. It lived in the little kitchen by the top of the stairs, and people came from yards around to admire its beauty and marvel at its generous range of drinks. Or something like that. The choice may have been wide, but it was also unusual. On the tea front, it could do black frothy tea, white frothy tea, extra white frothy tea, frothy tea with sugar, frothy tea without sugar, frothy tea with double sugar, and lemon tea (frothy). Pretty much any tea you wanted, in fact – apart from those fancy sorts that taste like soap – provided you didn't mind it having a covering of fizz and froth and bubbles. And, more to Steve's taste, it could also make an equally impressive selection of frothy coffees.

Steve chose black and frothy. The machine gargled internally for a few seconds and then dribbled something warm and wet into a small recycled plastic cup. Steve retrieved the drink from its little alcove, and the machine made its usual random deduction from his change and flashed its little lights in a gloating manner to remind him who was boss. To make a bit of a special occasion of it, he helped himself to a stale biscuit from the box that someone had left for sharing. It was always hard to resist free food, no matter how unappetising.

When he reached his desk he saw that his clever little computer had managed to find him a large stash of unread e-mails. He sighed, put the cup of coffee on the humorous coaster that Darren had once given him ('Only a mug would use this'), and started to flick through the pile of papers that had accumulated on his desk in the last week or two. The e-mails were probably more urgent, but Steve was well versed in all the arts of procrastination, and the paper documents probably offered him a gentler start to the working week.

He had only read as far as the second paragraph on the first page when Darren returned, also clutching a hot drink from the machine.

'There's nothing like a lovely cup of tea,' he said.

'And neither's that,' Steve and Simon chorused with him, in well-worn ritual.

Darren was his usual self, muttering and complaining about everything and everybody, some of it in jest but quite a lot of it not. He hadn't so much got out of bed the wrong side, he was more one of those people who had got out of the womb on the wrong side. Somewhere on his desk was a framed certificate from the ceremony when he'd sworn allegiance many moons ago to the Sacred Crested Guild of Whiners and Carpers Onners. His mood today was not particularly helped by Lisa asking him for some figures and calculations that she needed for a report that she had to send to Bob Scott, the Head of Corporate Indecision.

Steve took a sip of coffee and started to file some of the papers in the binders that lived on the shelf above his desk. His hole puncher had been abducted by person or persons unknown a few weeks back, so he had to use the end of a pencil to puncture each sheet, which was a rather unsatisfactory process. He made a mental note to ask Clare whether he could have a new one, then promptly forgot it when he went off to the chocolate machine for another seventy pence worth of happiness.

By half past nine he'd done enough paperwork to give himself a headache, and as his legs were again going numb he went for a saunter round the office. Darren was busy trying to write a summary of the latest Lemming test results without telling too many outright lies and he didn't look in the mood for a chat, but perhaps Simon or Lisa would be disturbable. Simon was rather non-descript, or at least I can't be bothered to describe him, but Lisa was attractive and vivacious and petite, with hair the colour of rich loam and an oh-so-kissable pout. She was always fun to have around, and her very presence seemed enough to energise her colleagues. She was liked by everyone. Well, almost everyone. Darren always said that he preferred sour miserable people like himself. Their romantic liaisonship had not been a great success during the four months it had lasted.

'Is your meeting on, this afternoon?' Lisa asked Steve.

He sighed. His fortnightly innovation meetings had been suffering falling attendances for a while but recently there'd been a lot of truancy and he was now lucky to get more than three people and a septic cat, metaphorically speaking. He couldn't really blame the no-shows, of course. Their lives were probably blighted with as many interminable meetings as his was.

'Well, yes and no. Barry wants me to use the slot for a kick-off meeting on the new project that he afflicted me with last week. I'm assuming you're still available?'

Lisa didn't exactly jump up and down with enthusiasm, but she was at least willing to attend, as was Simon. Darren didn't comment, but it was unknown for him to miss anything as jolly as seeing someone else floundering, so Steve had little doubt he would also be there. Everything was all set for a momentous meeting to start a momentous project, apart from the small matter of compiling some sort of agenda, which was Steve's next job, followed by starting a draft project plan, setting up a project budget and trying to concoct a provisional project charter and mission statement.

It being a Monday, Steve broke off at lunchtime for his regular hour of exercise in the swimming baths or, as Darren preferred to refer to it and Steve preferred not to think of it, his hour's thrashing about in dilute spit. He had been going swimming at lunchtimes since the previous Christmas, when, having noticed that what should have been his six-pack seemed to have taken to hanging over his belt, and having been told by Jackie (and Natalie) to take more exercise, Steve had resolved to take more exercise. That was the kind of guy he was: incisive, decisive. So it was off to the swimming baths at lunchtime three times a week. OK, twice, to be absolutely honest. OK, once a week, but the twice bit was only a little white lie, and everyone's entitled to their dignity and pride. Once a week. Most weeks.

***

The swimming bath temperature was, as usual, twenty-seven degrees centigrade according to the thermometer on the wall, and, also as usual, Steve failed to see what was wrong with thirty-five. Not as usual, today he had to share the pool with a group of thirteen year olds in pyjamas who were learning survival skills. It looked something like a teenage sleepover on board the Titanic, but presumably it was useful practice for saving the life of anyone who turned over and fell out of bed into a river.

Once in the pool, he set about doing his usual thirty lengths of slow breaststroke. He swam really inefficiently. Each length was an effort, so at least he had the comfort of knowing that he was expending lots of energy and presumably getting fit. All those supersleek people who whizzed effortlessly up and down around him had missed that trick: he was burning off far more calories doing his imitation of a whale in difficulties.

It was past half past one when he got back, and there was no-one around in the open plan office. The swimming session had not gone well. He'd had the suspicion that someone's corn plaster had entered his mouth as he first dived in. It hadn't, as it happened, but he'd been unable to quite shake off the doubt for the rest of the hour. On the positive side, it had also put him right off the thought of lunch, so the fact that he'd completely forgotten to pack any sandwiches didn't now matter. It was curious that all his colleagues had vanished, though. If something important was going on, he had perhaps better find out what it was.

Eventually, with a search of two floors of the building, Steve managed to track everyone down to a meeting room at the back of the ground floor. They were in one of Barry's crisis meetings and it was showing every sign of being likely to run on and on, into the time reserved for the project start-up meeting. He'd been going less than a day on his new assignment, and already his boss had hijacked his meeting time and stolen all the attendees.

Barry was brash and hearty. He was always one to host a meeting with noise and drama and meaningless buzz-words. Today was no exception. When Steve arrived, Barry was five minutes into his opening soliloquy, rallying the troops into action for a major offensive. There was only one chair left empty, in the far back corner, and to reach it involved clambering past a row of his colleagues, their briefcases and their laptop computer recharger wires. There must have been about fifteen people packed into the little room, but then it was a crisis meeting and you can't beat a good crisis, so it was bound to attract crowds. Somewhat self-consciously, and smelling faintly of chlorine, Steve sat down between Darren and Cathy, and opened his own laptop bag. Cathy, one of the customer key account managers, gave him a frown. That was no surprise, however, as she was well known for being cold and unfriendly, having held a grudge against the world since losing both her legs in a freak sewing accident some years previously. You only asked her for favours on the rare occasions she was in a good mood, and you never crossed her unless you wanted your boss to receive weekly complaints for the rest of your career. She and Darren made a lovely pair of bookends.

At the other end of the room, Barry paced up and down in front of a whiteboard on which he would occasionally add the odd hieroglyph. His motion had a peculiar and hypnotic rhythm to it because he walked with a slight limp, and his reciprocating strides were effectively tracing out what was technically a waltz. He always hoped that everyone would think it was some old sporting injury, obtained under the most heroic of circumstances, but in truth it was just an unevenness of gait, obtained by never quite bothering to learn to walk properly.

Steve had half a mind to query what he'd missed, but the confused looks around the room made him suspect that they'd missed it too, despite having been present. Barry's speeches were like that. Every sentence made sense as he uttered it, but when he'd finished the whole thing you hadn't got a clue what he'd said. He clearly was passionate about something, and felt strongly about several other somethings, but nobody was too sure what.

By comparison, Steve's meeting was a low-key affair when it finally started. No rousing speeches, no cryptic symbols, just a group of eight people chosen by Barry for the new project team despite his earlier promise to leave some of the choice to Steve. There were three Supporting Team Members, the sort who usually 'attend' team meetings by dialling in from their own offices while they get on with other work. There were the four Core Team Members, who had to physically show up in the meeting room but could bring their laptops and do something more interesting while they half-listened. And there was the Team Leader, the one who couldn't actually be doing something else at the same time during the meetings. And there needed to be a lot of meetings, because no one else paid much attention and hence very little was ever properly sorted out on any one occasion. And the Team Leader was of course Steve, the living proof that it's not what you know, or who you know, it's how you say 'no' that counts, you know.

While having seven other people to support him didn't seem too bad, things weren't quite so good when Steve considered whom Barry had given him. First, there were Lisa and Simon and Darren from the development engineers group, plus Clare the secretary, and while individually all of them were reliable and competent (except perhaps Clare) and had reasonable personal drive (except perhaps Simon), all the usual inter-personal differences would need careful handling. Steve could anticipate at least three potential conflicts there, for a start. There was Darren and Lisa, Darren and Simon and to some extent Darren and Clare. Oh, hang on; there was also Darren and Steve himself. Four.

Then there was Chris Tomkinson from Manufacturing, who was rather an unknown quantity, and Adrian Redgate from the Quality Operations Group, who had plenty of experience and excellent judgement, but who was probably far too busy to do anything on the project apart from attend the first meeting. Finally, there was someone whom Steve didn't know, a woman called Liz from one of the other manufacturing sites. Steve didn't catch her surname, but it sounded a bit like Hindrance.

His preparation for the meeting had been a hasty list of 'must do' reminders, which he'd managed to compile that morning. It wasn't going to be a great start: he had occasionally been more organised before trips to the supermarket. There were so many things to consider that it was going to be hard to know where to begin, but top of the list was the need to decide the features of the new sensor. Luckily, Steve had Barry's in-depth expertise and professional judgement to help him there, provided by the man himself in a brief personal visit to the meeting.

'You need to come up with the best process sensor in the world, with the fastest response time ever achieved, at a rock bottom manufacturing cost.'

There was a pause while the greatness of his vision and the depth of his insight were appreciated by those in the room. He stood there as if he was expecting everyone to cheer.

'Quite something, eh?' More pause; still no applause. 'I'll leave the trivial little details of how to do it to you guys.'

Barry left at that point, as he had to make some decisions about restocking the stationery cupboard. Steve was left to fend for himself.

'OK,' he said, slowly. 'Now it seems to me that the most pressing things to do are to decide on the sensor's main features, and to come up with a list of all the things we need to do between now and January.'

To get things started, he pinned his sheet of pre-prepared scribble onto the wall, to an accompaniment of unimpressed silence. 'What have I missed?'

Nobody had much to add, though. They had all come to this cold, and Barry's preceding crisis meeting had left them feeling rather drained of energy. Only Darren was willing to volunteer anything to the process, and most – nay, all – of his comments were actually criticisms of what Steve had already written, rather than additional suggestions.

'Why do you feel you have to comment on every single thing?' asked Lisa, after ten minutes of listening to her ex-boyfriend challenging everything that he could decipher.

'Oh, it's just that I love the sound of my own voice. I can never really get enough of it. Isn't it brilliant?'

Lisa wasn't going to bother thinking of an answer to that one. 'Well do you have to be so negative about everything? Couldn't you try to actually help Steve by being constructive for once?' she asked, rolling her eyes. 'You can see that he's struggling.'

Steve hadn't particularly needed that to be spelt out.

'Oh I know it's easy to criticise,' said Darren, 'but what most people don't seem to realise is that it's great fun, too.' Ah, the old ones are the best.

This was going nowhere. No-one seemed in a mood to get to grips with the challenges that lay ahead of the team. Steve decided it might be best to abandon the process and to reconvene when everyone had had a chance to think a bit about the objectives of the project. The following Monday afternoon seemed to suit most people, so Steve decided to bring the meeting to a close until then.

'Anyone got any questions?' he asked.

Unfortunately, that triggered a barrage of enquiries from Darren about the precise details of the milestones, the timelines, the deliverables and the budget, none of which Steve could properly answer without Barry's help.

'What are we going to call the project?' asked Darren, as he watched his colleague silently opening and closing his mouth as he tried to address his various questions.

Steve scrabbled to grab at that one, as it was finally something that he felt he might be able to work with. Perhaps if they came up with an inspiring name it would be the spur they needed to finally have a success with a project.

'OK, let's brainstorm that, and then call it a day,' he said gratefully. He turned the flipchart pad behind him to a blank sheet, and started to write down suggestions as team members called them out. For some reason, naming projects was an activity that everybody liked to contribute to. For three and a quarter minutes the process worked well, but then it started to get a bit bogged down in what rapidly became the team's first squabble. In fact, it was over twenty minutes before they had all agreed on a name. The entire useful output of an hour and a bit of eight people's time was a single word scrawled on a flipchart. Steve wondered whether he should laugh or cry.

Barry poked his head round the door at that point, intending to remind them all that the team would also get first call on the services of the new technician that they were planning to choose at interview the next week. His gaze fell upon the five pages of suggestions for project names, culminating in the triumphant offering ringed at the bottom of the last sheet.

'You've decided to call your project Suck?' he asked, his eyebrows arching wildly.

'No,' said Steve, 'it says Slick.'

'Hmm. OK then. Project Sling it is,' said Barry, 'I'll let the other managers know.' And with that, he vanished, leaving them to wrap up the meeting and tidy the room. Steve had originally hoped to be in a position where he could allocate action points to the other participants, in a bid to get things moving, but having failed to achieve anything he couldn't even do that, and they all had to leave empty-handed.

He stayed behind when the others had gone. It was a bit of a struggle even to summon up the energy to go home. On the one hand, it was always nice to see his wonderful family, but on the other he knew that Natalie and Chloe had plans for him to build them a large wooden ark and that Jackie was insisting he have a look at the shed door, which had got itself jammed. It looked like he had an evening of carpentry, bruises and splinters ahead of him.

3

Unusually, Steve had no meetings in his diary for the Tuesday. It gave him a chance to think about what to do first on Project Sling and to have a proper look at the latest results from the lacquer curing experiments on Project Lemming. He was also hoping to get round to reading through the CVs for the six candidates for the technician's job. Barry had asked him to be involved in the interviews, so he thought he'd better see who his boss had short-listed.

Planning Sling was the most pressing task, so to put it off he started with the Lemming lacquer experiments. Judging by the measurements that Simon had made and the microscope photographs that Darren had taken, they were still failing to get a proper pressure seal. The lacquer just didn't seem to be doing its job: it wasn't managing to get into some of the nooks and crannies around the probe head.[1] They would have to try to change the properties of the mix yet again. The runniness, or whatever the proper technical term was.[2]

By quarter past nine, Steve was thinking that he'd really have to try to get to grips with the new project, so he went to get some coffee to wake himself up before he started. Then he went to empty his bladder so that he could get on without further interruptions, but then he noticed that he was feeling hungry so he made a detour via the chocolate machine on the way back to his desk.

'I thought you were on a diet?' said Lisa.

'I've got to keep my figure,' replied Steve, defensively. By now, his throat was getting dry, so he went back to the machine for another coffee. It was almost five to ten, and he hadn't started doing any project planning yet. Luckily, he was not quite out of ideas for constructive dawdling, because there were the CVs to read through. It was an important task. On each of them rested

---

[1] One of life's little mysteries, really. Why do nooks always go around with crannies? Why do you never hear of one or the other on their own?

[2] By the way, if you're one of the 98% of people who read the footnotes as soon as you turn the page, please stop it. You'll spoil the story for yourself.

the hopes and dreams of one of his would-be colleagues. He had expected to be able to judge something of their characters and their attention to details from the way the documents were written, but he had forgotten that these days they're all typed and spell-checked. Worse, five of the six appeared to have been written by the same CV preparation agency, as the glowing descriptions of the candidates were almost identical. They sounded so good that Steve was vaguely surprised that they were applying for a technician's job rather than to be the next Secretary General of the UN. The sixth CV was written in Romanian, so was hard to judge.

The phone rang, and Steve answered it to find it was a man from a small London design company who wanted to come up and see him, one day next week. Offers of expensive help always seemed to come from design companies, never people who knew anything about formulating lacquers. Steve didn't want to waste anybody's time, so he politely but firmly told the chap that they weren't interested. Well, actually, he wasn't quite brave enough to do that, so he expressed fake interest and gave him Barry's name instead. It would amount to more or less the same thing in the end.

'Right,' thought Steve to himself after he had extricated himself from the phone call, 'I'm having ten minutes off for good behaviour and *then* I'm getting down to my plans for Sling.'

The rest of the morning was spent in similar vein. He filled in a purchase form for a different solvent to try in the Lemming lacquer mix. Clare told him it was the wrong form, so he went back to his desk to hunt for the right one. Finding it took ages and ages, and by the time that he did, he suddenly realised that he couldn't for the life of him remember what it was that he wanted to order. He spent twenty minutes improving the layout of his list of important phone numbers, as it had been nearly a year since he had last updated it. It was twenty minutes that he didn't really have, but it was definitely worth it because the majesty and beauty of a well-designed computer spreadsheet is something to behold. Before he knew it, it was lunchtime. Well, actually it was always lunchtime, as far as Steve was concerned. It was just that the canteen only opened at twelve.

'Come on, Mr Adventure. Let's go for some lunch,' said Darren. He had been calling Steve that ever since the previous Christmas's company raffle, in which Steve had won the first prize of a day's hot air ballooning and paragliding, and had traded it in for an Introduction to Watercolour Painting course. Steve was more than happy with the idea of lunch. He was so hungry that his stomach seemed to be trying to eat him.

They were faced with a tempting choice of fare once they had passed through the hallowed portals of the canteen. Should they go for the fat with a hint of gristle, or the gristle in a coating of fat? After two minutes of indecision Steve decided to go for the vegetarian option, despite the fact that that too seemed to be mostly tendons and ligaments. Darren went for the meat and gravy pie: he didn't like vegetarian food. To him, a meal wasn't a meal unless something had had to die in its preparation. It had been one of the main reasons why he and Lisa had proved incompatible.

Their lunch was interrupted by one of the production line supervisors, who stood up to present a long service award to one of his operators and to congratulate him on having exchanged twenty-five years of his life for a rather nice framed certificate and a ten quid gardening token. Despite having shared the same canteen with him for a decade and a half, Steve had never noticed the lucky recipient before. You could spend half a working lifetime next to somebody and not even have time to speak to them.

He went to get himself something healthy for dessert. Rather unusually, the fresh fruit counter was bare. Normally Sally, the woman who did most of the serving in the canteen, kept it well stocked. Today there was just an empty space and a couple of strange stains on the top of the counter. There was also no sign of Sally, so Steve went to the kitchen door to peer in and ask whether there was any fruit. At a table in the furthest corner, Sally looked up from where she had been individually labelling the price on each apple, banana, pear and grape with a marker pen.

'Yes?' she said, through teeth that didn't entirely fit within her mouth. She would have added 'Can I help you?', but only if she'd been more helpful a person than she was.

'Is there any fruit?' asked Steve, wishing as always that life wasn't full of opportunities for getting shouted at. He knew even before he'd finished the question that the answer was likely to involve sarcasm seasoned with a hint of outrage.

'What does it look like?' Sally snapped. This clearly wasn't a conversation that was going to lead anywhere but Pain City or Embarrassmentville.

'It doesn't matter; I'll wait till tomorrow,' Steve replied.

The way things had been going all morning, getting anything started on the Sling project would end up having to wait until tomorrow, too, which wouldn't please Barry. So he certainly couldn't afford to fritter the afternoon away as well. He took three deep breaths when he got back to his desk, leant back in his chair and gazed for some big-brotherly inspiration at the picture mounted on his wall. It was an exquisite piece of fine art – a framed side-on portrait of a young woman on the porch of a Mediterranean villa – and all the more impressive when you realised that his brother had produced it under exam conditions. Unfortunately it had been a maths exam, but the fact that Paul had sketched the girl purely as a distraction did not detract from its artistic merits.

It was quarter past one when Steve eventually made a start on drawing up his plans for his new project. The process took him the rest of the afternoon, the last three hours of it as a solid unbroken session. By six o'clock, he had made himself an outline high level plan, an annotated low level plan for the first month of the project, and a draft action point list. Each was about as interesting as it sounds, I'm afraid. Nevertheless, they were a weight off Steve's mind and he was pleased he had got them done. As Darren often said, planning seemed so much more productive than doing any real work, but only if you actually started it.

***

That night Steve had a dream about shopping, in which he managed to buy a pet squirrel instead of a new ironing board and in which he agreed to put down a deposit on four thousand wicker footstools instead of buy the bread and milk and cheese that Jackie had asked him to get. He'd just plucked up the courage to tell her the slight change of plan, and had been very much looking forward to finding out what his sub-conscious thought she might say on the subject, but unfortunately at that very moment the shopping centre had turned into the works canteen and Jackie had turned into the Duke of Wellington, who started shouting and woke him up.

He lay there for a moment, slightly damp with sweat, until his heart stopped pounding. To his relief, Jackie was still fast asleep and looked quite content, so he thought he'd probably got away with the footstools business.

***

Barry had scheduled a meeting for eight-thirty on Thursday, and Steve could see him standing silhouetted in his office as he and Darren came down the corridor towards the open door. He seemed to be in a brasher, haler and heartier mood even than usual, a wide grin on his face as he stroked his in-growing beard.

'Congratulations, come in, congratulations!' he boomed.

For a moment, Steve thought he might be about to receive another motivational key-ring or something, but he wasn't. Perhaps it was just as well: the previous one had cut through his trouser pocket into his thigh and had given him a scar that lasted nearly a year.

'Welcome to my ten thousandth meeting,' Barry beamed.

'You keep count?' asked Steve, with no real sense of surprise.

'How can you manage things if you don't measure them?' Barry asked, rather too rhetorically for Steve at that time of the morning. 'And speaking of managing things, by the end of the day I need your estimates of what you want to spend in the next two months, because I'm seeing John first thing tomorrow.'

'I'll do what I can,' said Steve. John was Barry's boss, and if John wanted something it tended to mean that Barry really really wanted it.

'Will we be able to use external consultants, or is there still a consultancy ban?' Steve asked as an afterthought.

'No, no. You're perfectly free to use consultants. Just make sure the consultancy costs don't exceed what we spent on them in the last quarter.'

'The quarter when there *was* a consultancy ban?'

But Barry wasn't listening and didn't reply. His attention had been diverted by an interruption from Lisa, whom Barry always found infinitely more interesting than Steve. All women fascinated Barry, apart from his wife. Disappointingly for Barry, the fascination was not reciprocated by any woman presently in his life. Lisa, though, did tolerate him, for it certainly made it easier for her to get on with her job when her boss was always willing to see her at a moment's notice. Today she wanted permission to spend a couple of thousand pounds on a small test jig to allow them to test how well their Lemming prototypes coped with vibration.

After Lisa had left the room again, armed with a promise of two thousand pounds plus another thousand for the road, Barry, Steve and Darren were left to get on with their meeting. Barry's intent seemed to be mostly to impress upon Steve the importance of the Sling project and how he mustn't let it fail. There seemed to be some dark undercurrents in the way that he said it: as if all their recent woes were somehow marked on Steve's slate.

'Steve, this time it's death or glory. Et cetera.'

'Yes, I know. But the plan is already coming together,' (that bit was true) 'and it's looking good.' (There was a bit of poetic licence there, however.) 'Anyway, Darren's working on defining how we'll do it and what components and technologies we'll need to make it best in class. We're a winning team; we're the experts, after all.'

'Excellent,' Barry said encouragingly. 'I know I can –'

He broke off, and turned to stare at Darren. '... er ... What on earth are you doing?'

'I'm trying to lick my elbow. Did you know that it's impossible?'

'Then why are you trying to do it?'

'Challenging the boundaries. Raising the bar. Pushing the limits.' Management-speak always went down well with the boss.

'Moving on...' said Barry, proceeding to lift from his desk a thick stack of papers that he had randomly pulled from his filing cabinet before the meeting. 'See if any of these are any use. If not, bin them.'

'Can we discuss which trade shows we're going to be taking this to?' Steve asked.

'No idea. That's up to you. Just make sure we launch in January. Time's not on your side.'

Time was never on Steve's side. It hadn't picked him for its team in his whole life.

'Are we going to be saying anything about it in November?' Steve persisted.

But Barry had lost concentration again. He'd remembered that he had to get back to a man from some small London design agency who had left him an interesting voice message a couple of days previously, and all he heard from Steve now was a vague mooing noise in the background. He herded them out of his office.

'My door is always open,' he said, closing it behind them as they left. 'Go Sling!'

'Go-wrong Sling,' echoed Darren to no-one in particular.

***

Steve spent the rest of the day and most of Friday sketching out possible configurations of sensor probe heads. Measuring temperature, magnetic field and nearby electrical currents in a single system looked as if it might be possible, but adding an accelerometer function was going to be interesting in the small space they had allowed themselves. This was rapidly turning into another assignment from hell.

He was still thinking about it all as he drove home on Friday, an hour and a half later than he had promised Jackie. The technical problems looked considerable, and Barry was about as much help as the diagrams that come with self-assembly furniture. Steve switched on the car radio but '*Wossit and Why?*' was on again. Prang, or Prod, or whatever his name was, was starting to have a hit on his hands. A very irritating hit. He switched the radio off and returned to his turbulent thoughts.

It had not been a particularly good week. But then, the weeks to come are going to be worse.

***

Steve and Jackie had set Saturday aside for trying to get the back garden into some sort of shape before autumn. It was always good to get tidied up before Mother Nature dumped her old leaves everywhere. The first item on Jackie's agenda was for Steve to get the ivy off the back of the house before it started getting between the roof tiles, while she went to the supermarket to spend their life savings on another week's food. Steve, not having a great head for heights unless there was something at least as solid as a mountain to hold him up, did not actually own a ladder of any worthwhile reach, so it would be a matter of borrowing one from one of the neighbours.

The couple who lived in the house at the back were probably both nearly fifty. He had lost most of his hair to natural causes and the rest to a daily routine with a razor, so from a distance his head bore a passing resemblance to an egg. She was a platinum blonde. More relevantly, Steve knew they owned an extending ladder. Steve thought that they were called Ian and Katie, but as he was hopeless at remembering names, and as Jackie had not been there when they'd introduced themselves over the back fence soon after the Oscrofts had first moved in, he always tried to be very careful never to accidentally address them by name in case he was wrong. When you have known someone for four or five years it is a little late to ask them to remind you what they are called.

At least Steve could be certain of their surname, though, for it was he who had christened them as the Empties, on account of the number of cardboard boxes full of wine bottles that accompanied them on their regular trips to the bottle bank. Steve and Jackie got on with them very amiably, although they never visited one another's houses and, since Ian and Katie were by no means keen gardeners, they rarely saw them in their garden except in the height of summer when the sun loungers were out by their small swimming pool. It was thus quite a surprise to find them outdoors on a changeable September day like this. Katie was pruning things, while Ian was fishing leaves from the pool with a large rake, an activity made all the more necessary by the tree that Steve and Jackie's predecessor had vindictively planted upleaf of it.

Steve went down the garden to take the opportunity to ask to borrow the ladder. Absolutely no problem, but would it be alright if they brought it round now, so that they could set it up on Steve's side of the fence and prune the offending tree back a bit? Like almost completely, if possible? Steve agreed, although he was actually rather fond of the tree, and ten minutes later Ian and Katie appeared with their fifteen foot ladder.

'We'll try not to tread on your match-stick model of Stonehenge,' said Ian, as he picked his way past Steve's mildewed roses and weed-choked onions.

'That's not Stonehenge,' said Steve a little tightly. 'That's my slug defence system. They're cocktail sticks, actually, if you notice.' Steve was very hopeful that his miniature Agincourt of sharpened sticks would save what was left of his hostas from the local slugs and snails. Well, it had worked for dealing with French horsemen; why shouldn't it work for snails? As he'd said to Natalie, if they were lucky they might get some ready-made slug-on-a-stick kebabs out of it, as well.

'I was only joking, you know,' he'd said as he saw the horrified look on his elder daughter's face.

Katie held the foot of the ladder while Ian went up to send a steady stream of small branches back down around her. In no time at all, the job was done and Steve had a large pile of twigs and branches and leaves to dispose of. The tree itself now resembled a ball on a stick.

'Oh my goodness,' said Katie, noticing the back of her own house from that angle for the first time, 'you can't see through my frosted glass can you, when I'm going to the shower?'

'Katie,' quipped Steve, 'We've been checking your breasts for lumps for you.'

Katie appeared to take offence at this. 'Steve,' she said slowly, 'my name is Jenny.'

She and Ian departed, leaving Steve feeling rather stupid. He spent the next half hour trying not to catch their eyes as he moved the branches from his lawn and they dismantled their metal-framed swing seat and put it away in their garage for the winter.

Jackie took the girls to play in the local park at half past three, leaving him sweeping the leaves from the lawn and the patio. It was a lengthy job, as he only had the oldest and scraggiest of brushes with which to do it. Jackie had once tried to persuade him to replace it with a new one, but it had been in the family for generations, and had great sentimental value. Where other people have silver tea services and priceless ornaments, the Oscrofts' heirlooms consisted of a broken spade, a bent lawn rake and a brush with about three bristles. Steve was very attached to them all, and his affection showed in the way he lovingly held the handle as he swept. It may have been slow, but at least it didn't make the row that a leaf-blower did. Old-fashioned ways; old-fashioned virtues.

When all neighbours on all sides had finished their various gardening activities, Steve decided that the coast was clear for him to have a go at climbing the ladder to get the ivy off the house. He knew that he was going to look less than brave or agile, and he wanted no witnesses to his trembling efforts. In actual fact the ascent was OK to begin with; indeed it started rather better than he had hoped, but the higher he climbed the more nervous he got and the less far he dared reach out from the ladder. Eventually, unable to climb any higher, he looked up. Frustratingly, he still couldn't reach much of the ivy. He looked down. He had climbed four steps. With a sigh, he went carefully back down to pick up the secateurs and then, with a slightly less than superhuman effort that even Natalie was unlikely to be impressed by, he climbed five steps up and carefully cut through the main strand of the ivy as high as he could reach[1]. Then he retreated to the kitchen and made himself a mug of coffee. Unfortunately, he was still shaking so much that he pulled more than just the mug out of the cupboard[2]. By the time Jackie and the girls returned, Steve had cleared the bottom ten feet of the back wall of the house, but the ivy higher up remained and the ladder had been returned.

Jackie had no time for immediate inspections of progress, as she had two wounded princesses in tow. Natalie had ripped her jeans and bruised her leg falling off the roundabout, while it was stationary, and Chloe had cut her hand on a pine cone[3]. Bandaging Chloe up took a little while, thanks to the assistance of Nurse Natalie, and counselling took a little longer, thanks to the advice from Doctor Natalie ('It looks highly infectionous. You're going to die'). It wasn't until after five o'clock that the results of Steve's handiwork could be scrutinised.

'Well that's disappointing. You're going to have to spend tomorrow trying again,' said Jackie who, to save time and complication, was acting as judge, jury and prosecuting counsel.

---

[1] No plants were harmed during the making of this book. Er, except for the ones on which it was printed.

[2] Two cups and one saucer were harmed during that bit, I'm afraid.

[3] Several children were gratuitously maimed in the research for this bit.[*]

[*] No they weren't, obviously.

'Oh, and there's a dead pigeon on the roof that could do with removing. And don't go and leave the shears and the secateurs out, because it's going to rain overnight.'

She marched inside to organise baths for the girls and sandwiches for tea, leaving Steve with an instruction to do something to prune the pyracanthas away from the herb garden. It was probably less life-threatening than going right up the ladder, but pruning pyracanthas was still a job he hated. He and they had worked up a mutual loathing over the years, and it was reinforced with each and every thorn. After the last time he had tried to trim them, a casual observer might have been forgiven for thinking that they'd done more to refashion his features than he had done to theirs. This time, he had learnt from his previous defeat and had improved his tactics, so that by half past six the result had been more or less a draw.

He was just tidying everything away when Natalie came out to call him in for tea.

'Tea,' she called. There, told you so.

'Wow,' she added, peering at a small something on the ground near her foot. 'It's a tribolite!'

'A trilobite? Are you sure? They've been rather rare around here these last few hundred million years. Are you sure it isn't a woodlouse?'

'Maybe. If it is a woodlouse, can I have it as a pet, please?'

'Sorry, no,' said Steve. 'Nothing with lots of legs.'

To reinforce the point, he turned and came face to face with one of the biggest, leggiest, Daddy Long Legses (*Latin: Crane Fly*) he had ever seen. He'd had a lifelong dislike of the things, stemming from his unshakeable belief that their mission in life was to leave spare legs dangling in his hair as they flew off to drown at the bottom of his coffee. Once, at the tender age of about twenty-five, he had taken a big swig of water in the middle of the night from the glass beside his bed, only to find not one but two of them practising doggy paddle in it. Finding out visually would have been bad enough, but to do it by taste and by wriggle haunted him still.

Flapping the insect wildly away from his face, he chivvied Natalie into the house for her tea and her violin practice. He shut the back door heavily behind himself and shuddered. Then he went to wash his hands, pausing only to remove a leaf that was stuck to the bottom of his shoe with a slug.

**

Steve had another strange dream that night. Jenny (née Katie) Empty was climbing down a ladder from her bathroom window, wearing only a thin veil of leaves, when Ian suddenly appeared with a leaf blower, the noise of which woke Steve up, but not before he had answered one of the great unsolved scientific mysteries of our time: can you dream in colour? Yes you can, apparently, as proved by the distinct flash of ginger that he glimpsed just before he woke.

4

Steve was rather later than usual into work on Monday morning, largely on account of his legs and back being so stiff after gardening that he'd only been able to move about the kitchen at breakfast time at a slow hobble. He parked his car, signed himself into the building, pulled himself slowly up the stairs, and creaked his way past Barry's glass-walled office and along the corridor to his own desk in the open-plan area.

He switched his computer on and sat back in his chair with his eyes closed for a few moments. He couldn't remember a time when he hadn't felt tired, to a greater or lesser extent. Privately, he had a theory that he needed ten hours sleep a night, whereas unfortunately he only ever seemed to get about seven. Worse, he was pretty sure that the need for sleep was cumulative and that his lifetime deficit had therefore been increasing at the rate of three hours per day for the last many years. That made him about twenty-six thousand hours short of sleep by a rough calculation, which certainly explained how he was feeling.

He had only managed to deal with about three e-mails when Barry came to see him. Ostensibly, it was about sorting out the packaging process for Lemming, but as was sometimes the case with Barry, there seemed to be a hidden agenda. It didn't take long to realise that it was something to do with the car park. The conversation was all about packaging speeds and packaging risk mitigation, but Barry's eyes returned time after time to the area of tarmac outside the window. Steve felt his own attention gradually being dragged away from the finer points of pick-and-place machinery and on to the need not to ask Barry what he was looking at. There was obviously something that he was supposed to get drawn into, but he really didn't want to be. Knowing Barry, it was almost certain that he had either just got a new company car or that one of the people he hated had damaged theirs.

Steve was right first time. It didn't take his boss long to move on to the rather less subtle approach of announcing the arrival of his latest roadster. Steve tried to stay seated, but was eventually made to stand up and look out of the window.

'It's that brand new one over there,' Barry proclaimed, waving his hand airily towards a top-of-the-range silver Pompous parked at the top of the car park.

'The one parked next to that dirty old blue car,' he added, pretending he didn't know that the Mundane was Steve's.

'Have you sold your Camber then?' Steve thought that a modicum of interest might be the best way of hurrying the conversation towards a conclusion.

'Yes, yes. The funny thing is, I'd never noticed before, but since I've been driving this one these last couple of days, I've noticed that Camber drivers are idiots.'

Steve had noticed that long ago.

'Anyway, that's not why I'm here,' Barry lied. 'I just wanted to sort the packaging stuff out. Thanks.'

He went off in the direction of Clare's desk, and for the next ten minutes Steve could hear fragments of automotive technical specification wafting across the office from where he had cornered the secretary.

Steve went to get himself some coffee from the drinks machine, but it was in a mood and only gave him about an inch in the bottom of the cup. He arrived back at his desk just in time to find Clare pinning up the latest group photograph of the department. It was really most unfortunate. It had been taken on quite a warm day a few weeks before, and Steve distinctly appeared to be in the process of falling asleep. It reminded him of the worries he used to have in his schooldays, in the weeks after a class photograph had been taken. The desperate hoping that he hadn't been the one captured at a bad moment, eyes half closed, mouth half opened, and silly leer on his face. And inevitably, always, Steve was the one who had to take home to his parents a picture of himself lapsing into brain death.

He spent the rest of the morning taking advantage of the relative peace and quiet in the office to make some inroads into his 'to do' pile, and was so engrossed that he almost forgot that it was his lunchtime swimming day. He had very little enthusiasm for it today, but knew that he had to burn off some calories. In honesty, he didn't care about his weight; it was more his volume that he worried about. It didn't achieve a lot, as it happened, because all the good work was almost immediately offset upon his return by the compulsory cakes provided by Clare in honour of her birthday the day before. With impeccable timing, the others came back in just as the cherry slices were being laid out alongside the chocolate éclairs. And their reappearance in turn brought Barry back, who had various urgent things he needed to discuss with them all, and a car park he had to gaze at. Steve excused himself after the first four hundred calories and went to get himself another cup of coffee. This time the drinks machine offered compensation for his last visit by double filling his cup, first with a cupful of black coffee and then with an equal amount of cold dilute milk that he hadn't asked for. His train of thought on the subject of his diet was broken by it overflowing and splattering over him.

Walking back to his desk with the gait that nature reserves for those with milk all down their legs, he passed Barry, who was heading towards the row of upstairs offices that looked down on the car park. The others had obviously been excused the window-gazing for now. Perhaps the sun wasn't glinting on the bonnet at the correct angle or something. Darren was busy at his computer, trying to out-spam his co-workers again. His frenetic typing was almost drowning out the sound of his mad mutterings, but Steve could catch the gist of his grievances with the world: he had been about to achieve truly great things of near-impossibility, but someone in manufacturing had let him down yet again. Although he didn't really want to know the details of the problem, Steve felt obliged to ask.

'I've just had an e-mail from Chris Tomkinson. Apparently, if we don't have the overall design of Sling laid out by mid October, they won't be able to use the high speed line to assemble it.'

'But that's only two and a bit weeks away!' exclaimed Steve, waking up to the fact that this was a problem heading in his direction faster than a tabloid newspaper in pursuit of a scandal.

'AND Barry needs you to pull together the manufacturing cost estimates by next Monday, so I think you'd better get on the phone to Chris.'

'I don't have time right now. We'll have to talk about it at the team meeting at three o'clock.'

Darren made a 'didn't forget, honest' sort of face and resumed his manic typing.

'Get Chris together with Alex Deese from Accounts,' he suggested. 'But wear body armour and a riot shield, because apparently they hate one another.'

That was news to Steve. He had always thought that people only ever hated him, apart from Darren who was much less choosy. He went to phone Alex to arrange an initial meeting, but accountants are very busy people and it would be two weeks before they could meet to discuss manufacturing costs and returns on capital. In the meantime Steve had to console himself with an extended e-mail exchange with Chris Tomkinson, mostly in the form of a series of queries about assembly equipment, each answered with a question along the lines of 'How can I plan assembly when you can't yet tell me what it's going to look like?'.

Compared with that, the three o'clock team meeting was very productive. Compared with anything else, it wasn't. I'll spare you the details.

***

Steve drove home and climbed out of his car. For some reason, there was a high-pitched wailing emanating from the house. A little concerned, in case Chloe was trying to put make-up on the neighbour's cat again, he fumbled for his keys and let himself in as quickly as he could. He needn't have worried: the sound was coming from Tom Alderson, which was a perfectly normal event when he was in the house. And he was often in the house because Jackie often cooked him a meal after school if his mother was still at work.

Tom was the son of Angela, who was Jackie's best friend. He was eight years old, and was the brightest child in Natalie's class at school according to his mother. He also seemed to be a bit unlucky, through no fault of his own. The wailing on this occasion appeared to be related to the four wooden cocktail sticks that were embedded in the palm of his left hand. It transpired, according to the varied accounts of the three female Oscrofts who were tending his wounds, that he had been cycling with his eyes closed round the garden to show off his innate gyroscopomorphic navigation skills while he waited for his mother to pick him up after tea. For purposes of additional guidance, Natalie was shouting 'left' and 'right' as she deemed fit - which was always going to be a bit iffy with Natalie – but unfortunately he collided with one of Jackie's flower tubs on the first lap. Luckily he had saved himself from landing in a heap on the lawn by putting his arm out straight onto Steve's slug defence system. The defences were flattened, although in the process they had at least proved themselves capable of fending off encroaching children as well as molluscs.

Although it took quite a while to coax Tom into letting them near his injured hand, the results were well worth the effort because the wailing finally stopped. Suitably bandaged, and mollified with a double dose of chocolate mint chip pain-killer from the freezer, he was almost smiling by the time his mother arrived to collect him. He had even built himself a cocktail stick model of a jet fighter, although it wasn't particularly good because Jackie had only allowed him to use the four sticks that had been plucked from his hand.

With imitation jet noises in his ears as Angela led her pride and joy out to the car, Steve went upstairs to listen to Natalie's violin practice.

'What did you do at school today' he asked, helping his daughter get the instrument out of the case.

'Can I have a chocolate, please?'

'Not till you tell me what you did at school today.'

'Oh, I don't know. We did something about circles and squares and triangles this morning, and then we learnt about healthy eating this afternoon. Now can I have a chocolate?

Steve agreed, but only on the condition that she ate an apple with it. He went down to the kitchen to get it for her, while Natalie started a tentative trial run on her first new piece. He was greeted on his return by music that had a distinctive style all of its own, having what Jackie euphemistically liked to refer to as a certain mournful quality and that the music teacher liked to call dreadful.

'What did Miss Blatherspit think about your free choice story, Natty?' asked Steve, after they had agreed that it was possible to practise too much.

'She wanted me to change it. She said it wasn't right for mangoes to be evil.'

Teachers had never recognised latent genius in Steve's day, either, he reminded himself. But Natalie would one day rise above them all, her abilities plain to see. Who knows, perhaps eventually he would too? He listened to her read her school book to him, and then he played a couple of simple board games with both girls before tucking them into bed and reading them a story each. He said goodnight and switched the lights out. Chloe fell asleep at once, but Natalie required ten minutes of reassurance that next door's cat, Poddle, wouldn't get scurvy despite having no fresh fruit in his diet. It seemed that she had almost as many things to worry about as her father did.

***

Tuesday was to provide blood, sweat and tears before the working day was out. Things started peacefully enough. Indeed they started much as the preceding day had, with a visit from Barry who just happened to be passing and just happened to mention his new Pompous.

'How are those packaging trials coming along? Has the machine got enough things we can control?'

'Yes, I think so. Simon is planning to run some experiments this afternoon,' said Steve.

'My new car has lots of controls, you know. Lots of knobs and dials and gadgets.'

'Um.' *Super.*

'It's got so many features that the instructions are nearly five hundred pages long. I'm learning one set of controls a day. Today it will be the heated mirrors; tomorrow, the self-levelling headlights.'

'And the day after that, the clutch,' muttered Darren to himself, under his breath.

'Does anyone want to come out and see it?' asked Barry, appearing to suddenly come up with the idea.

Only Darren responded. 'In the immortal words of Churchill, I think it was, no thank you.'

'Oh. No problem. I'm sure there'll be lots of other opportunities.'

No-one doubted that there would.

'Don't forget you're interviewing on Thursday. I've got a dream selection of candidates lined up for you.'

From what he'd seen of their CVs, Steve wasn't quite sure he could yet agree, but he said nothing. There would be time enough to come to a conclusion later in the week. What was curious, though, was that Barry wasn't going to be choosing the latest addition to his fiefdom himself. He usually cancelled all his meetings when there was some juicy interviewing to be done. He felt it was important to get the right people and to make sure that they were suitably inspired. And what better way to do that than by his own towering example of achievement?

'We need someone with vision: a bold leader of the future. This is a chance to add real strength to the team. I won't be around for ever you know.' And with that he went, possibly to polish his tyres, or perhaps to read up on the rain-sensitive wipers.

'Eeh,' said Darren, sipping his lukewarm coffee, 'that *was* motivational. I've not felt this good since I caught myself in my zip.'

'I thought we were recruiting a technician,' said Simon, 'not a captain of industry.'

Steve didn't have a good answer to that one, or at least not an interesting one. But energised by his boss's deep words of wisdom, and newly assisted by the peace and quiet that descended now that he had left the room, Steve thought he had better get his head down, and he spent the rest of the morning engrossed in calculations of manufacturing costs. It was past twelve before he realised what the time was.

Lunch time. Steve hurried after the others to the canteen, where Sally was presiding over a selection of hot food that Steve's mother would have described as 'unusual' – not necessarily the word you would most want attached to that which you were about to eat. After a careful perusal of the dishes on offer, Steve selected a packet of crisps and a couple of pre-wrapped toffee muffins. It didn't look a lot, but that suited his new-found healthy living regime provided that he didn't look at the calorie counts on the labels. He paid, and went to sit next to Simon and Darren who were already tackling what looked like stickleback in brine. He opened the crisps, and discovered that he hadn't picked up the cheese and onion ones he'd wanted, but had a packet of smoked salmon and gooseberry. Now that was undoubtedly an unusual combination.

They walked back in silence after they'd eaten, and had only been back at their desks for a few minutes when there was a loud yell from across the office and Darren grabbed his left hand in his right and started groaning.

'Oh dear,' he exclaimed, 'that was a rather unlucky thing for me to do, wasn't it?' Or words to that effect.

'What's happened?'

'My scalpel slipped – I've just cut my finger open.'

Lisa went over and prised Darren's hands apart. 'Ooh, dear, that is pretty nasty – it's gone right along the side of the finger. There's quite a lot of blood.'

Judging by the look of Darren, most of it had come from his face. 'Will I be OK?' he asked weakly.

'Well I think you'll live,' said Lisa, 'Nothing's fallen off – it's just a bit flappy, that's all.'

'For goodness sake, bandage it up quickly, before Helen comes to give me the Kiss of Life.'

Helen lived in an office down the corridor, and was the most enthusiastic first-aider in the building, if not the world. Her favourite thing was blood, the squirtier the better.

'Please,' begged Darren, 'Please don't let Helen see it.'

Lisa set about sticking Darren's skin back with a boxful of plasters, while Steve looked away and Darren lapsed into a mantra about Helen, or the Curse of Life as he sometimes called her. In no time at all he was as good as new, which wasn't saying much, and the room was filled with the excited babble of multiple voices all trying to top one another's injury stories.

Just as all the excitement died down, Jon and Neil from the workshop came to see Steve, bringing with them an assortment of five hundred small plastic parts that he'd asked to borrow to see if any of them might be useful as prototypes for the casing of the new sensor. Steve was surprised to see the two men, as they rarely left their little cubbyhole in the workshop. Although they were supposed to help any project team that needed it, to be honest they weren't actually a lot of use, though they did radiate a bit of heat in the winter months and could provide some useful shade in the summer.

Steve was just starting to peer at some of the jumbled up parts in the large plastic bag that Jon was holding when, inevitably, the phone rang. It was Barry, who had a sudden urgent need for him to go over to his office.

'I'm on my way,' Steve lied, as people are wont to do when trying to finish off what they were doing. He motioned to Jon and Neil to leave the parts on his desk, rummaged through his desk drawer for the few notes on costings that he had yet compiled, put the phone down, swigged the remains of his after-lunch coffee, picked up a notebook and a pen, and headed over to Barry's office.

His boss was actually in the middle of being shown some Pyrenean mountain photographs taken by Mike Marshall, a keen weekend rock-climber who spent his spare time during the week earning a living in sales at SLSL. Neither of them looked up as Steve knocked and entered. That wasn't a problem, though, as

Mike was one of those people that Steve knew by sight but had never actually spoken to, even when they'd sat side by side in the canteen.

'I was thinking,' said Barry, 'I'm sure they keep all the parts from old projects down in the workshops. Why don't you give Jon or Neil a ring, and see what they've got that you could cannibalise until Sling has its own custom parts?'

Steve politely thanked him for his wisdom and bold leadership, and left him to his study of Mike's vertiginous photographs of northern Spain as viewed from the end of a nylon rope. He got back to his desk to find that Jon and Neil had gone, taking their plastic bag with them but leaving all the hundreds of plastic bits heaped all over his desk, his chair and most of his little patch of floor. Even as he watched, a couple more fell to join their fallen comrades on the carpet. Rolling his eyes up so far that he could almost see the inside of his head, Steve set about picking up the old discarded prototypes and sorting them out into separate bags. The process took much of the afternoon, and he was aware that he should really have been finishing off the manufacturing cost estimates for Sling, but sorting plastic parts was one of those strangely satisfying jobs, like removing the fluff from the filter screen in the tumble drier[1].

He left as soon as it was four o'clock, for he had promised Jackie that he would do the week's main shopping run at the supermarket on the way home, in return for her letting him have an uninterrupted couple of hours to get some work done once the girls were in bed. Lucky Steve. Accordingly, he put most of the papers on his desk into his briefcase, picked up his jacket, left the office, and started to cross the car park. By one of this book's funny coincidences Barry was on a converging collision course with him, speed-sauntering across to his new car.

'Nice evening for a relaxing drive home,' ventured his boss, by way of small talk.

---

[1] Oh well, the world would be a very boring place if we all liked the same things.

'Mm, yes. I have to go to the supermarket though.'

'Well I hope all the stuff fits in your car then,' said Barry walking nonchalantly off in the direction of the silver monster.

The supermarket was as supermarkets usually are, unfortunately. Even finding a parking space was difficult. The whole area was filled with a seething and aggressive mass of circulating SUVs and 4x4s, and it was ten minutes before a certain clapped-out Mundane was resting safely against a concrete bollard. Steve didn't normally call in at this time of day. He much preferred going after tea, when he could take Natalie with him so that they could have some fathery-daughtery time choosing the wrong brands of food together.

It was past six when he got home to unload the shopping. The house was somewhat in chaos, as Jackie had been plagued with interruptions all afternoon. Her sister Diane had rung at two o'clock to moan about how she had the cowboys in for the week, fitting a new bath and retiling her bathroom, and that things were already starting to go wrong. Then five minutes after she'd finished that conversation, she'd had Angela on the phone, relaying the saga of her latest attempt to make things more permanent with her boyfriend. ('So I told him that *I'd* decide where and when and *how* he should ask me to marry him. And he had better make it a romantic surprise!')

'Don't you think you should divorce Tom's father first?' Jackie had asked, immediately wishing she hadn't as a great wave of hysterical sobbing came washing down the telephone line. She had still been trying to sort that one out when the time arrived to pick the girls up, and the end result of it all had been that she was still struggling with some part of her great weekly laundry-go-round when Steve came home.

He made tea for them all – it was only sandwiches, so he could just about master it – and then went upstairs to help Natalie with her story-writing homework when he had washed up. She had chosen to write a story about a girl with toothache, possibly because she had a new tooth coming through. So far, she had written eight lines and had used the word 'tooht' six times. It was about as good as some of the progress reports that Simon wrote, and Steve vaguely wondered whether he should introduce the two of them so that they could get together and swap writing tips.

'What's that noise?' he asked, noticing a hissing and thudding coming through the wall.

'Oh that's Chloe's radio. It sounds like Prod,' said Natalie, a trifle too innocently.

'I think he's called Progg actually,' said Steve. *Or Prat.*

He went in to see Chloe, who was sitting morosely on her bed, red rings round her eyes.

'What's the matter, Sweetles?'

She burst into tears, but between her sobs he managed to establish that she was very upset because her big sister had told her that there was no such career as trainer of space hamsters and she would have to be a secretary instead. We all have to learn these things eventually, but it's still painful. Even now, it's still painful.

Steve worked hard to cheer her up, with a careful balance of provision of sympathy and explanation of harsh reality. After a while she stopped crying and agreed that openings in inter-galactic hamster training might open up some time in the five years before she was a grown-up. She sat on his knee and he read her a couple of animal stories, and before very long it was bedtime.

'Animals are my favourite thing you know,' said daughter number two, as she settled down under the duvet.

'Oh. Not parents, then?'

Chloe gave that a few moments of careful thought. 'Well, parents are alright, but animals don't answer you back.'

Steve patted her on the head, kissed her forehead and switched the light off. In the adjoining room, Natalie was also settling down in bed. She didn't normally get ready so willingly, but she had been looking forward to probing her aching tooth with her tongue. 'I wonder if it still hurts? ... Ooh, yes. ... I wonder where it hurts the most? ... Ooh, there. ... I wonder if it STILL hurts? ...' Steve switched her light off too, and went downstairs to get his laptop out so that he could finally make a start on the work he needed to get done. Unfortunately, though, in his haste to leave for home he had forgotten to bring his laptop with him. There was almost nothing he could start without it. It was so frustrating that he had to drain three cans of beer before he felt calm enough to sit down and join Jackie in front of the TV, where she was watching a programme on the illegal global trade in identical twins, deliberately separated at birth to satisfy the growing demand from the makers of social documentaries.

***

Steve and Darren went up to the spare office at the back of the building where the interviews were to be held. They had only been there five minutes, and were still arguing over how best to arrange the furniture, when the phone rang. It was Barry, reminding them yet again of the critical importance – until he thought of something more important – of recruiting a technician with the potential to develop into a technology group supervisor within three years.

'A bold leader, of drive and vision,' he added, as he put the phone down.

Clare poked her head round the door at that point, not to bring in the first candidate but to remind Steve that he needed to submit his September timesheet by the end of the morning.

'But there's another day and a half of the month left yet!'

'I know, but it's the end of the quarter and we need to get them in early, so you'll have to make something up.'

Steve always made something up, but it still took time.

'OK.'

'I'll be back after you've finished this interview,' said Clare. She disappeared, leaving Steve wondering how he was supposed to do his monthly timesheet at the same time as he interviewed would-be technicians.

'Shall we tell them the job prospects?' asked Darren.

'What, that if they work really hard, and do really well, and have lots of luck, they might end their career earning seventy per cent of what some lawyers get paid for lawying as soon as they leave university?'

'Yeah, that kind of thing.'

'Perhaps not in those exact words.'

There was a knock on the door. It was Clare again.

'There's a gangly little youth biting his nails out here. He might be the bold leader of drive and vision that Barry keeps saying we're looking for. Are you ready for me to send him in?'

Steve wasn't, but he nodded because he knew that Clare wouldn't listen and would send him in anyway. She beckoned to a spotty lad who was hovering indecisively outside the door.

Dean was smartly dressed, politely spoken, meek of character, and instantly dislikeable. The first problem was that he had the enthusiasm of a wet blanket and the interpersonal skills of a biscuit. Not only that, but he appeared to be a couple of bricks short of a wall. In fact, he was probably a couple of bricks short of having three bricks. Although he wore top-label designer clothes, he either hadn't had enough money left over to buy himself a handkerchief, or perhaps he simply lacked the skills or training to know how to use one. Every few seconds he sniffed.

The interview did not go well for any of the participants. Steve didn't have any four-piece jigsaw puzzles with which to challenge Dean's intellect, Darren looked as if he had lost the will to live, and as for Dean, he had been rather stumped by the question of why he wanted the job.

'Do you want a few minutes to gather your thoughts?' asked Darren, in resignation.

Or a few hours, thought Steve.

Dean sat there, sniffing, for what seemed like an eternity. There was a puzzled look on his face, which suggested to Steve that something might be happening internally, so he gave him a bit more time. The sniffing continued. Steve held on until he could stand it no longer. Using all his mental strength to stifle the temptation to scream 'Will you PLEASE stop shuffling your mucus collection, you revolting youth?', he tried exploring Dean's personal interests in an effort to see what made him tick, but every line of enquiry led nowhere and Steve was left to conclude that Dean's internal clock had perhaps got stuck.

'Oh dear, oh dear,' he said, once Dean had left the room.

'Perhaps we shouldn't be too hard on him. We were young once,' Darren pointed out.

Steve thought for a moment. His own youth had all been a bit of a blur, if he was honest. A blur interspersed with moments of pain. But he couldn't have ever been as useless as that, surely?

Darren rang Clare, who duly reappeared with another of Barry's interviewee selections together with a further reminder to Steve for his monthly timesheet. This next candidate seemed to be everything Dean wasn't. For five minutes, Sim gave quite an impressive performance. He answered every question directly and decisively, and certainly seemed to know a lot of stuff. Unfortunately, it gradually became apparent that he didn't just know a lot of stuff, but he knew everything. Worse still, for many of the questions that Steve and Darren asked, Sim knew different answers from the ones that most other people did. For example, although it is considered traditional for the average of two numbers to lie somewhere between them, Sim didn't hold with that particular tradition, nor with the general consensus that methanol is flammable.

Steve decided to change tack a little for the last five minutes of the interview. He asked Sim why he had chosen to do an engineering apprenticeship when he had left school, rather than go to university to get a degree.

Sim positively snorted with derision. 'Anybody can get a degree these days! I came up the hard way, you know. It was the School of Hard Knocks and the University of Life for me.'

But not, evidently, the Polytechnic of Originality.

It was quite a relief when the interview finished and they had time to grab a cup of coffee before the next candidate. They didn't need Sim; they already had enough loud-mouthed know-nothing know-alls in the organisation.

Once they had settled down again with their drinks and had reminded themselves of the contents of the next CV, they rang

Clare to send in its subject. Two minutes later she appeared again, armed with another candidate plus a couple of questions from Barry about project resource needs. The third interviewee was different again, which was perhaps just as well. For a moment, Steve wasn't convinced she was in the right place. From the look of her clutched wicker basket with a tea towel over it, she might be on her way to the local craft fair, and from the way she was dressed, that was probably where she bought most of her clothes. Her shoes didn't go with her skirt, her cardigan, or one another, and her hair looked as if its owner had been attacked by a group of short-sighted delegates to a convention on abstract topiary[1]. Lizzy Knowles hardly looked as if she would set the organisation on fire, unless perhaps they asked her to try to cook something in the little kitchen by the stairs.

Steve started the interview by asking her to say a bit about herself. It was a mistake, producing as it did a flurry of blinking and a couple of false starts before she settled for 'Well, I started at the school of hard knocks...'

Oh blimey, they're all at it now.

Steve was struggling to weigh her up. He wasn't sure whether she was having problems with her contact lenses or whether his ruthless questioning had made her tearful. She was clearly disorganised and messy, as her rambling covering letter amply demonstrated. And yet there was some quality in her manner that encouraged him to think that she might have useful experience of coping with long years of disappointment and non-achievement.

Darren was also showing signs of having seen something in her, a certain vulnerability perhaps, and Steve wondered whether he'd already made his own selection. If he had, it was not influenced by the standard of her answers to the technical questions that they asked. She considered each one carefully, rolling it around inside her head for a bit before providing an

---

[1] Actually, thinking about, there's no such thing as abstract topiary, so that bit didn't really work.

answer that almost-but-didn't make sense. After her fourth consecutive slightly strange reply, Steve came to the twin realisations that this was the best that they were ever likely to get from her and that they were only three minutes into the interview. It was going to be rather embarrassing to stop it there, and in any case there were another twenty-seven minutes to fill until the next person. With significant help from Darren, who was unusually chatty, they managed to spin the questions out for more than another quarter of an hour. They even persuaded her to reveal what was in the basket – twelve balls of home-spun wool that she was taking to try to sell at a homespun craft show that afternoon.

Steve waited until she was safely out of the room before pronouncing provisional judgement.

'Possibly useful? I think not. Rejected.'

Darren looked for a moment as if he had something to say, but in the end just shrugged. Clare appeared with a couple of cups of coffee – interviewing is thirsty work – and a 'remember your timesheet' look, and Simon popped in with a purchase request form for Steve to sign. It was half past eleven. They had a few more minutes to prepare themselves before it was time to call in their next intended victim, a Miss Charlotte Smithers. The procedure in this case was going to be slightly amended, as Barry had passed her as she came into the building and for some reason had decided that he would sit in on her interview. When they were ready, Steve picked up the phone to Clare and asked her to show her in.

The elegant Miss Smithers entered the room with considerable grace and refinement. Her posture was exquisite, and her divine countenance would not offend the eye of any beholder. She also had a nice pert –

'- Ask away,' she interrupted, with a mischievous smile that gave Barry the distinct impression that if he played his cards right the rest of his life could be something really wonderful.

Steve cleared his throat to start the proceedings, but before anything could leave his vocal cords Barry had launched in with a question about her industrial development experience. After that, it was question after question, interspersed with light-hearted little quips and amusing asides from Barry, and answer after answer, mingled with the sweetest of smiles, from Charlotte. She really was *frightfully* well spoken, and clearly had *impeccable* deportment, but unfortunately she didn't actually seem to *know* anything. She was supposed to have technical qualifications, but Steve couldn't help but notice that she had to turn the screw top on the bottle of mineral water both ways to find out which way it opened. He had the suspicion that her parents hadn't been able to keep up with her private school fees and that the bailiffs had come and repossessed much of her education.

'Oh well. We've still got two more. Let's not panic just yet,' Steve reasoned, after Charlotte had stridden elegantly from the room with Barry hurrying along to open the doors in the corridor for her. He shuffled his pile of CVs and interview notes. 'Come on. Lunch time.'

'OK,' said Darren, 'I'm ravishing!'

'I think the word is ravenous.'

When they reached the canteen they were greeted, if that was the right word, by both Sally the Servery and her recently acquired assistant, Attila the Till (which might not have been her real name). They were both wearing red sashes over their normal uniforms and were handing out leaflets on healthy eating. What the relationship might have been between the fine words of nutritional encouragement on the leaflets, and the varicose cutlets that sat on the serving counter, was unclear.

'They're good for your heart,' urged Sally.

'Good for its chances of appearing in a jar of formaldehyde within the week,' Darren muttered.

That rather settled it for Steve, and he went for the option of a couple of dry and crusty salad rolls instead.

They sat for a few minutes once they had finished eating, partly to let their stomachs come to terms with the latest digestive challenges, and partly to avoid having to walk back with someone from Maintenance Engineering whom neither of them liked. Darren reminded Steve of the interview that had led to Simon's recruitment three or four years back. Simon had worked for a now-bankrupt company that made speaker systems for rock concerts, but there'd been some problem with the design of their bass units, such that – at full volume – some of the larger audience members with weaker skins had come very close to bursting. Although he had heard the story many times before, the mental imagery stayed with Steve all the way out of the canteen, back across the car park and up to the interview room again.

'Now who's next? Ah, Glenn somebody or other. Perhaps he'll be better: his CV talks a lot about work experience.'

Glenn turned out to have jug ears and nothing much between them. His work experience turned out to be three short periods stacking shelves or operating a check-out, with nothing much between them either. He had one vocational qualification, in lurking and looking morose. The numerous other achievements to which his CV made passing reference amounted to half a term spent at Reading University. Shame it wasn't Reading and Writing University, thought Steve, mentally throwing his application form into the waste paper basket. Thank you; don't call us. Darren did question how a transient attendance at university could amount to 'numerous' achievements, to which he got a half-hearted reply that, well, one's a number, innit?

As Glenn loped out of the room, Steve had to fight to stop himself from peering down to see whether his knuckles were dragging along the floor. One thing was becoming clear: they weren't going to have a problem meeting their government social inclusion quota.

Barry returned from escorting Charlotte to her car at that point, well over an hour after her interview had finished but still only halfway through showing her the classic lines and gleaming paintwork of the shiny new Pompous.

'She'd be a great asset on the team,' he said hopefully. 'Very professional. Very focussed. What d'you think? Shall we cancel the rest of the interviews? Hasn't she got great presence?'

'No thanks,' murmured Darren, 'I don't go for simpering.'

'There's only one more candidate anyway,' Steve pointed out.

Indeed there was, and Rachael Bryce it was. The final candidate from Barry's dream selection looked a little as if she had just stepped out of one of Steve's nightmares. At some time in the recent past she had sprayed along the centreline of her hair, and forehead, with a green spray can, and she had more metalwork embedded in her face than there was in your average reinforced concrete retaining wall. On her neck was an unusual tattoo, which seemed to portray two slugs mating, unless it happened to be a love bite that had become infected.

Oh dear, oh dear, oh dear. These days there seemed to be more and more people around who qualified as weirdoes, by at least one of Steve's many criteria. He might have been narrow-minded, but his narrow-mindedness was wide-ranging and comprehensive. He did try to accept that the world was changing, but it wasn't really his forte. People would just have to take him for what he was, old-fashioned and rather bigoted towards those who modelled their heads along the lines of a mediaeval mace with verdigris.

The allotted half hour had barely started before it became clear that her experience of school exams had left Rachael convinced of how the world expected to have its questions answered.

'Why do you want the job?' asked Steve.

There was a long pause and a blank look.

'Yes?' prompted Steve.

'Oh, sorry – I was waiting to hear the options.'

'Options?'

'You know. Multi-choice. A: because LSLS are a really great company to work for. B: because I could contribute a lot and develop my skills. C: because I like the idea of working flexitime and having a good canteen on site. That sort of thing.'

'Well, which? A, B or C?'

'No, it's D: none of the above.'

Steve groaned and let his head fall forwards onto the table, hopping[1] for unconsciousness or at least concussion. Why was he wasting his life like this?

After a few seconds, realising that he was undeniably still fully conscious, and starting to become somewhat self-conscious, he sat up again so that they could continue the interview. He picked up Rachael's CV, in the hope of finding a subject or interest that might get her to talk freestyle, without needing to be given choices. It wasn't easy to find anything specific amongst the flowery agency-written prose, though. Eventually, with a bit of diligent searching, he managed to ascertain that she enjoyed listening to music and drinking with her friends. Well, fancy that, there was a surprise. Nevertheless, it was something to try to hang a conversation off. Unlike her face, Steve thought to himself, which looked more like something to hang a set of keys off.

The interview rambled on, increasingly informally, for another quarter of an hour. Although Rachael was quite an authority on the music of the last six months – Prod was her personal hero, apparently – she appeared to know diddly-squat that might be of any use in life's great battle to invent, develop and commercialise competition-beating sensors. Steve would have finished the interview much sooner, but he was starting to find a fascination in the way the studs in her face moved as she talked. Eventually, though, they exhausted even the subject of disco track drum beats, and Clare came to lead Rachael away. It was decision time.

'Who can we eliminate straight away?' asked Steve.

'Nearly all of them. Make your next question harder please,' requested Darren.

'Well who was the worst of all?'

'Yep. That's harder all right.' He paused for reflection. 'I'd say that Glyn or Glenn or Gland or whatever his name was, was about the worst, but that first one was the most annoying. I'm not working with him.'

---

[1] Sorry, that's a typo. It should say 'hoping'.

'Hmm. OK.' It was hard to disagree with Darren's conclusions, but the upshot is that they would be left with only four possibilities. A combination of Sim's grit and Charlotte's polish might go quite a long way, but even playing pick-and-mix wasn't going to assemble a single decent candidate. And yet these were the only people they had left, and it was imperative they recruited someone as quickly as possible.

Steve went back to the pile of CVs and his scribbled notes on the four remaining applicants. They agreed that Rachael was probably number four, but after that things became more tricky. Steve was reluctantly forced to conclude that it came down to a choice between Mr Loud Mouth and Lady Air Head, whereas Darren admitted preferring Lizzy, to whom he had clearly taken a bit of a licking[1]. It was all rather academic as it turned out, however, as Barry reappeared at that point and promptly awarded himself the only and casting vote. To spin the process out, and to give it a thin veneer of democratic accountability, he did produce a long and rambling justification of how he'd been impressed by many of Charlotte's fine qualities, except for her looks which he hadn't even noticed. He interspersed the speech with the occasional reflex reference to some of the qualities of his new car, while Darren consoled himself by checking through Lizzy's form to find her phone number so that he could ask her out later in the week. By half past two the recruitment process was complete as far as selection was concerned. Clare was instructed to prepare a job offer letter, with the 'help' of course of an army of bureaucrats in HR, and a desk was found for Charlotte for when she started after her notice period at the air traffic control centre.

They never did establish why Dean's CV and covering letter were written in Romanian. Nor did they ever find out from Barry how he had selected him for interview when he couldn't have understood a single word of his application.

---

[1] Sorry, another misprint. It's meant to be 'liking'.

***

Lizzy Knowles let herself into the flat that she shared with her best friend Jo. The interview had gone really well, she felt. They hadn't asked her any difficult questions at all. In fact, most of the time they'd just had a very pleasant chat about the traffic and the weather.

It's truly astounding how many people reason like that. A little simple logic should lead you to the conclusion that being grilled is a sign that you're a serious possibility and it's worth making the effort of seeing just what your limits are. Cosy chats are reserved for situations in which you've already been classified as hopeless and where the interviewers can't bring themselves to sit and watch you squirm.

Still, let's not disillusion her just yet. If Lizzy thinks it went very well, so be it. The truth could hardly be more different: she hadn't got the job, and she was about to end up with Darren.

She went into the kitchen and naïvely made herself a cup of celebratory tea.

***

Barry was so disappointed. All the adverts for the car had promised him twisting open roads across heathery moors, or the chance to drive across fragile ecosystems to the top of unspoilt mountain wildernesses, and yet here he was stuck in stop-start traffic with a van driver behind him who was more intent on finishing his crossword than he was on avoiding Barry's shiny rear crumple zone. In front of him stretched a long line of vehicles, edging forward intermittently in a series of slow compression waves. Up in the distance, some yellow earthmovers were starting the long slow road-widening process that would allow the traffic jams of the future to be short fat ones instead of long thin ones. He was already late for his meeting and it was abundantly clear that he would get later yet. He bitterly hated being late. He couldn't bear the thought of meetings wallowing inefficiently along without the brilliance of his personal contributions.

He pressed a button to bring up the traffic news on the radio, but all that happened was that the boot flew open, scattering dozens of sheets of paper into a sudden gust of wind that carried them like giant confetti into the hedge at the bottom of the motorway embankment. For a second, he panicked, but then he realised that it was only Steve's various project plans and all that stuff. He would have to get him to print them out and reannotate them again on Monday morning. Oh well, it wasn't the end of the world. He got out and closed the boot, found another button that *did* summon the traffic news guru, and inched slowly forward with the rest of the queue.

***

Back at SLSL, Steve had been dreading Friday for some days now, on account of his six-monthly health check-up with the company nurse that had been scheduled for ten o'clock. He'd never been good with matters medical. When he was a small child he'd sometimes nearly passed out when his father had cut his fingernails for him, and now he'd grown into someone unsure as to whether he was one of the Worried Well or one of the About To Be Diagnosed With Something Serious. The only thing he was pretty certain about was that he was not one of the Unworried anything.

This week had already been over-blessed with medical interventions, what with Tom's skewering and Darren's scalpel. Now it was Steve's turn. He gritted his teeth and braced himself. The nurse had a wicked sense of humour that could be distressing. It was rather alarming to squeamishly turn your head away as she took a blood sample, only to have her yell out 'Whoa! Artery! I've hit an artery!' every time.

He knocked on the door as quietly as he could, in the hope that she wouldn't hear. To his distress, though, he was immediately called in, and he entered the small office-come-surgery to see a large number of tubes on the desk, each with a different coloured cap, each ready for a sample of his precious blood. There seemed to be rows of them: it really looked as if she meant to drain him completely this time. Steve had suspected for a while that health care professionals inflict extra tests on hypochondriacs in order to discourage excessive repeat business.

In the event, it turned out that there was to be no large-scale blood-letting that morning, at least as far as Steve was concerned. And boy, had he been concerned. No, instead she was going to focus today on exploring his lifestyle and measuring some of his related vital signs. Judging by the tut-tutting and the worried tapping of her pencil against her teeth, it did not look too good. After telling him that he was heading for a burn-out and possible stress-death, she then turned her attention to criticising his diet, his drinking habits and his lack of an adequate exercise regime. Apparently he was going to have to choose between pushing weights or pushing up daisies. The former needed to be three times a week, the latter once each spring. It was his choice. Or he could go swimming more often, perhaps three times a week, or he could go for a brisk walk three times a week. It didn't really matter which, so long as it left him slightly out of breath and raised his pulse by twenty or more. Steve tried to argue that reading his e-mails often made him feel like that, and usually more than three times a week, but nursie wasn't going to be budged on the subject, so an improved exercise regime it was to be. And he wasn't to forget to improve his diet, either.

Before he limped out she did take a single small blood sample, just to show willing, and she gave him a leaflet on environmentally friendly burials.

'See you again soon,' she beamed, slapping her stickiest plaster onto the hairiest bit of his arm.

Steve returned to his desk via a much-needed pick-me-up cup of coffee substitute from the drinks machine. Only Clare and Darren were in the office. The others were elsewhere, testing prototypes, attending meetings, or breaking things. Clare was in the middle of trying to help the marketing department by thinking of words rhyming with sensor, while Darren was having a ten minute tea break while he wrestled with the problem of trying to decide what to buy someone as an apology that he didn't really mean.

The morning finished with an hour of compulsory safety training for everyone, after Lisa had conscientiously reported Darren's scalpel accident of Tuesday. Such training was a fairly frequent occurrence at SLSL, and was a complete waste of time. After all, despite being retrained and told to be more careful on about a monthly basis, the minor injuries kept on coming. Labs and factories are dangerous places. As are meeting rooms, corridors, stores cupboards and coffee machines.

The safety officer turned up about fifteen minutes late, having gashed his hand on the edge of his car door, which gave everyone else another chance to reminisce about some of their favourite past incidents. There had been that time when Clare had sustained a minor injury whilst using her pencil sharpener, and afterwards the entire department had been made to undergo twenty minutes of pencil sharpener awareness training. Then there was the time that Simon had accidentally dropped a heavy box of redundant equipment on Darren's foot, and the time very shortly afterwards when Simon's chair had mysteriously collapsed while he was quietly sitting in it.

Today, training consisted of being told that scalpel blades had sharp edges, with the suggestion that safer alternatives be used. Quite how they were supposed to use a screwdriver to accurately trim small plastic prototypes was quite beyond Steve, but he didn't want to argue the point, because he had more than enough other things that he needed to be getting on with. They were then shown a short video nasty, demonstrating the consequences of getting it wrong. Suitably chastened, they all filed out of the training room.

'Wow. That was worse than Tuesday. I've not seen that much blood since that cucumber went through my finger a couple of years ago,' said Darren.

'Surely it was the other way round?' suggested Simon.

'No, I definitely blame the cucumber.'

Steve gave a Steve sigh. Life – or at least Darren – could get a little weird at times.

Scratching at the skin next to his plaster, which was starting to itch, Steve led the way to the canteen for lunch.

***

'Right then!' announced Miss Blatherspit to the Year 3 class, on a beach somewhere on the east coast, 'what can you find in the rockpools?'

The answer, after twenty minutes of diligent exploration and research, was almost nothing, as they'd been quite worked through by four preceding school parties that morning. It would in fact have been absolutely nothing, had Tom not ended up sitting in one of the pools when he'd tried to jump across three of them at once.

'Never mind,' Miss Blatherspit consoled them, 'we've got another lovely treat lined up for you all now.' And with that she led the way back to the coach, which was waiting to take them off to a reconstructed iron age village and craft re-enactment centre. There would be weaving, pottery and goat-milking to try, and, for the boys, stabbing one another with sharp pieces of iron.

Nobody got hurt, though, except for Tom who managed to stab his own leg.

5

Saturday was the day of Woody's funeral.

Natalie had got the idea from her friend Rebecca. Rebecca's guinea pig had died the week before (in somewhat suspicious circumstances, it has to be said), and had been given a large state funeral in their back garden. Reports circulating the school playground of the solemn magnificence of the occasion had reached Natalie's ears, and then Chloe's. Chloe was in fact so taken with the idea that she wanted to have a funeral for next door's cat. When she had asked Jackie whether they could have a 'fumerool', the answer had however been an emphatic no, they would have to wait for him to die first. Chloe went into a deep sulk and Natalie went into the garden to try to find something else that they could bury. She was just about to give up and use one of Chloe's favourite dolls when she came across a dead woodlouse, curled up against the pair of rusting secateurs that Steve had left out since the previous Saturday.

The memorial service for the deceased woodlouse was conducted by Natalie, assisted by Chloe. It started with the whole family having to sing Woody's favourite songs. Whether a 'yee-ha' hoedown is really what he would have wanted was a matter of some conjecture to Steve, but before he'd had time to reach an opinion the service had moved on to a graphic description of Woody's tragic and fatal accident and the girls' part in trying to prevent it. When the grisly details had finally all been recounted, which took some time and much improvised dramatic recon-struction, Chloe bowed, expecting applause. The lack of it looked set to trigger another sulk, but the situation was skilfully saved by Natalie calling for a two second silence in which to remember Woody. She then announced loudly, 'I will now bury him!', and swung Jackie's trowel high above her head ready to plunge into the ground.

'Not in the lawn, you won't. Can't you do it over there by that bush?'

'OK, then. That's his favourite place. Well, it would have been if he'd ever gone there.'

'Woody has gone to a better place,' Chloe added sombrely, not to be left out.

'Dear woodlouse, we miss you and we're sorry that you're dead. Amen,' intoned Natalie.

She proceeded to hack at the soil until a suitable grave had been created for the last mortal remains of the recently departed much-legged one. (Or, at least, much-legged up to the time of his accident.) Natalie then committed Woody's body to the grave and his soul to heaven. Steve's mobile rang at that point, as Natalie had forgotten to ask the congregation to switch them off, but a stern glance and the formality of the occasion combined to persuade her father not to answer it. She covered the sad little corpse with a sprinkling of soil and a piece of dead worm, and then planted into the earth a simple tombstone that she had fashioned out of that morning's empty cereal packet. She spoke a few more solemn words ('Oh woodlouse, we worship you...'), there was a bit of hymn singing, and they were finally done. Not the jolliest of ways to spend quarter of an hour, thought Jackie, but at least it would be good practice for Grandma, although she would need a rather larger hole.

***

After lunch, Natalie and Chloe took their parents across to the local village fête. My, what a time they all had. Steve was made to try to guess the name of the Teddy Bear. I don't know: Fred? Nigel? Aloysius? Then he had to guess the weight of the woman behind the cake stall, and then he had to guess the number of fag-ends in the jar. Steve guessed nine stone three for the cake woman, which he knew was far too low, but diplomatic. He guessed fifteen hundred for the number of fag-ends. He knew that that was too high at the moment, but he'd noticed that a couple of eleven year old lads behind the marquee were working on a few more. It didn't really matter though: he had no intent on claiming his free ashtray, even if he won. It was the fun of the fair, of taking part, that mattered.

Jackie and the girls had hurried on ahead, and Steve strolled after them. The next tent was hosting an Ugliest Dog competition, which had only one entry, and the one beyond was proclaiming an Ugliest Baby competition, which had no entries at all which was odd considering the ones that Steve had seen as he walked through the crowds. Jackie had halted in front of a small fenced-off area, where a group of bearded men in white shirts and short trousers were hopping backwards in some sort of a square formation. Natalie and Chloe seemed to be rather transfixed by this, but Steve carried on towards the attractions beyond. He didn't much care for all that slap whacky diddle, whacky hey-hey stuff that went on, with its accompaniment of skipping around and waving of hankies and young birch twigs, on village greens across the thatched parts of the south of England. It was somehow comforting to know that someone somewhere was doing it - a bit like gentle games of cricket on rustic village greens – but it was also comforting to know that it wasn't him and that he didn't have to watch it.

He couldn't avoid the two raffle ticket sellers, though, because they had hit upon the underhand tactics of (a) putting an arm each round his shoulders and (b) being young, female and scantily clad. With Jackie perhaps only a minute or two behind him, he did not have time to stay and argue with them for long, and he ended up paying five pounds for five chances to win an adventure experience that he knew he would never have the courage to do.

The others caught up with him at a line of trestle tables where a vast selection of everything was being sold. He didn't exactly intend on being there, either, but nothing pushes and shoves like an old person at a second hand clothing stall, and somehow he had got himself tangled up. It took a concerted family effort to extricate him from the grip of a pensioner who had convinced herself that he was somehow concealing a pair of slippers that she wanted, but eventually he found himself free and standing in front of the boy scouts tent. He was about to lead the girls off in the direction of a helter-skelter that lurked in the corner of the field, but Jackie had seen a chance to put his hunter-gatherer skills to the test, and before he knew it he was furiously rubbing two sticks together in an attempt to start a fire and win ten pounds. Ten minutes and four blisters later, having failed to win a prize, he was being marched back towards a hook-a-duck stall that Natalie had spotted. On the way, he couldn't help but notice that they still hadn't managed to get any entrants for the Ugliest Baby competition.

They passed a fortune teller's tent, whose occupant loudly called out from her doorway to Jackie that 'He's got a very healthy aura, dear. That, or his hair is on fire.' For a second, Steve thought that perhaps he had managed to kindle a wayward spark after all, but a quick check with his hands reassured him that nothing was ablaze aloft. Madam Mysteriosity's psychic powers were perhaps having an off-day.

Not so for the man on the hook-a-duck stall, who was clearly very psychic indeed because he was able to reach straight for one of the 'small' prizes even before he'd checked the colour of the spot painted on the underside of Chloe's hooked duck. Another one pound fifty gone; another shapeless soft toy that even his daughter was not much bothered about. Steve couldn't believe he was actually spending so much time and money at this fête worse than death when he had an important report to write and several important e-mails to send. It wasn't even as if Natalie or Chloe or Jackie actually enjoyed doing these things, surely? But his thoughts were interrupted by Chloe, who was now clamouring for twenty pence so that she could have a go at guessing the number of marbles filling a large glass jar. The prize appeared to be the marbles, but not the jar.

'What will you do with them if you win?' asked Jackie.

'I could build a castle,' said Chloe.

'?!'

'Or you could play marbles with them,' Steve pointed out.

'How do you play marbles?'

'I'm not really sure, actually. I think you roll them into each other and hope that glass splinters don't fly off and blind next door's cat.'

'Oh, don't worry about that. He could have one of the marbles as a glass eye,' said Natalie.

They wandered on, round the rest of the stalls, and then round them all thrice again. On the final lap, Steve saw that the addition of a fifty pounds cash prize and the chance to appear on local television had now produced a queue a hundred yards long outside the Ugliest Baby marquee. Three stalls further on, the teddy bear's name had been revealed as Teddy. A scribbled chalk notice proclaimed four winners, three of them being members of the organising committee and one of them being 'Emily Benson (aged five)'. Perhaps the little girl sadly cradling a damaged teddy bear was she, and perhaps the pile of scratching and gouging middle-aged ladies were they.

***

Steve put the light out and closed his eyes. He wondered how many people had choked to death on marbles during the course of human history. Then he pondered the question of where you'd go to buy a death bed. Anyone's thoughts can have a tendency to the unusual as they drift towards sleep.

'Have you had another look at the shed door yet?' asked Jackie suddenly from the patch of blackness to his left, somewhat interrupting his musings.

He lay there for a second, blinking at the darkness. How had he got so quickly from the frontiers of philosophy to discussing a shed door that wouldn't shut properly?

'I had a look this morning, but I think it's going to need some new wood to fix it.'

'What's wrong with it?'

'It's all distorted and starting to rot at the top.'

Jackie grunted a vague 'oh' of acknowledgement and rolled over to go to sleep. Steve lay there for a moment, thinking. And then, lest he died unexpectedly in the night and those became his last words, he quietly added 'Good night, sleep well.'

***

Sunday dawned bright and clear, the sort of day where the air was crisp and you could have seen for miles if it wasn't for next door's house getting in the way. Outside, just below the overhanging corner of the shed roof, the Steve Oscroft of the spider world was frantically trying to untangle itself from its web. Indoors, the other Steve was pouring breakfast cereal for the two girls and Jackie was supervising the kettle. They were always up early on a Sunday, as it was Natalie's swimming morning and they needed to have her in the water by eight thirty.

'I don't want that, I want *that!*' said Chloe, pointing to a cereal packet that was lurking near the back of the cupboard.

'Oh. I didn't think anybody liked that one,' said Steve.

'Then why did you buy it?' asked Natalie, with faultless logic.

While Steve was thinking about that one, Jackie stepped in to point out that she had been the one who had bought it, because she thought that Natalie might want to collect the tokens on the back that would get them a free CD of Prod's new debut album *Changed My Tariff.* Free if they could eat twenty kilos of tasteless cereal before the special packets disappeared from the shops.

'Pronk are that good are they?' asked Steve innocently.

'It's Prod, Dad, and it's a he.' It seemed that even Chloe was a fan.

They got to the baths at twenty-eight minutes past eight, and Jackie ran in with Natalie while Steve locked the car and followed behind with Chloe and Chloe's doll Osmarelda. The previous lesson was still going on, and the water was teeming with brightly coloured little swimming outfits, their tiny owners splashing around like multicoloured tadpoles working on their frogstroke.

Natalie's lesson started ten minutes late and today was back crawl. She could already do a passable breaststroke, plus a front crawl reminiscent of a wounded helicopter, but she had never actually tried swimming on her back. Thirty-five minutes later, she was more or less able to do it, but very slowly and only in circles. In the best family tradition, she had made a weak start and then gradually declined. Perhaps it wasn't a problem, though: it was hard to imagine a set of circumstances in which back crawl would be your stroke of choice in any sort of an emergency, unless perhaps you needed to keep a lookout for vultures.

Steve was just musing on why crawl is the fastest stroke in the water and yet the slowest on land, when the tannoy announced the end of the session and the children all climbed out. Having got that out of the way, and having driven them all home, he was then free to get on with some of the work that he'd promised Barry he would do over the weekend. He went upstairs to the spare room and settled down with the draft Sling project plan for an hour or so while Jackie did some baking and the girls went into the lounge and played at trolls going shopping. Peace and quiet only lasted ten minutes, however, before Chloe realised that great fun could be derived from impersonating her sister's swimming teacher. Five minutes of chanting 'Don't windmill, Natty, don't windmill, Natty' was enough to drive Natalie out of the room and into the kitchen to enlist her mother's support for administering a regime of corporal discipline in the direction of little sister.

'How many pairs of arms do you think I have?' asked Jackie. (Do all parents say things like that?)

Natalie was pleased that the principle of punishment had been so readily accepted and that they were only haggling over resources, but was rather less pleased that it was she who was then unjustly ordered to go somewhere else and do something else, away from her sister. (Do all parents do things like that?) Accordingly and grudgingly, Natalie went upstairs to see whether Steve might be ready to play something with her now?

'Can I have ten minutes to finish this?' asked Steve, who had not actually yet started anything.

Natalie conceded that he could, and came back in five. They played a board game together for half an hour, and then Natalie wandered downstairs to see whether she could help do anything to get lunch ready, such as lick out the cake mixture bowl? Steve switched on his laptop and finally started to look at the report and the project plan. From that point on, he got on famously, and made enormous progress during the rest of the day. True, there was lunch to be eaten and then dishes to wash up, and he did get dragged away from his desk four more times during the afternoon: once to play at trolls, once to tickle Chloe, once to help turn an old shoe box into a miniature theatre to attract hedgehogs, and once to judge a fainting competition.

By tea time, he decided he had done all he could do without consulting Barry, and he put the computer away and went to see what the rest of the family was doing. The girls had been diligently and dutifully visiting Woody's grave every time that they thought about it for more than twenty four hours now, but even the most patient child can get bored and by four o'clock Natalie had been asking to dig Woody up again so that she could see what a woodlouse's skeleton looked like. ('I bet his little skull is so sweet.') Jackie had said 'no', though, and refused to get the trowel out of the garage, and in no time at all the girls had in any case lost interest and wandered away to go and feed some grapes to Poddle who had been sitting on the fence watching the world. Jackie meanwhile was on the drive, washing her car and shouting over to the old lady across the road, who was out pruning her nettle display. The old dear had some time ago finally lost all feeling in her hands, which had brought a merciful curtain down on all the swearing and cursing that had disturbed Steve's ability to work at home at weekends in years gone by.

That evening, after they had all had tea and watched a bit of TV together, Jackie decided that they had better agree what, if anything, to do with the October half-term that was rapidly approaching. Would Steve be able to have the week off, because he was starting to look a bit stressed? He was indeed a bit stressed, but he felt he actually needed a week to catch up at work and get things done, not seven days of restyling the hair of orange and green trolls or deciding which daughter's swoons were the most convincing. It might be best if he postponed his time off for now, and he was trying to think of a way of saying so that wasn't going to offend or upset Jackie, but his face had already alerted her to his lack of thrill at the prospect of a week at home.

'Well how about going away somewhere then?'

'Well,' he started, hesitantly, 'perhaps...'

'Good. That's settled then. We'll go to the Lakes.'

Steve loved the Lake District, and they'd spent many a holiday there over the years. October half-term was one of his favourite times of year, with the trees changing and the clear autumn air. He remembered one October there when they'd climbed twenty hills in six days. Mostly in sunshine, and some of it in heat, so it might not have been the Lakes, thinking about it. He did need a break, and it should be good provided Jackie could find them a nice cottage at such short notice. But it would mean having to fit all the Lemming and Sling stuff around that week, and that wouldn't be easy.

He sighed. He noticed that he'd been doing a lot of that lately.

***

In no time at all it was Monday morning, and time to start the daily routine all over again. Get up, get dressed, have breakfast, hear Chloe announce that she's just chosen what she wants for Christmas, see the girls off to school, and go to work. It was a bit of a bad hair day for Steve, but that was pretty much routine as well. His hair was his crowning glory, and like most good crowns it had a tendency to stick up at the corners, at least when it was in a bad mood. And having been kept awake much of the night by his rumbling stomach, the rest of him was indeed rather grumpy.

Being the first working day of the month, Barry was in particularly high spirits, and that made things even worse.

'This morning is a new opportunity; a fresh shiny new day!' he boomed.

Everything was running in its usual rut now. That one was so hackneyed that Darren was able to echo it when he arrived ten minutes later: 'Another month! Another opportunity!' He slumped down in front of his desk. 'Gosh, it's depressing.'

Steve had switched his computer on a few minutes earlier, but like all computers it had got slower and slower and took longer and longer to warm up. Too full of viruses and anti-virus software, no doubt. Eventually his e-mail inbox did open, but to his surprise there was nothing new in it. Normally messages came in overnight or over the weekend. He glanced across to where Simon was busy filling in an application form for unauthorised leave, but *he* didn't seem to be having any troubles with the computer network. Steve was just about to call across to Darren to see if he had managed to get into the system yet when suddenly about thirty e-mails pinged up on his screen. Well, they didn't actually ping as such, but it made his life a bit more exciting if he thought of it that way.

So he had his messages and his extra set of problems and he could settle down to fighting the day. It was going to be yet another one where things accumulated on his 'To Do' list faster than he could even count them. Steve had spent his entire life searching for the elusive way of organising his task list that would allow him to be lean, mean and efficient. Unfortunately, he'd never quite found it. All he ever seemed to do was to lurch from one format to another. It had been a hand-written book at one stage, with everything added in chronological order. Then he'd decided he needed to organise everything by category instead. A couple of months after that he'd decided that it was better to have it on loose sheets, and then later on, cards. Then he decided to go electronic, and spent three evenings typing it all into the computer. Then he felt that a spreadsheet would be better than a simple list, so that he could sort and prioritise tasks by different criteria. Then he realised that he needed a printed-off paper list that he could carry around and update or annotate on the spot. Then he decided that keeping the paper list reconciled with the electronic master copy was taking too long, so he went all-electronic again, with the idea of editing it every three or four evenings to keep it up to date. Finally, in hair-tearing desperation, when he realised that he was never going to find the time to do that, he decided to buy a pocket book that he could write jobs into as soon as he thought of them.

If only he had realised that storing the list in the shredder was the answer, he might have actually had time to get some of the jobs done.

***

'No.'

'Oh. OK then.'

That was that. Charlotte had decided not to come to work for SLSL and was refusing to change her mind. They would have to choose a different candidate. Barry was bitterly disappointed, not least because he was sure the salesman had said that if he bought a Pompous he would be able to attract women without any problem whatsoever. All his powers of persuasion had failed, though, and he was now reluctantly forced to call an impromptu meeting of himself, Steve and Darren to choose a different candidate to complete his crack team. The conversation swung back and forth between the principal demerits of each of the other five people they had interviewed until Barry decided that Sim was his next choice, on the grounds that he might bring some fresh thinking to the place, from what he'd heard from the other two who had actually bothered to meet him.

'He certainly might,' agreed Steve. Along the lines of think-ing that they needed to sheep-proof their accelerometers for when they did field trials, for example.

'Excellent,' said Barry, and nipped out to tell Clare to give him a call. He was back within two minutes, having been in-formed that Sim had already phoned them previously to invite them to get stuffed. They were on to their third choice candidate. More debate. More judgement from he who hadn't been there. Lizzy Knowles next. Barry trotted out again to see Clare.

They had to wait ten minutes before she came back to inform them that Lizzy would take the job but couldn't start until after some big meeting she was attending.

'Oh dear. When's that? Are we going to have to wait for weeks?'

'Oh, I don't know. I didn't ask. I'll go and ring her again and see if we can negotiate with her current employer.' Clare disappeared again for a few minutes.

'She's not actually in work at the moment,' she said when she returned. 'The big meeting is some quilting exhibition she wants to go to on Thursday. She can start on Friday at 9.30.'

'9.30's a little late in the day. Couldn't she make it earlier?'

'Apparently not. She's not an expert on getting out of bed early, she says.'

'Isn't she? Well we'll have to look forward to seeing her on Friday at 9.30, but after that perhaps somebody can work on her levels of expertise.'

Barry happened to look at Darren as he said that, which rather startled him out of his reverie. Thinking about getting Lizzy out of bed hadn't been uppermost in his mind. He felt he had to say something, though, so he said 'Uh', but by the time he had got any further Barry had looked at his watch and stood up. It was ten twenty-five, and he had to dawdle off to a meeting with the Head of Strategic Incompetence. He left them doing whatever it was they did. In Steve's case it was trying to finish a report on the Lemming lacquering experiments.

By quarter past eleven Steve had more or less completed the report, ready for a final read-through before he distributed it around all the relevant departments of SLSL. Thirst things first, though: time for a cup of coffee.

The drinks machine was in another of its moods, and refused to take any of Steve's coins. It was always quite happy to give fifty pence pieces out in change, but it never seemed to accept them. He often wondered where it got them from in the first place, but in the meantime he was (very) gradually accumulating the entire world's supply of them.

His lack of acceptable money gave him an excuse to wander down to the chocolate machine, to see whether that might be any more obliging and might in the process give him some change that the drinks machine might like. He told himself that all the snacks he ate were a protest at stick-thin catwalk models, but in reality they were a protest at the protestations of his ever-hungry stomach. Anyway, chocolate was good for you. Apparently it contained antioxidants, and he certainly didn't want to risk oxidising.

When he got back with his cup of coffee and his slightly quietened stomach he found Lisa standing on a chair hunting for a couple of safety folders that were somewhere on the top shelf, and Darren sitting at his desk with his eyes closed. He was probably thinking profound thoughts about sensor attenuation factors or some such, but then again he might have been asleep. Steve put his cup down and was just about to settle down with his laptop for a final on-screen re-reading of his report when Lisa's telephone rang.

'Can you pick that up, please?' she shouted down to Darren, he being the closest to her desk.

'No.'

'You're being unusually awkward today, even for you.'

'I know. I'm making a special effort.'

'Darren!' she shouted.

'Hell's bells!' he grumbled, and pushed his chair back to go over to her desk, but Steve had already beaten him to it.

'Good morning, Sense Less Sensors Limited,' he said.

It was only Barry, who wondered whether anybody had a spare copy of the planning folder that the Head of Strat Inc had managed to lose. They hadn't. No-one had planned on the only copy getting lost.

As soon as Steve put the phone down, Lisa turned on Darren.

'Why can't you do me a simple favour?'

'I was busy. I was just thinking some profound thoughts about sensor attenuation factors. And then I fell asleep.'

'What is it with men? Can't you ever do two simple things at once?'

'Of course we can. But I'm not your slave, you know, so you can stop bossing me about.'

'I see we seem to have a new office Chief Moaner.'

'Yes, I appointed myself last night. The duties are largely ceremonial, if you'll pardon the pun.'

'Please shut up,' said Lisa, stepping down from the chair with the safety folders.

Her ex-boyfriend settled down to chuntering about men's ability to handle several complex tasks together, interspersed with the occasional 'Hell's bells and buckets of teeth', and Steve returned to his drink. And then, with the sort of time-efficient multitasking ability of which only a man is truly capable, he managed to simultaneously delete three sections of report and pour his coffee into both his lap and his laptop.

***

Steve took a shorter lunch break than usual, and spent most of it worrying about the fact that he'd been so busy of late that none of the recent work on his computer had been backed up properly anywhere else. He tried to print off a paper copy of the Lemming lacquer report for Barry, who liked things he could scribble on, but it was clear that his laptop was not at all well, and twenty past one found Steve's hands splayed across the keyboard in a sort of desperate Ctrl-Alt-Delete-Break-Escape sort of manoeuvre while his nose rhythmically tapped the space bar. It was to no avail, though: all the buttons had turned into placebos, and his frantic keyboard prodding wasn't even able to summon up any of the computer's nonsensical error messages, never mind its indecipherable icons. It seemed irremediably jammed up, and the space bar, it had to be admitted, smelt strongly of coffee. Even unplugging the battery pack didn't help. The laptop was in some sort of irreversible silicon trance. The life of his previous computer had been ended back in the spring by an under-engineered shelf that he'd erected in the spare room at home, and now this one appeared to be about to join its predecessor in microprocessor heaven.

Steve gave a silent curse. It looked as if it might be time for a new computer, and he was going to have to explain to Barry the reason for this one's demise. In the space of three weeks his coffee spills had wiped out one satnav, most of a major report, and a laptop computer.

His chance to break the bad news came sooner than he had expected, for Barry was no different from any boss and instinctively turned up whenever someone was in the middle of making a mess of things. On this occasion he came in to announce that he had managed to negotiate half of Jon and Neil's time to help on the Sling project, in a bid to speed things up. Steve felt he was in little position to argue, although privately he rather doubted that having Sicknote and Workshy on the team was going to ease his lot a whole lot.

After a suitable hushed pause of gratitude – four seconds – he broached the subject of his recently caffeinated laptop and then closed his eyes and held his breath. Barry didn't exactly congratulate him, or if he did, he chose some strange phrases, but he did eventually accept the situation and suggested that Steve try to get a loan one from the IT department.

Steve was just about to express real thanks at that point, but Barry then ruined the moment by breaking the news that he wanted him to fly out to the USA at six days' notice to try to persuade a potential new customer that the new SLSL sensors were worth buying. Steve treated himself to a drawn-out inward groan. He hated overseas travel, and this was plainly one of those assignments that had 'ordeal' written all over it. He could now suddenly see that last week, when he'd felt so very very stressed, was actually a kind of golden age of worry-free relaxation, a bygone time of carefree innocence and easy living. He desperately tried to think of an excuse, but nothing would come. Or at least, nothing credible.

'What does Jane think about you going away on business trips?' asked Barry.

'She's not pleased, but she accepts it,' replied Steve, ignoring his boss's ignorance of his wife's name.

'Oh, that's good. My wife seems to be in a bad mood whenever I'm about to go away on business,' said Barry. 'In fact, thinking about it, she always seems to be in a bad mood.'

Steve couldn't possibly imagine why. And he couldn't think of a reason why he couldn't go, either, which was rather more serious.

'I'll have to tell you later in the week what it involves,' said Barry. 'But you'll need to tread carefully because there's wheeling and dealing afoot, and we can't have you insider-trading and getting rich, can we?'

'No, Barry,' echoed Steve slowly, 'you can't have me getting rich.'

But his boss had already gone to finish waxing his car. He'd got most of it done while the others had been interviewing on the previous Thursday, but he still had the colour-coordinated spoilers and valances to do. He wanted to do it in company time, because it gave him an underling-free opportunity to think his profound managerial thoughts.

Steve was left with thoughts that were equally profound, in their own way. He was thinking of how much he was looking forward to flying the Atlantic once again: the endless waiting around, the cramp, the fear, the refreshing towelettes. It was all rather special.

***

The dead computer situation went better than Steve dared to hope, and while he was being briefed on Thursday morning by the Marketing Department ready for his American trip, Lisa took it upon herself to persuade the IT department to lend him a spare laptop. By half past nine it had shown up on his desk, right next to where he placed his cups of coffee.

'It had been returned to IT because it was infested with Keyboard Borer larvae, but they sprayed it with cheap aftershave and they think it's OK now,' Lisa reported.

What hadn't shown up yet was Barry. It was quite a misty morning, so there was the possibility that his journey in had been disrupted. When it reached five to ten, though, Steve went off to see whether perhaps he had gone straight to his office without bothering to come in to say 'good morning' to them. He needed to discuss how he was to play the meetings in America, so it was important he spoke to him while there was still time to prepare anything else he might need, but as there was no sign of him in his office either, he returned to his desk.

Darren was just replacing his telephone receiver as Steve entered the room.

'That was Barry's mother,' he announced. 'Barry won't be in until the fog lifts, because he can't find the switch for the fog lights on his new car.'

'His mother? Does he still live at home, at the age of forty-nine?'

'I think he moves back in whenever his wife leaves him.'

Steve didn't respond to that, but instead asked whether they'd yet had the results of the Lemming response speed tests from Sarah-from-testing.

Lisa waved a piece of paper at him. 'Yes, they're here, Neil dropped them round earlier.'

'Crikey, it's not like him to be that helpful, or that quick.'

'He's not one to sit around. At least, not if he can lie down,' quipped Darren, crawling under his desk for a pencil that had rolled off the edge. He proceeded to make further disparaging remarks, but they were too muffled for anyone to catch and in any case Steve was by now studying the test result graph. To his alarm, the results were awful: they had just spent eighteen months developing a sensor with the slowest performance he had ever seen. Even when he turned the graph the right way up, the results were embarrassing. The only consolation was that Barry wasn't in, so they had some time to decide what to do about it.

'Can you all come over here for a quick meeting about these Lemming results?' he asked.

'I'll be with you in a moment,' shouted a voice from under Darren's desk, as Lisa and Simon gathered round Steve and the graph of shame.

'How bad is it?' asked Lisa, peering over Steve's shoulder.

'We're achieving response times of about thirty-five.'

'What, typically, or worst case?'

'It's, er, best case, I'm afraid. Most of the time we get somewhere in the high sixties.'

'Ouch. We're going to have to try something else, aren't we?'

Steve was starting to sweat. He absent-mindedly rubbed the inflamed patch on his forearm where nursie's plaster had been a few days earlier. It looked more red and angry than ever, and was beginning to resemble a map of France. Or possibly Brazil judging by its recent deforestation.

'Are you joining us, Darren? I thought you said you'd be with us in a moment?' Lisa sounded irritated.

'I did. I just didn't say which moment.' He was still crawling around on the floor, rediscovering things that he'd lost or that he'd dropped halfway through chewing.

Simon was still scrutinizing the graph. 'I'm sure that better results are in the offing. Whatever an offing is.'

'...but I wouldn't bet on it,' added Darren, finally emerging.

'Perhaps they'll be better when we assemble them on the real production line?' suggested Simon. 'Or if we went back to the old style of cover?' He was warming to his theme now, and managed to get another three suggestions in before Darren told him to put a plug in his one-man think-tank.

'Let's just see what happens with the second lot next week,' Steve suggested.

'I'll give Sarah a ring, to see when she's going to be testing them,' Lisa volunteered, reaching for the internal telephone directory.

'No need! I'm going out for lunch with her,' said Darren, noting with some satisfaction the effect he'd managed to produce on Lisa's face. Humming quietly to himself he got out a pad of paper and started to sketch out his design ideas for the new Sling sensor head. It took Steve about fifteen minutes to understand the drawings, partly because he thought one of the doodles was a key component, but when he did he realised that Darren had solved the thorny problem of how to lay everything out. It was a little galling, but Darren could be a clever little so-and-so when he wanted to be. He might be cynical and negative, but his contributions always seemed to overshadow any that Steve managed.

It was more than a little galling, in fact.

***

Despite his private breakfast time resolution not to bring any work home that evening, by the time he'd left for home at six o'clock Steve's briefcase contained fourteen separate documents to review or action. He probably wouldn't get round to looking at them, but at least they were there, to hang over and spoil his evening. He parked the car and let himself into the house. The girls were watching a children's film on the television and Jackie was at the computer in the spare room, peering at pictures of holiday cottages on the internet.

'All the ones with damp-proof courses and working toilets have already gone,' she said.

'Shall we try somewhere else? We don't have to go to the Lakes you know.'

'No, I like the Lakes.'

'But you've been at it for days,' Steve pointed out.

'Well, we could wait until February and then go skiing.'

Jackie had been suggesting skiing holidays throughout their ten years or more together, but Steve knew with absolute certainty that it would never be for him. Apart from anything else – and there were quite a lot of anything elses - he was practically guaranteed to slip over on the drive every year at the sight of the first snowflake of winter. Jackie had once suggested, the year before they were married, the idea of having a go at cross-country-skiing, on the grounds that it was gentle and safe and might overcome his fear of icy slopes, and in a fit of youthful bravery he had almost agreed to it. Then he had thought about it a bit and said 'no', and then Jackie had thought about it a bit and had suggested she went without him. In the end, they had decided to find a compromise between her desire to try going off-piste and his desire to try sitting down for hours with a cool drink under a palm tree in the Maldives, but the results had been disappointing, frankly.

'How about the Scottish Highlands?' suggested Steve.

'I'll think about it,' said Jackie. It was a long drive, and the days would be rather short for walking, especially at the speed the Oscrofts usually managed, so it wasn't going to take her long to think about it.

Steve left her searching the internet, and went to see how the girls were doing. Their film had nearly ended, so he waited a few minutes until it had – the good guy won – and then switched the television off.

'How was school?' he asked.

He was worried how Natalie was getting on. Everything seemed to be a bit of a struggle for her, whereas her friend Sherry - Super Sherry – had been winning so many gold stars for her work that her mother was well on the way to the coveted title of Most Hated Parent At The School Gates. Steve needn't have worried, of course, because by the time Natalie would come to do her GCSEs, the relentless rise in educational achievement would mean that pretty much everyone would be getting at least 180% in every subject. But that's a year or two off yet, and outside the scope of this book.

'It was alright,' she said after reflecting carefully on an afternoon spent learning about the Battle of Trafalgar Square.

Steve was just about to ask whether she had done any violin practice, when Jackie called out to say that she'd found a cottage for half term. After he'd left the room previously, she'd decided in her infinite wisdom to try to find somewhere in northern France. And then she changed her mind and decided they would go to Wales. And lo and behold, almost at once she'd found a place that sounded perfect, right in the middle of nowhere and yet handy for the beach and the shops. It was in a small group with three other holiday cottages, so if they were lucky the girls might have some other children to play with during the long balmy October evenings. It was another compromise, between the girls' need for sand and Steve's cravings for peace and quiet and solitude and starry skies.

He peered at the cottages' website closely, but eventually grudgingly accepted that they were going and that he would be spending time that he didn't have, sitting on a British beach in October. What a pleasure it would be to squat contorted on a collection of sandy towels and coats and plastic mats for hours on end, trying not to make any bodily contact with the several acres of damp and windswept grit on which everything had been carefully arranged. And all the while he would be wondering, of course, whether his happiness would next be disturbed by a marauding seagull looking for a sandwich, by a marauding dog looking for somewhere to shake itself dry, or by a marauding dirty nappy blown over from the next windbreak and looking for nothing in particular. And two weeks afterwards, all he would have to remember it by would be a slowly healing cut on his ankle from paddling by the rocks, a set of grey photographs of people huddled in the rain, and the tendency to flick sand across the room whenever he took off his socks. He couldn't wait.

***

Lizzy's first day at SLSL did not go entirely well. She had turned up in Reception on the dot of seven minutes to ten, clutching the same wicker basket that she had brought to the interview, and Clare had gone down to bring her up to introduce to the others. They came into the office either side of Lizzy's basket. It seemed to go everywhere with her.

After handshakes all round and a slightly goofy smile from Darren, she settled down at the desk they'd cleared for her while Clare ran through some of the basic admin procedures. In any large organisation such things are never-ending, of course, so there was only time for the highlights, such as the timesheet rules, the absence reporting system, the emergency evacuation procedure and the Friday cream cake rota. Excitingly, it was Lizzy's turn to get the cakes that very day, as it happened.

At half past ten, Darren went to fetch her a cup of tea. None of the others were quite sure they had ever seen such a thing before, and Simon even had to have a brief lie down on the floor, but all the witnesses were later to recount the same tale, so their eyes were perhaps not deceiving them. Lizzy pulled the cover off her basket and today revealed a folded bundle of cloth that turned out to be the quilting sample that she'd entered into the previous day's exhibition. It was clearly work in progress, but some of the little embroidered figures had a definite grace and poise as they danced their way across what appeared to be a minefield. It wasn't really Steve's taste – he didn't like to see flying limbs, even in needlework form – and perhaps he let it show in his face.

'Please be impressed, because I've put a lot of effort in on this one,' Lizzy begged, as she glanced over at him.

'Mmm, yes, it's very, urm, nice,' he mumbled.

'It'll be better when I've finished these other ballet dancers,' Lizzy said, pointing vaguely at some of the disconnected arms and legs.

'Ah, yes, of course.'

'Did you win any prizes?' asked Lisa, also a bit relieved that dismemberment wasn't part of the deal.

'No, I didn't,' said Lizzy, catching a sudden sob. 'I've never won anything, because I never get enough panels quilted together in time.' She went on to explain how she had wanted all her life to win a cup or a rosette or even a 'highly commended', but how she could never match the output of many of the other quilters. They had more ideas, better ideas and a fantastic work rate that meant they could produce twenty times as much work for each show as Lizzy could.

'They use performance enhancing drugs,' she confided in a loud whisper, a tear appearing in her eye.

Oh yes, even patchwork quilts have their seamy side.

***

Their new technician's day really went wrong when they showed her the lab. The problem was the new safety footwear, issued in a rush after Darren's recent accident with the scalpel. No, logic doesn't always come into safety committees' decisions. Unfortunately, the new steel toed, armour plated safety boots were very heavy and for someone as slight as Lizzy made it almost impossible to walk. A bit like those textured bits of pavement that they put near zebra crossings to trip blind people into the road, they were almost guaranteed to cause an accident. In this instance, they served to promptly trip Lizzy straight onto the fireproof cabinet that held the safety equipment. She might have been alright, but she hadn't finished buttoning up her lab coat and it had caught on the corner of the bench as she stumbled, aiming her head straight at the cabinet's solid metal edge.

She didn't hit her head particularly hard, but it was enough to give her mild concussion, and she lay for a while in a crumpled heap on the floor while Lisa and Darren fussed around her, Simon went to call a first aider and Steve wondered where they might hide a body. He hadn't really expected basket girl to become basket case on her very first morning.

Darren managed to sit her up against the front of one of the lab cupboards, her face tight with pain, while Lisa ran a wad of paper towel under the cold tap and held it against her head and Steve sat down and tried to look vaguely useful in a crisis.

'Isn't it ironic,' he mused as they waited for the ambulance to take Lizzy away, 'that to avoid accidents you're meant to remove any items of loose clothing, and then when you've had one, you're meant to remove any tight ones.' It rather left you, um, well, naked. And with some of his colleagues that was never going to be a pretty sight.

6

Steve sat at his desk, very conscious of the fact that he was probably alone in the building. It wasn't entirely a surprise, of course, at this time of night. It had been good of Barry to change his mind and let him negotiate with the Americans by teleconference instead of in person – albeit on cost-cutting grounds rather than from any consideration of Steve's undesire for travel – and it was kind of him, too, to offer to meet the Americans' preferred start time. But only for the Americans, not for Steve. And nor was the 8 p.m. start the only problem – Steve hadn't missed his boss's semi-audible comment that he thought the thing would take three to four hours.

Two minutes before the allotted start time, Steve switched on the speaker-phone and began to dial. Having forgotten the 9 for an outside line, that just got him the nice pre-recorded message that the switchboard gave to overnight callers. The one about caring, minus the closing exhortation that he didn't bother to wait for. He tried again, and on this second attempt was overjoyed (sort of) to make it through to Beauchild International in America, and then to their boardroom. This was it, his big moment to show what he could do; his chance to redeem his reputation with a polished technical presentation and an order for half a million sensors.

Unfortunately, his presentation was more confused than it was polished, despite the hours that he'd spent tinkering with the wording. On top of that, the clear mind that he required to do this well was already tired before he started. The evening was going to be a challenge.

In a most un-British fashion, the Americans on the phone launched into introductions without spending even ten minutes discussing the weather. And Steve was then so busy trying to concentrate on introducing his own name properly that he only managed to pick up about one in three of theirs. He hadn't expected better, of course, because it's a matter of national pride in Britain that we forget names as soon as we've been introduced to people. It's just one of our lovable little quirks, like wanting to stand in queues and having bad teeth.

The one name that Steve did catch was Randy's. Randy was a self-made man, though first impressions indicated that he was one who'd forgotten to install a personality or to fit himself with any charisma. He'd joined Beauchild back in 1978 and had risen rapidly through the ranks to be Chief Operating Officer. If Steve was to fulfil his brief and sell hundreds of thousands of sensors a year to them, then this was the man he was most going to have to impress.

'OK, well, 'um, good evening, I mean morning, or is it lunchtime, or, er, something over there?' started Steve, once he'd worked out how to position the phone so that it didn't buzz his own distorted voice back at him.

He was interrupted at that point by Randy, who cut in to enquire 'What the hell are you on about, son?'.

If he was impressed yet, he wasn't letting it show.

Steve thought he'd better try a different conversational tack, so he made a clever comment along the lines of 'Why don't you drop dead, Dad?'. With hindsight, which came a few seconds later in the depths of a sudden profound silence, Steve realised that he'd made a mistake. He wasn't to know, of course, that the father of one of the women present had three weeks earlier done just that, but on the other hand he could perhaps have checked more carefully that he'd pressed the 'mute' button properly. It didn't help that the woman then spent most of the rest of the teleconference bursting into tears.

Steve's sales pitch was meant to have started with a five minute clip of inspirational scenes of SLSL products in action, but unfortunately he couldn't get the necessary video link to work properly so instead he moved straight on to the main part of his presentation, which described SLSL's various families of sensors and then went in depth into the performance that they expected from Sling when it was fully developed.

The Americans were actually very polite. It was all 'Help me to understand what you mean', not 'Don't talk c**p'. And once all the technical people had finished their in-depth technical grilling, it was over to the business people, led by Randy, to ask their in-depth business questions: how much would it cost and when could they have it? They then called a coffee break prior to the rest of the teleconference, which resumed with a project risk analysis session. Beauchild were very keen to make sure that any sensors that they took would not cause them problems, so Steve had been asked to prepare a comprehensive summary of the possible failure modes. He had done his best to comply, even though he always questioned the worth of such exercises. They just stifled creativity, in his opinion. After all, if formal risk analysis methods had been around in earlier times, would the zip fly ever have been developed?

As it turned out, the risk analysis session was very nearly the final killer blow to any hope of a deal. Steve had always been an open and honest sort, and his imaginative ability to suggest additional potential failure modes knew practically no bounds. By the time he'd finished, he'd inadvertently let slip the five things the project team were most worried about, and had helpfully suggested seventeen further ways in which the new sensor might potentially fail. Barry had coached him not to overdo the honesty factor ('Let them find any problems for themselves'), but his tongue had repeatedly run away with him and when someone had asked him how the encapsulation and mounting resin survived in high vibration environments, he accidentally let the word 'crisis' slip from his lips. It was the final straw for the US contingent. They called a quick 'time out' and put their phone on mute, but not before Steve had thought he'd heard Randy say that he'd seen stampedes that had been better organised, though what he was referring to, Steve didn't know. He needed to concentrate on mentally composing how he was going to tell Barry that he wasn't likely to be getting any major orders from the Americans after all.

At length, the Beauchild executives unhuddled themselves and came back on the line.

'You've got until the big European conference in Germany in January to prove yourselves,' said one of them.

'We'll be ordering five million high speed sensors from someone,' said Randy, promptly then spoiling the effect by adding 'But I think you have about as much chance of overcoming all your technical problems as you Brits have of introducing fox hunting on the moon.'

***

2.30 a.m. Steve was now six and a half hours into his teleconference with Beauchild, and he was now most definitely the only one in the building. Several times he'd thought the call was about to end, but although most of the Americans had drifted off, Randy and one or two others still remained. It was Steve's own fault, of course. They'd been about to hang up hours ago when his garbled account of the anticipated benefits of Sling had failed to properly answer any of Randy's probing questions. Steve had realised that things were going big-time wrong, and that he probably needed to do something dramatic to keep his foot in the proverbial door, when by undeserved luck he managed it: he accidentally let slip that Sling would have a composite halide coating, and because composite halide coatings were supposed to be an SLSL secret until the patent applications had been published, he got their full attention back.

The whole pace of the teleconference changed. Randy stopped multi-tasking on a separate call and suddenly found time to pay attention, someone paid Steve a couple of compliments on his earlier presentation, and the woman in the background made a concerted effort to stop sobbing. It was almost as if time, and everything in it, was slowing down to a new pace. Everything except Steve's pulse, at any rate. If anything, that had accelerated further, from the crisis zone into the panic zone. He had somehow blurted out one of Barry's most treasured secrets, one of the things that SLSL were relying on for some sort of competitive advantage over Sensandetect Limited, and now the whole world effectively knew it and had an early chance to do something about it. Or they soon would.

'Would you keep that to yourselves?' asked Steve quietly, in lieu of a plan to reverse time.

'Sure,' said Randy, with a worrying smile in his voice. 'But we would like exclusive access for the next two years.'

'We'd want to sell you quite large numbers in that case,' reasoned Steve, not unreasonably. He did consider adding that in future Beauchild would also need to deal with someone else on the technical side because Barry would be turning his intestines into an executive puzzle, but he could hear popcorny sorts of noises going on and he didn't want to put anybody off their food. He sat there increasingly miserably as the Americans tried to find out more about the coatings from him and he tried not to tell them anything of value while appearing not to be rude. Eventually, very very eventually, Randy must have conceded that there was nothing further to be gained from the session, and he drew the meeting to a close. He thanked Steve – possibly mockingly – for his openness, said something about arranging a follow-up call, and made no mention of any orders or contracts.

Steve was just about to hang up, when he overheard someone in the background say something about a new product from Senssertive Solutions Inc., who were perhaps SLSL's bitterest commercial rival. It was strictly unethical to listen in to such conversations of course, but what he overheard as he accidentally pressed his ear to the speaker filled his veins with cold dread. He didn't catch all the details, despite turning the volume on the speaker phone right up, but from what he could make out, Senssertive were about to launch a new sensor with specifications of which SLSL could only dream. Barry was going to have to find a lot more resources, and a fair chunk of luck, if Sling wasn't going to be a too-little too-late laughing stock when it was launched.

***

'Lemming's gone over the edge,' Darren announced, quietly.

Steve sat down, in an attempt to take it in. Lemming had been part of his life for something like three years now, and its passing would affect him in multiple ways. For a start, it would take away any Lemming-based excuses for lack of progress on Project Sling, which might be quite a problem. More significantly, it was a bit like losing an old friend. The sort of old friend who causes endless heartache, grief and stress and the sort of old friend who is qualmless about taking up hours of your time without notice, invitation or reward, but an old friend nevertheless.

Lemming had had a chequered history. It had originally been called project Eternity three or four years back, but it had dragged on and on and had eventually had to go into hiding for a bit and then reappear under an alias. For longer than Steve could remember it had waxed and waned, ebbed and flowed, bloomed and whatever the opposite of bloomed is. And now it had gone; gone to join Albatross and Possum and Dodo and a whole string of other failures that Steve would really rather have forgotten, were it not for the fact that he actually had forgotten some of them. He struggled to know what to say, but it didn't matter because Darren had gone back to his paperwork and was amusing himself by announcing 'You're fired!' every time he crossed an item off his list of things to do. Steve was left to check his e-mails. Most of them were the usual trivial rubbish, and so were the rest. There was only one from Barry, which was something to do with an SRT that Steve had to sort out. SRT's were Supplier Relationship Terminations, which were never the easiest things to carry out, but Steve braced himself, phoned the Legal Department for help with the precise wording, and composed a suitable e-mail to inform the company concerned of the bad news, and then he followed it up with a confirmatory voice mail message that said much the same thing but was padded out with a lot of distracting dithering and grovelling in a bid to break it to them gently.

By now, sleep deprivation had turned into exhaustion, and exhaustion had Steve almost ready to turn in for the night. However, Barry, being one who never liked to let a month go by without issuing a new set of instructions, had recently decreed that all e-mails should be dealt with on the day that they arrived unless you happened to have died, so Steve resolutely set about firing off a series of pointless electronic answers to pointless electronic questions, and pointless electronic comments to everything else. If he hadn't been such a positive, happy-go-lucky kind of guy there were times when it might all have got him down and he might have just sat there weeping over his keyboard at the thought of all the wasted hours and years. It was just the hope that any day now he'd actually do something useful or actually achieve something that kept him going. That, and the biscuits.

***

Jackie was preparing a snack for Natalie when Steve got in. It consisted of a peach, off the bone, fifteen grapes – Natalie had been very insistent upon that point – and a large slab of chocolate, 'because I've been so good'. Both girls ran up and gave him a hug, and then Jackie gave him a hug, and then all three of them went to watch something on telly.

Jackie had ordered home delivery pizzas for tea, because she had again been delayed by another episode of Angela's life story on the telephone earlier in the afternoon. As well as everything else in her wildly tempestuous world, Angela was in the middle of trying to move house. So far she'd been at it for three months and was now the proud owner of a solicitor, an estate agent and two surveyors, but not, sadly, a new home.

The pizzas arrived at five to six, and two minutes later the phone rang again. Weariness and exhaustion were vying for the prize of the life form once known as Steve, but necessity is the mother of valour and he had to stay awake and valorously chop up slices of rapidly cooling pizza. Pineapple for Natalie, double pepperoni for Chloe, beef and peppers for Jackie, and watery red goo for Steve. *Yummy*, he thought, putting his straight in the bin to save time. He took Jackie's through to the hall, where she was deep in what passed for conversation with her sister.

'Mm', 'Yes', 'No', 'Mm.'

She was rewarded between each syllable with a lengthy buzz of high pitched indignation. Diane hadn't been easy to deal with for quite some time. She was forty-two and had been publically trying for a baby for a couple of years now. Well, she'd been talking publically about it for a couple of years. The actual trying hadn't been in public, as far as Steve knew.

He cast his mind back to the time when he and Jackie had first been trying to conceive. That hadn't been easy, either. Neither of them had been sure whether you were supposed to take folic acid and Omega 3 fish oils during pregnancy or during sex, which hadn't made for a terribly romantic time, all in all.

His thoughts were interrupted by Jackie, who had managed to interject enough words to unslave herself from the phone and come back into the kitchen. Diane still wasn't pregnant, but the main purpose of this particular conversation had been to moan about her husband's brother, whose turn it was to invite them round for Christmas but who had instead cleared off to Africa to teach them Western democratic family values, presumably along the lines of disrespect for your elders, prejudgement of teenagers, and the spoiling of children. Steve tried to take an interest, but even with the best will in the world, which he didn't have, sleep had by now almost won its long battle. Offering his apologies to the rest of the family, and taking a brief passing interest in the beautiful dimples that Chloe had just decided she had ('I don't think they really count if you have to hold them in with your fingers, Chloe, I'm afraid.'), Steve went up to bed. Five minutes later, his head hit the pillow. A minute after that, Natalie started her violin practice.

***

Friday the thirteenth dawned bright and sunny. Unfortunately, that was a few hundred feet above the ground. Lower down, it was foggy, apart from the small clear patch over SLSL's car park that induced Barry to forget to turn his lights off. A warning buzzer had buzzed, but there were so many of them that he was already in the habit of routinely disregarding them all. By great good fortune, though, Clare noticed that they were on when she came into the building a few minutes later.

'Whose is the big silver car?' she asked, although how she couldn't know was a complete mystery.

Steve had had a respectable night's sleep and was awake enough to manage to pick up the phone to tell Barry. A few moments later they were rewarded with the sight of Barry's middle-aged spread wobbling frantically as he ran out to his car.

'I don't know why he's making so much fuss about switching them off,' grumbled Darren. 'They'll go off by themselves eventually anyway.'

'Morning,' said Steve to his boss when he reappeared in the open plan office a few minutes later, immediately realizing that he'd just said the same thing on the phone and hoping that Barry hadn't noticed.

He got a slightly quizzical look in return. 'Morning. How are you today, Steve?'

'Well,' said Steve, 'I'm not sure I'm...'

'Good,' said Barry, who wasn't listening anyway, 'because we've got a lot to get done today, not least the draft list of new equipment for next year. John absolutely has to have it by the end of the day. I've been meaning to ask you to compile it for me for weeks now.'

Steve made a strange noise in place of some of the unprintable words that he was thinking.

'How did you get on with the Americans?' Barry asked.

Steve had been expecting the question.

'Well, it sort of started off...'

'So we're likely to see big orders from Beauchild?'

'Well...' Steve took a deep breath and broke the several aspects of bad news before he drew his next. For good measure he included the news he'd heard of Senssertive's impending new sensor and he asked Barry to take into consideration his inadvertent disclosure of the composite halide coatings. And then he closed his eyes and waited for Barry to pass sentence.

In fact, Barry passed several sentences, some of them peppered with worse expletives than Darren's favourite 'sh, - sugar' or 'sh, - shine a light'. When Steve plucked up the courage to open his eyes again, he couldn't help noticing that his boss's face had gone distinctly red. This was not good.

Not surprisingly, the next half hour was not easy, but by the end of it they'd agreed a damage limitation plan. Barry would check whether the wording of the confidentiality agreement that they'd set up with Beauchild International would cover the composite halide technology, Steve was instructed to learn what he could about the new Senssertive product, Lisa would be put in charge of future technical meetings with overseas customers, and Barry would get Mike Marshall to follow up whatever sales opportunities Steve hadn't destroyed. It wasn't exactly a plan that left Steve covered in glory, but at least it left his soft bodily parts intact.

'I take it you've heard about Lemming?' Barry asked, once he'd convinced himself that Steve's transatlantic woes could be sorted out.

Steve nodded.

'We've got nothing to launch at Birmingham now.'

Steve nodded again. It was the only tactic he could think of.

'So now all eyes are on Sling. It has to be ready for Germany in January. No ifs, no buts.'

Perhaps a couple of little maybes? thought Steve.

'Can some more resources be freed up, now that Lemming's been stopped?' It was worth a try.

'No. They're needed for manufacturing support on the existing products. And speaking of manufacturing, your cost estimates for Sling are still much too high.'

***

By lunchtime, Steve was more than ready for a little liquid motivation, and he had no hesitation in accepting Darren's suggestion that they all walk over to the pub across the road for lunch, rather than go to the canteen. After all, it was Friday. Lisa and Clare opted not to join them, for respective reasons of a report to finish and a friend to share sandwiches with, so it was just Steve, Darren and Simon. Barry never got invited, as it would leave them with a lot less to talk about and fewer people they could collectively hate.

As always, Ye Merrye England was full of dour, miserable people. Whether the development engineers from SLSL fitted in or stuck out was a matter of opinion. As usual, Steve somehow found himself at the bar trying to order the food and beers while the barmaids concentrated on drying glasses and sipping their own drinks. When he was eventually and grudgingly served, each of his 'friends' immediately set about choosing a different brand of lager and considering complex combinations of side-orders, all apparently designed to make his task of ordering as difficult as possible. Meanwhile his own choice was straightforward enough: he'd had the double cheeseburger with chips and beans the last twenty times he'd been in there.

'I thought you were on a diet,' Darren challenged Steve when he sat down to join the others.

'It's alright,' Steve said, 'I'll walk it off the week after next, in Wales.'

'Whereabouts?'

'I haven't a clue: I'm leaving all that to Jackie.'

'Oh.'

They sipped their lager for a moment.

'When are we expecting Lizzy back?' asked Simon.

Darren looked rather pleased with himself. 'I'll ask her tomorrow evening. We're going out for a meal.'

'So she's out of hospital then?' checked Steve.

'Well I hope so,' said Simon, 'or it won't be much of a first date, even by Darren's standards.'

The food arrived just then, suspiciously quickly, and there was the usual round of puzzling who had ordered which dish and, indeed, which dish was which dish. For a moment no-one was owning up to having ordered the bacon salad, but then a man on another table called out that it was his and the three engineers were spared the smell of scorched lettuce.

'We haven't got any cutlery,' Simon observed. 'Would you do the necessary, as they say, please?' he asked Darren. 'I'm going to get another round of drinks in.'

'As the great Noggin the Nog himself probably once said – no.'

'I'm surprised you have any friends,' said Simon.

'Pah – friends are for losers,' growled Darren.

In similar comradely solidarity and bonhomie they passed the rest of lunchtime before walking back to work. They had all enjoyed themselves as much as anyone could expect to do in Ye Merrye England, but within five minutes of being back at his desk, Steve had Barry round, nagging, cajoling and criticising. His current top two priorities seemed to be the draft of the departmental equipment list for John and the need for brilliance at Steve's Sling team meeting on Monday afternoon.

'By the way, did you sort out that Special Request to Tender that I asked you to do for Gilmore and Jenkins Limited?' asked Barry.

'Er,' said Steve, as befitted a man who had some sudden knowledge to digest.

'It is quite urgent,' Barry went on, 'because they're no longer a bit player. The board has just agreed to enter into a major supply agreement with them for components for several of our best-selling sensors, and now they want to forge closer links with them in development, too. We might even end up doing some co-developments with them.'

Steve looked as if he was about to say something, but whatever it was, he swallowed it heavily and gave a wan smile.

'I'll see what I can do,' he said, eventually and faintly.

The phone rang at that moment, which gave Barry the chance to wander off in search of better attractions and Steve the chance to go dizzy with fear. The call was from Alex Deese, postponing their meeting until some time yet to be arranged because the previous day's arrival of a box of new pencils in the Accounts Department had proved a little too exciting for the inhabitants, and they'd all had to go home for a few days for a lie down.

'What's an SRT?' Steve asked Darren quietly, when the coast was clear.

Darren looked up from the improvised crush test that he had been performing with the small vice on the edge of his desk, and without a moment's hesitation put Steve further into his misery. 'It's a Special Request to Tender.'

'Not a Supplier Relationship Termination?'

Funny looks time again. 'No.'

'Oh.'

That was that then. He'd dug himself a hole deeper than a multi-storey coal mine, and he was going to have to think of a way to tell Barry. The sooner the better, obviously, but after the weekend better still. There was always the chance that something would happen before Monday morning that might get him off the hook. He might worry so much that he had a heart attack, for example. Barry wouldn't feel he could shout at him then, especially if he was dead.

***

If anything, Steve felt more tired on Saturday morning than he had the day before, but Jackie insisted he got up and went for a good walk. Steve loved good walks, especially on crisp autumn days like this one, but not when he was struggling to raise the energy to raise as much as an eyelid. Not only that, but the radio was announcing a severe weather warning, with extremely overcast weather expected for the next few hours. The risk of disruption to solar panels and postcard photographers had been put at over ninety per cent. Under the circumstances, as he tried to persuade Jackie, it might be best if he stayed under the duvet until perhaps Wednesday. Jackie was having none of it, though, and although she agreed to postpone their morning walk until after lunch, its inclusion in the day's schedule was strictly non-negotiable. In the meantime, perhaps he'd like to drive over to somewhere he could buy some suitable wood, so that he could get on with mending the shed door on Sunday? Oh, and how were his plans coming along for having another go at tackling the ivy on the back of the house and the dead pigeon on the roof?

Steve retreated under the sheets, but the battle was lost, as well he knew, and by half past ten he had bought the wood and was driving home again, one frontal lobe thinking about the traffic and one his worries. He had spent Friday evening and half of Saturday morning wondering whether he should tell Jackie of his wee faux pas with the SRT business. In the end he decided he wouldn't, which was a good call because she already had enough on her own plate. Apart from the endless phone calls from Angela about whether or not she should leave and/or divorce Tom's father in order to elope with her latest boyfriend, there was the daily update from Diane about her bathroom refitting and there was the little matter of getting everything ready for going to Wales for half term the following weekend. As well as the usual washing, ironing, planning and general coordination – which she wasn't even going to imagine Steve trying to do – there was the problem of trying to decide whether to leave the curtains open or closed at this time of year. And on top of that, she was getting stressed about Natalie's toothache, which had got better once but now kept coming back intermittently, seemingly triggered by a whole host of different stimuli: having to eat carrots, having to eat cabbage, having to go to bed too early, to name just three. With all that to deal with, it was just as well that Steve chose not to bother her with something as trivial as the strong possibility that he was about to be sacked for gross incompetence.

Their afternoon walk did help him to keep his mind off his problems at work to some degree, and the evening also passed reasonably SRT-free. Occasionally there were as many as ten minutes between worryings. It was unlikely that he could have managed to sleep much, though, had he not still had a significant dose of exhaustion in his blood to help him. But he did, and he might even have been asleep before nine-thirty had it not been for Chloe, who for some reason couldn't sleep. Jackie had tried making her a hot milky drink, Natalie had tried telling her to shut up and just close her eyes, and Steve had tried telling her her favourite bedtime story, the one about Mr Barry Angry and the overdue project report, but it hadn't made her any the more inclined to surrender to sleep. Presumably she did at some stage, but Steve did not know when because some time around ten seventeen he went to lie down for a couple of minutes to think what to try next, and fell into a troubled slumber.

***

He awoke on Sunday morning to the alarming realisation that it was almost time to start getting ready for Christmas. Considering that he didn't usually enjoy it a whole lot more than your average turkey did, it wasn't a great thought. How could it have come round so quickly? One minute it was the beginning of January and the next you found yourself here in the middle of October, for goodness sake! Just sixty shopping days left before he might have to start thinking about buying something. He could have been quite agitated had he not at that point remembered the thing that he was meant to be agitated about. He looked over at Jackie's side of the bed, to see if she had noticed the extra worry lines on his brow, but she was already downstairs, preparing to take Natalie swimming. She had just broken off to console Chloe, who was upset because she couldn't find where she'd stuck her poster of a chameleon, but as soon as she'd done that she came back upstairs to clean her teeth and put her watch on.

'We've found another dead woodlouse,' Natalie called up the stairs as Steve struggled out of bed.

'Oh dear. I'll come down,' Jackie shouted back.

'It's OK, Mum, we've buried it.'

'Where?'

'In the kitchen bin.'

Steve had his breakfast while Jackie reeled off a list of ten or so things she wanted him to do before she got back, and Natalie went upstairs to tidy her room for five minutes. As soon as he'd finished the one slice of toast that he was allowing himself on his new diet, Steve set to work on his chores. Job number one was to round up the dirty laundry and put it into the new environmentally friendly low water consumption eco washing machine. That was less than straightforward, as Chloe had hidden hers and wasn't telling, but Natalie's was easy to find because her idea of tidying up was to hang her clothes all over the floor.

Steve shoved everything into the machine, waited to make sure it was heating the thimbleful of water that it used, and went to make himself a mug of coffee. Then it was off to dust the curtains, upstairs to answer Chloe's question about how they got the ponies out of the swimming bath at the end of a water polo match, and outside to sort the week's rubbish into metric and imperial.

Chloe had gone to the toilet to have what she'd long ago christened Muddy Bits, or MB for short (Steve's alternative suggestion of Fool's Chocolate having been vetoed by Jackie), so while she was busy, he quickly put the vacuum cleaner round upstairs. Normally he made it more fun by sprinkling grit into the carpets so that he could hear it rattle satisfyingly around inside the tubes and other innards, but time was a little pressing so today he had to settle for the sound of Jackie's lost diamond earring. After he had sorted Chloe out (we'll gloss over the details), he organised the soup tins into alphabetical order as Jackie had requested, and then he went to check on the washing machine. There wasn't a lot to see, though, as it had just gone into its thirty minutes hope cycle where the water was somehow supposed to clean itself up ready for the next bit, so he moved on to vacuuming the lounge.

'I've found another dead woodlouse,' Chloe called down from the bathroom, where she had been polishing Osmarelda.

'Burial at sea,' announced Steve briskly, marching upstairs, flicking the tiny body into the toilet and flushing it. He was doing reasonably well now, and Jackie's inevitable disappointment with his progress was likely to be towards the lower end of the scale. In fact, he even managed to iron the tea towels and demould the bread bin before Natalie rang her usual fanfare on the doorbell and Jackie came in with tales of parental swimming rivalry and goodness, haven't you done that yet?

Steve spent the rest of the morning dismantling the shed door and then trying to remantle it with the new wood. It was a slow and painful process, especially whenever any hammering was involved. Steve's ability to hit his own fingers was a thing to behold. Ah, if only Paul, with his superior do-it-yourself skills and his superior big brotherly confidence, had been there to help him. *His* expertise with wood and screws and putty was legendary. Most of Steve's experience of DIY was related to splinters, stripped threads and broken glass.

An hour and a half of solid and frustrating labour later, the rotten wood was all gone and the replacement strips and planks were covered in pencil hieroglyphics and, in some cases, cut.

'Have you just started?' asked Jackie as she came out to call Steve in for lunch. He quickly washed his hands, gave the toilet another quick flush to get rid of the woodlouse, washed his hands again and went into the kitchen. The whole Oscroft family dined together for once, while they swapped stories of the excitements of their various assorted mornings. Steve's we already know about; Jackie's had mostly passed in a flurry of chauffering, organising and cooking. Natalie and Chloe had spent the latter part of the morning working on Natalie's latest project, which involved designing and building a nursing home for injured woodlice, complete with swimming bath and exercise paddocks. Perhaps in deference to the risk of having inherited her father's tendency towards misfortune with sharp or heavy tools, she had chosen to use cardboard and sticky tape as the only building materials.

Steve did manage to get the shed door rebuilt by teatime, although it was a close-run thing with all the interruptions from his daughters. The door still tended to jam, which was annoying, but this time it was something to do with the way he'd fitted the top hinge, rather than a consequence of mouldering wood. And to Chloe's delight, the offcuts of timber could now be earmarked for the ark that the girls had so long been promised.

After tea, Steve settled down to compile a list of all the things they needed to pack for the cottage in Wales, but he'd only got as far as socks – and that wasn't alphabetically - when Chloe came into the room clutching a plastic sandwich box with breathing holes, which she had made temporary home to her temporary pet, Vanilla.

'Look Daddy, look, it's trotting round the ring!'

Cautiously, Steve peered under the lid. Inside, a small woodlouse was exploring the perimeter of its new-found prison.

'Where did that come from?'

'Natty found him. Can we keep him? Oh can we? Oh please oh please oh please oh please!'

'Just for this evening,' said Steve, making a mental note to have a further go at flushing the other woodlouse away again. Chloe squealed with happiness and ran out of the room to tell her sister, poor Vanilla being rattled around like the vacuum cleaner grit that Steve hadn't bothered with earlier in the day. He returned to his list of things to pack, and this time got as far as Chloe's unicorn net before she returned, this time with plastic sandwich box plus breathing holes plus Natalie.

'Daddy, Vanilla's learnt to show-climb!'

Another peer in revealed the solitary inmate to have his front legs up against a small pebble. Steve conceded defeat, put away his list, and went to play with the girls for the rest of their evening. By half past eight he was worn out. The previous night's sleep had been fractured repeatedly by his dread of the Gilmore and Jenkins SRT situation, and the sooner he could get the two girls settled and asleep the sooner he might be able to start his next tussle with the forces of insomnia. He never slept well on a Sunday night, presumably because the shadow of another week of problems hung over him, and today was set to be worse than most. And so it came to pass, in the inevitable nature of these things, that both girls chose that night not to calm down after their day of woodlousy excitements. Massive intervention, by their now massively tired father, was required to get them dressed for bed, with their teeth all cleaned and with their heads on their pillows. But as soon as he'd quietened one set of vocal cords, the other would strike up again. He looked at his watch, and wilted. It was nearly half past nine, and Chloe was still bouncing around on her bed whenever he went into Natalie's room. Steve realised with an inward groan that he was no better at getting girls into bed now than he had been when he was eighteen. He admitted defeat and went off in search of the cavalry, or Jackie as she preferred to be known.

While she was successfully tucking the girls in, which took three minutes, he started to get ready for bed himself, diverting just once to give the toilet another flush.

***

Steve's first port of call on Monday morning was Barry's office, so that he could explain to him what he'd done with Gilmore and Jenkins in his confusion about what an SRT was. Unfortunately, Barry wasn't in port; he had been invited to attend a meeting of the manufacturing engineering group and was delivering one of those management motivational speeches that leaves everyone ready to down tools and go to the pub for the rest of the day. Clare didn't think he would be finished much before he had to attend another meeting at eleven-thirty. Steve had little option but to wait and hope that he might catch him then. He went off to his desk with a heavy heart in his mouth.

'Have you had a good weekend?' Simon was asking Darren with a loud yawn.

'Yes, I have, thank you,' said Darren. A look of slightly wistful concentration crossed his face. 'It was back in 1995 if I remember rightly.'

'What happened to your hot date with Dizzy Lizzy?' asked Lisa.

Darren made a sort of snorting noise. 'She came out of hospital with some kind of a bug, so we're having it next weekend instead.' He fixed a defiant glare in Lisa's direction to dissuade her from further questioning.

'The poor girl,' Lisa murmured, enigmatically.

As good weekends went, Steve's had also been a little lacking. Three nights of disturbed and tortured sleep had taken their toll, and he was beginning to think that he must have stepped on a crack, somewhere along the pavement of life.

'I've had better ones, too,' he said, though no-one had asked him about his weekend.

'And this is going to be the sort of week I could wish away,' he added helpfully.

'You're a long time dead,' Lisa pointed out to him.

Steve sighed. Sometimes he couldn't wait to get started.

***

Just before half past eleven, Steve made his way towards Barry's office, walking with the air of someone who has just been conscripted into a lion taming act. Barry was there, but as he approached Steve could see through the glass that he was with someone Steve didn't recognise and he was clearly in the middle of venting his spleen, which was a rather messy process. As it happened, Barry saw him and beckoned to him not to go away, so he waited in the corridor while Barry finished ranting at the man.

'Can you come along to the Achilles Room and present an update on Sling at the directors' meeting, please?' asked his boss when he was allowed in.

'Erm, OK. When is it?' Steve didn't have his appointments diary with him.

'It's now. I should be there too, because they're covering all the development projects. Can you come along at twelve?'

Steve said 'yes', but his face said 'no'. Even with Barry's track record of last minute announcements, this was a bit much.

'I need to tell you something.'

'In the meeting, please, I really do have to go.' And with that, true to his word, Barry was gone, leaving Steve in a pool of sweat and a haze of fear. Today was showing all the signs of turning very ugly indeed. Back at his desk, collecting together a few files that might support his case that Sling was proceeding to plan but urgently needed more resources, he was confronted by Lisa who could see that he was in even more of a state than he usually was on a Monday morning. She could sense when an animal was in pain, and she instinctively knew when to provide calming reassurance and emotional support. Steve briefly explained how he'd mistakenly managed to terminate their supply relationship with Gilmore and Jenkins just at the moment that the SLSL board was about to make them their key development partner.

Lisa whistled. 'Steve!'

As reassurance and support went, he might have expected a little more.

'I think you're going to need a fairly heavy duty excuse for this one,' she said, following a long pause and after she had sat down fairly heavily on her chair. 'How on earth did you manage that?'

Steve briefly explained his mix-up over the meaning of an SRT, his face flushing red but with slight relief that he was at least sharing his problem with others.

'I think you're going to need a Best in Class excuse,' said Darren, whose ears were like radar for tuning in on other people's troubles. 'Now let's see. What have we got? Alarm clock eaten by next door's baby? Car eaten by aliens? Train driver took a wrong turn in the fog?'

'Barry knows I'm in. This isn't helping.'

'Well you'll have to hope he's in a good mood then.'

That didn't seem likely. The scene in Barry's office that he'd witnessed earlier had not been a particularly pretty sight. To make matters worse, the Achilles Room was reputedly haunted by the ghost of someone who had underestimated the strength of desire of senior management teams for good news.

'I should have told him on Friday afternoon, when I first realised my mistake,' Steve mumbled dejectedly. 'He's not going to be very pleased that I kind of told him everything was OK.'

'No. I shouldn't have thought he is.'

'I'll just have to face the music.'

'Firing squad,' corrected Darren.

Steve finished pulling his things together while Darren tried to cheer him up with a reminder that dying in the course of duty made him eligible for a wider range of company awards.

Clare was just wheeling a trolley-full of executive buffet into position in the corridor as Steve reached the door of the Achilles room. From inside, he could hear the sound of hearty laughter, which was no surprise because for the directors their get-togethers were not so much meetings as lovely chats, once a fortnight. Steve cleared his throat, knocked on the door, and was rewarded with a curt 'Come in'. Adjusting the tie that he had forgotten to put on, he opened the door and entered the room. Around the table with Barry and John were most of SLSL's biggest cheeses. Clockwise from the luxury biscuit assortment were Bob Freeman (Head of the Coatings Business Unit), Tony Roe (Head of Operations), Dilshad Patel (Head of Business Development), Ben Saville (Head of the Legal Department), Annabel Weaver (Head of Marketing), and Joe Reedman (Head off Early for Lunch). Finally there was John, with Barry sitting behind him rather than at the table. There was also one empty seat at the end of the table, into which Steve was motioned to sit.

'Hello Steve,' said Tony, who was chairing the meeting while the managing director recovered from his hair transplant.

'Morning. I mean, afternoon. Or is it just Good Lunchtime?' Why did they have to confuse him with all this intellectual stuff? He sat down, and shuffled his papers a bit. His pen rolled onto the floor.

'How's Sling?' asked Dilshad.

'It's coming on,' said Steve, slowly and with one eye on Barry. He started to fumble for the printout he had of the latest project plan, but he couldn't find it, so he just waffled a bit for a few minutes.

'This isn't very impressive,' observed Bob. 'Sort it out now.'

'Come back in two weeks and prove to us that you're back on track for a January launch in Germany,' said Annabel, who was too busy typing away at her laptop to look up. She was too important to bother with all that nicey-nicey eye contact stuff, especially when it came to nobodies from Research and Development.

'Let's hope you're getting acceptable results by then,' added Dilshad, with an encouraging smile.

Bob snorted. 'The results need to be excellent. Just being acceptable isn't good enough.' He gave a violent stare at Steve, who gave a stare at the table. Perhaps he would tell Barry about the SRT problem later in the day.

'Before you go, what was it you wanted to tell me?' asked Barry. Perhaps not, then.

Steve took the deepest breath of his life, and explained how he'd accidentally cancelled all of their business with Gilmore and Jenkins. 'I'm sorry,' he ended. 'It was all a misunderstanding. I thought an SRT was a Supplier Relationship Termination.'

He continued to stare at the table. There was a long silence.

***

A very long silence.

***

When Barry eventually spoke, at the third attempt, all he managed to say was 'Good grief', thereby proving that he didn't grasp the concept of grief desperately well.

'This is literally going to kill us,' he added, proving that he didn't understand what the word 'literally' meant, either. Or so Steve hoped.

'Look,' said Tony, after another long pause. 'This is a bit of a mistake, but for goodness sake, I think a phone call can get it sorted. It's not exactly the end of the world. Leave it with me.'

'Or I can sort it,' volunteered Ben.

Steve nearly cried. He had to fight the urge not to hug and kiss them both. Never had he imagined in his entire three days of misery (well, greater misery than usual) that there would be a happy ending. He almost punched the air, but instead he settled for thanking them politely and taking the opportunity to escape, relieved beyond relief despite Annabel's parting reminder to 'find a way to make Sling happen, all tout de suitish' ringing in his ears.

Lisa was waiting for him in the open plan office. Using that intuition thing that women have, she sensed that it had been a happy outcome and immediately looked relieved herself.

'You've survived,' she smiled. She seemed genuinely pleased.

'I surprise myself, sometimes.' Nobody could be more pleased than he was.

In fact, he managed to stay happy pretty much all afternoon. Even when Chris Tomkinson and Darren both failed to turn up for his team meeting[1]. He stayed happy even when the drinks machine gave him two worthless foreign coins in his change, and even when Barry delegated him the task of arranging a meeting with Cathy Banfield to tell her exactly what had happened in his teleconference with one of her key American customers. He was even OK about having missed his Monday lunchtime swim again.

His unusual cheerfulness saw him through the rest of the day, all of Tuesday and almost into Wednesday. And once that, and its meeting with scary Cathy, was out of the way, it was really just a case of clearing a few little jobs and leaving everything else until he came back from holiday. His life was all demob fever and counting the hours.

---

[1] It transpired that Chris had rung in that morning claiming to have suffered a bedclothes injury, while Darren had simply thought of something more interesting to do.

7

Friday lunchtime finally arrived, and Steve started to clear his desk and check his e-mail in-tray so that he could leave work in time to get home for a quick sandwich. He had booked the afternoon off to get the packing done before Jackie fetched the girls from school: there was a lot of undie hunting and suitcase stuffing still to be done. Taking plenty of wet-weather clothing was going to be a high priority: the long range weather forecast was for five days of intermittent drizzle followed by three weeks of unremitigating[1] rain.

The plan had been to set off at about half-past-four-ish, before the traffic started to build up, but in the event Steve didn't even leave work until nearly half past two, courtesy of helping Darren to unjam the desk drawer that he'd managed to wedge his Corporate Efficiency Award in.

By four, the girls were home from school but Steve was still only half way through finding the things he needed to pack, and he hadn't even started checking the car over. He was pretty sure the back tyres would need a bit of inflation if they were going to get to Wales with all the stuff Natalie and Chloe had earmarked to take. Fitting it all in was going to be quite a challenge, helped only slightly by Jackie's merry shouts of moral support and encouragement, along the lines of 'Don't forget to leave plenty of space for presents and souvenirs and things'.

By five, Steve had filled and closed his suitcase. He couldn't find his waterproof alarm clock, but they'd manage without it. The girls were having their tea. Jackie was looking at her watch.

By six, Steve had pumped the tyres up with the foot pump, had topped up the screen-wash, and had removed from the boot and back seat all the detritus that had accumulated since the last major trip. He was now going round the house, checking that all the doors and windows were locked. The girls were upstairs, arguing over what the trolls should pack. Jackie was pacing up and down in the kitchen.

By six thirty, Steve had gone out to practise the ancient and manly art of trying to cram too much stuff into the confined and

---

[1] It's my book; *I'll* make the words up.

oddly shaped space of the car boot. The vehicle was meant to have seven hundred and fifty litres of luggage space, but if it did, six hundred and fifty of it must have been on the roof rack they didn't have. Meanwhile, Natalie was reading a book, Chloe was running around the hallway pretending to be a wild pony at a gymkhana, and Jackie was getting rather fraught.

By six forty-five, Steve had finished loading everything in, the front door was locked, everyone had got their seat belts on and they were finally off on the long and winding road that led them to the holiday cottage.

It had probably been the rich Welsh television voiceover entreating her to 'While away a while in Wales' that had persuaded Jackie that they should for once metaphorically turn their backs on their beloved Lake District and head instead Walesward. Although there were apparently plenty of local attractions, if the tourist board lleaflet[1] was to be believed, the cottage they'd chosen was somewhere in the remotest and most beautiful depths of the Welsh countryside: it was going to be a real break from everything. No cares, no scares, no worrying about sensors, for seven whole days. Except that, on the way, there was the ordeal of an overnight stopover at Steve's mother's to face....

***

The journey seemed to last for ever, especially as it was dark before they set off. Chloe had worked her way through the bag of 'things to keep her amused for hours' in 3.5 minutes. That left her stuck for something to do, so she started arguing with one of her dolls and then with her sister. Jackie intervened to tell Natalie to ignore her and Chloe to count the lamp posts. Five minutes later they were squabbling again, so Jackie turned round to tell Chloe to ignore her sister and Natalie to count the lamp posts. Steve gripped the steering wheel and tried not to get distracted.

---

[1] The Welsh spelling.

'I'm going to hold my breath until I die' announced Chloe.

'How do I unwrap this sweet?' complained Natalie.

'Where are we on the map?' queried Jackie.

'How do horses find their stables when it's dark?' pondered Natalie.

'What's the difference between a pony?' asked Chloe.

'Why's the chocolate gone all gooey?' demanded Jackie.

Have I had some sort of free transfer to the Stupid family? wondered Steve. He switched the radio on, in the hope that it would drown out the racket going on all around him. It didn't, but it did at least give Natalie and Chloe the chance to sing along to '*Wossit and why?*' and several other songs of similar musical accomplishment, interrupted by the occasional witless remark by the semi-articulate disc jockey.

After forty-five minutes they had covered about thirty miles and the traffic was perhaps beginning to thin out slightly, which was good, but as they joined the motorway Steve suddenly wondered whether he'd remembered to switch the immersion heater off, which was less good.

***

Mary Oscroft put down the pile of forms and her knitting with a heavy sigh. She glanced at the clock on the mantelpiece in the vague hope that the battery was now feeling a little better or that she'd managed to find a new one and had managed to forget that she had. The clock said five to three, so clearly the battery wasn't and she hadn't. She pulled her carpet slippers towards her with one stockinged toe, and with much reaching and bending and a small release of wind she got them onto her feet and shuffled off towards the kitchen.

They still hadn't turned up or telephoned, and she still hadn't decided whether or not to enter any of the classes at the village show next week. She had been rather tempted to have a go at the triathlon (best home-made fruit cake, best arrangement of fresh cut flowers, best bungee jump) but the element of danger had got the better of her and she had decided not to finish filling in the entry form. The degree of risk seemed just too great: if she out-baked old Mrs Collins at number six she'd never hear the end of it. She decided to make herself a cup of tea instead. She tapped the clock against the mantelpiece on her way to the kitchen, and it sulkily started to tick again. It knew better than to try to argue with Grandma.

Five minutes later, she was just settling down with the drink and her local free newspaper when the doorbell finally rang. She pulled herself back to her feet, with a small volley of tutting and sighing, and went to the front door to let Steve and Jackie and the girls in. Natalie and Chloe came into the hall with all the enthusiasm for the company of an old person that you would expect from tired children, and Steve and Jackie carried in the overnight bags that had been threatening to avalanche across the back seat onto their daughters every time that Steve had moved the steering wheel more than an inch.

Mrs Oscroft enjoyed seeing her younger son and his family – it at least beat the times when Mrs Briggs from down the road came round to let her know what the doctor had said about her knees – and she'd laid on a special welcome of a chocolate cake, a large plate of stale biscuits, and three light bulbs that needed changing. She also made some reference to Steve sorting out a problem with her computer, but he chose to be temporarily deaf as he knew that all its problems stemmed from her inability to understand the first thing about it. On his previous visit it had come to light that she thought that the monitor was the computer, while Natalie, who had been trying to help, thought that the keyboard was. Neither of them had noticed the box sitting on the floor beneath the table.

They all shuffled awkwardly round the mortal remains of last year's Christmas tree, which was still guarding the way into the lounge. The free newspaper was lying across the sofa, open at the Crime Watch column on page six. Steve had never understood why they didn't name the whole paper Crime Watch, as ninety-five per cent of the rest of its contents were indistinguishable from that bit. Usually the only non-crime features were the adverts for new cars (useful for doing crime) and for houses (useful for burgling). Just every now and then the editorial department managed to liven up the occasional issue with a touching short article commemorating some old local or other who had managed to reach their eightieth or ninetieth birthday before they lost the will to live. Once a year they did a feature on the local carnival, with a photograph of a gap-toothed six year old in an embarrassing costume holding up a bad painting. And not being entirely on the ball, they usually repeated at least one photograph or article on more than one page.

'Tell Grandma what you did at school today,' Jackie instructed Natalie, once they had all cleared spaces to sit down. There followed a five minute sentence about story writing, about ex- best friend Abigail, about new best friend Megan, about a painting of a frog and two princesses and about shepherd's pie and custard. She finally drew breath to take questions, glanced over to the settee where Steve's mother was now lying back with her eyes tightly closed, and plunged into another seven minutes worth. I'll spare you the details.

'Natalie's passed her Grade One violin exam,' said Jackie proudly, when her mother in law re-woke.

'Oh, it must be wonderful to be able to make lovely music!'

'No,' said Steve, 'that's Grade Four.'

Now if there was one thing that gave Chloe the fidgets, apart from having to sit nicely and make polite conversation, it was talk of her big sister and her achievements. It was marginally worse than having to sit next to James Pinch-and-poke at school. She looked around the room, to see if there was anything that might liven things up a bit. Her grandmother's big glass-fronted cabinet full of porcelain plates and figurines was obviously one possibility, but Jackie – despite being secretly tempted to relive her coconut-shy days - had made it clear before they got there that touching that carried a likely death sentence or – worse – a month without chocolate. The rest of the room contained nothing of interest, assuming no-one would switch the television on for her, just the furniture, papers, balls of wool and her relatives. She would have to see what she could do with those: the alternative was going to be boredom followed by bed time. She wasn't sure whether playing with the wool, or trying to get the adults to talk about more interesting things, was likely to be the less dull. She decided she would start with the latter.

Her chance came a few minutes later when Grandma had finished complaining about the price of gussets[1] or some such, Natalie had passed further comment on how much she enjoyed school, Jackie had patted Natalie on the head, and the conversation was on a bit of a general go-slow while Steve tried to think of something he could talk about that wouldn't set his mother off. Nothing much was coming to mind. Even the weather could be tricky. Perhaps something in the house would give him inspiration? He glanced over towards the cabinet of china figures. They were quite a varied set, with no single theme or common scale, but he did sometimes find himself wondering what they might one day have been worth if many of them hadn't been chipped through over-zealous dusting over the years. He noticed that a new one had appeared since their last visit, sitting proudly on the top shelf between the fly fisherman with the broken rod and the King Charles spaniel that was missing its head. This one was a girl in a flowing blue ball gown, being sick. Unusual maybe, but certainly more interesting than discussing where the red and white cake tin might have got to.

'It's a messy business,' Chloe announced brightly.

A sudden hush descended, and the clock on the mantelpiece seized its chance to tick as loudly and as slowly as its age and weak battery would let it. Grandma looked across at her youngest descendent.

'Kissing boys. It's a messy job.'

The hush became a silence. Even the clock held its breath. And then everybody tried to talk at once, apart from Natalie, whose facial features spelt the word 'disgust'. Grandma was probably the most shocked. She hadn't entirely been prepared for that

---

[1] What a wonderful word.

sort of frankness in the conversation: the children were obviously growing up rather faster than she could keep up with, especially with the infrequent contact she had with them. She had still been treating Natalie as if she were five, and Chloe as if she were about two. Mind you, come to that she often treated Steve as if he were eleven and a little dense.

To change the subject, Steve's mother fished around by the side of her chair for the photographs of the previous summer's coach trip to some tropical greenhouse. The four younger Oscrofts dutifully passed each print round in turn and Jackie thought up a question to ask her mother-in-law about each one, in a stoic display of interest beyond the call of duty.

It was getting late, or at least it felt like it by the time that they'd discussed ferns and mosses for twenty minutes, and Grandma took it upon herself to order the children upstairs. It was quite clear to her that their parents weren't giving them enough sleep. In Mary Oscroft's eyes, more sleep was the answer to almost everything, which was rather interesting as Steve had remembered her spending much of his childhood and most of his teenage years chivvying him to get out of bed in the mornings. Jackie might have stayed to argue the point, but she was rather relieved to have an excuse to get up and stretch her legs, so she and Steve ushered the girls out of the lounge and up to the back bedroom. As he passed the ornaments cabinet, Steve noted upon closer inspection that the new figurine was actually bent double ice skating, with one hand across her stomach as she cornered. And missing one foot.

***

As usual, Steve's mother had taken the opportunity created by having so many potential driers bearing tea towels (i.e. Steve and Jackie) to wipe and wash every item and surface in the kitchen. She had spent much of the afternoon washing things, in fact, and as soon as the girls were tucked up in bed she directed her small army of 'volunteers' into the kitchen, where they remained until half past ten when they eventually finished and went to rejoin Grandma in the lounge. She was sitting ensconced in a pile of cushions on the sofa, watching a film on television. She liked a good chain-saw disembowelling, particularly if she could relax with a glass of sherry in one hand and a box of chocolates in the other, as she had now. Steve tried to attract her attention to ask her about -

'Sssh!' she hissed, 'This is a good bit.'

Steve risked a quick glance towards the screen and immediately wished he hadn't. The good bit had clearly been good for the make-up and special effects departments, but perhaps not for the young man in the chequered shirt. Or young woman: it was getting hard to tell. The ketchup manufacturers were going to be happy for quite a long time. The man with the chain-saw also looked quite pleased with his work as he strolled back to his car, or at least he did until he realised with a mild curse that he couldn't find his keys.

Steve's mother grabbed the TV remote control, stabbed at the 'Off' button and slumped back on the sofa.

'I'm fed up with all the bad language on television nowadays,' she complained. Steve had her full attention.

'Is there anything you need, that we could bring you back from Wales?' he asked, while Jackie shook her head violently and mouthed the words 'We're not calling in on the way back' somewhere over by the edge of his field of vision.

'A kilogramme or two of Welsh butter, perhaps?' said Steve, who had started so felt the need to finish.

His mother shook her head. She refused to have a clue about metric measurements of any description, despite it being over thirty years since their official adoption in Britain. Even if she could still learn new tricks, she wasn't going to, on principle. Not even for Steve. Perhaps especially not for Steve. She lapsed into silence again, which wasn't really like her, because normally she could talk the hind legs off an Eskimo, or whatever the expression is. Embarrassingly, she had reached an age where her usual topics of conversation were other people's medical problems, recent deaths, and the manifold failings of her younger son.

Of the three, she didn't have a particular favourite – she was quite happy to expound on any one with equal relish, particularly at the breakfast or dinner table. Living on her own she generally took any opportunity she could get to talk, as it made something of a change from her usual routine, which was to spend most of the day dozing, breaking off only occasionally to attend a doctor's appointment or go on an expedition to the hospital in a fruitless search for a cure for the latest of her endless ill-defined symptoms.

Today she was very weary, though. There had been all the pacing up and down, at least mentally, while she waited for Steve and Jackie and the girls to arrive, and she had perhaps overdone her assault on the kitchen cleaning earlier in the day. She was also still tired from having spent much of the morning cooking a hot meal for her housebound neighbours down the road, only to take it round and find that they were out.

As a result, they sat there largely in silence, punctured from time to time by Steve whenever a new potential conversational topic came into his head. He tried to tell his mother how things were going at work, but somehow ended up being given a list of the household appliances that needed fixing. He mentioned Wales, but it triggered an outburst about foreign places and how she didn't like foreign food, such as all that Pilates stuff. Against his better judgement he even found himself asking her what she might want for Christmas, instantly regretting it as she read out the list of provisions that her newspaper advised for cases of civil emergency. He'd temporarily forgotten that she always took such warnings to heart and liked to keep her pantry shelves well stocked up. If there were ever to be a major terrorist incident or a war or an outbreak of pigeon fever, she wouldn't be short of air freshener refills for the vacuum cleaner.

Jackie attempted to throw in the odd comment, here and there, despite the difficulty in trying to think of subjects that weren't taboo. There is only so far you can go with a theme of the difficulty of opening milk cartons, however, and pretty soon she gave up and left Grandma to chunter her unrelated comments in response to each of Steve's attempts at dialogue. Somehow, she managed to refer to council flower bed replanting policy, blocked guttering, and the overprice of bread, none of which remotely fitted with anything Steve had said. His sainted big brother only got one mention, which was an improvement on usual, but it was offset by Mrs Truman from down the road getting three. By twenty past eleven, even Steve had run out of ideas, and they all retired for the night, Steve to lie awake worrying for two hours about his mother, about completing the development of Sling and about the state of the world.

***

In the morning, Steve was keen to be off before his mother could share some more of her problems. They weren't quick enough, though, and he found himself changing the light bulbs, unjamming the toaster, and fixing the dripping bathroom tap. As the cottage wasn't going to be available until mid afternoon, Jackie had been hoping they would find some sort of attraction for the girls to visit before they reached Llanaberllan, but the way things were going the attraction might be watching Steve cleaning out the kitchen sink overflow. To fill a bit of time in, while he was re-grouting the bath, Jackie took the two girls out into the back garden to visit the tortoise. He (or she) had been part of Steve's family since childhood, and he had been old and slow then. After a brief search, he was found underneath a bush where he had decided to hibernate for the summer: he was perhaps getting forgetful, too.

Now your average tortoise is not much different from a rock, but with a marginally higher top speed. And old Streak probably didn't even come up to average in the running department, but what he lacked in speed he made up for by also lacking in brains. He had stashed away a pile of gravel to tide him over during those long cold summer days – now he just had to remember what he used it for. He didn't appear to know why he was still awake, either, and after a while he seemed to concede defeat and started a long slow shuffle in the direction of a rose bush that was growing about half an hour away in the direction of the side gate.

Grandma came out into the back garden herself at that point, partly to lead Steve out to where the washing line post needed reinforcing, but mostly to tell Chloe to leave Streak alone. Steve's mother seemed to thrive on negativity like that. His own childhood seemed to have been lived to the accompaniment of a long string of restrictive instructions, designed to guide him towards good behaviour and to give him a profound and enduring sense of general guilt. 'Don't play with your food. Don't forget to wash behind your ears. Always tie your shoelaces properly. Don't eat with your mouth full.'

'Don't stand on my flowers,' she said to Natalie, who had moved to within three feet of a cluster of waterlogged sticks that stood in a small puddle in the middle of the lawn. Grandma's approach to plants seemed to involve the belief that if you water dead things often enough you end up with something other than wet dead things.

She didn't appear to notice that Chloe was now for some reason on her way to the shed to get the rat poison from its secret hiding place. Jackie spotted her re-emerge with the bag of pellets, though, and the sight was enough to convince her that they should perhaps be on their way. Rather unsatisfyingly abruptly they repacked the car, said their goodbyes, rejoined the road to Wales, and ended the paragraph.

***

'There it is!' cried Natalie helpfully, as she spotted the strangely shaped oak tree that marked the turning off the dual carriageway into Grandma's road. When Steve had been a child, it had always looked to him a bit like an Edwardian girl holding a bag of sweets in each outstretched hand (well, you had to use your imagination). One branch had been broken off years ago, though, and now it looked more as if it was pointing out the direction of escape from his mother. Or perhaps pointing the way towards Wales, which is really where they should have been by now, had Chloe not taken it upon herself to bring Streak along for the ride. She was sitting with her arms folded crossly now, glaring down at her feet, but at least she had been magnanimous enough to use a pile of luggage to prop the aged tortoise up against the window, where he could see the countryside flash past, in case speed turned out to be his thing after all.

It took them another while to re-extricate themselves from Grandma's house, and then it was at the expense of having to force down a slice each of her forty megacalorie walnut cake. Grandma had also had the chance to read the first few pages of her Sunday newspaper, which led to the usual one-sided discussion about how she thought the world was going mad, interspersed with the occasional request for advice on whether or not now was the time to go and start hiding in the cellar and putting sticky tape round the doors and windows. Not that she was going to let the world and its problems beat her, oh no. Or that she had a cellar, come to that.

Chloe was talking again by the time they passed the oak tree à la one-armed Edwardian girl holding a bag of sweets, etc, for the third time that morning, and within half an hour she was back to her usual, excited and bubbly self, rabbiting on in the back of the car about all the animals she would see on holiday. In fact, she got so loud and distracting that at one point Steve found himself instinctively trying to turn down the volume knob on the car radio, which wasn't even on. His road stress was creeping on again, especially after an altercation at a roundabout with a member of the costs-money-to-indicate brigade, so Jackie took it upon herself to try to get the girls to play a quiet game while he tried to concentrate.

She suggested they counted the yellow cars they passed, but Chloe was having none of that, and suggested counting horses. Steve suggested counting the shiny new sections of replacement crash barrier that marked recent pile-ups, but horses won.

Even Natalie, who was far too timid to go anywhere near a real horse in real life, was excited by the game. 'Wow – that's five horses now. How many more will we see before we get there?'

'Oh at least a hundred, I bet,' said Steve.

'I don't think we'll see that many,' said Jackie.

'I'm sure we will. In fact, I'll drive round and round until we do, if necessary.'

Jackie glanced over at him, to check that road stress wasn't turning into road-crazy, but they'd just gone past a sign saying Soft Verges, and Steve's wandering brain was now busy wondering whether that was a good thing or a bad thing. He did know that he wasn't ever going to risk driving onto one, just in case. It reminded him of the 'contains sulphites' message on wine bottles. Was that a healthy thing for a wine to do, or not? Was it a claim, a boast or a warning? And then there was the little matter of that last junction: should he have gone left, instead of straight on? Certainly the road looked very minor to be an 'A' road, even though Chloe and Natalie were both thrilled by the now rapidly rising horse count.

As people invariably do when they are concerned that they might be heading in completely the wrong direction, Steve speeded up a little, as if attempting to be in the wrong place sooner. The pile of bags between the girls started to wobble more alarmingly than it had earlier, and the odd small item cascaded from the top one every time that Steve made a slight navigational adjustment, or U-turn as they are sometimes called.

It was twenty minutes before they regained the correct road, and by then Steve had to contend with Natalie's repeated wailing ('I'd never seen a fox, and now I've gone and seen a dead one') and Chloe's questions as to whether the toilet at the holiday cottage could have a dead woodlouse floating in it, like their toilet at home had.

Steve sighed. Roll on Wales.

***

Eventually, Steve swung the car through the gateway of the old farm that had been turned into a cluster of holiday cottages, somewhere in the middle of Welsh nowhere. He parked at an incompetent angle in the small car park, and they all got out and stretched. The country air was surprisingly warm, and full of bovine goodness.

'It's very prettyful,' said Chloe, a trifle doubtfully, as she studied the nearest cottage, a small slate-built structure with peeling paint on its window frames and a crooked hand-painted sign announcing its identity as Two Tree Cottage.

'Ours is the one beyond the little grassed area,' read Jackie from the brochure that she was clutching. She indicated a rather larger but no less depressed looking building that stood thirty yards away, beyond what might have been the advertised wild-flower meadow.

'It's by a herd of trees!' exclaimed Natalie, trying to be upbeat and positive.

Steve was about to take the brochure from Jackie's hand, to see what it might have to say about obtaining the key, when a heavily built forty-something man wearing mortar spattered trousers came lumbering out of a doorway in another of the former out-buildings, followed by a decrepit dog. Steve presumed he must be the owner, Mr Rhys ap Llewellyn. By the looks of it, he had just been putting the finishing touches to a flight of three stairs that he was adding to the entrance to one of the cottages, perhaps to help elderly or disabled visitors to get some exercise.

'Yow must be the people fer Four Lawn Cottage,' said Mr ap Llewellyn in a strong Birmingham accent. 'Mrs Oscroft,' he added, to show that he knew what was what and who was who. 'And yow need to use the end parking space.'

He fiddled with the front door until it opened. Steve followed him inside, almost tripping over the dog in the process. He was expecting some sort of tour, or at least an explanation of how the wood-burning stove worked, but Mr ap L had only come in to read the electricity meter that formed the centrepiece of the small sitting room at the back of the cottage. For some reason he wasn't happy with what he'd written, and appeared to change it twice as he went out. He was followed out by his ancient dog, neither of them saying a word, although the dog did leave a trail of ancient slobber.

'Right,' said Jackie, who was never one to let fate get her down. After all, she'd married Steve. She set about exploring the cottage with the girls while Steve went out to start unloading the car. That was the great thing about holidays, he told himself, you didn't have to put up with them for ever. So what if there were bits of forest growing from the foundations and the owner had a dog with tail rot? It didn't mean he couldn't have a break from the stresses of his normal routine, a chance to escape from SLSL and its senseless sensors for a while.

Laboriously bringing in all the luggage single-handedly would normally have taken him something like ten trips back and forth across the rough grass of the 'lawn', but with the owner sitting watching his every move from the comfort of his new steps, Steve decided he would try to do it in six. It was perhaps not the wisest of his recent decisions, particularly for his back, his left wrist, and Natalie's suitcase.

Once everything was in, and he'd unpacked, he finally got to collapse into one of the armchairs in the cottage while he tried to regain his breath and to remember where he'd seen the bottle of red wine so that they could relax with a glass or two each after the girls had gone to bed, but almost at once Mr ap Llewellyn pushed his head round the edge of the front door.

'Yow can't stay here,' he said.

Steve took a few moments to respond, partly because he had almost swallowed his tongue.

'Pardon?'

'Yow can't stay here.'

'Sorry?'

'Oi'll help watch yow put everaything back in yower car.'

'Why can't we stay here? What's the problem?' Steve had gone from wanting not to stay in Four Lawn Cottage to wanting not to leave it in rather less time than he could have anticipated.

'Someone called Garay rang at lunchtoime and left yow a message. Yow must go back fer a secret Monday morning meeting about the secret croisis.'

'What secret crisis? Who's Gary? I don't know anyone called Gary.'

'Well he knows yow. Said he wuz yower boss. He said yowr Sling sensor project has gone titz up.'

'Oh, Barry.' Steve's stomach lurched, tripped, and fell. He made hand signals to Mr ap Llewellyn to indicate that he was going to go and make a mobile phone call to Barry to find out what was going on, and Mr ap Llewellyn gestured back that he should go immediately.

Unfortunately, their little rural idyll was not over-blessed with mobile phone connectivity, and within five minutes Steve found himself in the little pay phone cubicle that had been installed behind One Horse Cottage. Even from that, the line was terrible, and when Barry eventually answered the phone it was as much as Steve could do to make himself heard. From what he eventually managed to establish, either Sling had run into extreme difficulties over its latest test results, meaning that Steve needed to come back to work for the week to discuss what to do, or possibly that gubble boice fritty salvo shed friggy perble oop.

'Couldn't I just do it over the telephone from here?' asked Steve.

'Jittles wig-wig crody samling Monday,' Barry seemed to say.

Steve continued to plead with him for something over two pounds fifty, but it was no use. A combination of Barry's resolution that things were really bad, combined with his telephonical translation into some dialect previously known only around the upper reaches of the Zambesi, meant that Steve had conceded defeat and was offering to return by the time he ran out of coins. He managed to win the argument that there was no point in returning immediately – for one thing, there was no way he had the energy to drive straight back – but he ended up agreeing to travel back on the train the next morning, so that Jackie and the girls could keep the car. For his part, Barry agreed that Steve could resume his holiday again later in the week if he came in to work on Monday, and that he could have a couple of days off in lieu some time. He then proceeded to wish Steve a peaceful night in Wales and a zisblat grotoff spaglorsgettle blot.

Steve put the phone down and stood for five minutes watching a robin hopping about in the fallen leaves while he summoned up the courage to break the news to Jackie. She was actually surprisingly sanguine about it – perhaps she wanted a holiday from more things than home – and agreed to run him to the station if he could locate some more change and phone up for the train times. This time he rang from up in the village.

By the time they should just about have been finishing off the bottle of Merlot, it was all sorted, and he was able to relax with a spot of light repacking. Chloe and Natalie were too busy with the gymkhana that they were holding on their parents' bed to notice that he was spending the first and, for now, only night of his holiday luggage-wrestling on his own.

***

Long after Jackie had fallen asleep, Steve lay there, his mind in turmoil once again with thoughts of sensors, until finally, some time after two, he fell asleep, lulled by the sound of a gentle breeze in the trees and by the noises of Mr ap Llewellyn distressing the plasterwork in one of the other cottages deep into the night.

8

The last remnants of mist were just clearing from the higher slopes of the surrounding hills as they set off from the cottage, Jackie at the wheel, the girls subdued and rather upset in the back, and Steve in the front passenger seat, worrying about what might await him at work. The valley looked serene and beautiful on this October Sunday, steam gently rising from the farm muck-heaps and flocks of wood pigeons grey against gold in the fields of stubble down the lane as the car slipped through the tranquillity of this dew-encrusted Eden.

Such poetry, such penmanship. Where's that Booker prize?

Jackie dropped Steve off at the nearest station, Llanqwerty-uiop or some such, so that he could catch the train back home. It was quite an emotional send-off. Steve gave each of the three of them a hug in the station car park, but as he extricated himself from Natalie's arms he saw tears welling in her eyes, and Chloe sobbed as her father placed her down on the ground after kissing her cheek.

'I'll see you all on Tuesday, all being well,' said Steve, with a bit of a lump in his throat. 'Try to enjoy yourselves.'

'Take care, Steve,' said Jackie. She turned to her daughters as he picked up his hold-all and walked towards the solitary platform. 'Come on girls, let's go to the bunny farm.'

'Yeah! Cool!' shouted Natalie, and both girls bounced back across the car park and into the car in a series of giant joyous bunny hops.

Steve had a ten minute wait amidst the excited chatter of a group of young-at-heart walkers who were setting off to climb one of the hills near the next station. They were laden with cameras, camcorders, binoculars and picnics, and it was quite clear from the sky that the weather wasn't about to let them down. Three long months without a single day off apart from weekends, and Steve's first chance to get away to the hills for a few days was already fast evaporating. It didn't have to be nice weather as well, to rub it in.

The train duly arrived, and he got on and found himself a window seat on the left hand side, opposite two women in their mid twenties. The multicoloured fabric that covered the seats, the floor and much of the walls wouldn't entirely have been his choice, looking as it did distinctly as if it had been designed by somebody with either a good working knowledge of hallucinogenic drugs or some sort of kaleidoscope fixation, but the seat was at least comfortable and the leg room more than adequate even for people with more than the average number of legs, such as Steve[1].

With a mournful 'parp' from the horn the train resumed its twisting and snaking journey out of the middle of Wales, through a series of hidden wooded valleys and past a string of wayside stations in remote outposts with unpronounceable names, such as Shrewsbury. The views alternated between stunning and beautiful, or sometimes both at once. There were more golden fields, overgrown green lanes, sudden glimpses of kingfisher patrolled rivers, and even the occasional sighting of a red kite as it made its way towards the bunny farm. For miles, too, the railway cuttings were cloaked in a pink duvet of Himalayan Balsam, a plant that was rapidly taking over the British countryside in the absence of any native predators willing to touch it. While fighting one interloper with another is not a great recipe for ecological stability, Steve couldn't help wondering if it wouldn't be a good idea to import a yeti or two to keep it under control.

The two women spent the journey reading bits of their identical newspapers to one another. Most of the stories were semi-plausible at best, and some seemed to be downright nonsense, but the two members of the talking newspaper club didn't seem to care or notice. You can't believe everything you read in the papers, of course. In fact, whenever you happen to have any inside information about a story, or to know much about a subject in any detail, you can always find errors and inaccuracies in the newpapers' reporting of it. Books, on the other hand, you can always rely on absolutely. Trust me on this one, I'm an author.

---

[1] For a human; not for a woodlouse.

Steve's thoughts were interrupted by a sudden explosion of discordant musical notes, apparently played on a xylophone by an outraged orang-utan. Either a dustbin lorry was reversing (a little unlikely on a moving train) or one of the women's mobile phones was ringing. Steve groaned. When he was a lad, having a telephone was all about waiting six months to have it installed; now it meant changing the way it rang on a weekly basis. And it meant having to listen to everyone else reciting every trivial detail of their worthless lives to one another. The intrusion on his ears was highly irritating and compulsively addictive in equal measure. In particular, he soon became very keen to hear what had happened to Lindsey after she'd discovered that her missing underwear had been found in the drawer of the till. Annoyingly, the conversation got diverted off in the direction of Happy Hour drink prices before Steve could get to hear what the manager had done when he found it, and soon after that the women reached their station and Steve was left alone to sit and marvel at how fast sheep can sprint when they think that a train is about to chase them up the field.

***

The house was cold and unwelcoming when he let himself in, although there was a small pile of mail behind the door to remind him that their gas and electricity suppliers, and three credit card companies, were eagerly waiting to hear - and to receive cheques - from him.

He spent the rest of the daylight hours trying to prune bits of the garden in the drizzle, and then settled down in front of the TV to half-watch a documentary about jellyfish while he half-worked on his statistical analysis of Sarah's Sling test data. By half past ten he'd concluded that there was more to jellyfish than any ordinary person could possibly take an interest in, that the world's foremost jellyfish experts knew an incredible amount about the origins, distribution and physiology of jellyfish, but absolutely nothing of any use whatsoever about treating jellyfish stings, and that the Sling test data were about as depressing as depressing does.

The drizzle outside had turned into the sort of rain you felt you had to watch. It was certainly better than the television, where the documentary had given way to a sofaful of celebrities who were earnestly interviewing each other about nothing. At least, Steve presumed they were celebrities, on the grounds that he'd never seen or heard of any of them before and that they all took themselves terribly seriously. He switched the TV off and went to bed. He hadn't had much sleep the night before, what with his difficulties in falling asleep and then the doves doing a war dance on the roof tiles at four. He closed his eyes and tried not to worry about what tomorrow's meeting with Barry might bring. Even in the most extreme of past circumstances (the time they'd had six thousand sensors fail in a customer's new product; the time Barry needed urgent help writing an after dinner speech for an industry get-together; the time Barry had scratched one wing of his previous car), Steve had never been called back from holiday. It did not bode well. The omens were ominous.

It wasn't looking good for a happy ending.

Whoops, that's given it away.

***

The mood in the office was quiet, but tense. Barry's idea of a Truth Morning, where all pretensions were swept aside in the interests of getting it off your chest and of team building, was not going well. Clare wasn't speaking to Simon. Simon wasn't speaking to Lisa. No-one was speaking to Darren. And Darren was speaking to no-one, at least not civilly. Steve, meanwhile, was still in suspense about why he'd been called back so abruptly from his holiday. As Barry was shut in his office with the factory manager, and as pretty much no-one else was communicating anything to anybody, he had to content himself with twiddling his thumbs until just before eleven when Clare gave him the tip-off that Barry was at last free.

His boss's office door was open when Steve got there, and Barry, who was stabbing some numbers into a calculator and muttering something about those further up the corporate food chain, beckoned him to come in.

'I didn't know you were in. I thought you were in the Lake District this week,' he commented idly.

Steve nearly choked. 'Wales,' he said, though that wasn't really the point.

'Is something wrong? Is Jane not well?'

'You rang me on Saturday and called me back for an urgent meeting, remember?' spluttered Steve.

'Ah,' said Barry, who had just realised that he might have forgotten to ask Clare to contact everyone to tell them that he'd changed his mind again and was postponing the meeting. 'While you're here,' he continued, eager to move the conversation on, 'would you mind seeing how Darren's doing with the supplier stuff? Has he chosen someone yet? Oh, and can you have a word with Anthony – he's going to let us do our first pilot manufacturing run some time in November and he needs to know when you'll be ready.'

With an invitation to enjoy the rest of his holiday ringing in his ears, Steve turned and moved towards the door. He'd come all the way back for this? Even for Barry, it wasn't much of a pep talk. And Anthony was one of Steve's very least favourite colleagues, with a reputation for always being ready to help others to be less fortunate than himself.

'One question: when *are* we going to have the urgent meeting about the Sling test results?' Steve asked.

For a moment, Barry seemed caught off guard. Then he looked up and motioned for Steve to close the door.

'I've had some exciting news – I've got a job at head office in London,' he said, sitting back with a proud look on the bit of his face that wasn't hidden by beard.

Lucky old head office, thought Steve.

'I hadn't planned to tell anyone until the department meeting on Friday, but since you're on holiday this week –'

In theory, thought Steve.

' – I decided you could be the first to know the good news –'

Steve wasn't necessarily going to argue with that last bit.

' – but you mustn't tell another soul.'

That bit was less clear: whether or not Darren had a soul had recently been a matter of some debate between Lisa and anyone who would listen.

'So what is the job?'

Barry's chest puffed up further. 'I've been given a special assignment to lead a project to drive down the costs of managing our technical facilities and procuring professional services.'

Steve hoped that his raised eyebrows weren't noticed. It might have been a lot of big words – in fact, it was a lot of big words – but it rather sounded like a bit of a sideways move, with hints of downwards about it.

'And will someone be brought in to manage the department, or will it be one of us?'

'I don't know,' said Barry, and 'I don't much care,' added his body language. 'There'll be an announcement soon, I think.'

'And what about meeting to discuss the test data?'

Again, Barry evaded the question, this time with a request for upper and lower cost estimates for the composite halide coating process.

'I sent the costs through on that at least two weeks ago,' Steve pointed out.

'Well, they were too high,' sniffed Barry, returning to his calculator and punching the keys with renewed venom, 'and I still need the lower end estimates.'

'Those *were* the lower end estimates,' said Steve, in a rather affronted tone.

'Then we need another technique, because the marketing folks have decided they need to halve the price if we're going to sell anything against Senssertive's new offering.'

'But -,' said Steve, and shut his mouth. Perhaps it wouldn't be helpful to remind Barry that the alternative protective coating processes had both been casualties of Barry's departmental cost-cutting exercise of the previous year, when he'd not so much pruned as bonsai'd the lab organisation.

'Darren might have some ideas about something we could buy in,' said Barry. 'He's supposed to be looking for cheap new technologies when he isn't busy with his own brilliant ideas.'

Steve decided not to bother with further protestations until he'd mulled it over with Darren, and Barry wouldn't have heard them anyway because he was now too busy reminding Steve that he expected nothing less that a hundred and fifty per cent from him and that a hundred and ten per cent was for shirkers. Steve did make one final attempt to ask him about the test results meeting for which he'd come all the way back from Wales, but there were no chinks in Barry's blank-faced look of denial and in truth he was beginning to doubt himself now. His boss's exact words on the telephone might have been something about a Sling test results crisis, but then again they might have been gloggle likk-likk truvbit smack.

'The meeting was to discuss the Beauchild International situation. It was nothing to do with your Sling results,' said Barry. 'I think you must have got the wrong end of the stick.'

'What Beauchild situation?' asked Steve, acutely aware that this was likely to be another stick with at least two wrong ends to grab at.

'Who did you talk to, in that teleconference you messed up?' There was sudden steel in Barry's voice.

'Randy somebody. Hedgehog or something.'

'Randy Hodgellog,' said Barry. 'He's their Chief Operating Officer, and he owns nearly half the company.'

None of this was going anywhere fast, as far as Steve was concerned, yet it seemed to be of great interest to Barry, whose voice was rising so alarmingly that Steve wondered if it might go into a feedbacky scream. He'd always been a bit of a dramasmith, of course, but Steve was struggling to see what this particular drama was about.

'Do you know what the plan was?' shrilled Barry, his previous new-job bonhomie now clearly behind him.

No, but he was obviously about to.

'We were going to merge with them!' hissed Barry, the veins at his temples pulsing in time with the gesticulations of his hands.

'Oh,' said Steve, but Barry didn't seem to be interested in Steve's input.

'It would have been a marriage made in heaven,' he went on, a certain sudden bitterness in his voice at the contrast with his own union with the woman he liked to call – behind her back – his first wife. 'A little spot of vertical supply chain integration. They would have had their own in-house source of sensors and we would have got a massive ready-made market to sell into. Did you know that they use nearly ten million strain gauges a year? There was even a name planned for the merged company – Strainbeau Inc.'

'Is it off?'

'Yes, it is off. Dead as a – ' Barry searched for an analogy. 'Dead as a lemming.'

Steve swallowed. 'They seemed nice enough people,' he lied weakly.

'Yes, they were. But then someone told them about all our problems, and now they've dropped the whole thing.'

Steve was not, repeat not, about to ask for any more information about that. From the look in Barry's eyes, the main sewage outflow was already about to hit the offshore wind farm. If trouble was coming his way, he didn't mean to go out and greet it.

'I warned you as much as I dared that things were volatile with the share price, and that wheelings and dealings were going on,' said Barry. 'A reverse takeover like this could have safe-guarded all our jobs, but I couldn't tell you more because of the Due Diligence secrecy rules.'

He sagged back in his chair, his energy spent. Steve didn't know quite what to say. From his boss's expression, he couldn't help but wonder what he'd done to his career prospects.

'We'll have a meeting next week about how we hide all this from senior management.' Barry gave a wan smile and opened the door. 'In the meantime, nothing to anyone. You'll be lucky to get away with this.'

Steve walked back to the open plan office, making a mental note to have his midlife crisis good and early.

The ever brilliant Darren was busy trying to save space on his desk by balancing his pens and pencils on end, and as one or two of them were wobbling like a pensioner on a tightrope, Steve thought it best not to disturb him. Before he tackled either Darren or Anthony, job numero uno was to phone Jackie, to see how things were going in Wales. Unfortunately, it was hard to tell how things were going, though, because his wife seemed to be somewhere with a hundred over-excited children in the background. It sounded as if they were doing something that involved rushing through the air at great speed. As far as he could make out, the girls' trolls were in on the act, too – the whole happy family, except him. They'd all just come back from a boat trip round the bay to see the seals (if Steve's interpretation of Chloe's description of 'fat sausages' was correct) and Natalie had named the horses in the field near the cottages as Squish and Squash, but that was as much as he learnt before they abandoned the phone and ran off for more ice-creams.

He was left with a disconnection tone, and Anthony to negotiate with. It took a while to track the guy down, but he was eventually found by the pallet-wrapping machine in the loading bay, carving another tally mark into his copy of the plywood R&D Mission Statement plaque. Fixing a date for the November pilot plant run took a surprising amount of juggling with dates and angry snorting (on Anthony's part) and much begging, pleading and humiliation (on Steve's), but they somehow agreed on Tuesday the twenty-first.

'We'll definitely be ready by then,' Steve reassured him, trying to look as if he believed it.

'Good. If you're not here by seven a.m. that day, I'll give you a ring. And if you're not here by ten past, I'll give your neck a ring.'

By the time he had finished laughing over-heartily at his own joke, he was alone.

**

Steve arrived back at his desk just as the clock on the wall would have reached twelve if it had had any batteries in it. The prospect of canteen food was enough to tempt Darren out of the office, and he and Steve walked across together and sat down with their chosen meals.

'I'm not sure that Sarah is doing the testing properly,' Steve confided. 'I wonder if there's anyone else we could get to help her?'

'There's Andrew,' Darren suggested, but Steve shook his head. Andrew was basically a waste of precious oxygen. It was hard to see how a five times winner of SLSL's Idiotic Mistake of the Week competition and recipient of the corporate silver cup with oak leaf cluster for the biggest technical blunder of the year, 2005, was likely to be an asset on the team.

'Well what about Nell then? She'd probably be willing to help, if you asked her nicely.'

'What, Nell in Quality Control? You seriously want me to go and ask Death Nell for a favour?'

Darren shrugged and lapsed into silence. His well-meaning suggestions were manifestly adding to his colleague's stress burden.

'The more you look at it, the more it all seems to be a can of worms,' Steve sighed, at length.

Darren looked disturbed. 'Oh, I was hoping it was perhaps shepherd's pie.'

A sudden thought struck Steve. 'How did your meal with Lizzy go on Saturday?'

Darren grinned, which wasn't a pretty sight, nor a common one. 'We're going out,' he proclaimed.

'Congratulations,' said Steve, making a mental note to commiserate with her.

Another thought occurred to him. 'When is she coming back?'

'She isn't,' said Darren. 'She's resigned, and Barry's agreed to her not working her notice, as a cost-cutting exercise. She's got a job in a made-to-measure curtain shop.'

Steve worked on his pie in surprised silence. Most pop groups have longer careers than that. Darren, though, became unusually talkative, and explained at some length how Lizzy had restored his faith in women. From the strange look in his eyes, it was clear that he'd found at least the love of his week.

They returned their trays to the kitchen and headed back to the office, Darren babbling on merrily about love, romance and pencil pleat ruched pelmets.

'I'm sorry to interrupt,' Steve interjected, a few minutes after they'd sat down in front of their computer screens to allow their distressed digestive tracts a chance to make a truce with lunch, 'but Barry wanted me to find out whether you've got anywhere with finding a new strategic supplier or a cheap new coating process yet?'

Darren dragged his eyes up from his screen. 'Why don't you go to hell?'

That was a little unexpected, even from Darren.

'...? ...!' said Steve.

'No, H.E.L. – Hindsight Electrolysis Limited. I've got their website up – it looks pretty good.'

Steve wasn't entirely sure about their motto ('With Hindsight, you'll find a better way'), but he had to agree that he was otherwise impressed – you can't beat a bit of snazzy graphics and a dancing cursor in the shape of a golden spanner - so he and Darren set about arranging a trip to H.E.L. and back. The only slight snag was that the company was based on some forsaken industrial estate in Doltburn. And the only question was why Darren had found them an electrolysis company when he was meant to be looking for lacquer suppliers and coatings experts.

'If we start electroplating things, we're going to need to use acids, right, and we'll end up with corrosion problems and goodness know what, right?' said Steve, as if to a dim child or senior manager.

'Yes, and if we look a little further down the website – if I can ever get this damned spanner thing to move out of the way – you'll see that Hindsight have now developed their electroplating process into the basis of a high performance encapsulation system for holding and protecting delicate components in extreme environments, and which *doesn't* use acids. Right?'

'Ah,' said Steve.

They agreed that a visit to Doltburn was probably going to be necessary, but Darren did offer to have a list of alternatives drawn up for when Steve finished what was left of his holiday. With a bit of luck they might end up with a shortlist of coating technologies they could license or acquire that wouldn't involve a trip to a town with a reputation for having an accent so thick that none of the locals could understand one another.

***

According to a message left on his telephone's voicemail recorder, Steve had finally been granted an audience with Alex Deese at three o'clock, so at five to he made his way to the Accounts Department ('If it can't be priced, it's worthless'). He found all the offices dark, deserted and locked, and for a moment wondered whether they'd perhaps sacked themselves to save money, but a small handwritten sign on one of the fire doors read 'Gone for an economy drive', so he scribbled a note on the bottom of it, requesting Alex contact him with another date. He wasn't sure he remembered exactly what the meeting was supposed to be about, but he did know that Barry was insistent that it must happen. And at least the walk over would help to improve his waistline.

He got back to his desk to be greeted by number eleven in a long series of e-mails about how to send less e-mails. These days, sanity at SLSL was about as common as photographs of the *Titanic* in New York. With a sigh that could have powered a wind generator for a week, he settled down to plug some numbers into some equations, in another bid to try to understand the almost implausibly bad test results.

'Steve,' said a voice, 'what do you think of Barry's move?'

Steve hesitated for a moment. He was shocked and felt rather cheated. 'You're not meant to know about that.'

'Oh, everyone knows,' scoffed Darren. 'It's one of those secrets that you're allowed to tell one other person.'

'Hmm.' Steve hadn't yet formed an opinion on losing Barry: he had been intending to set the evening at home aside for thinking his way round that one.

'If you ask me,' said Darren into the silence left by Steve's internal thought processes, 'it'll make no difference. It's a non-event.' He pulled his coat on to go home. 'It's like stirring lumpy custard. Different lumps rise to the top each time, but nothing's really changed.'

And that analogy could have been so much worse, believe me.

9

Steve arrived back at Four Lawn Cottage at eight o'clock on the Tuesday, courtesy of another lift from the station with Jackie and the girls. They had both been promised that they could tell Steve all their news, but not until he was back at the cottage. They respected the request, but you would have needed a good stop-watch to measure the pause between car stopping and chatter starting. Natalie was first off the mark, telling Steve how they had named the nearest three sheep in the field adjoining the cottage. They now rejoiced, as much as sheep can rejoice, in the names of Blossom, Twilight and Hairy.

Steve was practically thrilled. 'And how are Slop and Slip, or whatever you called the horses?' he asked.

There was a condescending look from Natalie. 'You mean Squish and Squash, Dad.'

'I think Slop and Slip suit them better.'

'Hmm. Moving on...,' said Natalie, with a withering, crush-ing sort of a look.

'Moving on,' echoed Chloe. It was her turn now to recap some of the events of the past two and a half days. They'd been to the bunny farm, found a dead ladybird, seen a blackbird and a brownbird, and Natalie had nearly trodden on a baby spider.

'Anything else?'

'A snail fell in the pond, but it was OK – we fished it out and it was still working.'

Steve was rather relieved about that. He still shuddered from time to time at the thought of the long-dead starling that Chloe had wanted him to revive the previous summer.

Then it was Jackie's turn. On Sunday afternoon they'd gone to visit the lost mediaeval village of Bryngwynllpox, but Jackie hadn't been able to find it, and neither had any of the locals. So instead, Mrs Ap Llewellyn, who worked as a part-time adminmaid at the trinket shop up in the village, had been persuaded to take them for a walk to look at some of the fascinating Celtic monuments in the vicinity, and Mr Ap Llewellyn had then given them all a tour of his latest project – a barn conversion at the side of the existing cottages. To save money for more expensive things, such as Eisteddfods, he'd been doing all the work himself, and although he informed Jackie that he had been by trade originally a crease-folder in a map factory, she was able to report that he had been doing a truly professional job, with some exquisite craftsmanship. The one question that she had only just brought herself to ask, though, was exactly why it was that he'd decided to convert the cottage into a barn. 'Itzferpoh-onaysloik,' had been his answer, which hadn't entirely helped until she'd worked out that it was aimed at families who wanted to take their daughters' ponies with them on holiday.

Having caught up with all their news, and having briefly explained to Jackie about losing Barry and about getting the chance to visit an industrial estate in Doltburn, but not about having gone back for nothing nor about messing up the Beauchild deal, Steve went into the kitchen to open a bottle of wine and to cook a late and lonely meal for one using the few things in the cupboard that were within his repertoire. Not that boiled eggs, pasta and mint sauce wouldn't have been a good meal, if he hadn't burnt them and had to settle for two glasses of Merlot and a bag of crisps.

***

Wednesday morning was a kind of good to be alive sort of morning, clear and cool and fresh. The early light was pretty much perfect, and even his daughters were surprisingly keen to get started on Steve's proposed expedition up the nearest mountain, spurred on no doubt by his unkeepable promise of chocolate at the top. Steve didn't mean it to be unkeepable, as it happened: it was simply that he had completely forgotten that he had raided the chocolate cupboard in the night and had finished off the week's rations. The girls were so eager, indeed, that they almost forgot to take the trolls, and ten precious minutes of sunshine were lost while Jackie went back into the cottage to find them. Not a problem that Hillary and Tenzing had had back in 1953, presumably.

They parked in a little layby with a couple of other cars, near the stile that marked the start of the footpath. Steve got out and went round to help Natalie put her walking boots on, while Jackie did the same for Chloe. It was nice to be outdoors, ready for exercise and adventure. Ready for heathery slopes, hill-top tarns, wide open spaces, wilderness, lark song and gentle October sunshine.

Natalie waited patiently while her father pulled her socks on for her, then gently explained that they needed to be the other way out and have the tops turned over. Steve wilted under the realisation that he couldn't even operate a pair of socks correctly now. Eventually, though, everyone was ready, and slightly after eventually they were beginning the climb up Steve's cleverly crafted 'keep the boots dry' watershed route.

The first part of the path crossed two fields, before veering left towards a series of small crags. Fifty yards further on, Steve led them off the path and up through ankle-breaking tussocky grass towards the start of the main southern ridge of the hill. Like many leaders, he was doing it from the back. Already he was beginning to have some doubts about the route. Even at these early stages the going was beginning to separate the men from the, er, everybody else, who were rapidly leaving him some way behind. Before they had set off, he'd worried a bit about making Chloe walk up such a large hill, though not enough not to. Those concerns were thoroughly dispelled now: up in front she was quite happy, chasing about over the hillside after sheep, trying to catch one for Natalie as a pet. Natalie was not quite so happy. She had seen a squashed beetle as she climbed over the stile, and now she was having to keep her eyes on the ground to make sure she didn't nearly step on any others. Jackie walked with her, not appearing to notice the gradient at all.

Steve's clever route up the watershed, predictably, missed all the streams, but, also predictably, found all the squelchy marshy bits. And like every walk they did, it zigzagged backwards and forwards annoyingly over the fold of the map. Not that it really mattered, because the other three were now way ahead and climbing strongly. He only managed to catch them up when they stopped by a stream to look for dolphins. Sweating profusely, he might have contemplated a couple of mouthfuls of the water, but it looked a little too organic for his liking so he opened a small carton of apple juice instead and drank the bit that he didn't squirt over his trousers. He studied the map, one way up and then the other, and then looked up to offer a few words of encouragement and motivation, along the lines that they were already four per cent of the way to the top. It obviously worked, because the others were immediately on the move again and Steve was once more left alone to his own devices at the back, trying to make the most of his enforced solitude in a world in which it was rapidly become a commodity available only to the rich and the hard of washing.

After many twists and turns and a couple of false summits, Natalie finally spied the top and went charging off towards it, only to discover with a loud 'Oh my blimey!' that there was still more mountain beyond. Although he had the maps, and despite life having many times tried to teach him that it was all about disappointment, Steve was equally surprised to find that a further summoning of energy was still necessary.

The weather chose that exact moment to turn character-building, i.e. wet, but if anything the next fifteen minutes saw a deterioration of his character as he plodded slowly upwards until, with a stumble and a slight trip, he found himself alongside the others at the summit cairn. For some reason his relatives weren't experiencing the oxygen deficiency that he was, which he presumed was how they were able to remain standing while he slumped against a rock and waited for his heart to stop thumping, preferably in a reversible, non-fatal way.

'If you look carefully, you can't see my house from here,' Chloe was announcing proudly in the direction of anyone who would listen. As the only anyones around apart from Steve and Jackie and Natalie were sheep, she didn't get much of a response. There was two minutes of silence.

'Come on Dad, now we have to unclimb it all again.' Natalie's words broke into his thoughts as she set off with her mother and sister down the path back to the valley, leaving her father to contemplate the panorama before him for a few minutes before he followed on.

This is the point at which, in the blockbuster film of this novel, the helicopter will circle round taking aerial footage of Steve sitting on his own at the summit, in an attempt to make a poignant metaphorical contrast between being on top of the world and being at a low point in a mediocre career and a fraught life.

The descent was uneventful. For most of it, Steve was behind his kinsfolk, struggling to keep them in sight and thinking turbulent thoughts about his project and his workload. The drizzle continued on and off the entire way down, and the temperature gradually fell, so by the time he reached the others back at the car – and the sun finally reappeared – he was damp and miserable.

'Now, how about borrowing some racquets and going up to the tennis courts in the village?' suggested Jackie, with one eye on the rapidly expanding patch of sky-blue sky.

Steve winced. 'Definitely not,' he said.

'Oh, you're not still going on about that silly bird, are you?'

Steve confirmed that he was indeed still going on about that silly bird. The last time he'd picked up a tennis racquet he'd missed just about every single ball, yet somehow, freakily, he'd managed to hit a swallow with the racquet as it swooped over the hot tarmac of the court. One swallow might not make a summer, but it does make quite a splatter, and a hell of a mess of a brand new white tennis shirt.

'Oh never mind,' Jackie frowned, obviously minding. 'Let's just go back and I'll do something to eat.'

She had been rather hoping to convince them all, if not to play tennis then to go for a walk in the Great Squirrelly Woods instead. There was always the chance they might spot or even photograph that shy elusive forest creature, the red squirrel. Mind you, the last time she and Steve and Steve's flat feet had gone looking for red squirrels, when the girls were still being carried, the only shy elusive forest creature that hadn't heard

Steve coming was a slug. And they'd both resisted the temptation to photograph what is after all basically slime in a skin.

To try to persuade her husband to walk in woods with twilight approaching was probably always going to be a lost cause. In all honesty, he wasn't a country lad. Until he was fifteen he'd thought that badgers were two-dimensional animals that liked to sleep at the side of dual carriageways. And although he nowadays professed to crave the peace of a rural evening whenever they were on holiday, some of the noises of the night still spooked him if he was out in the countryside after sunset. It might be best if she let him spend the evening with that project plan that he'd been hiding inside his reading book, or the laptop computer that he'd secreted behind the sofa.

***

Like the previous day, Thursday dawned bright and clear, and the girls bounded out of bed demanding a day at the beach. With Jackie on their side, and unable to think of a good enough reason why not, Steve capitulated almost at once. After all, it was supposed to be a family holiday near the seaside, and the area did have some lovely beaches, albeit rather cold at this time of year. Ten minutes studying the map over breakfast found him a likely looking place, and as a slight compromise so that he could stretch his legs a little and also avoid having to drive down a vertiginous hill, he persuaded them that they should park in the little car park on the headland and then walk along the cliffs to the bay. The walk down should provide them with half an hour of gentle onshore breezes and glorious views over the sea.

As soon as they had finished eating and he had helped Jackie make the sandwiches for lunch, he loaded the car with everything they needed for a day at the British seaside: buckets, spades, sandals, towels, wind-break, cagoules, and arctic survival suits. The car park turned out to be a patch of rough gravel in a small field by a two hundred foot drop, and theirs was the only car there, which always made him feel uncomfortable, but it would have to suffice. They divided the paraphernalia between their various rucksacks and bags and set out along a small barbed wire corridor along the far edge of the field.

Perhaps it was because the gentle onshore breeze was enough to freeze a polar bear, but there were not many other people about. Soon after they set off they did go past a middle-aged man caught on some brambles, and a little further on they passed a couple of professional birdwatchers in pursuit of a chuff-bunting or something similar, but that was it for most of the way until they rounded the last corner on the cliff-top path where Natalie, who had been leading, was confronted by a barking and snarling black Labrador. With a tiny whimper, she turned and hid behind Steve. Steve tried to hide behind Jackie, as he had always been rather allergic to large dogs with sharp teeth and he had visions of spending the afternoon unembedding them from his leg.

'He won't hurt you,' announced a middle-aged woman who was walking along some way behind the dog.

Steve was not too sure about that, and Natalie was clearly also unconvinced. Even Chloe appeared to be thinking twice about making a fuss over this one.

'Perhaps it should be on a lead,' suggested Jackie.

'No he shouldn't,' snapped the woman. 'I've never put him on a lead. He wouldn't hurt anyone. He's never even barked at anyone before.'

Steve thought about questioning how she could be so sure that it wouldn't bite when she didn't know it would bark, but he had long ago learnt that there's no point in arguing with the sort of people who are never wrong. Besides, there was still the little matter of her darling killer dog, which was growling at his nether regions. So he meekly led the family past its bared teeth and didn't stop to look back for two hundred yards, by which time it had run off in pursuit of somebody's grandfather.

Despite the cold, the beach when they reached it was by no means empty. Not much, it seems, can deter the British from enjoying their little patch of damp sand. As man of the family, Steve of course took it upon himself to select the appropriate spot to spread out their things, having due regard to the cleanliness of the vicinity, the quality of the sand, the direction of the wind and other things that men are best left to judge. And Jackie, being a woman, took it upon herself to point out – to no avail – that the spot he'd chosen was going to be under water within an hour and a half.

Having emptied out the contents of the beach bags so that the blowing sand could start to bury them, Steve pulled off his shoes and socks and walked down to the edge of the sea, the better to survey the scene. Chloe accompanied him, as she was hoping to sight a passing shark that she might catch as a pet. When they returned to the towels and the others – Steve hobbling after standing on a razor shell – they found a family of about eleven something like six feet away. Father, aided by grandfather, was busy setting up a windbreak so elaborately ambitious that the adjoining patch of beach was a major construction site for the half hour that it was being hammered into the sand. While they were doing that, two of the children got started on a set of industrial scale earthworks (well, sandworks) and three of the other children instigated a rowdy game of cricket that threatened to spill over onto the Oscroft's already sandy possessions. Grandmother, who looked as feeble as a politician's excuses, had been left holding a kite that had a wingspan to put a passenger jet to shame. It could have been a typical British beach scene from any one of several post-war decades.

Steve put his socks and shoes back on, sandpapering the tops of his toes in the process, and set off along the beach and up past the chandelier shop until he reached a small café where he bought a couple of takeaway coffees, two cartons of orange juice and four ice creams. As he did so, over by the rocks at the foot of the cliffs in the distance a flock of seagulls was just starting to rip the flesh from the bones of a middle-aged woman and a black dog who had tripped and fallen from the coastal path.

This book rights wrongs and settles scores, however implausibly.

***

While Steve sat and inspected the wound on the sole of his foot for a few minutes, Jackie took the girls down to splash in the edge of the waves. They were gone for half an hour, most of it spent watching a group of people bandage up a surfer who had misjudged his rip curl calculations, and they got back to Steve, who hadn't dared leave his post guarding their pitiful little collection of beach equipment, just as the first drop of rain hit the end of his nose. Within twenty seconds it was pelting down, and it was all the four of them could do to get everything scraped up back into the bags before the lot was sodden. The whole length of the bay, people were trying to get off the beach and into shelter faster than a sea-borne assault force under fire. Even the British have limits to the hardship they will pretend to enjoy. Only the large family next to them, somewhere within their inner fortifications of woven nylon, seemed willing to sit it out.

As the rain was getting more intense by the minute, and as lightning was now flashing round the sky, Steve and Jackie had little alternative but to seek cover. In a rare stroke of genius, Steve remembered the little museum a few buildings up the road. He hustled the others inside and paid the impressively ambitious entrance price for them all. It wasn't easy to move about once they'd got in, as absolutely everyone seemed to have developed a sudden burning interest in the area's local history at exactly the same time. The displays seemed a little random. For example, the first room housed an old rowing boat, a dozen or so photographs showing the history of the beach ball, and a highly polished collection of spare parts for a Belgian telephone exchange.

'What does obsolete mean?' asked Natalie.

'Well, it sort of means old fashioned; no longer useful,' said Steve.

Jackie already had a word for that, which was Grandma.

The girls found the second room more interesting, as that was mostly given over to something that was titled a wildlife museum but which, as far as Steve could tell through the massed rainwear of a couple of dozen people, was more of a deadlife and stuffedlife museum. The only thing he learnt from the entire hour long experience was that the Celts didn't have a word for 'Well fancy that, it's finally stopped raining'.

Eventually, when they could all take no more of displays of lobster pot stitching down the ages, Jackie led the way past the rather doubtful diorama of a Victorian airport and back out into the street.

They emerged squinting into the sunshine that had replaced the rapidly receding dark clouds. The puddles everywhere were glinting silver, and people were emerging from shops and cafés left, right and the other one. Judging by the happy looks on most of the faces that Steve passed, no-one else had water trickling down the back of their necks in the way that he did.

A fakely rustic sign at the end of the last row of cottages denoted a little art gallery, and Jackie being Jackie they soon found themselves in it. The pictures were 'interesting', which in this context means hideous, and the prices were very, and despite the number of people outside, they had the place to themselves for the fifteen minutes it took Jackie to look round. They came out just as the rain was starting again. Most of the visitors had now gone – probably to relax in nice hotel rooms before four course dinners – and there was only one other person on their side of the road. Nevertheless, Steve almost succeeded in walking into him and then realised, much to his considerable surprise, that it was Mike Marshall from Sales. The near collision was embarrassing from several angles. First of all, it made Steve look clumsy, which of course he was. More problematical, though, was that Mike was one of those people whom Steve never acknowledged when they passed in the corridor at work. Now, however, he had no option but to take a great interest in him and his health and in what he was doing there. And that was the third embarrassment, because it was quite clear from his harness that Mike had been rock climbing somewhere in the vicinity, and he looked an awfully lot younger and fitter than Steve did.

Steve made introductions all round; Jackie wrinkled her nose as she puzzled why Mike's name should be so unfamiliar to her when her husband was clearly so close to him at work, and the girls shuffled uncomfortably from one leg to the other.

They talked for a few minutes about the local rock outcrops, at Steve's self-conscious insistence, and then a little bit about people at work and about sensor sales. Finally, with a 'Look, I need to be going', Mike tore himself away and hurried off down the road towards the pub by the beach. The bedraggled family of four pulled their collars up and set off up the narrow path through the soaking vegetation back to the cliff top car park.

***

Over in England, Barry was also watching the rain splash in the puddles and was wondering whether it was ever going to stop. It had rained for nearly forty-eight hours now, and he was starting to worry about what it might be doing to his pride and joy parked outside. For the life of him, he couldn't remember reading in the handbook whether or not the rain-sensitive wipers were meant to be going rusty like that.

The day before, he had announced his job move to all the people in the department – who all already knew – and already he could feel the influence and respect ebbing away around him. The other thing that was bothering him was the thought that he would be leaving his successor with a development project that was in deep trouble. This wasn't entirely altruistic concern from a man who might have bequeathed his replacement a burning office if it had suited him, but was more the fear that all the problems he had hidden from senior management would come out of hiding and point their fingers at him.

On top of that, the department's financial results were rapidly heading south. He hadn't shared it with the team, but their salaries would soon be coming from the flipchart budget. He was also irritated at having wasted over an hour trying to track down the laptop computer that had been lent to Steve Oscroft. Its new replacement had now been delivered and the loaned one had to go back, but it couldn't be found anywhere despite the half-hearted efforts of most of the department plus several suggestions from Darren Searston. They could only assume that Steve had locked it away in some obscure cupboard that they didn't know about. Simon had tried ringing him for clues, but it was a waste of time as Steve only switched his mobile phone on for special occasions.

Barry watched a silver hubcap bobbing along the stream that now ran down the middle of the car park, and pondered the future. He'd been looking for months for a job where he could spend less time with his family, but now that he was going he wondered whether he was doing the right thing. A senior role in Facilities Management had sounded so impressive until he had overheard Darren mockingly telling everyone that it meant being in charge of the toilets. Perhaps he was making a big mistake.

***

Friday started as another beautiful morning in the heart of Wales. Unfortunately, in the time it took the Oscrofts to eat their cardboard breakfast cereal, the weather had completely gloomed over, and by the time they had decided which beach looked best on the map, it was raining again. Steve was accordingly sent out to sit in the car and listen to the weather forecast on the radio. Not that he believed them any more. Long ago, in the days before litigation with everything, the weather forecasters told you what the weather was most likely to be. These days they told you what the worst possible weather could conceivably be, so that you wouldn't sue them. It wasn't entirely helpful. Nevertheless, today they seemed pretty certain that heavy squally showers would be the dominant theme, and when Steve reported this back to his superiors, no-one quite fancied the beach any more. He tried to suggest another hill they might climb, and Jackie suggested he tried to find a different set of mugs to climb it with him.

So it was time to find an alternative, and as luck would have it, they had been left a pile of dog-eared leaflets by the previous occupants of the cottage. The first two were none too promising – a supermarket trolley test centre and an eyebrow museum – but the third looked more hopeful. Sadly, however, the Junior

Explorer Interactive Play Experience didn't admit children, and was in any case over eighty miles away, back in England. Rather more locally, a nearby market town was hosting a sheep herding show (or was it a sheep flocking show?), but it wasn't today. And there was the local thimble fanciers' annual autumn gathering and floral tribute to the international siblinghood of thimblers past and present, which *was* today but wasn't of any interest to anyone.

'Shall we just stay here until it stops raining?' Jackie suggested.

Steve was 100% ready to agree, when Chloe came over with a pamphlet that she'd taken from the pile before breakfast.

'I want to go here!' she announced firmly, and that was that.

The Marine Farm underwater zoo ultimately proved to be disappointing, though. There are only so many waterlogged horses and cows that one can take, and the children in particular were very upset by all the drowned lambs and piglets. They'd had barely a quarter of their money's worth before Jackie bundled them all out to the combined picnic and dog exercise area while they tried to decide what to do next. They weren't out there long: the weather had settled into a kind of permadrizzle, the picnic benches were all too wet to sit on, and from Steve's observations, the only exercise that most of the dogs were getting involved the relaxation of a single muscle. To overcome the trauma of the things they'd just seen, the girls hit one another with damp trolls while their parents struggled for inspiration. There wasn't much indoor entertainment to be had in such a remote area in October. There had been a notice board by the phone box up in the village, but the only event that Steve had seen listed for the week was the monthly Scrabble night at the dyslexia club. He had half a mind to concede defeat and to plonk the girls down in front of the television in the cottage, and then get on with some work while they fathomed out that it didn't get any reception. But that wasn't really what he wanted for his little princesses: the whole idea of the holiday had been to spend some quality time together as a family, not to dump them in front of something with less picture than a Bakelite radio.

Jackie took charge of the situation at this point, and after a considered fifteen second debate they all agreed to drive somewhere to try to find a decent café. However, whether the Ceffyl a Sglodion was such a place was a matter of conjecture. Not only that, but Steve unfortunately took the 'open' sign on the glass door a little too literally, and he walked straight into it, arriving at the counter in a shower of broken glass and mutual ill-will.

'Damn and blast!' cursed the owner. 'That's the third time today!' He went into the back room to find a dustpan and brush and a first aid kit, while his wife dialled the glazier.

'Now what can I get you?' she asked, once Geraint the Glass had been summoned. She was remarkably civil under the circumstances. They ordered drinks – and cakes, for, as Steve said, they were walking it off - and Steve also had a couple of sticking plasters and a paracetamol. The tea came in one of those white pottery teapots with walls so thick that there is only space for a dribble of liquid inside. It didn't matter much, as it was cold the moment it hit the walls of the pot, so nobody wanted to drink it anyway.

They came out some time later into sunshine, and on an impulse they didn't drive straight back to the cottage but followed a brown tourist sign to a picnic site by an attractively wooded stretch of river. They got out to look, and soon found themselves following a good path along the river bank signposted to a world famous viewpoint of some considerable obscurity. As at most beauty spots, hardly any of the people there had got more than two hundred yards from the car park, and the rest were sat in it, either in their cars or on folding chairs or picnic rugs. The actual scenic attraction itself, which was nearly a quarter of a mile away, was utterly deserted. Even today, in these increasingly overcrowded little islands, you only need to go somewhere that involves five minutes of physical effort to reach it, to find your own space. Especially when the wind's blowing the wrong way from the sewage works.

***

After breakfast on Saturday, Steve set about packing every-thing up and loading it into the car as best he could, with a little 'assistance' from Natalie and Chloe, while Jackie washed good-bye to the hideous chintz crockery. They'd agreed the night before that they would try to book a week in the same cottage for the next summer – when perhaps the rain would be warmer – and Steve was duly despatched to negotiate with Mr ap Llewellyn. That took about ten minutes, as Mr ap L couldn't understand a word of Steve's accent so early in the morning, but by ten past nine he was back, having been relieved of a surprisingly substan-tial non-refundable credit card deposit.

'There's a big dumbozer digging up the field!' announced daughter number two, and Steve looked up to see a large yellow earth-mover trundling across the field towards the hedge at the back of the cottage. Indeed, a whole robotic army of excavators and tipper trucks was rumbling down the lane past the cottages, followed by a gaggle of workmen staggering along under the weight of a huge wooden sign that proclaimed the start of work on the new motorway link road. The Department of Transport had spotted a few fields that they hadn't yet concreted over.

Scarcely able to wait until the next year to see how they were progressing, Steve put the key into the ignition, and they set off for home. On the way they made a long detour to pay a surprise visit to Jackie's Uncle Dennis, her only living relative apart from the three of them and her sister Diane. The visit was a surprise not least to Steve, as Jackie hadn't mentioned the idea until they were an hour into the journey. Protestations had been useless, despite their solid grounding on the point that Uncle Dennis could be quite difficult at times, as Jackie had insisted that they couldn't not visit him when he was facing his first winter alone after thirty-seven years of marriage, following the death of Jackie's aunt in February.

The route to his house involved many circuitous miles along a winding A-road that ducked and weaved its way through the Welsh Marches. Most of those miles were spent trundling along at thirty-eight miles an hour behind a small silver car occupied by two small silver-haired people. A stream of traffic the other way meant that they couldn't overtake, and it was beginning to look as if they wouldn't make it to Dennis's house before he went out for his regular Saturday afternoon at the football match.

By a quarter to twelve they had reached the town before the town before his village. Curiously but typically of people who drive at thirty-eight in a sixty zone, the man in front continued at a steady and oblivious thirty-eight as he passed the twenty sign near the local school. Three hundred yards after that he used a speed hump as a launch ramp and a bit beyond that he sent a frightened heavy goods vehicle swerving for the safety of somebody's front garden. In the next town he braked abruptly to give way to a parked car and Steve nearly ran into the back of him. As fraught as ever, they reached Jackie's uncle's house at ten past twelve.

If they'd thought that the death of his wife might have changed him at all, they were wrong. The moment he opened the door, it was obvious that he was just as irritable and cantankerous as he had ever been during his years with Ann. It had been just four days after he'd come out of the navy that he had met the right girl, but within six months of their wedding she had turned into the wrong woman. From that juncture onwards they'd spent their whole time scoring points off one another. Over the course of a long and difficult marriage, he'd scored 511,761 points off her and she'd scored 427,909 points off him. In fact, he'd have increased his winning margin (which was attributable partly to scoring points while she was asleep) still further, had he not grudgingly relinquished about five thousand from after her death. Not that he could be sure precisely how many of them had been post-mortem, as he hadn't taken a huge amount of notice of when she'd died.

He beckoned them inside and shut the door rather heavily behind them. The cause of today's ill-humour, it transpired, was that he'd spent half the morning hunting for the code that he needed to prevent some obscure piece of software from automatically renewing itself at a cost of two and a half ransoms. Not only that, he grumbled, but his computer had recently taken to adding a strong blue colour cast to everything it printed out.

He led them through into the kitchen, switched the kettle on, led them through into the small utility room that he used as a white elephant store, asked them why they were all following him, and shooed them into the lounge. Then he bustled in quickly himself and scrabbled around picking up a dozen or so pictures that he'd left strewn on the floor. Jackie wasn't going to comment, but she couldn't help but think that the blue cast on his printer might be the result of the red and yellow inks having been used up on all the flesh tones on the pictures he'd been printing off the internet.

Once the tea had been poured – coffee for Steve – they sat down and looked at one another. Dennis rarely said much, so Jackie started the conversation with tales of their time in Wales. It wasn't entirely clear that their host was listening, although his ears did prick up slightly at mention of the boat trip they'd gone on while Steve had been back in England. Like all men with a maritime past, Uncle Dennis loved the sea and loved hearing tales of it. He himself though would never talk of his own service days on HMS Lacklustre, no matter how much anybody pleaded or how drunk he got. He had once muttered something about a collision with their sister ship, HMS Lethargic, when the two had drifted slowly into one another in Plymouth Sound, but that and the occasional reference to maggoty biscuits were all anybody had heard of his time before the mast.

When she had recounted their Welsh tribulations, Jackie tried to engage him in talk of more general family matters. She reminded him that Chloe's birthday was coming up – not because anyone was expecting a present from a man so mean that he'd once tried to have his light circuits put on to Economy Seven – but for something to say, and because she needed to remind herself to remind Steve to send out the party invitations. Dennis made an oblique reference to Steve's brother's love of parties, which caused Steve to lapse into a broody silence, but otherwise he said little and glanced at the clock a lot. What passed for conversation ebbed and flowed, then ebbed a bit more, and finally evaporated completely.

'I think we'd better leave you to get to your match,' conceded Jackie, who was beginning to see her late aunt in a new and saintly light. She rounded her daughters and husband up, there was a little awkward goodbyeing, and within five minutes they were on their way again, and ten minutes after that they had stopped for a belated lunch at a burger van in a layby. It wasn't exactly food, any more than Dennis had exactly been company.

For Steve at least, though, there was the considerable relief of knowing that, apart from the two lieu days that he was going to carry over into the next year, he had used his annual leave up and wouldn't have to face the stresses and worries of finding things for his loved ones to do in the rain again, at least until Christmas.

10

It was an hour and a half into the working day, and Steve was beginning to regret having changed the password he needed to get onto the SLSL computer network just before he had left the office to go back to Wales. He'd already been through all his usual themes (girls names, places his parents had had big rows on family holidays, even the proper medical names of the bones that Angela's son Tom had broken over the years), and he was just about to give up and go cap-in-hand to the computer department to beg and grovel, when he remembered that he'd set it to Osmarelda as the first of a new theme of dolls and trolls.

Having finally got into his e-mail account, and having satisfied himself that all his e-mails could wait, he went off to get himself a cup of coffee. He'd already had all the expected brief back-to-work conversations with his colleagues ('How was your holiday?' 'Fine, thanks.'), and thought he'd better go and report in to Barry. If nothing else, it might help to fill the gap until lunch. Apart from about a thousand things, he had nothing else to do.

When he got to Barry's office, he found Darren sitting there on his own. For one second, he wondered if the appointment of Barry's replacement had all gone horribly wrong.

'There's been a bloodless coup,' said Darren, in answer to his unasked question. He paused a moment, to admire his new kingdom once more, then added 'Or at least it's bloodless now I've finished wiping up.'

'Where's Barry?'

'Oh, he's in a meeting actually. I just needed an office to make a few threatening phone calls from. Can I help you in some way?'

'No, not really. I was just going to ask Barry what he wants me to say in Birmingham next week, and to ask him how things are.'

'Things aren't too bad,' said Darren. 'We had a better week last week on the Sling project, while you were off.'

'Hmm.'

'Yeah, the speed response is finally looking slightly better, and John's given the go-ahead to pull together the marketing and launch plan.'

'And what's that going to involve?'

'Well Step One is your presentation at the Birmingham conference. Barry wants a strong, positive message, to generate a bit of excitement in the industry.'

Steve hoped they'd had a *much* better week on Sling while he was off, or the only thing he was likely to be exciting in the industry was laughter.

'Any news on Barry's replacement?'

Darren glanced towards the open door, and lowered his voice.

'There's a rumour that it's going to be Mike,' he said.

'Mike from Sales? The rock climber?' It was always good to show off your local knowledge.

'No, Mike from Quality Engineering, the social climber.'

'Oh,' said Steve heavily. Mike from Quality Engineering, the social climber, was a serial jobhopper, moving on every couple of years to positions of ever increasing greatness. It was a strategy that worked very well, both for him and for many others throughout the land. He was never in one job long enough for his mistakes and lack of action to become apparent. By the time they did, he'd moved on and his successor was getting the blame and the negative comparisons; his own meteoric career continued unblemished and unabated, despite the fact that he made fewer useful contributions than a broken chair. He was loved by everyone he worked for, and hated by everyone who worked for him or with him or who came along and had to pick up the pieces. He played the game so well he could have been a politician.

Gosh, I'm glad I got that off my chest.

'D'you think the rumour's true?' asked Steve, though he knew full well that almost all rumours are.

'Well it ought to be,' said Darren. 'It's me that made it up.'

Barry came to reclaim his office at that point, welcoming Steve back with an enquiry as to where his postcard had got to.

'We even had one from Mike Marshall from Sales,' Darren pointed out.

Steve could see that. It was taped in pride of place on Barry's cupboard door, across the spot where the photograph of one of the Lemming prototypes had been.

'It sounds like he got higher up the mountains than you probably did,' taunted Darren.

Barry laughed.

'But then, he was there all week,' Darren added as he went out of the door.

Steve was left to get his news update from Barry. As news went, it was somewhat dull, comprising mainly a list of extra things for him to do, think about, or worry about. There was also a report that Steve had written so long ago that he had quite forgotten about it, which Barry had now been through with a red pen, adding confusion and removing value. And there was a reminder that the two of them were going to Doltburn a week on Thursday to visit Hindsight Electrolysis, which came as a surprise as the plan had been for Steve and Darren to go. Without Barry.

Steve had intended to ask whether the five million Beauchild sales were still a possibility, but it didn't seem to be a good news morning, so he didn't. In any case, Barry seemed a little preoccupied with the fact that the directors had now insisted it was him that attend their fortnightly R&D review meeting to give the promised progress report on Sling. The fact that he was distractedly pulling out large tufts of his beard suggested he wasn't entirely confident they'd be pleased with progress. Steve quietly excused himself and went away to panic about who their new boss might be.

Being a Monday, it was a swimming day, and being a swimming day Steve told himself that he'd had lots of exercise the week before in Wales, and went to the canteen with Simon and Darren instead. Regular exercise was all very well in principle, but sometimes he wasn't sure whether it was adding years to his life or years to his age.

Coming back from holiday can be unnerving for anyone, with all sorts of developments and changes even in a few days. Today, though, nothing had changed and there was no gossip. Sally was at her customary place behind the serving counter, waiting to lure passing custom with a selection of pulpy fruit, Simon looked as if he'd been up until two, as usual, and all the forks were covered in yellow slime. According to Darren, the week's only excitement had been that the local fire brigade seemed to have got a new set of ringtones for their sirens.

The canteen appeared to be celebrating some special occasion, possibly the demise of something large and meaty that had been rather slow crossing the road the night before, and had laid on a magnificent carvery, with all the trimmings. Well, a carvery, with a few lumps of concrete stuffing and a bit of congealed gravy. Forty thousand years or more of accumulated masculine hunter-gatherer skill and pride meant that Geoff the Chef, rather than Sally the Servery, was in charge of the electric carving knife. As well as a choice between two different some-things on the carvery, there was also an enticing range of leftovers from the week before. Steve opted for a few slices from a large amorphous lump of animal tissue lightly patterned with a cross-ply motif. The chef looked at him expectantly as he took the plate, a response seeming to be necessary. Steve forced his face into a grimace of pleasure and gratitude.

'One of your best, Geoff,' he said.

The chef beamed. It seemed to have done the trick. With a worryingly enthusiastic grin he retreated into the kitchen to do some rearrangement of chicken entrails.

'Rain tomorrow,' his voice boomed through the kitchen doorway. 'And Swarf's Bottom will win the 3:15 at Musselburgh.'

At the corner table, Darren fumbled for a pen to record next Saturday's winning lottery numbers as Geoff shouted them out. Damn clever things, disembowelled chickens.

***

That Wednesday, only one evening behind everyone else, Jackie allowed Natalie to have her school friends round after school for a small Hallowe'en party. They were getting to that age where ghouls and witches were cool, and in any case it gave Jackie a chance to spy on the other children's homework books. Out of a sense of fair play, everyone in the class was invited, apart from the three boys whose names Natalie couldn't remember, but most of the boys gave it a miss because they were busy counting or spending the proceeds of the previous evening's juvenile protection rackets[1].

The party went quite well. They started with a game of musical broomsticks, followed by pinning the tail on the starfish and then lemon bobbing. The final game, before sending them all off with toffee apples and brandy snaps and a few other things, was a bat hunt. Jackie had invested in a box of black rubber vampire bats, as you do, which she had tied to the trees and bushes in the garden. She'd painted the numbers 1 to 10 on them, and the idea was to cross each number off when you found it. A bit like train-spotting, but more slow-moving and considerably less interesting. Steve's contribution had been to rig up outdoor lighting (four small torches, three of them working, clamped to gardening canes), so that the black wasn't quite pitch. To spin the game out a little longer, and to keep the kids outside while she got on with the party bags in peace and quiet, Jackie had removed bat number seven. Two of the little boybrats, not surprisingly, still claimed to have found it, though. So half rations of party bag sweets for them.

Tom, however, got double sweets to take his mind off the ankle injury he sustained. Jackie had bought extra – and a supply of bandages – for just such an eventuality: even though he was only eight, his reputation for misfortune was already legendary. You just knew that he would ultimately end his days caught in some large rotating machinery or embedded in quick-

---

[1] A reference to Trick or Treating, that ancient rustic practice of demanding money with menaces.

setting cement. As it happened, he almost choked on one of the sweets.

***

After three days of hard work on his presentation, and a long debate inside his head about which set of test results to present, the ones he liked or the ones he believed, Steve was ready to try a dry run in front of a discerning, not to mention critical, audience, viz Darren.

The practice session didn't go terrifically well, though, as he kept forgetting points he wanted to make and he erred and ummed so much that he overran the time limit by ten minutes. When he finished there was a bit of a lengthy total silence.

'Some feedback would be nice,' he prompted.

'OK. It was pants,' said Darren.

It wasn't the most positive of portents.

***

The Birmingham sensor conference and trade show wasn't actually being held in Birmingham, it was taking place in a hotel some miles away. Steve, being late, got the last space in the car park, accessed only by an elaborate, inching eleven point turn. Why was it that car park spaces had got narrower as cars had got wider? And why was his sun-roof jammed, the one time that he needed to climb out of it?

There weren't many empty spaces in the room where the conference talks were being given either. The ones that there were, unsurprisingly were on the front row. As it turned out, that wasn't too bad a thing, as the room had all the acoustic charms of a bus depot. It was also quite stuffy, and none of the talks was exactly rivetting, not even the one that was about rivetting, so it was quite a relief to reach lunchtime. The fare on offer at the free buffet wouldn't have been Steve's choice (whoever decided that beetroot was good to eat?), and he could imagine what Darren would have thought of all the quiches and salads and herbal infusions. Nevertheless, it was free, which meant that Steve ended up filling his plate with finger rolls, quiche slices and sandwiches as fast as he could stack them. Sometimes he wished for the sake of his diet that they'd give him a tenner and then charge him back a pound an item, instead of making it free at the point of use.

The afternoon was little more exciting than the morning, and Steve learnt nothing of any use to Sling. The highlight was probably the talk given by the final speaker, who was six foot three with a Mohican haircut and a nose ring. He spent most of his talk – which concerned testing to destruction, but whether of sensors or competitors wasn't quite clear – staring malevolently at Steve, so when his talk ended and he turned out to be quite a nice chap and Steve turned out not to be dead, Steve's relief was palpable. Indeed, they ended up discussing the finer points of test results analysis for nearly half an hour afterwards until Steve suddenly realised the time, bade farewell to his new best mate, and went to check into his room for the overnight stay that Barry insisted he made ('for networking purposes').

The one perk of the conference was the formal dinner in the evening. The organisers had conveniently laid on coach transport to the stately home where it was being held, which was thoughtful as it allowed everyone to over-drink and then be sick.

Everyone has their problems. Some people have to walk fifteen miles in sweltering African heat every day to fetch half-clean water to drink. Others have the pain of sitting next to someone boring at the free conference dinner. The level of hardship is very different, of course, and yet it's the latter who feel hard done by. Life is strange.

Being fairly stoic, Steve resigned himself to suffering in silence as the monotonic man next to him started upon a long story about a lost suitcase and a mislaid passport. It turned out to be the highlight of the evening, conversationally. Soon after that, his neighbour steered the talk towards his fascination for modern shelving, and once they were on that subject he never stopped. By the time he'd repeated to the point of nauseum his one funny line (it involved brackets and a witty play on the word 'screws', but it loses something in the telling), Steve made an excuse (involving a clever play on the words 'domestic' and 'emergency') and fled to the bar where he spent a small fortune on having the charmless staff serve him short measures. Unfortunately, his ex-companion noticed that he was missing after less than an hour, and joined him at the bar.

A century or two later it was eleven o'clock and time to get on the coach back to the hotel. Steve was joined by his uncharismatic and thick-skinned 'friend', despite trying to spread himself over two seats. There was the usual twenty minutes delay waiting for someone who had already made their own arrangements and had a lift, and then they were off, Steve finally locking his room door behind him at quarter to twelve. He might have read for a while, had he had more to read than the card listing the internal telephone extensions, or he might have reflected on the positive experiences of the day, but he couldn't think of any. So instead he switched the light off and went to sleep.

Or he might have done if the person in the next room hadn't switched on their hairdryer, full blast. Steve was less than two-fifths of one third of pleased, so he responded by sighing quite loudly at the wall. The noise promptly stopped, five minutes later. Then the T.V. went on instead, also full blast. Steve retaliated by tut-tutting. That wasn't quite so effective. An hour and a quarter less effective, in fact.

Long after it finally fell silent, Steve lay there, trying to make sleep happen. He tried lying on his left side. He tried lying on his right side. He tried covering his head with the pillow. He told himself that it didn't matter, that a rest was as good as sleep. Yeah, right. By the morning he was exhausted. He had perhaps managed three of his forty winks, and even those were marred by a bad dream about having to assemble twenty-three flat-pack wardrobes. And why is it always the most annoying songs that go round and round in your head all night?

Steve's choice of seat for the second day of the conference was driven by an overwhelming feeling that he couldn't face another minute in the company of the bore-aholic from the previous evening. Luckily, there was one seat in a small alcove near the back of the room, where you couldn't really see or couldn't really hear, but where you could at least hide from those who might want to mutter things about built-in bookcases while you were trying to listen to the talks. Steve had half thought he might skip the opening presentation on 'Twenty-five years of membranes in pressure sensors', but in the event he nodded off and missed it anyway. Most of the rest of the day was little better, and only the last talk of the conference offered any real excitement, and that was only because he was the person who had to give it.

It really wasn't the best of slots on the agenda. He had to follow an overweight – sorry, circumferentially challenged - lady who was wearing a pink tent, and many of the audience had already sneaked out to go to the station or the airport or the bar before he'd even started. His occasional presentations at industry conferences were typically delivered to about fifty to a hundred people: about a hundred at the start and about fifty at the end. Today there were eight left when he was introduced, five by the time he'd reached the podium. His talk was about recent trends in the design of high performance multi-purpose sensors, but as things were going so snail's-pace badly at SLSL, it couldn't exactly be the launch platform for Sling that Barry had wanted it to be. Instead, Steve had to waffle on vaguely about the evolution of sensor specifications and design requirements until everyone wished the bulb on the projector would blow, Steve included.

As has become the custom, the conference organisers had left speaker feedback forms on every seat, and just as Steve was inviting questions on his talk one of the women in charge of proceedings stood up to interrupt him with a reminder to members of the audience, or at least those that now remained, to fill them in. With the diversion created, Steve thought he might get away without getting any questions, apart perhaps from the token one that the session chairman felt he had to ask, but no, a hand went up on the back row. It was Tony Russell from Sensandetect Ltd., with whom he'd clashed microphones before, waving his feedback form in one hand.

'I have one small technical question.'

'Yes, Tony?'

'Is piss-awful hyphenated?'

***

When Steve got home, Jackie was busy on the first three hour DVD training module of a three module package, trying to understand the rules of the latest TV fame-chick-dance-talent-home-voting-eliminator-competition-show. From the glazed look on her face, she had already had enough, and Steve's arrival gave her the excuse she needed to give up completely.

'Chloe's been invited to Emily's party on Saturday,' she said.

'Who's Emily?'

'I've no idea. One of the kids in her class, I think. Her mother rang up, but I couldn't catch much of what she was saying over the sound of her slurping her chewing gum in my ear.'

It was to be Jackie's longest speech in this entire book. (Go on, check if you want.)

'Oh,' said Steve.

'And then there's Chloe's party on the eighteenth.'

'Oh, whose is that one?'

'It's Chloe's. *We're* doing it, remember?' said Jackie after a tiny irritated intake of breath.

Steve knew there was no facial expression he could pull that was likely to convince anybody he'd not forgotten, least of all Jackie, but he went for one anyway. The results were a cross between confusion and indigestion.

'We'll have it here,' said Jackie, who had started from the premise that Steve wouldn't be contributing much to its organisation. 'But you can phone round for a suitable children's entertainer.'

Steve nodded. He knew what was coming next.

'And that does not mean Darren Searston.'

No, it didn't. Not after his little jokes with the balloon animals, the year before.

It took Steve only five minutes to find the perfect amusement artiste from the phone book, and two minutes later he was booked. That sorted, he settled down at the computer in the spare bedroom to design the party invitations while Jackie phoned her sister about helping with the catering. It took him an hour because he kept missing off vital information, such as the date and the venue, and he did wonder for a bit whether it was enough just to provide boxes to tick for *Yes I'd love to come* and *No, I can't come* or whether they should also be providing a third *I can come, but I don't want to* option. He had just realised that the ink cartridge had expired part way through the second of the twenty-eight invitations that he'd just printed, when Jackie came in for a bit of sympathy. Diane had spent half the afternoon preparing a dinner party for her new boss who had forgotten to mention his fish allergy and the other half watching the builders try to find the leak in her new bathroom's plumbing, and she hadn't been in the mood to start taking prisoners. Jackie's request for ideas for universally acceptable children's party food had therefore been about as welcome as a sneeze in a snog, and Jackie had had to endure quite a binge-moaning session.

A shared bottle of wine seemed to be the only answer, soon followed by a second one, but although they undermined his resolve to get anything done, they didn't provide as much relaxation as he'd hoped, and they certainly didn't help him sleep. Indeed, he was still awake at two, thoughts in turmoil and heart pounding. He got up for a glass of water. He opened the windows by just less than the wingspan of the average moth. He tried adjusting his pillows, he went to the toilet, and yet still he was wide awake. He tried listing in his head all the reasons why he couldn't sleep, but although he got to nearly fifty, even that didn't seem to help. Finally, at quarter to four, he did sleep, but it was a cruel, shallow sleep of restless thoughts and nameless fears. In his half slumbers he saw the oak tree near his mother's house, as it used to be in his childhood, with its two extended branches and its imaginary bags of sweets. Yet whenever he resurfaced into half wakefulness, the second limb was torn off and the sweets were scattered and dashed. And no amount of wine was ever going to change that.

**

Wednesday went down in history, a bit like the *Mary Rose* but less so, as the day that Steve finally got to see Alex Deese to discuss the financial figures. Alex was an accountant with all the charisma of an accountant, and spent the first twenty minutes of the meeting going on and on about the cut and thrust world of accountancy and lecturing Steve on the importance of all sorts of things from accruals to amortisation. So many accounting terms he didn't understand, and they had only reached A in the alphabet. Steve assumed that he was meant to feel rather awed and quite belittled by it all. Half an hour in, he was beginning to understand why Chris Tomkinson might hate Alex and had made an excuse not to join them, but he wasn't beginning to understand abatements, apportionment or arbitrage.

The lesson in financial analysis and economic modelling continued for another two aeons or so while Steve sat like a rather dim rabbit in the headlights. Alex then pulled up several screenfulls of figures that were something to do with Project Sling. To Steve, it was all a blur of numbers, but judging by the look on Alex's face, it was bad news.

'Did you realise that you will need to hand-build the first hundred thousand units before you can afford to customise the assembly machine?'

Steve glumly shook his head. He had been busy wondering whether or not it would be a kindness to introduce someone from the cut and thrust world of accountancy to the minus sign. Would it be helpful and time saving, or would all those years of brackets and red and black ink be suddenly seen for the waste they were, and lead to deep and crushing embitterment? He could but hope.

'Unless you can get the component costs down,' the accountant added, opening the door and sending Steve on his less-than-merry way to share the bad news with the team.

If nothing else, the poor financial case for the project led to a renewed drive to finish addressing some of its outstanding technical issues. The trip to Hindsight Electrolysis in Doltburn to assess their revolutionary encapsulation process had been scheduled for the next day, and plans for the pilot manufacturing run later in the month were also in hand. Barry was even happy to allow Steve to get on with the project with fewer meetings. And just to emphasise the point, he organised one for him for that very afternoon, so that they could discuss the main learning points from Steve's time at the trade show ('We may have missed the boat') and hear Steve's considered plans for evaluating H.E.L.'s technical capabilities the next day ('We'll suck it and see').

'Why are they called Hindsight?' asked Simon, at the team meeting.

Don't worry; they'll find out in the fullness of time.

***

Since he was losing the next day travelling, Steve stayed late to get things done. By half past six he and Lisa were the only two left in the office, and having finished the more important things, he was just moving on to contemplating why rows of staples – 'cloches' in the trade – always come in lengths too long for the stapler, when Darren came in from wherever he'd been lurking.

'I've just learnt who our new boss is going to be,' he announced breathlessly.

'Mike, from Quality Engineering?' ventured Steve.

'No, it's Barry: he's changed his mind and decided that he'll do both jobs part time – some weeks in London, and some weeks here.'

'And who told you that?' chipped in his ex.

'I put a few rumours together,' said Darren, 'And then I rang him at home and asked him. Am I not a talented man?'

'You're right: you're not,' said Lisa.

'You're only jealous, because you wish you could be Lizzy and have me back.'

Lisa gave the sort of snort that only warthogs usually make, and then only when they're stuck in something.

'I can't believe you're still together. Haven't you irritated her to death yet?'

Darren shook his head as he collected his things for home, but a slightly doubtful look had flashed across his face.

***

Steve woke with a groan, and rolled out of bed with another one. Then he remembered that it was Thursday, the day of his trip to H.E.L. with Barry, and he gave another groan. Another day of having to listen to Barry's philosophy on life; another three hundred miles of motorway hard shoulder to admire. If he was lucky, the day would comprise ten hours of tedium. If he was unlucky, and the meeting dragged on or if the traffic was bad, it might be twelve.

Barry had agreed to meet him in the car park at work, to avoid Steve having to trail round to his house. That rather suited Steve, for Barry had an unpleasant tendency to show off any recently acquired possessions. Accordingly, after a mug of strong coffee and two slices of weak toast, Steve drove to work, his journey largely traffic-free at this early hour. Even the traffic lights were kind to him for once.

Barry's beloved was already sitting in the car park when Steve pulled up, bristling with vanity mirrors and a vanity registration plate and gleaming metallically even though it was still dark. The driver's door was open, and Barry was waiting for him. It was the first time that Seve had seen inside the car, and privately he had to admit that it looked stupendous, which I think means stupid. The dashboard, or perhaps flight deck, was covered in row after row of LCD screens, lights, buttons, knobs and cup-holders. Closer inspection revealed that most of them seemed to relate to the audio system, which would not have disgraced a medium sized recording studio. Somewhere right of centre, Steve thought he glimpsed a steering wheel. He climbed into the passenger seat, fastened the gold-trimmed seat-belt and gripped the real leather armrests. With a gloating glance towards Steve and a flourish of his arm, Barry pressed a button somewhere, and nothing sprang to life. He said something that Steve didn't catch, pressed and adjusted a few more things, and they were off.

Barry was not the most considerate of drivers. He went everywhere with his headlights on full beam to intimidate other motorists, and he did his best not to let other drivers know what he was about to do because he liked to maximise the element of surprise. He also tended to get very animated in conversation when he was driving, and they'd gone less than a mile before he'd illustrated some point or other about Project Sling by waving his hands about in a dramatic gesture that tempted two cars from opposite side roads into violent head-on collision behind him.

It turned out that they weren't going to Doltburn but to Barry's house, as he'd somehow contrived to forget all the papers he needed. By great good fortune, though, it also gave him a chance to show Steve some of the home improvements he'd made since last time his colleague had been there. In fact, Steve hardly recognised the house, which now had a large neo-Georgian portico stuck onto its mock Tudor frontage. Barry bade him (it's the sort of thing one does, if one has a neo-Georgian portico) go into the house for a moment while he searched around. Rather reluctantly, Steve followed him in, past the large orange sticker in the front window which proclaimed that his other house had a porch. Barry went off upstairs, leaving Steve to be greeted by an elderly spaniel that tried to jump up to lick his face but instead only got as far as giving his left knee a sort of damp kiss. The poor animal was probably weighed down by the heavy brass name tag round its neck, if not physically, then perhaps at least psychologically: it takes a special kind of person to name their dog *Tosser*. Steve had quite forgotten that Barry had an animal, but then, his memory wasn't as good as he remembered it being. He'd thought that recent mentions of going home to the dog had been Barry's references to his wife.

'I see you've met Towser,' said Barry, coming downstairs with a clutchful of papers. Perhaps Steve's eyesight wasn't as good as it had been, either.

They got back into the car, Barry pressed a few more buttons, and they were off again, manoeuvre - signal - mirror.

'You know,' said Barry after a few minutes of silence, 'if you work really hard, when you next get promoted, or the time after, you might perhaps be able to afford a second-hand Pompous, you know. They don't half accelerate.'

To prove his point, he put his foot down, and Steve was left bracing himself against his seat and wishing that his boss could hold a conversation without having to look round at him every time he spoke.

As it happened, the brief bout of speed lasted about as long as a seagull in a jet engine, because almost at once they came across a large yellow sign announcing that roadworks start here for the next hundred and seventeen years. In honesty, Steve was surprised they'd be finished as quickly as that, as the council appeared to have run out of earth movers and pneumatic drills, and were widening the road using a single garden spade. It might have been the low point of the journey, but it wasn't. A couple of miles further on, as they started to round a long left hand bend, Steve saw that there was a tractor in front, mud flying off its tyres as it charged along. Barry changed down to fourth gear and moved out slightly in a bid to see round it. 'Overtake! Overtake!' urged the synthesised voice from the sat-nav screen. Barry started to accelerate. 'Go for it,' directed the sat-nav. Barry put his foot down hard, and swept out across the solid white lines. 'Go go go!' shouted the sat-nav enthusiastically. Steve closed his eyes, which didn't help but was slightly comforting. 'Perhaps not,' suggested the sat-nav quietly. With a great screech of brakes and a shower of flying earth, Barry swerved back across the road, missing the implements on the back of the tractor by about the length of a small parsnip and missing an oncoming livestock lorry by perhaps the width of a malnourished piglet. The experience had come very close to being literally harrowing, and yet Barry's only response was to comment in hushed and reverent tones that the sat-nav was so clever that it could download new skills and teach itself new tricks as it went along. Like taking them over cliffs looking for short cuts, presumably.

Once the tractor had turned into a field and they were safely past it, Steve decided to strike up a conversation, in a bid to take Barry's attention away from planning any more life-threatening manoeuvres.

'How are your lads getting on?' he asked, trying to sound as if he was interested but keeping his eyes firmly fixed to the road for new hazards.

'Let's see. Gary's still working at the supermarket checkout. He's getting quite settled there, being with all his mates.'

Well, he certainly wouldn't get lonely. Steve remembered Barry telling him a couple of years earlier how almost all the students from the Mediocrity Studies course at the University of Hugh's Oak had ended up working in one supermarket or another. Perhaps that was the nature of going to a university that until a few years previously had been a small edge-of-town B&B. At least Gary could perhaps take comfort from the fact that he was on the checkouts rather than spending his days in charge of opening the tops of plastic bags for little old ladies.

'And Harry's at drama college now, studying to be a professional footballer.'

'And how's your brother these days?' enquired Steve.

'Oh Larry's over in Europe somewhere, trying to teach them about queuing and personal space.'

'Wow, he's ambitious.' Steve lapsed into silence. Despite heavy traffic and several small detours around gangs of men in fluorescent jackets, most of the remainder of the journey was uneventful. At one point they passed another Pompous, and the two drivers gave one another the Pompous wave, but apart from that and a near miss with an oncoming village green nothing much happened until they were nearly in Doltburn.

What happened nearly in Doltburn was that they nearly didn't find Doltburn at all, due to a confusing road sign that was large enough to be seen from the Great Wall of China but which for some reason only bore the abbreviation D'b'n where it had space to display the name Doltburn several times over. Barry's sat-nav then made things worse by taking them for a 'scenic' (in very much inverted commas) detour via Little Point and Motheaton. Luckily they chanced upon a small service station where Barry was able to refuel the car, Steve was able to defuel his bladder, and they were both able to ask for directions and get almost identical answers.

They didn't realise it at that moment, but there were clues a-plenty as to the nature of Doltburn in the garage on its outskirts. There were the sweet wrappers all over the floor, the heavy-duty padlock on the till, and the fact that the cashier had a black eye and his arm in a filthy sling. It was the sort of place where you could have removed the wash basin from the toilet and none of the regular clientele would have noticed.

Ten minutes later they got their first sight of Doltburn and its quaint architecture of pebbledash walls and plywood glazing. Collections of pre-loved sofas and mattresses adorned every car park and front garden, and the bottom six feet of most of the buildings had been heavily moronised with a spray can. The local council had rather bravely put up a sign to welcome visitors, but the police had almost obscured it with their own bigger one, warning of pickpockets, bag-snatchers, sneak burglars, car-jackers and paedophiles. Both signs had been liberally sprayed with graffiti. Long before the Scilly Islands and the remoter fells of the Lake District were the only bits of England where you could be sure of not getting mugged, Doltburn had been rough. In fact, the sat-nav's synthesiser was perhaps the very first voice that had ever sounded cheerful at the prospect of arriving there. Probably the only thing that could be said in the place's favour was that it was not pretentious.

Downdraught Industrial Estate turned out to be on the far side of town, and Paradise Way turned out to be on the furthest edge of that. Unfortunately, find it they did, and ten o'clock caught them standing in Hindsight's car park. Barry was just running his hands round his beltline to tuck his shirt back into his trousers, in the way that important business people always do after long car journeys, when a portly gentleman came bounding over to welcome them. Or at least he bounded to the extent that portly people can bound. His name was Andy Fisher, or at any rate that's what Steve thought he heard, and he was Hindsight's Commercial Manager. As Barry walked in with him, deep in conversation, Steve followed behind and took the opportunity to phone Jackie and tell her that he had arrived safely despite the harrowing near miss with the harrow on the back of the tractor[1].

They were ushered into a small meeting room with walls embellished with samples of electrolytically coated components and a floor adorned with threadbare blue carpet tiles. The meeting lasted for one mug of coffee, three biscuits and ten minutes. It might have continued considerably longer, but Barry was quickly and easily persuaded that they had found the answer to all the remaining technical challenges on Steve's project, and he was keen to move on to the promised *pièce de resistance* factory tour to see how H.E.L. achieved the remarkable results they did, but unfortunately...

'Our new process is a closely guarded secret and the only person in the world who knows its precise details is our Chief Technical Officer, Dr Carmichael. He'd be able to tell you how it works, apart from the very secret bits, but I'm afraid he's not here this morning because his quintuple-bypass open heart surgery has been brought forward to today.'

'Perhaps in two or three weeks?' suggested Barry.

'Yes, um, Tuesday the twenty-eighth should work. No hang on a minute, he's doing his charity parachute jumps that day. How about the fifteenth of December?'

Barry didn't bother to check with Steve, but nodded, and scribbled a note in his diary.

---

[1] Oh, you get it now, do you?

'Will the machine definitely be operating then?' he asked, stroking his beard.

'Oh yes,' said Mr Might-Have-Been-Fisher, 'it runs day and night, night and day, without fail, three hundred and sixty five days a year. Perfect results every time.'

Even Steve was beginning to dare to hope that they had found the last piece in the jigsaw needed to give their new sensor a world-beating competitive edge.

'We'll need to get you to sign a confidentiality clause,' their host added, herding them through the door out into the car park. The sun was coming out, but it didn't make Doltburn look any nicer, which wasn't surprising because nice things in Doltburn were rarer than Remembrance Day poppies on people younger than thirty.

And of all the things about the place that were unsavoury, perhaps the worst were the inhabitants. Indeed, at that exact moment, a group of bored teenagers (is there any other type?) was moping around the car park of the pub opposite, as they had been doing for an hour or two already, occasionally spraying words like 'scum' across the bottom of its wall with no obvious hint of any sense of irony. Like most of the locals, they each sported a shaved head and diamond ear studs as a sign of their individuality.

'Great data,' said Steve. 'I really think it's what we need to get Sling sorted.'

'Yes,' agreed Barry. 'Shame we've got to trail back again to see their machine, though.'

'Mm. I'm not too fussed with having to brave the scenic delights of this place again.'

'Come on, let's go home,' said Barry, unlocking the car doors.

Behind them, as they headed east towards the motorway, one of the lads threw his cigarette end into the front garden of one of the derelict houses that lined the street. There was a half-second's pause while the hot stub flew through the air towards the methane emanating from the rubbish piled there, followed by a very loud bang as the youth was engulfed in a large fireball, followed by the sound of life (though perhaps not his) going on as normal.

Different towns get their names in different ways.

***

It was one of those rare spring-like days, with barely a cloud, that only February and March can produce with any frequency. Except of course that this one was in November. Once Chloe had been dropped off at Emily's party, Steve and Jackie had a chance to get some gardening done before the onset of winter, and Natalie had a chance to be made to do some violin practice in the music room, a.k.a. bathroom. In fairness to her, there were some aspects of the violin that she did quite like. She enjoyed staging mini-concerts for her parents in the orchestral hall, a.k.a. lounge, and she *really* enjoyed rosining. She rosined everything she could. On one memorable occasion, she'd even rosined next door's cat. Her musical progress, meanwhile, was slightly less exciting. Steve had originally hoped that the violin might prove easy to learn and had been very disappointed to discover that a four-stringed instrument could play so many notes. He did, though, have a sneaking suspicion that Natalie was inventing a few of her own.

Outside, Malcolm next door was also out enjoying a spot of gardening in the green and verdant space that was his very own little piece of England. He'd already trimmed the hedge and mowed the lawn for the last time of the season, and was now spending the rest of the morning rearranging the piles of fallen leaves with his Canute 2 petrol driven leaf blower. He just loved the tranquillity of nature at this time of year.

Steve's first job was to reseed the corner of the lawn that Poddle had dug up after another of the experimental beauty treatments that Chloe and Natalie had given him. The box of grass seed had kind of set since Steve had last used it a few years previously, but five minutes with a chisel yielded enough to scatter over most of Poddle's patch. With an eye on the sparrow that had an eye on the grass seed, Steve raked a thin layer of dirt over where he'd sown, and then finished the job by hanging a few give-away CDs from the branches of the nearest rose bush to act as bird scarers. If he'd not been a devoted and hen-pecked father, Prod's album might have joined them. To be fair to Prod, though, the music escaping from the bathroom window from his greatest fan was not much better. Natalie had her own unique playing style, and at the moment she was labouring her way through her music practice book, '101 Merry Violin Tunes'. Although he could only hear a few strains (which really was the word) above Malcolm's leaf blower, Steve guessed that the piece she was currently massacring was Winter Wonderland.

While Steve had been delivering Chloe to the party, Jackie had been up to the garden centre to buy a new weeping cotoneaster treeling to replace the one that he had snapped off a few weeks before, and his next job now was to plant it where its predecessor had been. That looked like the sort of job best performed after an infusion of coffee, so he nipped into the kitchen, where he found Natalie helping herself to a sneaky chocolate biscuit from the cupboard. The pile of chocolatey crumbs by the table suggested that it had not died alone.

'It's sounding, erm, interesting,' said Steve, in his best tone of fatherly encouragement.

Natalie pulled a slight face.

'Don't listen too loudly yet, until I've practised a bit,' she insisted, going back up to have a go at Thank You For The Music.

Steve made the coffee, and took it back outside with him. There was little chance of hearing any music except during the occasional short lulls in next door's leaf rearrangement activities. Oh well, it was marginally quieter than that power shredder that their old neighbours had once hired, where you fed in a garden at one end and it spat out a stream of chippings at the other.

Having downed his coffee in two, Steve set to work on digging a hole to plant the new sapling in. Like all holes he ever dug – or drilled – he ended up settling for little more than half the depth he had originally intended for it. On this occasion, his excavations were frustrated by a large stone, a root from his prize

Leylandii, and something that looked suspiciously like the foundations of the house. At least that answered one mystery, for he'd been wondering where they had got to ever since he'd discovered that most of the property was underpinned by nothing more substantial than an ants' nest.

By now, the funereal closing bars of Ode To Joy from the bathroom had given way to the mournful lament Happy Birthday To You, followed by that well known dirge, If You're Happy And You Know It, Clap Your Hands. Steve planted the cotoneaster, nearly broke the top half off trying to straighten it up, and watered it in. He had made the executive decision to again put off doing anything with the ivy on the back of the house, and was just tidying away the gardening implements when Natalie called him in to answer the phone.

The caller was Malcolm's partner, Karen, inviting him and Jackie round for dinner the Saturday after next. It was now approaching a year since the fateful night of his cling-film casserole, so they were about due for another get-together.

'What time?' Six-thirty? Seven?' he asked, above the sounds of Chloe disciplining an errant troll that she'd just brought back from Emily's party.

'No, sorry, it will have to be after seven forty-six' said Karen, a little uncomfortable that Malcolm's social life had nowadays to be organised around internet auction bidding deadlines.

Steve accepted provisionally, subject to being able to find someone willing to have the girls for a sleepover. As he put the phone down he glanced out of the window to where the birds were queuing up to take it in turns to have a ride on the new bird scarers, which were now swinging to and fro in a gentle breeze. Banging on the window had no effect, although one of the birds did turn to look at him, its face a picture of feathery disdain. (Do birds have faces?) With a cry of 'That does it!', Steve ran out and tripped over a bucket. This time it was Jackie who gave him a condescending look, as she came over from her fight with his jammed shed door.

'Never mind them, how about getting those two dead pigeons off the roof?' she asked, as she helped him up.

'Ah.'

Steve had forgotten about the pigeon, and hadn't realised it had now found company. He wondered whether its new friend had given up the will to live when it had heard Ode to Joy. On the positive side, they were both lying in positions where the girls weren't likely to see them, so he wouldn't have to invent any stories about them just having a lie down before Christmas.

'Can't you just think of them as free extra insulation?' he tried. They were going to be harder to reach than the ivy.

It was apparent from his wife's face that she could not.

'I'm not sure I can get right up there,' said Steve doubtfully.

'Well give it some thought,' she said, and went back indoors.

Steve gave it some thought. He thought that perhaps he could borrow the ladder from the Empties and Poddle from next door, and send him up. Being a great white fluff ball visible for miles, he wasn't much of a hunter, but he might just manage to stalk and over-power a couple of dead birds. It was a plan.

11

'Happy Birthday!' shouted Chloe, leaping onto the bed at six a.m. and waking Steve into Saturday with a tiny knee aimed yet again right at his sweetmeats.

'I think we're meant to say that to you,' said Jackie, who was already awake, worrying about having twenty or so children invade the house at three o'clock. And Steve's idea to invite the parents to stay for drinks had not been conducive to a good night's sleep, either.

'Five, five, five,' chanted Chloe, who wasn't sure that her parents were yet treating her birthday to the attention it deserved. This was her big day, hers and hers alone. True, some of Natty's friends were going to be coming along to her party, but otherwise it was all about her. She was five, and she was special. She was also far too young to work out that she was sharing her birthday with something like twenty million other people across the planet.

Truth be told, Steve was relieved that they were going for the children's entertainer idea again, as they had done in every previous year. He had initially wanted to organise something a bit different, but even at their tender ages many of the invited children had already done nearly everything that money could buy. Besides, with Tom on the invitation list many of the possible activities were ruled out on the grounds that he would probably find them too fatal. Or that Steve would find them too expensive. Or both.

Anyway, now all they had to do was to enjoy watching Chloe open her presents over breakfast and then sit back and relax, pour a few drinks, and prepare the party food and take-home bags.

By ten to three, the first parents were ringing the doorbell, and Steve went to man his post by the front door, clipboard of names in hand. There had only been one last minute cancellation – Hayley had had a bit of an accident that morning when she'd crashed her pony – and twenty-one of the little darlings were still expected, not counting Natalie and Chloe.

The first child at the door was a girl of about seven, wearing an outfit that somehow reminded Steve simultaneously of both

Alice In Wonderland and *Spider-Woman*. He was just thinking 'what a bizarrely dressed child' to himself, when out of the car popped another one, identical in every respect.

'Ah, these must be the twins,' he said in a flash of inspired guesswork to the woman with them. He glanced down his list until he found Melanie and Melody, and crossed them off with a flamboyant flourish.

'They're not 'The Twins', they're individuals, and they need treating as individuals,' snapped their mother.

Strange that she'd dressed them exactly the same, then.

'Sorry,' said Steve hastily, as the woman turned on her heel and marched back to her car.

He waited until she was just out of earshot, because he was at heart a coward. 'Sorry I offended the clones.'

Next at the door was Isobel, and then Emily, and then Tom and then a whole flurry of children that totally overwhelmed both Steve and his list. By five past three, they seemed to have more or less the right number, give or take a few, but Steve hadn't got a clue which one was which. Many of the parents had decided not to stay for drinks, but a few had; generally the ones Steve didn't know and/or like. At that precise moment, that was the least of his worries, though, because the entertainer – Wacky Robert the Bendy Clown – hadn't yet appeared.

Steve went through to the kitchen to survey the situation. As the weather was quite pleasant, Jackie had decided mid-morning to risk having the children outdoors rather than in the lounge, and most of them were out on the lawn, working off a bit of energy. The girls, being girls, were doing - or at least attempting - cartwheels and forward rolls, while three of the boys were standing in a small huddle contemplating their recent demonstration of the universal force that had most lately come to the attention of science, the special gravitational attraction of a football to a neighbour's garden. The fourth boy – Tom – was nowhere to be seen, although there was quite a commotion in the middle of the bramble and nettle patch.

With everything in the world generally going about its business as normal, Steve turned his attention to the parents. A quick headcount revealed that nine had stayed, including the two mothers who had nipped upstairs to have a nosy peek at the furnishings. The others were all standing in the kitchen, and were quite a mixture. Nearest the door was a manicured man perhaps a few years younger than Steve, wearing a suit that looked very expensive. By the window was a very overweight gum-chewing woman dressed in an ill-advised floral lilac shell-suit that was two sizes too small. In between the two of them was everything in between.

Thinking that he had perhaps better introduce himself, Steve picked up two bottles of wine of opposite persuasions and went over to the smartly dressed father by the door. Smartly dressed, but sporting a black eye from a touchline disagreement at his eight year old daughter's netball match the week before. The moment he realised who it was, Steve regretted starting a conversation with him. Leonie's father was a defence barrister, in court every day wronging rights and defending the indefensible. Lack of a conscience had held him back about as much as lack of an appendix or lack of a hernia might. He was rich, and flaunted his wealth in a way that made Barry look very modest. On the one previous occasion that Steve had spoken to him, at another kids' party where he'd tried to ask him why you get less time in prison for attempted murder than for murder – a reward for incompetence? – the conversation had rapidly turned to tales of a recent free holiday in the top hotel in Malaria or some such exotic place. Free, because when he'd arrived he'd threatened to sue them over some lost luggage that he had never actually packed.

As it happened, Leonie's dad was about as keen to talk to Steve as vice versa. Escape, therefore, was easy. Leaving him moaning about the quality of the two glasses of wine he'd just been poured, Steve left him and went through into the garden, nearly tripping over a couple of six year old girls who were swapping life stories in the kitchen doorway.

After spending as long as he dared pretending to check everything outside, helping himself to a glass of wine in the process, he went back into the house to see whether he could help Jackie. He found Tom flat on his back, with people picking their way over his prostrate form. The way the boy kept falling over, Steve sometimes wondered whether Angela oiled the underside of his shoes for some reason. She was the only person he'd ever met who was on first name terms with the people who answer the phone when you dial 999. He helped Tom up, with a slight shake of his head at the thought that someone could have trusted him to carry the tray with all the paper cups of juice on it, and then started to fill a replacement set of cups. Behind him, he could hear that Chantelle's parents, Nick and Wendy, had got into conversation with Leonie's father. That was OK; they might get on well together. Like him, they were unhealthily wealthy, having been quite lucky with their choice of career paths (no interest in anything at school, minimum wage jobs, lottery win, idle rich). Like him, they never seemed to have to actually spend any of their stash of money, in their case living from day to day entirely off the back of a string of insurance claims. Steve had at one stage wondered why Chantelle, Tiphanie and Admirée weren't at a private school, if nothing else so that their parents could cultivate other rich friends with villas and timeshares in exclusive locations. Wendy, though, said she didn't believe in paying for education. A state education had never done her or Nick any harm, after all. Too much education only led to one ending up in employment, like poor Steve had.

'Anyway,' commented Nick whenever the subject was raised, 'why shouldn't the state pay? After all, I've paid enough taxes over the years.'

That wasn't legally true, as it happened, but Nick was talking more from what he saw as a moral, rather than legal, perspective.

Steve passed the tray of drinks to Jackie to take out to the children, and went into the front garden to see if he could see any sight of the entertainer, leaving all the parents practising their mastery of a hundred thousand different ways to hint that 'my child's better than yours'. By good timing, he got there just as Wacky Robert the Bendy Clown was arriving, and he hurried him through the house and into the garden to face the children, armed only with a battered blue holdall and a hastily poured drink of orange juice.

Perhaps rather unadvisedly, the entertainer had decided to run a disco, a finger-painting class and a game of football simultaneously, all in the little corner of the realm that was forever Steve and Jackie's provided they kept up with the mortgage repayments. There wasn't a lot of space, and the three activities rapidly merged. Within five minutes there was chaos, and within ten the garden looked like something from the end of a Laurel and Hardy film, only in colour. Lots and lots and lots of colour: there seemed to be enough finger paint to smear over at least a hundred party dresses.

Trying not to worry about the mess, Steve stood and watched the various children in fascinated horror. Jackie had insisted that she would sort all the food out herself, and he had already had more than enough of mingling with the parents, so it seemed an opportunity to see how Natalie and Chloe compared with the other kids. The answer was pretty well, really. For example, Chloe would never throw stones at pigeons, even dead ones, and he had never seen Natalie trying to poke holes in next door's fence using somebody else's finger.

The children came in all shapes and sizes, from Max, the smallest boy in Chloe's class[1], to Jonnerphun - whose mother thought that using a 'ph' was the posh way to spell it – who was big and beefy and always in the thick of things, more or less by definition. In Steve's opinion, some of them were still a few obedience training classes away from civilised behaviour, but most were well mannered, at least in the 'notice how very polite I am, and please tell my mum' kind of way.

---

[1] Gosh, this is subtle stuff.

Steve went back into the kitchen to pour some more drinks for the parents in there, although they all seemed more than capable of helping themselves. He tried to join in with the conversation, which was all about Leonie's cousin Liberty and her living conditions, but he didn't have much to contribute as he didn't know anybody in prison, unless you counted the man from up the road who'd been sentenced to five days for mowing down and killing an elderly couple on a zebra crossing while he was finishing reading the sports pages in his paper.

Pinned against the freezer in the corner by a one-sided conversation from some woman whom Steve didn't recognise, Jackie was doing a gasping goldfish impression to indicate that she'd like him to make her a nice cup of tea while she still had a pulse. Accordingly, he squeezed his way past Rebecca, who was telling Natalie how she wanted her gerbil to die as quickly as possible because she'd been promised a kitten next, and switched the kettle on. Meanwhile, Jackie continued to nod in false enthusiasm to the unidentified woman at the same time as contortedly pulling packets of frozen sausage rolls out of the freezer ready to arrange on the stack of baking trays that someone had spilt wine over.

Most of the kids were outside, playing a game called 'Find five objects beginning with the letter X' while Bendy Clown the Wacky Robert helped himself to lager in the kitchen and Leonie's father started to regale an appreciative audience with a tale of adventures in the dormitory back in his schooldays. Something to do with having dislocated his skull while climbing a ladder made out of cricket bats fastened together with four belts, six school ties and a couple of the juniors. Steve had never met anybody who had been to boarding school before, except for a girl from the road where he'd grown up who had come back with a dislocated accent, though Natalie's school had had some limited boarding provision for three weeks the previous summer when a group of travellers was camped on the sports pitch.

A small bang behind him told him that it was time to fill the kettle with water and change its fuse, so he excused himself –

though no-one was listening – and went upstairs to find a screwdriver. He was passed on the stairs by Harry from Natalie's class, who gave him a toothy grin. Though, thinking about it, it was a bit odd that it should be described as 'toothy' when he was actually sporting a distinct numerical deficiency in the dental department. He had come out of the spare room, and inside Steve found Chloe sitting in the middle of the floor, crying her eyes out and sobbing the name 'Harry'. For a moment, Steve wondered whether his younger daughter might have just reached the boyfriend stage, perhaps a little early at the age of five, but a glance round the room revealed what Harry had actually done to cause all the tears. After the little monkey had managed to break several of his father's windows with heavy wooden toys on two separate occasions in less than a week, he'd been confined to objects of a light and fluffy nature for the rest of his childhood and he had just spent the previous twenty minutes playing upstairs on his own with Chloe's light and fluffy toy kitten and noting how easily its light and fluffy limbs came off.

Quietening her down took several minutes and multiple promises. There are things that make even cutting-edge sensor development projects seem easy by comparison. By the time Steve had coaxed her back downstairs and had accidentally broken both the presents in Harry's party bag, Bendy Robert had given up on everything but the disco and was playing endless hyperactive, frenzied songs about computer games, unlicensed downloads, cool video clips and cyber-bullying.

Music hadn't been like that in the sixties and seventies, Steve mused. In those days, songs were about simple but important things. Boy meets girl, girl meets boy, boy and girl fall in love, cake gets left out in the rain, that sort of thing. Now they all sounded like Prod's new record, *Broken off an' cryin'*, which was already a hit according to Natalie, who had been loudly declaring it the best song EVER.

One shouldn't blunt youthful enthusiasm, but it has, in fact, been scientifically proven that *Unchained Melody* by the Righteous Brothers is actually the greatest track of all time.

***

At half past four it was time to get the children sitting down for the party tea so that Steve could ask them who wanted sausage rolls and who wanted fish fingers. Some of them had shown initiative and hadn't waited to be asked: a hefty six-year old girl with a diameter that wouldn't disgrace a barrel was sitting at the table picking her nose with one hand and holding three cream cakes in the other.

'And which little angel are you?' asked Steve, through clenched teeth.

'Grace,' she burped.

Of course.

'And what would you like? Sausage rolls? Fish fingers?' *A bowl of swill, perhaps?*

'I don't like them things. Have you got anything nice?'

'I'll see what I can get you.' Perhaps they'd be able to rustle her up a lard bar, or whatever it was that she ate.

'I'll have burgers,' she demanded, as he left the room.

With his legendary lack of organisational abilities – he couldn't organise pulling the skin off a brewery – Steve had been made to leave all the catering arrangements to Jackie. When he reached the kitchen with Grace's cholesterol order, though, his wife had completely vanished, and just for an instant he panicked. Luckily, she'd not been abducted by aliens, nor was she slumped unconscious against the shed door like the entertainer now was. Instead, she was hidden in a mêlée of tipsy parents who were paying her not the slightest attention as she tried to wrestle Chloe's birthday cake into the freezer to reset it again after it had been left next to the oven to acquire a sort of pre-digested look.

The children's meals were all laid out on rows of paper plates waiting to be taken through, apart from those that had already been plundered by the drunken hordes in the kitchen, but there were no burgers, just sausage rolls and fish fingers. There was a single bowl of salad, but Steve couldn't help but think that ice dancing lessons would start in hell before Grace was likely to touch that, unless there was some meat hidden below the layers of lettuce and tomato.

Jackie fought her way back to daylight and asked Steve why he was running his fingers through the salad. He explained the situation and Jackie directed him in the direction of a packet of beefburgers that she had had the foresight to buy 'just in case'. Leaving him trying to find the 'on' switch for the grill, she started to take the meals through to the children in the dining room. It was quite some time before he had Grace's dietary requirements – the entire packet – cooked and ready to take in, and when he arrived bearing her plate he found Harry halfway through the second verse of 'Build a bonfire; put the teachers on the top' with Grace belching along in perfect time.

Amazing, Grace.

While Jackie went to find some paper towels to mop up the latest orange squash lake, Steve went back to fetch Grace some more tomato ketchup and a second helping of chips. In doing so, he managed to miss the moment when Hannah flamboyantly swung the heavy glass orange squash jug straight into the side of Tom's head. This time he landed face first, but luckily the cast iron door stop broke his fall. It took a minute or two to part the throng of children so that he could be picked up, and a few more to get his eyelids to open and his eyes to uncross, but then he seemed to be OK.

'Sorry Tom,' Hannah muttered quietly, as the adults dispersed back towards the kitchen. It was noticeable that she had only apologised once it was clear he was going to live. She'd been denying all responsibility up to that point.

Ten minutes later, the door bell rang and the beginning of the end began. The first parent to arrive was a young blonde woman, the trophy wife who had come to collect Leonie and her boorish father. She was followed by an older mother who was never going to be mistaken for a trophy anything, even in a good light, which in her case would have been dark black. It was the twins' mother.

'Right, party bags,' said Steve, grabbing a pink one with the name Melody on it, and waving it in the direction of the nearer twin.

'I'm Melanie.'

Steve rummaged in the pile for her bag, and then gave Melody's to the second twin.

'No, I'm called Melanie as well.'

'You're both called Melanie?'

'Yes.'

With only the slightest roll of his eyes, Steve grabbed a pen and changed the name on the bag. From then on there was a stream of arriving parents and departing children for fifteen frantic chaotic minutes. Only when things had all quietened down did Jackie go to revive and unbend Robert so that he could be sent on his way with his things and his money while Steve went round checking that nothing had been left behind, such as any of Tom's limbs or fingers.

Grace and Megan were the last two left. Grace was quite happily pigging her way through a pile of sweets while she watched Chloe listen to her still-wrapped presents for sounds of breathing, but Megan was beginning to show signs of agitation.

'My mum should be here by now,' she said to Natalie for the fourth or fifth time.

'Perhaps she's got stuck in traffic, or bumped into a friend and got chatting,' said Jackie.

'Or perhaps she's bumped into traffic and died in a giant fireball,' Grace chipped in helpfully.

Steve pulled a face and retreated inside his head to a day long ago. It had been the time on a warm July evening when the swallows were just finishing their shift and the bats were just starting theirs. Steve and Paul had both been staying with their mother for the weekend, on one of their frequent visits to give her some company in the months following their father's death that Easter. Like Paul, Steve was single in those days, a year or two before Jackie came onto the scene, and he'd had much more time for such trips. His brother had been celebrating it being the day before his thirty-second birthday by taking his new sports car for a spin round the local roads. He had been very proud of his 'mean machine', from its modified suspension and enlarged mudguards to its chrome plated exhausts and blacked out windows. It was fast and black and just the thing to be seen around in, except of course that it was almost impossible to see in through the windows. And quite difficult to see out, come to that.

Paul had always lived life in the fast lane, which was ironic considering where most of him was found after he came off the road and hit the old oak tree, that fateful evening. The inquest had concluded that he had been speeding, which was probably true, as he'd never shown much respect for the laws of the land when it came to such matters. Unfortunately though, the laws of physics were generally pretty strictly enforced in those parts, and they hadn't shown too much respect for him or his parts when he reached the reverse bends near the end of the dual carriageway. The large right hand branch had taken the full force of the impact, and had catapulted both driver and car quite some distance as it broke from the trunk. Even then, despite his terrible injuries, Paul would probably have survived if he hadn't been smothered by the airbag. From the policewoman's midnight knock on his mother's door to the chink of milk bottles in the cold dawn light had been the longest night of Steve's life.

The doorbell rang again at that moment, and Jackie opened the door to let in Grace's mother, The Massif. Like her daughter, the girl with the girth, her own fullness of form suggested that she was perhaps no stranger to a double portion of chips. In the four minutes she was in the house, she consumed most of the children's leftovers and all of the cheesecake that Steve had kept back for his own tea.

After they had driven off – in the direction of a take-away – there was only Megan still left to get rid of. It was over half a sob-filled hour later before her mother turned up to fetch her, having had a blonde moment that had lasted two hours until she'd finally remembered that the thing she had forgotten was collecting Megan. When she had departed and the door had been locked and dead-locked and double bolted behind them all, Steve breathed a sigh of relief. All in all, it had been quite a successful party. There had been a few bouts of 'Emily's not my friend any more', but nobody had died, not even Tom, and some of the children looked like they might have enjoyed bits of it. True, much of the next day was probably going to have to be set aside for trying to sell most of Chloe's presents on the internet, but there might be one or two nice ones. And the best thing – the very best thing – was that he didn't have any more social engagements for a whole week, until dinner at Malcolm and Karen's.

***

Steve felt a frisson of excitement on the way to work on Monday morning. It was the day of Barry's leaving 'do': perhaps not terribly exciting on a cosmic scale, especially since he was only going to be gone for certain weeks and the rest of the time his replacement had already been named as himself, but everything is very much relative and even sensor development projects could be dull without occasional entertainment like leaving speeches. It was kind of their boss to let them have an event for him even though he wasn't really going anywhere.

It seemed like Steve wasn't the only one who was looking forward to Barry's departure, for his cheeks hadn't even hit his chair when Clare brought the leaving collection in. Darren was the first to sign the card – a picture of an injured termite being expelled from the nest - and restrained himself to writing 'Congratulations. Please let you buy me a celebratory drink!' not very originally. There was then a lot of kerfuffle as he hunted through his pockets for the dodgy pound coin that looked like it'd been minted by a five year old. Then it was Steve's turn. Inspiration not being very forthcoming so early in the week, he had to settle for 'Best wishes' and a smudged signature. He wasn't too sure about putting anything into the collection, but under Clare's watchful gaze he grudgingly contributed a fiver.

At half past ten, people started to gather in the open-plan office that Steve called home, ready for the leaving presentation itself. As John had suddenly contrived to be away for the day on urgent business, Barry was left to deliver his own glowing eulogy on himself. He spoke for over twenty minutes, starting with his favourite tale of how he'd worked his way upwards towards his aspirations, and about how he'd had to sweat and sweat to achieve them. Steve had heard the story before, so it didn't much matter that Darren was muttering something into his ear about perspirations.

Barry talked movingly of the loneliness of command, and then waffled on about how he was leaving them with a firm foundation on which to build. That brought chunterings from Darren about that being a reference to morale being at rock bottom. Barry said that he rather prided himself on being a polyglot (Darren whispered that he'd bear that in mind if ever he had a problem with his grouting), and peppered his speech with historical references ranging from Herod the Wake to The Hundred Days War. He then declared that 'Whosoever can pull this staple from this status report will be ye true deputy manager of this office' while everyone just stared at him, apart from Simon who had had another very late night and appeared to be asleep.

'Seriously, ...' joked Barry, with a laugh both hearty and hollow. As opposed to unfunnily, presumably, thought Steve. The rest of the speech went undelivered because just at that moment somebody at the back of the room yelled 'Shut up, you big drama queen' and Barry lapsed into silence. For the only species on the planet to claim to have a sense of humour, humans can take themselves awfully seriously sometimes.

After an awkward pause, Clare stepped forward to present Barry with the card they'd all signed for him, together with an envelope containing the whip-round. He had asked for money so that he could choose his own gift, but Clare was worried he might be very disappointed unless his polyglotism extended to a love of foreign coins or old buttons. She needn't have worried. Barry hadn't bothered waiting to find out how much money would be collected and had already gone out and bought himself a large silver picture frame into which he'd inserted a very tasteful picture of himself leaning out of the open window of his new car. As a finishing touch he'd even had it engraved with the poetic words 'From your grateful colleagues'. Poetic as in gross poetic licence.

As it happened, none of his grateful colleagues – and they were, today, in a way – were too interested in the words carved into his leaving gift to himself. Everyone was more excited about passing round the card. The moment that Barry went off to dab away an emotional tear in private, the room exploded into laughter as they read out each others' subtle little acid-tipped barbs of double-edged wit, such as 'I hope your future career takes you far', 'You've taught us a lot', 'Thank you for giving me so much unexpected pleasure' and 'Shrivel up and die, you b*****d'.

***

After the excitement of getting rid of Barry, who had to leave immediately to go down to see his new extra part-time boss in London that afternoon, everyone returned to their seats or went to get themselves a cup of tea or coffee. The hush of productive work descended on the office, broken only by the noise of Barry coming back to show everybody in turn, and at great length and close up, his new picture. It was possibly, with the exception of one of his mother's cream of tuna casseroles, the most nauseating experience that Steve had had in years. Even Geoff's special lunchtime beef and ale pie with a hint of cat was more palatable.

They were still digesting the pie when the site manager's secretary, Pat, came round with a clip board.

'Right then,' she announced loudly. 'I'm taking names for the Christmas dinner and disco. What about you, Lisa?'

'Yes please.'

'Steve?'

'When is it?'

'Tuesday the twenty-seventh of February.'

'We're having our Christmas dinner at the end of February?'

'We left it a little late to find a venue big enough.'

'I'm not sure, I'll have to get back to you tomorrow, when I've checked whether Jackie will be in to have the girls.'

'Simon? Clare?'

'Yes please.'

'Yes please.'

'Darren?'

'I think he's nipped out to the tea machine.'

'Hmpf,' snorted Pat, in the way that secretaries to important people do.

A couple of minutes after she'd gone, Darren appeared. Whether that was cause and effect wasn't clear.

'You've just missed Psycho Pat – she was checking who wants to go to the Christmas party,' said Simon.

'I'd rather eat my own spleen,' said Darren.

'I think she's going to be sorting out the menu choices a bit nearer the time,' commented Lisa.

Pat, being nothing if not persistent, came back ten minutes later to give Darren another chance.

He curled his lip into a sneer at the invitation. 'I'd rather gargle with burning coals and have my buttocks branded with a red hot porcupine.'

'I'll put you down as a 'maybe' then.'

She turned to leave, but noticed Lisa's face. 'Are you alright?' she asked. Pat might have been battle-hardened from her days in the typing pool, but she was still technically human.

'I think so,' said Lisa. 'But I was just wondering why on earth I ever went out with Darren, even briefly.'

'Go boil your head,' muttered Darren, and then added as an afterthought: 'Oh sorry, it looks as if you already have.'

'Are things going badly with Lizzy?' Lisa sounded genuinely sympathetic, which was particularly irksome.

Darren shot his colleague a murderous glance.

'Things are fine,' he said.

'And how's that testing protocol coming on?'

'Things are fine,' he said again, more as a growl. They might have been finer if Barry hadn't made Lisa his second-in-command for the weeks when he was going to be away. Darren didn't need her to nag him about everything as well.

He set about thumping the keys on his computer with a vague murmur about his esteemed colleague shutting her esteemed face.

'What's the matter?' asked Lisa as the keystrokes rose in violence. 'Aren't you getting enough attention?'

Barry had only been gone an hour and already the place was falling apart.

***

Steve fished in his top drawer for the chocolate bar that he'd got from the machine on the way back from the canteen. He wasn't meant to be snacking so soon after lunch, of course. In fact, he was meant to have gone swimming, but once again his resolve had dissolved when twelve o'clock had come round. He reminded himself that it didn't really matter, as he'd walked loads of calories off the other week on holiday. In any case, you could overdo avoidance of chocolate machines: even obsessives need a break sometimes. Anyway, if the human brain uses twenty per cent of the body's energy requirements, then it ought to be possible to get into trim just by thinking harder, he reasoned. If he could just get his head round this long draft contract, for example, he ought to be able to burn off at least a couple of hundred extra calories. But his thoughts kept coming round to things along the lines of 'A biscuit would be nice'. He went to see what was in the biscuit cupboard.

'Did you ask Barry about that Hindsight Electrolysis contract before he left?' asked Lisa as he passed her desk.

'Ye-es,' said Steve, rather defensively. 'I sort of snuck it into the conversation when he wasn't really listening.'

'And did he get you to run it past our lawyers?'

'I've tried that. I told them how important it was, but they're all spending the week working on a new Vision Statement for the Legal Department, so I'm doing it myself.'

'I think you need to get professional advice when it comes to modifying contract documents, Steve.'

'Well I suppose so,' admitted Steve with the enthusiasm of an alcoholic for a soft drink. 'Who do you recommend?'

'I've no idea. I'd just go into town and find someone.'

'Oh, OK then. I'll see if I can find time on Thursday, once tomorrow's pilot manufacturing run's out of the way and we've had a quick look at the results.'

He went off in a biscuity direction, and returned a minute or two later with the realisation that he was supposed to be meeting with Darren and one or two others to discuss something or other. It was perhaps the meeting to discuss what they would need from H.E.L.'s encapsulation process if it was to solve their component protection problems.

'Are you coming along to my meeting?' he asked Darren, who had finally stopped sticking straightened paper clips into the voodoo doll on his desk.

Darren nodded. 'I've not had time to review your agenda. Is it the usual thing – you mumble, I half listen, you give me some action points, and I half apologise for not having done any of my previous ones?'

'Yes, more or less, except that I never actually sent you an agenda.'

'OK then,' said Darren wearily. 'Let's get started.'

***

Why do all firms of solicitors have ridiculously implausible names like Spine, Whitless and Crabfellow, or Pasty, Clutterbucks and Orifice? What exactly is it that causes people with funny names to want to go into the legal profession? Or do they change their names in some bizarre ritual when they qualify? About the only unusual name you never seem to find on a solicitor's door is Qualms. Or Scruples.

Steve's march along the tree lined avenue that housed every solicitors practice in town led him first to a large white Victorian villa with the names Pasty, Clutterbucks and Crabfellow etched into the glass of the downstairs windows. He rang the doorbell beneath the brass plaque that repeated their names, and waited. No answer. He rang again. No answer again. A small handwritten notice taped to the outside of the door caught his eye. It said simply 'Ceased trading – gone overseas.' He stood back from the door and looked down the street. The next property along also sported a brass plaque or two, so he went to try his luck there. Johnson, Brown and Jones didn't quite sound the part, but at least they hadn't fled abroad, which was something. Steve pressed the intercom buzzer and an officious female voice instructed him to push the door and come in.

'Do you have an appointment?' asked its blue-rinsed owner when Steve eventually found his way along a couple of meandering corridors to the reception desk at the back of the building. He was about to confess that he didn't, but the receptionist got there before him.

'No, you don't. And if you want Mr Jones, you'll be lucky.'

That was terse receptionist-speak that meant he wouldn't be lucky.

'He's in court today, dealing with some gardener's industrial injury claim,' she offered by way of explanation. Steve's face tried to convey the idea that he wasn't particularly interested in the details.

'A nettle sting,' she added, a provocative glint in her eyes.

Steve opened his mouth to speak – he hadn't joined in the conversation yet, after all – but it was clear from the defiant angle of his adversary's jaw that that wasn't on her agenda.

'Take a seat in the waiting room. Our senior partner will see you in fifteen minutes.'

She wrote something on a pad of paper. Steve hoped he wasn't being charged for that little piece of advice. He went through into the small waiting room indicated, and sat carefully on the edge of a stern, upright chair. There was a sprawl of magazines on a small coffeeless coffee table beside him, but none of them looked very interesting to non-enthusiasts of litigation.

After exactly fifteen minutes, the steely-eyed receptionist strode in to summon him into an adjoining office.

'Mr Bolus will see you now.'

Mr Bolus was a short fat man of about sixty, wearing an ill-disguised black toupée. He glanced up briefly as Steve walked in, and started a clock on his desk.

'Sorry about that,' he breathed, a little breathlessly. 'I was just suing my daughter.'

He closed a thick leather ledger. (I've no idea what a ledger is, but it kind of sounds right.)

'Now, what can I do for you?'

Steve explained the types of changes that he needed making to the draft legal agreement, bearing in mind Hindsight's various concerns and stipulations, and then he sat and watched Mr Bolus very slowly typing away at his ancient computer keyboard, one hesitant finger at a time. From the speed he was going, by Steve's back-of-the-envelope reckoning, each character was working out at something like £1.50. The situation wasn't helped by the fact that Steve, nervous at how much all this would cost SLSL, developed a sudden spontaneous stammer that probably added another £75 to the bill.

Eventually, though, the draft agreement was printed and ready for Steve to take away. It would be quite some hours later that he would realise that he'd come out clutching a document clearly dated the 243rd November.

***

Jackie risked a quick glance at her wristwatch. It was only five past eight. Steve had beaten his own record by more than three minutes. In less than a quarter of an hour he had managed to mention politics, religion and sex – and work, and money - and now sounded as if he was warming up for a discussion on private education. Jackie checked the coffee table, but any attempt at using it to hide a shin kick risked showering their hosts in sherry, dry roasted nuts and possibly a rainbow of fragments of best cut glass. She tried to skewer him with a scowl instead, but he never met her eye so she instead had to resort to a fake choking fit to shut him up.

'So how's things in the drains business these days?' she asked Malcolm, after a sudden recovery.

'Oh, pretty shitty.'

'Is that what happens after you've been doing it for a while, you develop an eye for the pretty ones?' interjected Steve. He half noticed that their hosts' bowl of nibbles appeared to have given his wife a second bout of spluttering and coughing, but he carried on regardless, in an attempt to hide her embarrassment. He was already quite tipsy, having knocked back two large glasses of wine on an empty stomach in an effort to calm his nerves.

'Do you mind if I just put the telly on to see the rugby scores for a moment?' Malcolm asked, ignoring Steve's previous question.

Steve made a gesture that was intended to show acquiescence and wasn't meant to tip white wine over his left knee. He saw, as he poured the remaining contents of the glass down his throat, that everyone else was looking rather stony-faced, so to jolly them all up a bit during the rugby highlights he started yelling 'Hand ball!' every few seconds, but even that didn't produce any smiles. No-one seemed to have a sense of humour tonight.

'Something smells good,' said Jackie, eager to try a new tack.

'It's chicken and leek casserole,' said Karen, glancing up at the clock.

'Oh, that's one of my specialities,' said Steve, helping himself to another glass of wine. 'You just shove a load of chicken bits into a pan, whack up the heat, and wait for it to sort of rot down a bit.'

'Yes,' agreed Karen, so icily that her teeth needed gritting. 'Something like that.'

Steve was starting to enjoy himself, although he might have enjoyed himself more if he could find a way to avoid slipping off their new leather suite onto the floor all the time. Karen went to give something a stir at that point, and Malcolm got called away to explain to someone on the telephone why he wouldn't be coming to deal with their constipated drains before Thursday. With both their hosts out of the room, Steve took the chance to go up to the mantelpiece to peer inside the birthday cards there, as you do, and then got caught with one still in his hand when their hostess returned.

'Nice card,' he said, a little lamely. 'I didn't read the bit about the vasectomy, you know.'

'I think it's possible to sit down now,' Karen said quietly. Steve presumed that that was an invitation to go through to the table, rather than a follow-up to what he'd just said, but to be sure he waited for Jackie to make the move.

The meal itself went quite well, and Steve didn't make any further faux pas. Or at least, he didn't think that he did, from inside his little bubble of alcoholic haze. And certainly not on the scale of the first time that he and Jackie had been round there for dinner, the night of the infamous murder mystery dinner party. There had been a dozen people there altogether, all of them in fancy dress except Steve who had only made a token effort when cast as the village tramp. Jackie had looked very cute as a glamorous young heiress, and Steve had hoped to be the dashing army captain, but Karen had given that role to Malcolm, which seemed a little nepotistic. Still, the party had got off to an enjoyable start as far as Steve was concerned, and it was nice to be awarded the prize for the best fancy dress, but the good mood most certainly didn't last, and he had no-one to blame but himself. Oh, he had told himself a hundred times since, if only he hadn't rushed in to reading his script and clue book so fast. How he had done it, he didn't know, but ten minutes into the party he had inadvertently read too far and blurted out 'Oh, it's me!' to a startled room and a sudden deathly silence. From thereon in, the entire evening had been one of the most uncomfortable episodes of his life. It said a lot for Malcolm and Karen that he had ever been invited back.

Tonight though, everything seemed to go well, apart from a slight tendency for his words to choose their own order of emergence from his mouth. It was nice to be able to make himself at home and to enjoy a bit of civilised company, and after he'd downed his third large whisky nightcap he even managed to persuade Malcolm to agree to come round sometime to sort out the smell from the drains.

***

The next morning, Steve had a bit of a hangover. Christmas planning doesn't care about such things, however, and Jackie was determined to put the previous evening behind her and to look forward to all the lovely, wonderful things that the festive season would bring. Starting with getting her husband to think about what to buy for the girls, and who to invite over. Steve knew what he would have liked the answer to the second question to be. He had for years been dreaming of spending Christmas, just the four of them, in some remote Scottish country house hotel. Of sitting in front of a blazing log fire with a glass of mulled wine as the stags roared outside in the snow-ravaged glen. It was one of several dreams that would never come true. And even if it did, he'd probably find that the drink, mulled or otherwise, gave him a headache.

Jackie waited until after Natalie's swimming lesson before asking the girls what they might want for Christmas. Chloe answered first, and was still listing animals five minutes later when her mother eventually managed to get a word in to ask Natalie what she might want.

'Can I have a pen, please?'

'OK dear.' Jackie was proud that she had such an ungreedy, non-materialistic daughter. She was proud of Chloe too, of course. Not every five year old can name seventeen sorts of lizard, as well as almost every species of mammal on the planet. She was even proud of Steve, in a funny sort of way. True, he had been a bit of an embarrassment at times the evening before, and true it might be some time before she could look Karen in the eye again, but he meant well and he always tried hard[1].

Jackie wanted to go to the shops, in the vague hope of finding a card for one of her friends at the meditation and relaxation class. Being a Sunday, the local shops were shut, but there was a newsagent's that would be open, about a mile and a half away. It was a glorious morning and it would make a lovely family walk if they cut through the park. (For those of you who don't understand why someone might walk a mile and a half when they have a car sitting available on the drive, I'm sorry, I'm not providing any clues. You never will understand.)

Although the crisp air and surprisingly warm sunshine provided an excellent cure for thick hung-over heads, the expedition failed to produce a 'Congratulations On Passing Your Blood Pressure Test' card. They did manage to buy a nice pen for Natalie, however, so the two hour trip wasn't wasted. They were just arriving back for their Sunday lunch of mushroom soup with an accompaniment of warm French bread and butter – Steve's favourite dinner, as it happened – when Angela's car drew up. Tom was out with his dad, so she had taken the opportunity to come and moan to Jackie.

Steve opened the front door to let everyone in and was nearly engulfed as a herd (flock? pride?) of woodlice scurried majestically past him across the twist pile.

'It's Vanilla's babies!' shrieked Natalie, and she and her sister rushed in and started rounding them up.

'I thought I'd told you to let Vanilla go,' said Steve, stepping out of the way as Chloe went crawling after Chocolate and Strawberry and something that might or might not have been little Raspberry Ripple. He was sure he'd been quite insistent on the point after spending thirty minutes earlier in the week trying

---

[1] No, I'm not going to do a joke about him always being trying; that would be pathetic.

to take a decent photograph for Natalie's school *Show and Tell* session of Vanilla relaxing at home in her plastic sandwich box.

'She's had babies, and they've come to visit us!' breathed Natalie in excited reverence.

'Yes, and now they're going into the garden,' said Steve firmly, although he was conscious that he was relying on his daughters to manage to find them all. Stepping gingerly over a small cohort on the right flank, he led Jackie and Angela into the house and left the girls going off in search of lavender leaves as a treat with which to tempt the tiny visitors back out of the carpet.

Angela explained that she had already eaten, so wouldn't be wanting any food. She then proceeded to help herself to half the bread as soon as it was buttered. Her main preoccupation seemed to be her endlessly drawn out house sale, and as she was obviously determined to spend the afternoon telling Jackie every last detail of recent developments, even though there hadn't really been any in an executive summary sense, Steve went off after a bit to play with the girls. They had finished their crustacean trap-and-release programme and were now sitting separately upstairs, Chloe lecturing Osmarelda and Natalie sitting with a pile of catalogues.

'Can I have my new pen now?' Natalie asked.

'It's meant to be a Christmas present,' Steve pointed out.

'Oh,' said Natalie, disappointed. She'd been using one of her mother's pens, but it had run out while she was going through ticking all the things that she might want for Christmas.

'Can we have a dolphin, please?' asked a little voice from the next room, sensing possible opportunity.

'And can I have Prod's new song?' she added, for good measure.

'Yeah. Can we buy the album, Dad, can we?' pleaded Natalie.

Steve wondered how to say 'no' and make it sound enough like 'yes' to end the conversation. From what he'd heard to date of Mr Prod's musical talents, it was a bit of an over-my-dead-body situation. Every track sounded more or less the same. The drumbeat surely *was* the same? In any case, he wasn't even sure how you went about obtaining music nowadays. Did you go on to the internet and have them beam it to you? Or did you do something clever with a mobile phone? He thought you could probably still get CDs, but he did wonder for how much longer. The ones that he was using as bird scarers in the garden might be the last of the line. He glanced outside to where a family of sparrows was swinging about. Judging by the state of the patio furniture, the disks were now a particular favourite of birds with stomach upsets.

Steve managed to persuade the girls to join him for a board game and a few rounds of *Snap*, and then they got him to help them play at Trolls at School, a game of Natalie's devising. Downstairs, Angela seemed to be in no rush to get back for her nearest and dearest, and was obviously intent on staying all afternoon: Jackie had quite a job prising her out before she ate their tea for them too.

After their soup and bread feast – Steve had been in charge of the day's catering arrangements – Jackie took charge of the girls and their entertainment while Steve got on with worrying about work. It was hard to know where to start. There were several megabytes of automatically generated data from Tuesday's pilot run to analyse. There was a launch and marketing plan to study and to comment on ('Why does every single sentence on your proposed information leaflet end in an exclamation mark?'). And there were several hundred accumulated e-mails that really needed reading and/or deleting. Given all that, he decided to settle on daydreaming as the first activity, and he was just wondering whether he'd walked off enough calories in Wales to justify a trip to the fridge when he was interrupted by Chloe, who had come to ask him the profound question 'Do you ever have to stand in the naughty corner at work, Daddy?'.

Although he denied it, it did set him wondering why it was starting to feel like an imminent possibility.

He closed his laptop computer down, and pausing only to pull a small dead spider from his ear he followed his daughter downstairs to help her judge a troll beauty pageant.

12

It was Monday evening, and Jackie sat with her head in her hands, surrounded by leaflets and charts, trying to work out the postage for the Santa mouse mat that she was sending to an old school friend on the other side of the world. If you followed the size and weight guidelines you needed four £1 stamps, but having a window in the envelope added another fifty to eighty pence depending how you interpreted the rules for the shape of its corners. Then there was the adjustment for the envelope's bendability, and finally there was a small discount for not using staples. She would just have slapped on all the stamps she had and been done with it, but the last time she'd done that the weight of stamps had pushed it into the next price band and the Post Office had brought it back for more.

'I can't remember – does the European Community or Union or Empire, or whatever it is this week, include New Zealand yet?' she asked Steve as he entered the dining room slash post office.

'I don't know, but I wish it didn't include Doltburn.'

'I thought you enjoyed meeting the locals?'

For a fleeting moment, Steve wondered if she might be serious, as she hadn't exactly seemed to be in a jocular mood. The only locals he'd seen looked like surly living proof that some Neanderthals had avoided extinction by somehow having the wit to interbreed with Cro-Magnons. 'Enjoyed' was too strong a word.

'I've got to go back for another visit. I might have forgotten to mention it. Barry wants a factory tour.'

'Couldn't you have done that last time?' asked Jackie.

Honestly, women could be so reasonable at times.

'No, apparently not. We've got to go all the way back, just so Barry can look at machinery he won't understand.'

'Anyway, I thought Barry had left?'

'So did I,' said Steve. 'But he decided he was only leaving for alternate weeks, and apparently then there was a problem with his new office in London and he's now changed his mind about going at all. So now our exciting new boss is our old one, but in a worse mood.'

'And do you really both need to go to Doltburn?'

'Well yes, apparently so. I'm the one who's meant to understand their technology and our draft legal agreement, and Barry's the one who's convinced this deal is the most vital thing in the whole history of things.'

'And doesn't Mrs Barry ever complain about these long trips and late finishes?'

'I don't think she can bring herself to talk to him much these days. Not since he sold her mother.'

'To be fair, it was only her ashes,' he added, in response to the enquiry written on Jackie's eyebrows.

Putting aside all thoughts of Barry the Boomerang for a few minutes, Steve went through into the lounge to see the girls. His enthusiasm for their company wasn't reciprocated right at that moment, though, as they were both engrossed in a children's TV programme about parasitic worms. Knowing when he wasn't wanted, he wandered back to the dining room.

'Have you had any ideas about what else we can get the girls for Christmas?' asked a voice from somewhere under a pile of envelopes, sticky tape, string and despair.

'I don't know. I haven't even started to think about it.'

'Well Chloe says she wants a pet.'

Steve expressed sarcastic surprise.

'She says she'll never want anything again if we buy her a rabbit,' added the voice.

'That's what she said about the swing for her birthday. And about the princess colouring book last Christmas.'

'Yes, well now she needs a house rabbit to complete the set.'

'And what about Natalie?'

'Still going through the catalogue,' said Jackie, emerging with a triumphant wave of a bent gift tag.

'I suppose,' said Steve carefully, sitting down at the table, 'that we'll have to have everyone over to stay.'

'Well your mother, definitely, and possibly my uncle. And I suppose we ought to have Diane and Tony over for the day at least.'

'Goodness me,' said Steve. Very nearly.

'Assuming Diane's not pregnant.'

Steve contemplated arguing the case for disappearing into the wilderness for a week, on the quite logical grounds that the presence of his mother in the house for more than ten nanoseconds would inevitably trigger stress-induced marital discord. But he didn't. He knew that his wife was right and that they had to share the unjoys of the festive season with everyone left on the family tree. But he did rather hate himself for not having the courage to challenge her, just once.

'By the way, don't forget that the girls have their school concert thing on Thursday afternoon,' Jackie reminded him.

Steve looked slightly startled. He'd forgotten that he'd have to find time for hoping that Natalie's contribution on the violin wouldn't sound like fingernails being scratched slowly down a glass blackboard. Not that anyone else in the Oscroft family was any more musical, of course. On the positive side, though, the school usually combined these occasions with prize-giving ceremonies, and Steve was hoping to perhaps win something for the model castle that he'd built as part of Natalie's half-term homework.

The phone rang at that point – Steve left the room when he heard it was Angela - and Jackie spent the next hour and a half in a long conversation about nothing. Angela was never short of things to say, especially when she was having one of her nights in, waxing her legs and de-waxing her ears. In fact, Steve was already reading in bed by the time Jackie finally emerged from the dining room.

'Did she ask how I was?'

'No,' said Jackie. 'She was too busy telling me about some man she's met at work who shares her sudden newfound interest in motorbike engines.' She got ready for bed and went to clean her teeth.

'Oh, and by the way,' she said, when she returned and climbed into bed, 'I told Natalie that she could have Rebecca over for a sleepover on Friday night, as it's our turn.'

Steve grimaced. Much as he wanted Natalie to have friends, he had rather hoped that they could have the weekend to themselves as a family.

'It's alright,' said Jackie, seeing his look of distress. 'She can't come, because she's taking her pet stick insect for a lethal injection that evening.'

And with that, she switched the light off, and that episode in their lives was over.

***

Steve arrived at work late, somewhat flustered by the tribulations of the morning's gridlock, to find a lot of anxious faces. For a brief moment he thought that his colleagues might be showing concern for his delayed arrival, but then he realised that they seemed to have something more important to worry about than the possibility of his involvement in an accident or breakdown.

'Barry's called an urgent meeting for everyone in the building,' Lisa told Steve, in answer to his dumb look. 'He's very agitated. Something's really wrong.'

'It might possibly be something to do with the fact that your project keeps failing to deliver and that we have nothing to take to customers,' Darren suggested, helpfully. 'I heard a rumour that Senssertive's new product is taking the market by storm.'

'It might just be another price rise in the canteen,' proffered Simon. 'You know how passionate he is about the price of the puddings.'

'No, I don't think so,' said Darren, 'He looked really upset when he popped in to tell us to wait here until nine.'

Nine o'clock was less than ten minutes away now, and the time soon passed in talk of the desperate state of the company's finances, the dire lack of progress on Sling, and the seriousness of the situation as judged by the look on Barry's face previously. By the time Barry came back, tailed by about thirty worried people from other departments, just about everyone in the office was hyperventilating or heading towards the early stages of cardiac arrest. Everyone except Darren, of course. He always enjoyed bad and exciting news, because it gave him something to make caustic comments about for days afterwards. Assuming that he was still going to be here and still have any colleagues to make them to, of course. Barry's slightly green and very drawn face did not look good.

Everyone arranged themselves in whatever space they could find between the desks while Barry cleared his throat with an unusual and elaborate nervousness. This seemed to be the first time that he had ever personally experienced any human emotions apart from heartiness and smugness.

'Good morning,' he said wanly, his voice wobbling slightly.

The room held its breath.

'I have some rather bad news for everyone.'

There was a drum-roll from thirty-five racing pulses.

'As you all know, the financial situation has been getting rather bad,' Barry said, choking slightly on his words.

Some of the people in the office exchanged nervous glances.

'And we really need our new projects to deliver us something that we can sell if we're to stay in the game.'

Several people turned to look in Steve's direction. Steve clenched his jaw and gritted his teeth. His stomach leapt in a freefall tumble down into his legs.

'I'm afraid,' Barry continued, 'that everyone is going to be affected by this.'

He took a sip of water.

'I'm sorry to say that stress has already claimed its first casualty. I called this meeting because I have very bad news – I've had a phone call to say that Mike Marshall from Sales is desperately ill in hospital.'

For two seconds there was a shocked silence. Then a great collective sigh of relief filled the room. No-one quite shouted 'Yes, oh yes, oh yes!' and no-one quite punched the air, but the buzz of relieved and excited chatter that followed was almost deafening. Never had so many people felt so close to losing their jobs. Not within Sense Less, anyway.

After a few moments, Steve managed to gather his wits enough to ask Barry what had happened to Mike.

'He had a rock-climbing accident at the weekend. They think he was distracted about the problems at work, and he tripped and stubbed his toe. Stubbed it badly, really badly, I'm afraid –' His voice wavered and broke. 'I'm afraid he's slipped into a coma. They're not sure he'll live. He might already be brain dead.' His voice trembled to a pause.

There was a short silence.

'Are you sure he wasn't trying to throw himself off something, when he heard that the new sensor still isn't ready to sell?' asked Darren.

***

Whether it was an automotive expression of artistic judgement will never be known, but Steve's car needed a significant dose of TLC before it would start on the afternoon of Natalie and Chloe's end-of-term school production. Indeed he only managed to get it going at all by threatening it with a tow to the garage behind Darren's battered camper van. Even recalcitrant Mundanes have their pride.

He drove home to collect Jackie, who had just come back from her salad'n'gossip lunch with Angela and was now dressed in the outfit she had selected as most suitable for attending a combined nativity play, concert, and speech day extravaganza. She had a thick coat, gloves and a scarf on, having learnt over the preceding two years how cold the school hall could be in winter. Steve picked up his overcoat, comb and camera, and a handful of loose change. With all Natalie and Chloe's various performances, their parents were rapidly turning into professional audience members.

They reached the school an hour before proceedings were scheduled to kick off. Any later and they knew they would get to see nothing but the backs of hundreds of heads. As it was, by the time they walked into the hall the front two rows were already occupied and bristling with more cameras and recording equipment than your average international press conference. How things had changed over the decades: the only movie footage of Steve's early childhood had been a faltering forty-five second sequence of him cycling along the pavement past his grandparents' house on the one occasion that his father had got round to borrowing a cine camera from somewhere. Steve hadn't seen the footage in years, though his mother probably had it ferreted away somewhere. It was too painful to watch, anyway. He could still feel the shock and humiliation when he wobbled off the kerb and split his ear open on the neighbour's car door. He wished he could consign the film, and indeed most of his childhood, to the dustbin rather than have it forever locked in his memory.

The hall was filling up quickly, and the noise from the audience-to-be was rapidly rising. Much of it emanated from two mothers who came in behind Steve and Jackie and sat down directly behind them.

'Gosh, this year's end-of-term production has come round quickly!' exclaimed one, in an *awfully* affected accent. 'It seems like only last week we were waving goodbye to another lot of disillusioned teachers.'

'I think the collective noun is a *whinge*, actually,' said her companion, with a haughty nasal laugh.

Steve glanced round. He half wondered whether to suggest she try to get the money back on her elocution lessons, but decided better of it. The conversation behind him moved on via their plans for flying abroad for some winter sun, past their thoughts on the latest cinema blockbuster, and had just reached the exchange of back-handed compliments on each others' outfits, when the headmistress, Mrs Buckland, marched to the front and clapped her hands together three times to attract attention. The noise level in the room fell away to a few sniffs and coughs and one small child wanting a wee-wee. The show was about to get underway.

Mrs Buckland made a few introductory remarks of a vaguely welcoming and entirely forgettable nature. Something to do with the school's pride in shaping the children of today and producing the footballers, cat-walk models and rap singers on whom the future of society would depend. She asked for mobile phones to be switched off, and then invited all the parents to mingle over mince pies and coffee at the interval. Steve could hardly wait. He had a major mountain of work to get on with, not to mention a foothill of Christmas presents to think about buying, and instead he had something like four hours of show to sit through PLUS the chance to get together with some of the wealth-equals-worth set at half time. It was going to be a long haul.

The first item on the programme was a nativity play by the youngest of the children. Chloe was sixth in line as they filed on to the makeshift stage, each of them looking nervously for their parents. There was a volley of 'Coo-ee's and 'Over here!'s and one 'Pull your hem down, Sophie!'. Jackie tried to get a photograph of Chloe in her donkey outfit, but the people in front were already standing up with their camcorders. Steve wasn't going to bother trying to film any more school productions, not after the time when he'd got all out of sync with the 'record' button and had captured all the scene changes but none of the scenes, thereby ending up with no footage whatsoever of Natalie in her first school nativity production, dressed as an armadillo. So there was no record of the moment when her love of woodlice had perhaps first been triggered.

The nativity was played at quite a lick, partly because little William decided to shout both of his lines out consecutively, thereby missing out seventeen scenes that should have come in between. There was then a little song, accompanied by a spotty faced young teacher on an untuned piano. The singing was interestingly freestyle, and the lyrics had obviously been written on a very tight budget, but it still drew quite a chorus of cheers from the back of the hall.

'Aah, aren't they sweet!' said one of the women behind Steve.

Sweet, yes, but clueless.

After the sheep and cattle and donkeys and wise men and zebra had all been rounded up and taken away for sandwiches by a couple of teaching assistants, it was time for the first instrumental piece in a programme of many, many instrumental pieces. First came five girls, one after another, each playing a violin solo. Natalie was not amongst these first five, and Steve was relieved to realise that the standards set by her class mates were not exactly leaving her behind, after all. They too seemed capable of notes entirely new to musical science.

The show wouldn't have been so bad if the parents weren't all forced to perch uncomfortably on those awful tiny plastic kiddies' chairs. Steve was already developing cramp and there were something like another hundred and fifty acts to go. Next up was what might be called a sympathy orchestra, and then it was the turn of an equally dire choir. Steve still had his own painful memories of school singing lessons at the age of ten, when the teacher, old Pimple Neck, had told him that he sang everything on one note, and what was more that it was the wrong note. Things like that tended to put you off ever singing in public again, and although their attempts at harmonies hurt, Steve did feel some empathy with the tone-deaf youngsters that Miss Blatherspit was attempting to conduct.

The man on the next plastic micro-seat to Steve turned out to be some sort of a stowaway, loudly announcing that 'I don't do this for fun, you know. I just come here to get out of the cold' once the choral pain-fest had ceased and Miss Blatherspit had retreated once more to the side of the stage. Steve did not reply. Another line of budding musicians was queuing up to play their solos. The first one on was Tom, after a short delay while the First Aiders got into position. His piece, a rhythmless rhythm bashed out on a bongo drum, somehow passed without incident. Then came two trumpets, then three trombones, and then a 'cello. The brass instruments were possibly marginally worse than the violins - the lengths to which the author went to research some of these stressful experiences are really quite phenomenal – but the 'cello at least provided a more mellow interlude. Steve wished that perhaps Natalie had chosen that rather than the violin, though he conceded that she might have had a job seeing over the top of it. None of the performances seemed to cut much ice with the man on Steve's left-hand side, though, who was muttering increasingly loudly between each piece now. Steve peered at his programme, in the hope that it might tell him how much more of this he had to endure before the interval, but it gave no clue. All he knew was that it was now the turn of a strange, rather thin boy called Nigel to show what he could do with a flute. Well, if you've got it, flaut it[1].

The man next to Steve muttered something that ended in the word 'rubbish'.

Mrs Buckland then announced that Leo, an eight year old in Year Four, was going to play one of his Grade Six pieces, based on Prelude From Te Deum with a few extra variations thrown in.

'I hope he's only going to play the Prelude and not the Lude and the Postlude as well,' grumbled Steve's neighbour.

The little lad went up onto the stage, clutching his violin. He stood in front of an empty music stand, looking for a moment uncertain as to what to do. Steve felt very sorry for him, having forgotten his music in such a public arena, when all of a sudden he started to play, and played absolutely exquisitely from beginning to end, twiddly bits and all. There was a fairly stunned silence from the audience, punctuated only by a low, rumbled 'Nobody likes a show-off' from somewhere on Steve's left.

'He's only eight,' hissed Steve. 'Give him a chance.'

'Hmm,' muttered the king of criticism. '*Some* children can play the violin *and* read music at the same time.'

Steve did not respond. He was beginning to get concerned that Natalie was never going to appear. The next child up was a dull looking lad with an earspan of about eleven inches who traipsed morosely onto the stage carrying a tambourine. If anything, his insipid and tuneless shaking was probably the worst performance yet. Mr Grumpy appeared to have finally

---

[1] I do apologise.

found one he approved of, however, and was wiping the side of his eye with the back of an index finger. 'Oh dear, I've gone all runny,' he said.

'Is he your son?' asked Jackie, leaning across.

'Yes, he is,' confirmed Mr Grumpy, his voice quavering and a lump in his throat. 'Could you tell?'

'Well, I just had a hunch,' said Jackie.

***

Finally, somehow, they reached the break and a chance to mingle with the other parents and to listen to tales of their offspring's achievements. Natalie's piece had come and gone without incident, or natural talent. Steve found himself in the queue for coffee and mince pies next to Elaine Smith, someone to whom he'd rarely spoken, but who had a daughter in Natalie's class and a younger son who had once scribbled on the walls in Steve's hall.

'You're Natalie's dad, aren't you?'

'Yes I am.' It was nice of her to take an interest.

'Never mind, dear,' she sniffed. 'Not everyone can play.'

She then launched into a pre-rehearsed list of things that her delightless children were doing with their high-calibre lives, leaving Steve remembering why it was that he'd not spoken to her much. He scanned wildly around for someone else to talk to. Jackie was nowhere to be seen, and the only person he recognised in the swarm of parents was Grace's mother, looking like a good candidate for stomach stapling but shovelling mince pies in as if she'd had her throat widened. Elaine was still pouring pity over Natalie's achievements and likely prospects, so under the pretext of needing the toilet Steve made his excuses and fled back to his seat in the hall, his next-of-seat neighbour shouting after him helpfully that 'I wouldn't go back in yet – you don't want to cut off the circulation to your buttocks before you have to.'

***

The second half got underway. Cunningly, all the children had been given bits in both halves so that none of the parents could sneak off home during the interval. Old Miseryguts, as the man on Steve's left was known to his nearest and dearest, appeared to have fallen asleep, and Steve was not bothered by any further comments, even when his talentless son stumbled over his own feet and off the stage.

This session started with a show of mime and dance by the six to eight year olds. Although the story appeared to revolve around a trip in a rocket to the stars, for some reason they were all dressed as pantomime animals. Natalie appeared to be playing the part of a weasel, or possibly a horse - the costumes that the teachers had helped them make were a little unusual – and Steve was pleased to note that she was one of the three space-animals to survive the impact when the rocket crashed into a space-whale. The final dance was particularly lively. A combination of half of them hopping up and down with nerves, or wanting the toilet, plus the consequences of being told to remain in character at all times, made it look a bit like a production at a school for ADHD sufferers.

After that it was time for another string of young musicians to scratch some violin strings, and then time for some woodwind. 'The haunting beauty of the descant recorder' was not a phrase you heard too often at the gates of Natalie's school at afternoon collection time, and nothing that happened in the second half of the show changed anyone's mind on the subject. By the time he'd heard fifteen separate squeaky renditions of *Rudolph The Red Nosed Reindeer*, Steve was almost at the point of giving each child a standing ovation just to ease the cramp. The whole experience was one of those occasions for which the word 'interminable' had been designed.

'Right. Last three,' announced Miss Blatherspit briskly. Teachers of her generation and tendency to wear tweed always tend to talk briskly.

Luckily, little Matthew, little Rosie and not quite so little Grace all took the hint, and four minutes later it was time for the final instrumental group piece of the afternoon, a trumpet fanfare in H minor with a tune more boring than scales. Steve was very grateful that Natalie had never shown any inclination to want to play a wind instrument. Watching the brass section now, their cheeks bulging like lawyers' wallets and their eyes crossed and almost popping, it didn't look very comfortable. In fact, some of them appeared to be in considerable pain, but then again that might have been the result of having to listen to their own output, and at such short range.

There then followed a short play performed by the older children. Two eleven year olds were dressed up as ugly sisters, pretending to be teachers, Miss Carriage and Miss Creant. Oh, happy, funny, day.

The play constituted the last part of the entertainment that had been laid on to thrill the assembled adults. There was still the little matter of the end of term speeches and prizes to sit through, however. Sadly, during the preceding three and half hours, two of the children had lost grandparents, and by the time it was all over another of the older audience members had given up the fight for life.

Prior to handing out any certificates, book tokens or silverware, the headmistress made a speech, thanking the governors and some of the teaching staff. Then the chairman of the governors thanked the headmistress, the dinner ladies and the caretaker, and then one of the dinner ladies thanked the children and the headmistress. After twenty-five minutes of this, Steve was quite prepared to thank anyone willing to not make a speech.

Eventually everyone except Mrs Buckland sat down, and it was time for the tense occasion that is a school prize-giving. Both Natalie and Chloe had already overtaken the one prize that their father had won in his school career. His had been a slightly tea-stained leather bookmark awarded for a third-form project about local wildlife. He could no longer remember many of the details, other than that he'd gone out counting frogs in the local woods one damp spring morning. Not well enough to get first prize, obviously, but he had always told himself that fourth wasn't bad. Natalie had won armfuls of certificates (swimming, running, jumping, English, maths, story-telling, story-writing, sitting up straight), and despite having been at school less than a term Chloe had already received two (a First Prize for colouring-in and a Highly Commended from the Institute of Advanced Ballet (Light Armoured Division)).

Neither Steve nor Jackie was a pushy parent, although Steve had dusted the glass fronted cabinet in the lounge just in case any silverware might be coming their way, but nevertheless they were both a little disappointed when all the good prizes – the ones that involved book tokens or gift certificates - went elsewhere. With a lack of any suitably accomplished former pupils, the role of guest of honour, principal speaker and prize giver-outer had fallen to Mrs Buckland's cousin the double glazing sales manager, who rattled on to the children for half an hour about the importance of sales force discipline. Daniel (the Head's son) won the Daniel Buckland prize for being Daniel Buckland, Grace won the prize for the child with the pushiest parents, and Jonnerphun received a silver shield on a plaque carved from non-sustainable wood for creative intimidation. Mrs Buckland's cousin then made another speech, this time about the glories of golf, and then there was a chance to watch the lesser prizes go to more of the teachers' own children.

Finally, very finally, it was time for everyone to join in the closing Christmas carols. From a musical point of view and a familiarity point of view they were ruined by the choir mistress's insistence on jazzing them up and speeding them up so that the children couldn't keep up and the adults couldn't sing them at all. Not that it stopped a couple of the fathers and one of the mothers from trying, mind you. However, from a point of view of getting the whole damned afternoon over with, it wasn't too bad a thing.

Mrs Buckland wasn't one to resist the lure of a captive audience as a chance to make a couple of concluding remarks. The first one was expected, as it had featured in her two previous sets of concluding remarks, at the Easter concert and the summer mime show. She was very sorry, but the school had blown the library book fund on three wheelchair ramps more than the law demanded, ready for when the new peripatetic dance teacher started.

The second announcement came as a complete shock, though. Miss Blatherspit was taking early retirement at Christmas and would be replaced by a Mrs Pottlesmirk. Mrs Pottlesmirk was asked to show herself, and everyone turned round to see a mad-looking woman of about six foot two who was standing by the rear doors. Judging by her expression she wasn't going to be standing for much nonsense, but at least she didn't look the sort of person who would ever instigate a witch-hunt, unless she had a hankering to discover how buoyant she might be.

Numb beyond words, everyone stood up and waited to file out and collect their children. Miss Blatherspit was standing by the door, looking rather forlorn, and Steve and Jackie felt they had to stop for a word. They could hardly ignore the woman who had enthused and inspired their elder daughter these last four terms. Though Steve did briefly consider it.

'All the best. Good luck,' he said, unable to think of anything eloquent for this important occasion.

'Have you got any plans?' asked Jackie, with slightly more flair.

'Not really, at the moment,' said the teacher. There was an awkward silence, only slightly filled by the sound of Steve dropping his car keys.

'Some of my house plants could do with re-potting, though, I suppose.' There was another silence, broken only by Steve scrabbling around near the inspirational teacher's feet.

'Have you enjoyed teaching, then?' asked Jackie, feeling that she had the task of keeping the conversation out of intensive care.

Miss Blatherspit looked slightly wistful, gave a small sigh, and said softly: 'It's been a bit mixed really – teaching has real highs and real lows. Parts of it are good.'

Jackie nodded, encouragingly.

'There are the rows of eager little faces every morning when I get into the classroom, for instance. But some of the other bits are OK.' She sighed again. 'My brother always said that I have what it takes to follow him into the legal profession,' she said, quietly and slightly sadly. 'But if I had done, I suppose I would have missed all this fun.'

She turned round to look at a couple of the children fighting while they waited for their parents, who were helping to massage Tom's knee back to life.

'They're all yours after Christmas, Margaret,' said the soon-to-be-former educator of tiny minds, turning to Mrs Pottlesmirk, who had just joined them. From close up, her replacement didn't appear to be any younger than herself.

'Oh, I'll soon sort them out,' Mrs Pottlesmirk reassured Steve and Jackie, unnervingly brusquely and unreassuringly. 'After all, I soon got the better of that husband of mine –'

'– the solicitor?' interjected Steve.

Mrs Pottlesmirk actually looked a little taken aback for an instant. 'How did you guess?' she asked.

'Oh, just a hunch,' murmured Steve.

They collected the girls, and left.

***

Steve's second visit to Doltburn with Barry was no more fun than the first. In fact, it followed what was already a weary routine. Same meeting in the work car park, same last minute need to call at Barry's house to pick something up and to notice the new uPVC-with-stone-mullions of the west wing, same traffic jams and delays. They even called at the same petrol station (with a Pompous it was less a case of miles per gallon and more a case of gallons per mile), where the proprietor now sported a head wound in the shape of a large dent. It probably wasn't too surprising, near a town that sold many a baseball bat but never a baseball ball. Perhaps the only change was that the local youths had recently been tearing round the nearby estate in their stolen cars so fast that all the resultant floral tributes on the lamp posts were in danger of winning the place a Best Kept Village award.

Apart from the usual cluster of smokers around every shop doorway, there was no-one much around. That might have been due to the fact that it was raining a light rain again, or it might have been something to do with the part-wit youths on the street corner nearest to H.E.L. Presumably going round as a gang gave them the chance to club together to make up one whole-wit. They had a gang of dogs with them too, of uncertain breed: probably a couple of thugsdogs, but one of them might have been a bull-chewer. The lads would have looked decidedly menacing if they didn't look so resolutely bedraggled and dejected and if any of them had looked bright enough to know which end of a knife to hold. You couldn't exactly blame them for having to loiter without intent, though: they'd had nuffinck to do since they'd burned down the local youth club. Except of course everything that there was to do in the old days, plus the internet, skate board parks, computer games, ten pin bowling alleys, mobile phones, multiscreen cinemas, frisbies, squash courts, cyber cafés, dry ski slopes, off-road cycle paths, indoor climbing walls, and a few other things. It was pretty awful for the poor dears[1].

A thin wiry man of about sixty, who turned out to be Dr Carmichael, came out into the car park to greet them, waved a five page confidentiality agreement and a thirty page legal disclaimer under their noses, got two signatures from Barry, and led them off towards the secret process and the infallible machine.

They were shown into a large building at the back of the site. The uneven concrete floor was puddled and oily, pipework festooned every surface, and the whole was pervaded by a strong smell of acetone. It didn't look terribly high-tech.

---

[1] That's right, the author IS over thirty.

'How's it running today?' their host asked the one man working the machine while another sixty-two people hurried around dealing with the paperwork. The man nodded solemnly, as if to convey that infallible machines and secret processes took a bit of experience and a lot of concentration. With a vague wave of tweed-clad arm, Dr Carmichael started to dart around the equipment, pointing things out in a state of mounting enthusiastic excitement. Steve found himself struggling to keep up, both physically and also in terms of understanding what he was being told.

'We take the etched substrates...,' Dr Carmichael was saying, as Steve scurried after him, deftly side-stepping a small puddle of oxygen dihydride with his right foot and putting his left one straight into a larger one of dilute sulphuric acid.

'... and we feed them into the – stop me if I'm using too much jargon – pointy end.'

He hurried on along the machinery, waving a hand in the direction of assorted buttons and tubes. The acetone vapour was beginning to give Steve a headache, and to add to his discomfort he could see some sort of fumes coming from the heel of his left shoe, where it was starting to turn into shoe sulphate.

Their guide continued to describe the special manufacturing process, but by now they were standing close to a collection of large metallic cylinders that were noisily issuing pulses of steam, and from his position behind Barry's shoulder Steve was only able to catch fragments of what was being said.

'...oxide coating.'

The acrid smell from the vicinity of his foot was beginning to get seriously alarming now.

'... and tough, but unpredictable.'

Like a lady, thought Steve, increasingly under the influence of both solvent and shoe vapours.

'Then we gold coat it.'

Like a rich lady, then.

'Then we pass it into this vacuum oven to allow it to outgas.'

Ah, like an elderly rich lady.

'And this,' said Dr Carmichael with a flourish of evident pride, 'is the heart of the process.'

Steve followed his gaze and peered into the gap between the tangle of hoselines and wires. The heart of the top secret process appeared to be a half-eaten cheese and pickle sandwich.

'Right,' said Dr Carmichael, 'now I'm going to switch on what you've come to see, the main hard-coating machine.'

Well that was news to Steve, but he waited while their guide pulled a small lever downwards and pressed a green button on the wall. With an inevitability to match that of next year's above-average pay rise for MPs, the infallible machine refused to start. An hour and a half of switch-toggling, unplugging and re-plugging, furtling, bodging and the occasional kick later, the machine still refused to start. The Chief Technical Officer looked a little crest-fallen.

'Would you like to borrow a pair of acid-resistant plastic shoes?' he asked suddenly and belatedly. As his left shoe was still emitting the occasional bubbling noise, and now kept sticking to the concrete, Steve had little option but to accept the offer, although he did feel a bit uncomfortable with the lime green colour of the only pair his size. Conventional wisdom has it that participants in inter-company business negotiations should feel comfortable and relaxed in what they're wearing, and here he was about to enter possibly crucial discussions wearing luminous green footwear. As it turned out, though, that part of their trip was also a waste of time. The Hindsight company lawyer had apparently, notwhereinforthwithstanding the fact that he'd agreed to the meeting, cleared off Christmas shopping for the afternoon. There was no alternative but to curtail the visit and to come back a third time. It was very frustrating, and by the time Barry had dropped Steve off back at Sense Less a solvent-induced headache had well and truly set in. The stiff plastic shoes did nothing for his clutch control, either, and the car did a passable impersonation of Skippy as he drove back home.

There were three new family members waiting to greet him when he opened the front door. With the Christmas holidays fast approaching, Chloe's teacher had needed someone to look after the three class goldfish, Gladstone, Disraeli and Palmerston. Steve couldn't be certain, but he got the distinct impression as Chloe was introducing everyone that Palmerston was staring mockingly at his feet.

As soon as the extended family's bonding session was over, and while Chloe was still trying to decide – out loud – which of her three temporary pets was the prettiest, which was the cleverest, and which was the coolest, Natalie went rushing up the stairs to continue something she was doing behind the closed door of the bathroom. Steve would have thought no more of it, particularly as he was now being asked for his views on the relative aesthetic merits of long tail fins versus deeper orange scales. However the sound of a significant quantity of water smacking against the upstairs floor, followed by sudden frustrated sobbing, sent him hurrying up to find out what was going on.

'What is it, sweetles?' he asked, cautiously pushing against the bathroom door.

'It doesn't work!' scowled Natalie, giving the closest thing to a stamp of the foot that Steve had ever seen her do. Or perhaps to a squelch of the foot, bearing in mind the puddle she was standing in. She then burst into tears, which helped neither the flood nor the investigation into its cause. Steve was a patient father, though, and willing to wait to get the full story sob by sob. It was possible that there was an element of sisterly jealousy – rare in Natalie – involved, but the fundamental problem had been the failure of her science homework, an experiment on dissolving things. No matter how much salt she had added or how hard she had stirred, she hadn't been able to get Osmarelda to dissolve in the bath. A little ironic, perhaps, given Steve's own recent experiment with footwear and acid spills.

Gently retrieving Chloe's favourite doll from the remnants of the bathwater, he managed to divert Natalie's attention much faster than he could have hoped by the simple expedient of promptly cutting his finger on Osmarelda's thing for getting stones out of horses' hooves.

'It's nothing, I'm OK,' he said, looking down at the welling red blood and immediately wishing he hadn't. The day's events had left him feeling particularly squirmish.

'Amputation!' announced Dr Natalie, suddenly cheering up and marching off towards her mother's bedside cabinet. She returned with a party size roll of medical gauze, followed by Sister Chloe who wore a white nurse's hat and a concerned but determined expression. Somewhat alarmingly, Chloe was carrying a stethoscope: clearly the infection might already be racing towards his lungs. Oh, and his knees, judging by the reflex testing hammer that Natalie was holding. They did all laugh about it eventually, or at least most of them did, but all in all it was an imperfect end to an imperfect day.

That night, Steve fell asleep into an uneasy dream in which Assettonii, the Greek goddess of dissolving things, was having an argument with Corrosivus, the Roman god of making things go rusty, as to who was chief deity and who was understudy in these matters. They decided to settle the affair using Steve's entrails, and might have done so had he not woken up in a sweat. The sizzle of the red-hot sword as they practised on a string of sausages had been all too real.

And, come to that, his finger really hurt.

***

Cometh the hour, cometh the man. Cometh five past the hour, cometh the bus, and the man being Steve, and Steve having long ago given up on the folly of city centre parking on a Saturday, the man got on the bus. As did his lady-wife and their two little lady-daughters. It was time for some serious Christmas shopping.

Now shopping was probably Steve's second favourite thing in the whole world, after not shopping. So the idea of at least four hours of it, followed by the pantomime matinée that was on at the playhouse in town, was really quite something. He understood neither why they needed to start so early – Christmas Day was still more than a week away, for goodness sake – nor why they needed so much stuff. He'd really hoped to make Christmas a rather more low-key affair this year, after the over-indulgence of last ('Look, Mummy, Santa's been sick on the carpet...'), but clearly it wasn't to be.

The journey into town was slow, despite the early hour, because the traffic was already building up badly. The main reason for this turned out to be a large black 4 x 4 outside a row of shops half way to town. Being a 4 x 4, the owner could drive or park it anywhere of course, and right at this moment it was parked exactly as you might expect a 4 x 4 to be parked: mostly off road, in this case at a rakish angle across the pavement, a bus stop, and part of the town-bound lane. Steve, and the other thirty-six people on the bus (plus driver plus two dogs) and numerous others in their cars, had to wait while its owner finished his business and drove off, but that was OK because 4 x 4 drivers are much more important than other people.

The first shop that Jackie led them into was RBV's, the big department store near the town hall. It was one of Jackie's favourite places, but for Steve it offered four whole floors of shopping misery. He had only agreed to set foot in there at all because he'd been assured that the first floor had a better Christmas display than he'd ever seen in his life. In fact, it took them half an hour to get even that far, because Jackie insisted they all went to the basement first so that he could try on some new shoes to replace the pair he'd just destroyed. Steve hated buying shoes. He hated having to undress in public, even a bit, and he was nothing less than mortified by having to take his shoes off. Then there was the long wait to see if the assistant could ever find a matching partner to the one he'd just tried on, while he waited in toe-curling embarrassment in his holey socks. And why, oh why do the people who work in shoe factories always go to the effort of lacing the shoes up wrong, but all the way to the top?

The best-ever Christmas display on the first floor turned out to be a lot of tat sprayed silver. Steve had tried to show some enthusiasm ('Giant inflatable Christmas tree (candles not included) anybody?'), but even Jackie only managed to find one thing to buy, a bundle of gold-painted twigs at £14.99, though it did come with a nice gold-embossed card that certified her good taste.

They eventually left RBV's, and Jackie marched them straight into VBR's. This was somewhat more fruitful, and by the time they emerged they were clutching four full bags of must-have Christmas stuff. Unfortunately, it had started to rain, which was annoying as Steve had thought originally that it looked quite bright. Mind you, he'd thought that about Tom. Jackie decided to head for the big shopping centre a couple of roads up, pointing Steve in the direction of his hairdressers so that she and the girls could have a chance to shop for girly stuff like nail varnish, hair slides and washing-up liquid.

It was quite late by the time he joined the others outside the café that he'd suggested for lunch. Jackie had wanted to go to the usual place, but Steve had been quite insistent they try this one. It wasn't perhaps the most sophisticated of eateries and its décor was nothing special, but it did offer the cheapest food poisoning in town and it was handy for the playhouse.

Being female, Jackie was biologically unable to come out of a shop without buying anything, and she had now added further shopping bags to her collection, as had the girls.

'Ooh, have you got something there for me?' Steve asked his elder daughter.

'We'll see,' said Natalie, who had already recognised that to be adult language for 'No'.

'You can have some of my fish food,' suggested Chloe.

Tempted though he was, Steve didn't want to spoil his appetite so he declined the kind offer and instead led the way inside, Jackie and the girls going off to get a table while he joined the customers already at the counter. It was a short queue but it was a slow one, because the rate-limiting hollow eyed youth in charge of the check-out had to look up every price from scratch, even though they only sold six different things. And then Steve forgot to pick up any spoons, and had to go back to the spoonery to get some.

They ate their slices of cake before trying the sandwiches, because the cake looked vaguely more edible. Steve had just finished his, and was peering into his sandwich, when the woman clearing the tables came over to ask whether they were enjoying their meals, using a tone of voice that suggested she was slightly less than interested in whether they were or not, or indeed in whether they lived or died. The food was awful, actually, but Steve and Jackie immediately and simultaneously said 'Great, thanks', because that's what you do.

The sandwiches were surprisingly filling, or at least no-one finished theirs, and the coffee was plentiful albeit nearly cold. It all made for quite a satisfying meal, only without the satisfying bit. The only positive part of the experience was that Natalie's reading was really coming on and she managed to decipher half of the graffiti in the ladies' toilets.

There was still a little time for shopping before the panto-mime, so Steve got the chance to lean patiently but somewhat forlornly against the railings outside a music shop with its window filled with copies of Prod's new CD, while Jackie and the girls inspected every single piece of cheap jewellery in the accessory shop next to the playhouse. He couldn't even remem-ber what it was they were going to see, which gives some measure of how interested he was in pantomimes. In fact, he didn't remember ever having enjoyed them, even when he was a kid. Come to that, he couldn't actually recall having been taken to one, thinking about it. In those days, entertainment largely consisted of pushing your nose against your bedroom window while you watched it rain for years on end.

The playhouse was one of those sorts of venues that put on shows starring people you only vaguely remembered from TV programmes of twenty-five years earlier that hadn't been very good. Despite that, Steve *almost* enjoyed the pantomime, except for the bit where everyone was made to stand up and sway and wave their arms about. Despite his discomfiture, he did join in, but was the first in the entire audience to sit down again, thereby winning Jackie's Christmas Killjoy award. Other than that, it was a tolerable experience, although he did somehow develop a cough during the performance. Some people cough in twos when their throats tickle, while others prefer to cough in threes. Just before the interval, Steve coughed in forty-sevens.

When it was all over, after three encores, six curtain calls and the odd standing ovation, Steve led them out into the cold dark streets, his pulse still racing (and Natalie's eyes still bulging like a barn owl with contact lenses) from the surprising enthusiasm with which the Principal Boy and the princess had kissed one another during the final scene. It had been a funny sort of a day. He'd gone into town hoping to get Christmas sorted, and all he'd managed to buy was lunch, a haircut, interval drinks and ice-creams, and an eighty-nine quid impulse purchase oil painting of a highland cow wearing a Santa hat. He was clearly going to have to make another present-buying foray or two before the twenty-fifth.

***

The weather the next morning was good, so Jackie decided that what they all needed was a good walk in the park before the annual round of Christmas gluttony got under way. There were few other people about, and Steve and Jackie plodded round on their own behind Natalie and Chloe, who had gone on ahead in pursuit of a pigeon that had flown off so fast it was leaving a vapour trail. Mostly they walked in silence, so as not to injure the quiet of the morning, but occasionally Jackie interrupted Steve's various thoughts of moss life-cycles or squirrel distemper with interspersions about organising Christmas. Pragmatic stuff, such as enquiring whether they should have the adults in the lounge for drinks, and the children in the conservatory, or vice versa, or all together? And then, after a few minutes more, asking him whether he was going to do anything about the conservatory roof panel that had slipped down in the summer to leave a gaping one-inch gap in the roof? As it happened, Steve wasn't required to provide much by the way of answers, as his wife was more than capable of supplying her own. A little further contemplation led her to the twin conclusions that the roof would probably stay leaking for a good few months longer yet, and that it would be better to have everyone together in the lounge, rather than to expect anyone to sit around a bucket, notwithstanding Steve's kind offer to put a bit of tinsel on the handle.

They got back to the house at ten past eleven, Steve feeling more calm and relaxed than he had in weeks as he unlocked the front door and checked for telephone messages while Chloe dropped a few pellets of food in for the goldfish - Scampi, Goujon and Whitebait as Jackie had now rechristened them. So it was poor timing for fate to pick that morning to leave him a message to say that his mother had tripped over her pile of medical encyclopaedias and would be in hospital for several weeks.

13

'Well, perhaps if you were prettier, it *would* be bigger.'

It hadn't been the nicest of ways to kill a relationship stone dead, and Darren regretted his words now, but what was done was done. His time with Lizzy had lasted a mere two months, which was all it had taken them to go from the every-little-thing-she-does-is-magic stage to the every-little-thing-she-does-is-irritating one. And now, it seemed, to the goodbye for ever and don't come back one. Darren Searston was a single man again.

Not that he, or anyone else in R&D at SLSL, had any time to mope, or to make the most of it, depending on your point of view; not with Christmas and the usual pre-Christmas rush coming up faster than a diver in a tank of piranhas. For Steve, things were particularly busy, what with the need to finish analysing all the latest Sling sensor performance data *plus* the long list of modifications needed to manufacture large quantities reliably *plus* the matter of using H.E.L.'s encapsulation process to protect the sensor's more delicate componentry *plus* Barry's request to move all the furniture in the office away from the windows so that they could be replaced with waterproof ones.

'It's been a long week,' he observed to Clare when she brought in the internal mail at ten o'clock.

'You wait another four days till Friday – it will have seemed even longer by then.'

Steve opened the first envelope while the secretary helped herself to one of the biscuits from Darren's snack tin. Everyone else was in one of Barry's scheduling meetings, which as usual was over-running, and she didn't seem in much of a hurry to go.

The envelope contained a strongly worded memo from Cathy Banfield, criticising Steve for not asking her permission before asking Simon to ask Dilshad Patel whether someone from the business development department could help Steve prepare the technical wording for the sales literature for the conference in Germany. (Got that?)

Sometimes Steve found himself wondering whether the accident that had put Cathy in a wheelchair had really been an accident.

'Are you planning to go to the New Year's eve party at work?' asked Clare, starting on another of Darren's digestives.

'I don't know. What day's that on then, the sixteenth of August?' Steve opened the next envelope, which contained a couple of pages of rough scribble from Barry, making a number of pertinent but semi-legible points that added up to the sum total of a reminder that Steve needed to get the project team focussed on the January launch. There was no comment on the fact that the underlying technology wasn't sorted out yet, nor that the sensor design wasn't finished. Those were presumably minor details – what seemed to matter was that their specification brochures were glossier than Senssertive's.

He was about to ask Clare whether she might help him move some of the desks away from the windows when she vanished in the direction of the cutting of somebody's birthday cake in another office, leaving him on his own for most of the rest of the morning. Jon and Neil wandered in at one point, and Steve did wonder about asking them to help, but he knew that he'd be wasting his time with two men who saw work as a spectator sport. They just hung around for a bit, loafer and loafer's apprentice, and then they ambled off in the direction of a tea break while Steve went through his e-mails. Apart from one notifying him that the Marketing Department wouldn't be using his photograph of Natalie clutching a handful of sensors for the sales leaflets, none of them were too annoying, and the rest of the morning went quite well: in a brief five minute break from his perusal of the latest magnetic field measurement results, he even won the correct change from the coffee machine.

His Monday lunchtime swimming session was not a great success, though – the more he did, the more he seemed to be wearing out – and he got back to find Barry in the middle of one of his motivational pep-talks.

'Thirty-five days to launch,' he was saying, 'and most of those are Christmas.'

Steve started to say something about a lack of help from Chris Tomkinson and the other manufacturing engineers, but only got as far as 'Er'.

'I can't tell you often enough how important this project is,' Barry cut in, though he could and he frequently did.

Steve managed an 'Um' before he was interrupted again, this time with a tirade about how variable the test results always seemed to be. Steve was slowly beginning to realise that he came somewhere below the tuna sandwiches in the great hierarchy of life. He wouldn't even be going to Germany to see the public launch of his new sensor, according to Barry: that honour was going to Lisa and Simon, plus a host of marketing and sales people. In a way, Steve was relieved not to be involved. After all, he hated flying. But on the other hand, there was an important principle at stake here: for some reason Sling was his project when it came to hassle and blame, but it was someone else's when it came to glory and exotic travel. And to make matters worse, he was fairly sure that Simon was a secret Sling non-believer. It seemed a bit unfair.

'Excuse me –,' he started to say, but Barry spoke over him yet again: this time it was a two minute rant about commitment and professionalism and not spending every weekend away from the office. He only finished when he finally felt the need to inhale again, and when he did there was complete silence, apart from his own gasps for breath and Darren's question 'Did you know you've got bits of custard in your beard?'.

Respect for one's superiors just isn't what it was.

***

Darren and Lisa found themselves alone together in the open plan office on Tuesday morning. It was never a happy combination these days, especially as Lisa was intrigued as to why Darren and Lizzy had gone their separate ways.

'Clare tells me you're a single man again.'

Darren responded by concentrating hard on not responding.

'Why did you split up, if you don't mind me asking? I thought it was going so well.'

'It was,' admitted Darren, opening up a bit. 'We'd even started to choose the Austrian blinds and voile tiebacks for the dream cottage we were going to buy together.'

'So what went wrong? Couldn't you agree on the colour of the linings?'

'Oh, ha ha. No, we had a blazing row over the photograph of her that I had on the mantelpiece.'

'You didn't photograph her in a compromising position, did you?'

'No, it wasn't that. It was just that she got mad that it was such a little photograph compared with the ones of my parents and of three of my ex-girlfriends.'

Lisa might have asked if she featured amongst them, but she was determined to keep at bay all memories of her foolish and misjudged past association. She changed the subject.

'Are you going to the marketing meeting in ten minutes?'

'Yes. Are you?'

'Well I suppose so. Somebody has to make sure the marketing claims bear some slight resemblance to what Sling can actually do, and Steve's over in the factory arguing about the assembly trials.' It's always useful when one of the characters helps to explain the plot like that.

Unfortunately, on this occasion she was wrong. Steve had left the factory and was walking slowly back with what was left of his dignity. He'd spent a very uncomfortable hour watching Anthony Archer show him the wide range of misassembled sensors, broken bits of sensors and tangled clusters of sensors that he had spent the morning manufacturing. All attempts to placate him had fallen on deaf ears, although in retrospect Steve was to concede that it hadn't helped to suggest that some of the robotic arms weren't straight. The only positive thing to come from their extended discussions was that Steve had probably lost half a stone in nervous perspiration. He'd suggested trying a couple of changes to the way the wires fed into the sensor and he'd proposed in desperation that they outsourced the difficult bits of the assembly process, but everything he said made Anthony redder and more strident: his long-held beliefs about the people in R&D weren't looking likely to change for the better any time soon. Eventual escape was only made possible by the offer of compensating the production department with some Design Specification documents plus a couple of rather nifty presentations on H.E.L.'s all-important (for Sling, anyway) Top Secret encapsulation process.

'Will you do me a favour, Darren?' pleaded Steve when he reached the sanctuary of the open plan office.

'What is it?'

'Hack me to death with your bare hands, please. I've lost the will to live.'

'I've got a teaspoon here. I could use that, if you'd like? It would probably be faster and more efficient, and make less of a mess on the carpet.'

'OK, whatever, I'm past caring.'

'Come on, Steve,' Lisa chipped in, 'don't let the pressure at work get to you.'

'Oh, it's not just work. There's a list of DIY jobs that need doing as long as my arm, there's Christmas to plan for, I've got to have Friday off to visit my mother in hospital –'

'I'm not visiting any of my relatives if they're taken ill,' said Darren quickly.

'Anyway, there's a lot to do,' Steve concluded, putting down Anthony's freakish misassembled sensor samples.

He settled down to write a report on how the trials were going. It would require some delicate wordsmithing if it wasn't going to bring Barry and John crashing down like a ton of bricks. He had already persuaded Darren to agree to proof-read it and to make any changes necessary; now he just had to get on with writing it. Slowly, and with much sighing.

In fact, it was to be more than three hours before he felt he had something ready to pass on to Darren, and Lisa was just putting her coat on to go home, when Clare came in with a bundle of Christmas cards.

'Only six days till Father Christmas comes,' the secretary announced, with possibly excessive excitement.

'He doesn't exist. There's no such thing.'

'Ooh, happy Christmas to you, too, Darren,' said Clare.

'There's no such thing as that, either.'

'Oh, for Pete's sake,' snapped Lisa. 'You're the most miserable person I've ever had the misfortune to work with.'

Darren wondered if there was a correlation between a person's miserableness and the length of time they'd worked with Lisa, but he wasn't going to wonder it out loud. He settled for rolling his eyes, instead.

'Right I'm off out to have some fun with my friends,' said Lisa, looking pointedly at Darren and leaving him muttering that fun was a rather overrated activity in his opinion and that going out was for losers. She picked up her bag and headed off into the rapidly falling outside temperatures, leaving a frosty silence around the desk where Darren was using his towering literary genius to perfect Steve's analysis of the assembly work.

Eventually, he put his pen down and stood up to leave. 'Goodnight Mr Adventure.'

'Goodnight Darren.'

Steve stayed another half hour and then closed his computer down and put his fleece jacket on. On the way to the door he picked up the Darren-modified in-depth summary report. It now comprised a single sentence. 'If the factory can ever make two the same, I'll buy Lisa Hemsley a diamond-studded flying pig.'

He switched the lights off and went home.

***

Thursday finally came, Steve's last working day before Christmas. As is so often the case, almost everyone had already melted away for the close-down period, and he was left to spend a quiet day alone with his work and his thoughts. The only time he saw another human being, unless Alex Deese counted, was at lunchtime in the canteen. That at least was a bit more lively than staring at a screenful of e-mail messages, especially since Attila was in a funny mood, taking great delight in announcing very loudly 'Cashier number one, please!' before each customer, and then giggling. It was hard not to think that the canteen might be a generally jollier place if she was allowed access to the sherry all year round.

***

Steve wasn't entirely relishing the idea of a family visit to the hospital to see his mother. Two-plus hours each way in the car together and then three more sitting round her bed while she complained about everything and everyone wasn't exactly his idea of fun. He locked the front door, got into the car, and took a deep breath. Oh well. It was going to be an unpleasant day, but at least it was an unpleasant day out.

The ward specialised in gerontology (that's the study of old people, unless that's genealogy), and the Oscrofts opened the door to be greeted by the undelightful smell of damp senior citizens. Steve's mother was sitting bolt upright in the next-to-last bed, bruised as if she had gone ten rounds with at least a light-middleweight, but otherwise looking as good as she ever did and certainly well enough to hold forth on all the other occupants of the ward. Steve hadn't even reached her bed before she was pointing at the woman lying in the bed by the window.

'She's dying,' she announced, with ill-disguised pride at having some worthy news. 'But she doesn't yet know.'

Natalie and Chloe sat down on the two bedside chairs while Steve brought another two over.

'And *she's* off with the fairies.' His mother stabbed a finger in the direction of an eighty year old woman who smiled and waved back.

'She's from a dysfunctional family. Her husband's dead –'

Well that's about as dysfunctional as you can get.

'- and her son's an alcoholic and her sister's a ...'

'And how are you?' asked Jackie, making a mental note that her mother-in-law had an identity tag attached to her left wrist, all ready for slipping into a body bag.

'Oh, I can't grumble,' she replied, launching into a long litany of moans and complaints. It was strange, but somehow, whenever anyone else was ill, she always managed to have a related but worse condition of her own. She had reached the age where every conversation, even when she wasn't in hospital, eventually came round to her symptoms or to how ill she felt. Conversely, Steve's father's chief delight had been to tell people how fit he was for his age. Until he dropped dead.

'I've been told that there's a ten per cent chance I won't make it,' the woman opposite shouted over, trying to join in with the fun.

'Oh, I wouldn't believe statistics,' replied Steve's mother, 'They're always wrong. My brother was told that there was a five per cent chance he would die during his stomach operation, and he did.'

'The girls have brought you some 'Get Well' presents,' said Steve, eager to move the conversation on.

'Happy Get Well,' said Natalie, a trifle unsure of the correct greeting.

'And this one's from me, Grandma,' said Chloe, saving time by starting to unwrap it herself.

Grandma had a cursory glance at the box of chocolates and the orange-haired party troll, and then announced that at the age of seventy-six she'd suddenly thought of having wanted to be a doctor all her life.

'Wonderful, skilled and dedicated people,' breathed Steve reverentially. (I put that bit in because even bestselling authors can become ill from time to time.)

They lapsed into silence for a bit, as hospital visitors always do when they've been there a long time and have run out of things to say. Natalie and Chloe were also getting fidgety after three minutes of sitting down, and went off to play hide and seek in the curtains drawn around one of the beds near the door.

Steve asked his mother whether anything was actually broken, and his mother said that no it wasn't, but then chuntered on for five minutes about how she'd had to wait to be x-rayed while they did someone who'd broken his leg in four places having sex.

'No, nothing's broken,' she repeated, 'but I'm shaken up.'

She didn't *seem* shaken up, but who was Steve to argue? Further mild interrogation revealed that she didn't know when they'd let her out, but that she wouldn't be available as guest of honour in the Oscroft household on Christmas Day, which she thought was just as well, as they always undercooked the sprouts and overdid the stuffing. Steve didn't know what to say. He was left walking an emotional tightrope between feeling sorry for her (which he did) and wishing that the old trout would shut up and stop moaning (which she didn't). Jackie did know what to say, though. She said that Steve would be coming over to visit her the day after Boxing Day, and that she wasn't to worry about a thing. And then they all sat more or less in silence for another two hours until they felt they could leave.

They bid their various farewells, Natalie asked the question that had been uppermost on her mind with Christmas coming up - 'If you die, can we have your snow please?' – she was always a polite girl - and they hurried out, Steve glad to be gone from a ward that looked very much like the one he'd been in for two weeks when he was ten, that time he'd misidentified a mushroom in the woods using the new book that his parents had given him for his birthday.

***

It was the twenty-third of December. For some, in touch with the earth and its place in the cosmos, it was a day of significance and hope. They were past the winter solstice. The sun was again reborn, and better days were on the way. It was a time to celebrate, and perhaps for a mild 'Yippee!'. But for Steve Oscroft it was a time for Christmas shopping. Nay, it was the *only* time he could do any Christmas shopping, as he'd left everything to the last minute because he'd been so busy.

Christmas had yet again taken him completely unawares. One minute it had been mid-February, and the next it was late-December. It seemed to have gone from one dull grey British winter to the next without bothering with summer.

He started in the large hardware shop at the top of the town. It wasn't necessarily the most obvious place for buying family Christmas presents, but looking at hacksaws and cupboard hinges and sandpaper broke him in gently for the difficult, serious stuff like having to make big decisions about dressing gowns and scented candles. In any case, he needed some light bulbs.

Less than an hour later, he had torn himself away from the exciting display of plumbing fittings and was standing –for once – in the shortest check-out queue. All the other queues had at least five people in them, but there were only two in Steve's, and the middle-aged woman immediately in front of him was only buying an earthenware plant pot. It wasn't often he felt smug – he rarely had anything to feel smug about – so he made the most of it until the woman started to fish out the twenty-seven items she had tucked inside the plant pot. And life was thoroughly back to normal when she started to hunt about for small change, having stood watching the sales assistant put every purchase into separate bags at her insistence.

And then it was time for some serious, desperate shopping. Clothes shops, toy shops, book shops, department stores, music shops, and – by mistake – one adult goods emporium. Like all Steve's shopping trips, it was hard work. He wasn't very good in shops. Normally when he went with Jackie he liked to wait outside, as he was allergic to the sight of his money being spent. And buying for other people was so difficult and so uninteresting. Whatever he bought Jackie was doomed to failure, for a start. She still went on about that 'Disgraced Politicians' thirty-two piece novelty table mat and coaster set that she'd once had for her birthday. And today it was stuff for her that he chiefly needed: she had given up on expecting him to help with buying much for the girls. The battery operated chocolate fountain had put paid to that.

The whole process took him another six hours, only two of which were spent browsing for things for himself. The rest of the time was spent adding to the collection of panic purchases he was accumulating. Some of them he agonised over, in a bid to get exactly the right thing. Some he just grabbed off the shelf, in the hope that raw impulse made for good judgment. And as usual, it didn't matter whether he chose the one at the front, the one at the back, or any one from the middle: he always ended up with the broken one. And throughout the entire afternoon, wherever he went, Prod's big hit *Broken off an' cryin'* was playing at him, sounding for all the world like a horse race commentary set to a hyperactive drum machine, but apparently popular with young people.

He got home to discover that, yet again, he'd bought screw-in bulbs instead of bayonet ones. He put them in the cupboard with all the others and went to make himself a mug of coffee. While he was in the kitchen, he remembered that he had been meant to buy a replacement for the vase that Natalie and Chloe had managed to break during high-fiving practice the week before. It was pretty much irreplaceable, as it had been one of Jackie's favourite ornaments and her last present from her late aunt Ann, but Steve had been told to try anyway. His failure was going to provide another pre-ordained source of stress when it came to present opening time on Christmas day.

There was, though, a costume drama just starting on television, followed by a big Christmas dance show. That was good: costume dramas and dance shows were by far Steve's favourite programmes. Not because he had the remotest interest in watching either of them, but because they gave him the odd hour or two when the rest of the family retreated into the lounge and he could get on with some chosen activity in peace, such as unblocking the kitchen sink. Or, in this case, finding the Christmas decorations.

Actually, the decorations were easy to track down because they were in his father's old trunk in the attic, but the key to the trunk was more of a problem. He knew where that was, too, as it happened, because it was somewhere amongst the two inch thick layer of old keys in the bottom of a drawer in the spare room. The missing trick was knowing which key it was, and Steve spent a happy hour trying several dozen of them before he found the right one. On the way he came across an interesting old postcard of an airport departure lounge where he and Jackie had once spent a holiday back in the days before the girls were born. And in the trunk, along with the plastic Christmas tree and broken baubles, was a shoe box filled with sentimental odds and ends. A few photographs, an invitation to a dinner and disco of long ago, a broken torch, and the remains of a tube of cream that he'd once had for an interesting skin infection.

He emerged from the attic in the middle of an advert break and a lot of commotion.

'Mum, Mum, Natalie's telling tales, Mum!' Chloe was shouting from the lounge.

'It's her fault!' Natalie shouted back from the dining room.

'Ladies, ladies –' Steve started to say, but couldn't think of what to follow it by, so shut up.

'I don't know what you've been up to, but I can't see much evidence of decorations,' Jackie said, rounding on the peace keeper in the traditional manner. For some reason, this confession of her own ignorance and visual failings wasn't preventing her from sounding annoyed with him, rather than with herself.

'This is all that's left,' said Steve, holding up the bent plastic tree and a bag containing the remains of the trimmings. He noticed that both were wet with condensation: it had been much colder in the attic than he'd realised. Jackie was just about to peer in at Steve's little collection of faded decorations, when fate dealt him a double blessing. The phone rang, and Jackie being the one free of plastic pine needles and what might have been a coating of mouse droppings, she scuttled off to answer it and to hear the news that Steve's mother had been discharged from hospital into the care of Mrs Collins at number six and her home-baking. On whose say-so wasn't apparent, but it was made very clear that she didn't want any relatives to visit her and set back her recovery, at least until the New Year. The visit planned for the day after Boxing Day was off: blessing numero uno. And blessing numero duo was that Steve had ten minutes while Jackie was on the phone to try to do something about the indelible green stain that had dripped onto the carpet where the condensation had caused the dye in the Christmas tree to run.

***

Christmas Day nearly got off to a bad start. When Jackie went downstairs to check that Santa had left the presents in a separate pile for each girl, as she'd instructed him the night before, she noticed that little Goujon seemed to have stalled half way through looping the loop, his fins drooping by his side. Luckily, even a child as animal-mad as Chloe can be diverted by presents on Christmas Day, so Jackie reasoned that she probably had at least twenty-four hours to come up with a story.

Her battle plan for the day had been deceptively simple. The girls would come down, unwrap their presents from Santa and from Mum and Dad, and then have a short fight and tears over something or other. Then they'd all have breakfast and get dressed. Steve would help her to cook the dinner, Diane would arrive two hours early and drain all the sherry, and they'd sit down to Christmas dinner as soon as Diane's husband Tony and Uncle Dennis turned up from the pub. Then after dinner they'd wash up, listen to Her Maj, open the presents from everyone else, play a disappointing board game, make tea, eat tea, put a DVD on for the girls, prise their visitors out, wash up and eventually stagger off to bed, their stomachs reeling under the weight of two boxes of chocolates each. It was a well-rehearsed routine, and Jackie had been steeling herself for it for weeks.

Bits of it went according to her master plan, and bits didn't. On the whole, Natalie and Chloe were very pleased with their presents and got nearly everything they wanted, plus one or two things they didn't. Although the ark wasn't finished, the girls were given what Steve had done so far. Chloe got the keel and Natalie got part of the hull. They also got one present to share, which was a puppy, although neither girl got to keep it, or even meet it, because they'd been bought sponsorship of it rather than the actual living, breathing thing itself. Steve and Jackie had debated for some while about what sort of puppy to sponsor, as Jackie had suggested a guide dog for the blind or a hearing dog for the deaf, whereas Steve had kept making silly suggestions along the lines of a licking dog for the tasteless or a thinking dog for the thick. In the end, after exercising her female prerogative, Jackie had decided on sponsorship of a trainee guide dog, and according to the literature pack its name was, curiously, Steve.

'I hope it's more use than you are,' she joked.

Because it was a special day, they went through into the lounge with their breakfast, and ate it from their knees while sitting bent double in front of a television cartoon about a family of disabled reindeers. Steve soon lost interest, though, and tried to count the Christmas cards arranged all round the room. As far as he could make out, though he never got the same answer twice, Natalie had had fifty-seven, Chloe had had thirty-three, and Jackie had had seventy-one. There had also been seven cards for Osmarelda Oscroft and four for Steve Oscroft. Three of his were from SLSL's suppliers, eager for business, and one from a confused customer. He also had a part-share in three postcards, all from Nick and Wendy and sent to prove that they could afford the most expensive of island retreats for their exotic midwinter holidays. Finally, in pride of place, addressed to the whole family, was a large and ornate card from Frenzy at the zoo, asking for another year's sponsorship money.

Perhaps if he'd carried through last year's threat to have the house named 'Freepost' he'd have had more cards, but at least the poor showing would save him some time, as he always felt he should reply to every card he got, even those from the garage and the butcher. Thinking about it, *they'd* both forgotten him this year, too.

After breakfast, Steve cleared the things away while Jackie started preparing the vegetables. She was interrupted three sprouts in by a phone call from Angela. Steve thought for one awful moment that she was trying to invite herself round as she sometimes did on his birthdays, but after a reassuringly quick twenty minutes he heard Jackie announce that she had to go because she had some presents to stuff and a turkey to wrap.

Although they were only doing one cooked meal for a total of seven people, they both seemed to have a never-ending number of things to do. By the time Diane arrived, followed within moments by Tony and Uncle Dennis, the prospect of actually eating anything they'd been cooking was rapidly losing appeal. Steve was quite ready to have an entirely liquid lunch, supplemented with the annual charade of pulling the crackers and throwing the cheap rubbish inside them straight into the bin.

As soon as they'd eaten, Natalie's great uncle made a speech about Christmas being a time for indulging yourself in your hobbies, which in his case happened to be watching football on telly, watching any other sport on telly, and interrupting people. And with that he went off to the lounge to see if anything might be on that was worth sitting in front of, leaving Jackie to wash up while Tony and Diane dried and Steve put away.

'Where does this bowl go?'

'Oh, that lives in the dining room,' said Jackie. 'And you can put the goldfish back in it now.' There was a short pause, and then she added 'Actually, you don't need to put Goujon back. Just the other two.'

***

At twenty past three, they all settled down for an after-lunch game of Hunt Mum's Contact Lens, and then it was presents time. Uncle Dennis presented Natalie some sort of a disappoint-ment-on-a-stick and Chloe some sort of disappointment-in-a-box. Steve got one of those rear bumper dangly things that touches the road to prevent static shocks from the furry dice that he'd had for his birthday. Tony got a six-pack of lager. Neither of his nieces got anything, because he'd forgotten. It was par for the course for Uncle Dennis. At least it was better than the year when he'd given Steve and Jackie a presentation boxed set of live surgical leeches.

Diane and Tony handed their presents out next. Diane had bought her sister some sort of a coffee table book and her uncle something that he didn't bother to open. Natalie and Chloe each got an identical parcel containing three cuddly toys (kittens for Natalie; puppies for Chloe), and Steve got a brown cardboard box, on the front of which was nothing but a large Union Jack. Cautiously, he turned the box over to look for clues. On the back was a small sticker that read 'Sold in Britain. Made in China.' Inside was some sort of a gadget, although Tony, who had bought it, was unsure exactly what it did, except that it had 'the capability to interface to the internet, so that you can download stuff, like viruses'.

'How did you get on with that crossword book we gave you last year?' asked Diane.

'It's got pride of place, on top of my To Do list.'

'Steven!' exclaimed Jackie, getting his name wrong in the way that parents and spouses do when they want to demonstrate something or other.

He would have said something in his defence, but was saved the effort by the timely intervention of Chloe who brought over a glossy pamphlet for his perusal. It seems that these days even cuddly toys come with an instruction manual and safety notes.

Jackie went to get the presents she'd bought people, while Steve went to put the kettle on. He came back just in time to be presented with a couple of hideous ornaments that would need dusting for the rest of for ever, while Diane got a cheque towards the cost of her brand new water-saving cistern, which had seven different programmes so that you could choose a flush to suit your mood and your needs. Tony got a couple of nice malt whiskies, and her uncle got what he'd asked for: a five-disk collection of highlights from the Saturday football scores from the post-war era.

After he'd finished making the coffees, Steve brought in the hastily wrapped flashes of inspiration that he'd bought for his wife two days previously. Now by and large (whatever that means), the best Christmas presents don't require any application of the questions 'What is it?' or 'What's it for?', nor are they greeted with the comment 'Interesting'. However, in the case of Steve's purchases...

'Interesting,' said Jackie, staring at the mango stoner.

'What does this bit do?' asked Jackie, pointing at one end of the spring-operated pillowcase inverter.

'What an original idea,' muttered Jackie, turning the wall-mounted hairbrush stand over and over.

'Crikey,' said Jackie, holding up something that even Steve had forgotten the identity of.

Steve was then given a nice tie by a small daughtery person and a nice pair of socks by a second, slightly larger, daughtery person. The socks had a picture of a bald old man on them, but it was the thought that counted. They weren't the perfect present, but they were very close to it: they were small, and they took up none of his non-existent time. He didn't have to read them, learn how to use them, play with them, or find much storage space for them.

Natalie's presents to Chloe were a clay modelling set (supplied by Jackie) and a beautifully hand-crafted book of Natalie's drawings of extinct animals. For some reason they all, from dodo to dinosaur, had similar faces, with an expression best described as 'concussed rabbit'. On the positive side, though, Natalie was nothing if not forward thinking, and had provided drawings of a tiger, lion, gorilla, orang-utan and, for some reason, cat, amongst her collection of curtailed inhabitants of planet earth. All that was needed now was for someone to attempt to translate her vowel-deficient captions into English. 'Grlr' was probably gorilla, and a 'dinsre' was probably a dinosaur, but what on earth was a 'ybtrl' or a 'wrrop'?

By now, there was wrapping paper everywhere and Steve was completely confused as to who had given what to whom.

Jackie was still exploring out loud the possible identity of her mystery present, Natalie was admiring the giant bar of chocolate that her sister had just given her, and Chloe was going round the room carefully peering into the bottom of each piece of wrapping paper in the hope of finding a present she'd missed. There was one small unopened package underneath the Christmas tree, clearly addressed to all the family in Angela's unmistakeable scrawl. The little 'something to share' was whisked away out of sight, though, the moment it turned out to be a family size tube of thong chafe cream.

Having opened everything, it was now time to test some of the new presents to destruction. First up was Natalie's dance console, a newfangled triumph of design over function that required sixteen various batteries of five different denominations, none of which they had except in other pieces of equipment.

'Please can you get this working?' requested Natalie, waving its microphone at Jackie.

'Dad will do it for you in a minute,' promised Jackie, demonstrating once again her incredible powers of prediction and premonition.

In fact, it took twenty-five minutes of effort, trial and error, and involved the raiding of all three smoke detectors, before Steve had it fully battered up and ready to go. The instructions had been printed in tiny dark grey text on pale grey recycled toilet paper to save the environment (and money), and were written in most of the world's six thousand languages, although not apparently in English. Oh, hang on, there it was, between Yurdoe and Eastern Splinach. It might have been easier to follow if the instructions didn't cycle between every language for each paragraph. And Steve couldn't help noticing that the 'English' was somewhat American: more gray on gray than grey on grey.

Even when it had its batteries, it took quite a time to make Natalie's present actually do anything, as the instructions were slightly less edifying than the small print on a credit card agreement, but after another twenty minutes Steve found what he needed, near the bottom of page three thousand four hundred and sixty-two: 'When wanting dancy fast starting, sliding starty upwards outings please.' Hey presto, although he'd not got it working, he'd at least got the console to light up, which was some consolation.

Before Natalie had had a chance to do more with her new toy than admire the fact it was now lit up, Jackie called everyone through to the dining room for tea. It consisted of a spread of sandwiches, cakes and trifle, followed by fresh strawberries picked with Jackie's own fair hands, off the shelves at the supermarket. It would have been one of the best feasts that Steve had ever seen, had there been a wider choice of sandwiches than turkey and sprouts. It was possible that Natalie was also thinking along similar lines, for as soon as she'd opened them all and surveyed what was inside them she announced that her toothache had magically come back.

'Here, have some trifle then,' said Steve, who could be pathetically easily taken in where his daughters were concerned.

'It does look particularly delicious,' he added, earning for his troubles a dark look from Jackie who had cooked, made, washed or otherwise prepared every item on the table except for the trifle.

Neither girl required much persuasion, and long before the first sandwich had congealed onto his taste buds, the dish of trifle was sporting two gaping wounds.

'Don't eat like a Hannah, dear,' Jackie admonished her elder child. Natalie understood the reference, even if you don't.

'These chocolate cakes are very nice,' said Diane, who had also started at the wrong end of the meal.

'Yes, they are,' agreed her uncle. 'I wouldn't mind a few more of these.' He grinned widely enough to show the sticky remains of the previous three smeared across his molars.

'Could you get me another spoon please Mum?' asked Natalie, looking forlornly at the spot on the carpet where the first one was now lying.

'Yes, and me,' added her sister.

Jackie quickly counted her limbs, just to be sure that she hadn't suddenly grown an extra pair of arms.

'Are there any more of the biscuits?' asked Tony, waving an empty plate in his sister in law's direction.

'Give me a minute, please! It's like working in a blasted soup kitchen here!' snapped Jackie. 'When the Twist family come in.'

Steve, vaguely aware that his wife was losing her usual calm composure, manfully decided to take charge of the situation after tea, and went off to entertain the girls and the male guests in the lounge, to give Jackie some quality time alone with her sister. Jackie's facial expression would not have been interpreted as gratitude by many dispassionate observers, but Steve didn't notice it anyway, as he was distracted by Chloe who was showing him her favourite Christmas present, a little misshapen knick-knack that had come from a cracker.

'Could you clear all the debris from the lounge floor, please, before you sit down?' Jackie shouted after him from the sink, but Uncle Dennis had already started to tell one of his tales about Christmases gone by, and she didn't get much of a reply, unless you counted what sounded like 'Glup'.

Unfortunately, Natalie and Chloe were not very interested in Dennis's long reminiscence about the Christmas when he'd almost died of nearly-but-not spontaneous human combustion, that time when he'd breathed over a candle after an evening spent downing whiskies. He put his survival down entirely to the single glass of wine he'd had mid-evening, and had sworn ever since that it was only the antioxidants in the grapes that had prevented him being completely turned to ash. Although a heart-warming story (literally, the way Uncle Dennis told it), its plausibility was not enhanced by each annual re-telling, and Steve soon grew impatient for his uncle in law to reach the final bit where the firemen all kicked his chest to put the last of the flames out. By nine o'clock the girls were asking to be allowed to go to bed, a request that somewhat backfired when Dennis offered to go up and tell them a goodnight story. While he was doing that, and while Tony was visiting the kitchen to see if anything needed doing, Steve took off his shoes and collapsed in front of the television, weak from the long battle to keep the central heating turned down.

Being Christmas, the TV schedules had for weeks been divided more or less evenly between adverts for chocolates and adverts for anti-ageing creams. Steve switched the television off again and casually picked up the coffee table book that Jackie had been given by her sister, a beautiful glossy work filled with informative chapters about activities that mainly appeal to women, such as cooking, ironing, sewing and listening. He was just wondering with some concern whether Jackie would ever try out the recipe for buttered kelp, when there was a commotion in the hall and he realised that their three guests were leaving. He stumbled to his feet so that he wouldn't deprive himself of the chance to make sure that they really had gone, and then he spent fifteen minutes shivering on the doorstep while Diane de-iced her car and Dennis waited for his pre-booked taxi.

Once they'd gone, it was time for that most traditional of all family Christmas traditions, the marital row. It started with a cat; never thought it would come to that, but in no time at all Steve and Jackie were fighting in the playground, or whatever the adult equivalent was. Steve had gone into the back garden to throw out the remains of the turkey for the birds. Yes, it seems a bit cannibalistic, but that's what he did. By chance, Poddle was sitting on the fence, avoiding the Christmas specials on television, and saw his moment to finally make his first kill and prove himself as a hunter. He pounced, but was too slow for the turkey, which rolled into the rose bushes. Feeling a little foolish, as cats can be inclined to, he pretended that he'd just been running towards Steve, and he proceeded to ingratiate himself by wrapping his tail round his leg. It worked, for he got stroked and he got to follow him into the lounge and settle on the sofa in front of the gas fire, where Steve sat and fussed over him.

'Have you put all the wrapping paper in the dustbin like I asked you to?' asked Jackie, poking her head round the lounge door.

'Not yet. I forgot.'

That was clearly not an excusable excuse in Jackie's eyes. 'It must have been tough sitting in front of the TV while I relaxed at the sink all evening.'

Steve started to say that he hadn't been sitting down for more than fifteen minutes, but it fell on deaf ears.

'I only asked you to do one job, while I've been slaving away here, hour after hour –'

'Right, so you've done two hours –,' said Steve, most unadvisedly.

'Am I to suppose,' asked Jackie in a tone of voice that led Steve to conclude that she already had, 'that you've gone on some sort of a strike?'

'It's Christmas. I was just enjoying putting my feet up for once. I was feeling quite relaxed.'

'Well I'm glad *you're* happy.'

Strangely, she didn't sound glad. In fact, he'd not seen her look so cross since the day that he'd accidentally coppiced her prize yukka back in the spring. Thinking that perhaps discretion was the better part of whatever it is, he followed her through into the kitchen where the washing up was stacked in a clean but sudsy pile, waiting to be dried and put away.

'These might do with a bit of a rinse,' he said, holding up a couple of side plates. He'd meant it to come over as teasing humour – more or less – but he'd miscalculated the mood that the day had left his wife in.

'You are such a ruddy perfectionist! What gives you the right to continuously criticise me?'

'Continually,' corrected Steve. 'Oh, and you split your infinitive.' Even as he said it, he knew that he'd gone too far, but there's something in the human psyche that means we can't quite stop ourselves, can we?[1] Jackie stormed off to bed, slamming the kitchen door behind her twice, once quite loudly, and then once more quietly so as not to wake the children. After she'd gone, Steve sat for a long time on one of the kitchen chairs, staring at the ever-changing colours of the fibre-optic tree on the work surface. He questioned how Christmas had yet again ended in a row. He questioned how all his best efforts and all his good intentions always seemed to leave him surrounded by people with grievances against him. He wondered where it had all gone wrong. He wondered why smoke was beginning to come from the base of the fibre-optic tree.

***

'Come upstairs, quickly, it's beautiful!' Natalie called out, on Boxing Day morning.

'Is it the sunrise?' asked Steve.

'Or is it another woodlouse?' Jackie shouted up the stairs.

Actually, for once Steve was right, but then he'd already seen the red-lined clouds. Bad weather was on the way. By the end of breakfast time the wind was getting up, by the time Steve had managed to help Chloe get her new troll hospital set out of all its eco-wrapping the sky was battleship grey, and by the time he'd reprogrammed Natalie's dance console so that it didn't crash passing milk floats, the rain was lashing down.

'Let's play with the new maths game, girls,' said their father, trying not to worry about what was happening outside. When he'd been young, he had used to love listening to the wind howling round, but everything had changed the minute he'd owned his own ridge tiles.

Natalie started to say that she didn't want to play at solving equations just at that moment, but she was interrupted by the sound of next door's wind chimes as they flew over the fence and smashed against the kitchen window.

'OK then,' said Steve, 'I'll go and get it.'

---

[1] Oh, is that not universal, then?

He went upstairs, ostensibly to find the game, but actually to look nervously out of the window to see how much the trees and lamp-posts were swaying. It really was a vile day: angry clouds were racing across the sky, heavy rain was peening against the windows[1], and the whole house shook and creaked and groaned more than Steve did on those occasions when he overdid the drink. Worst of all, the remains of next door's wind chimes weren't the only things swirling round the garden and threatening to come through a window: numerous other artefacts were starting to wander. There was nothing else for it: Steve was going to have to go outside and gather everything up into the garage or the shed. Or perhaps into the shed and then put *that* inside the garage.

Grabbing a waterproof coat that clearly wasn't, he went out into the back garden under skies that were hurling down enough liquid to test the professionalism of coat manufacturers and dam builders alike. With the sort of super-human effort that used to feature in 1950's films about the war at sea, and probably beyond anything Uncle Dennis had ever been called upon to do upon the oceans, he managed to collect together all the loose objects that might blow about and cause damage, such as some of the lighter paving slabs. Then he went in, and unable to think of a way of stopping the house blowing down, he drew all the curtains and switched the television up loud and tried not to hear the storm. And that's how they spent the rest of Boxing Day – with the TV turned right up and the curtains closed. Steve being Steve, he didn't really watch the documentary on the aerodynamics of reindeer or The Top 500 Celebrities of The Year Show of course, as he'd sneaked some work papers into the pile of newspaper supplements that he was pretending to browse.

The next morning, and with much trepidation and after two prods from Jackie, he went out to assess the damage. Things weren't too bad at the front, although the car had become festooned with bits of Christmas wrapping paper and the carcass of

---

[1] No, it really does say peening: go and look it up.

a turkey, but the back garden was a mess. The chimney pot was missing and several tiles had come off, one of them chopping in two Steve's new sapling and another punching a hole in the shed door. Yet somehow neither of the rotting pigeons lying on the roof nor a single strand of the ivy on the back of the house had shifted an inch.

The rest of the year, such as it was, was spent phoning builders, waiting for builders who didn't turn up, and eventually paying for different builders who did turn up but who spent most of the day making mobile phone calls, going to the builders' merchants to buy specialist equipment like hammers, or sitting eating sandwiches in their van. But everyone has got stories like that, so you don't need one here.

A couple of weeks later, Steve and Barry each received a three-line e-mail saying that H.E.L. were pulling out of the collaboration negotiations because their managing director had just done a deal to swap the company for a small lake in Wisconsin.

Sorry, that last chapter was rather cruel if Mummy or Daddy was reading you a chapter a night at bedtime. I promise there will be more tonight.

***

'It seems that H.E.L. have been sold to an American company, and they won't let us have access to their encapsulation technology any more,' said Barry when he came off the phone.

'Oh dear,' said Darren, with his usual profound gift for upbeat eloquence.

'It's worse than that,' said Barry. 'The same company has also bought Senssertive, which is why they've frozen us out.'

'Oh dear,' said Lisa.

'Who are the American company?' asked Steve, hopeful of a vestige of good news somewhere in this tale.

'Well...,' said Barry, turning to look him straight in the eye, 'Remember Beauchild International? The company that you were meant to sell half a million sensors to, but that you ended up killing our merger with?'

Steve nodded the nod of a condemned man.

'So now they've got the sensors, the component protection technology, and the market demand to allow them to invest in some serious development.'

Steve studied his feet.

'And we've got you lot, and a new sensor that doesn't work properly that we're launching in Germany on Monday,' Barry said, with a harsh touch of honesty that Steve felt unnecessary.

'So I think we need to do a little bit of thinking, don't you?'

Steve was trying very hard to think, right at that moment, but not a lot was happening.

'Don't worry, I'll be here to support and lead and inspire you, every step of the way,' said Barry, picking up his laptop and leaving the meeting room.

'Well,' said Darren, when they'd all had quite enough of the silence, 'in the words of Chaucer, this is another fine mess we're in.'

'Are you sure Chaucer said that?' asked Lisa.

'Chaucer in Accounts did, yes.'

'We should never have gone to Hindsight,' Simon rued, ruefully.

'It seemed a good idea at the time,' Darren said.

'All ideas seem to be good ideas at the time,' Lisa pointed out. 'Well, apart from the time that I thought you might be worth going out with.' She shuddered at the memory.

'So what are we going to do?' asked Steve.

'We could go back to the composite halide approach,' suggested Simon.

'The one that Steve gave away?'

'Well it doesn't stop us using it,' Steve pointed out.

'No, but the fact it doesn't work might.'

They had another silence.

'It's always darkest just before dawn,' said Steve.

That might or might not be true. Its scientific basis is unclear (at least to the author), but let's take it on trust for now. What does seem to be abundantly clear, though, is that the fact that it's darkest before dawn is not much of a basis in which to place your trust when your project's in freefall and you haven't a clue what to do. Still, any port in a storm, to throw another metaphor into the teacup.

'Let's buy a paddle,' said Darren. 'We'll still be where we are, of course, but at least we'll be where we are but with a paddle.'

'Look,' said Lisa, trying to inject a bit of positivity into things, 'we can either sit here and say unhelpful things while we wait for someone to just happen to come to us with the right technology to solve all our problems, or we can go out and do something about it ourselves before we're put out of business by the competition.'

Darren's vote was for sitting and waiting, and for perhaps having a few biscuits, but for once he didn't express his thoughts aloud.

'I think it's time to bring in the consultants,' murmured Simon. 'Find some internationally renowned engineers, or something.'

'Don't we have suitable engineers of our own? Aren't we good enough to solve this?' Steve tried to sound convincing, but even the office cactus looked a little unsure.

Darren looked thoughtful. 'There are people in our French office who hate me, which I think makes me internationally renowned.'

'Right, we're going to see if Barry's willing to relax his consultancy ban,' stated Lisa, taking firm charge of the situation. 'And we all need to go on the internet and see who we can find who might help us.'

'I've got to go to another meeting,' said Darren.

'Yes, and me,' said Simon. It was noticeable how everyone shuffled away from a project in trouble.

'But I'll give you a hand when I get back,' said Darren, somewhat to the surprise of Lisa who thought that her ears might be playing up.

'I'd better go and talk to Barry,' Steve volunteered.

'OK, then, that's a plan,' said Lisa, following the others out of the room.

It was a plan, but that didn't hide the fact that the situation was as depressing as one of Barry's motivational chats.

***

Barry proved surprisingly easy to persuade to overturn the embargo on using consultants. His principal comment to Steve was a request that they find an academic willing to do free consultancy before they resorted to anyone who might charge them money. He also asked to be involved in the decision-making process, because meetings like that were always more fun than real work. Besides, he knew the sorts of decisions he was likely to get out of Steve and Darren if he left them unsupervised.

Steve was not exactly ecstatic about going to the world of academia for advice. One of the most important things his student days had taught him – apart from the fact that too much beer hurts – was that academics are a bunch of fragile-ego'd prima donnas. He would never admit it to himself of course, but his feelings on the subject were tinged by a slight bitterness that although he'd done quite well at university, he wasn't bright enough to become an academic so instead he'd had to go into industry and earn twice the salary. It had left him feeling intellectually inadequate ever since.

When he got back to his desk, he found Darren in the process of sequentially reading out a list of possible consultants. (Well, reading them out simultaneously wasn't going to work, was it?) It was a bit of a pointless process, as no-one else – which at the moment was only Lisa – was listening, so to liven things up he'd been reading them out in silly voices and strange accents. He stopped and looked up when he saw Steve.

'We all had an e-mail from John Stokes ten minutes ago,' he said. 'I wonder –,' he stroked his chin, '- which is worse: when he's ballistic, or when he's incandescent?'

Steve felt his stomach knot as Darren continued. 'It's alright. I've reassured him. I sent him a reply to say that we're ninety-five per cent certain we'll identify a satisfactory solution, and a hundred per cent certain we'll identify a scapegoat for when the solution doesn't work.' Pleased with his humour, he gave a few unmanly sniggers and turned back to the list of consultants on his computer screen.

Steve ran his hands through his thinning thatch. It was going to take a long time to choose the right person, and he didn't really know where to begin. He was ignoring Darren's suggestion that they get someone in to advise them how to pick someone, but after that he drew a bit of a blank. Choosing where to go first wasn't straightforward. Just about every university in the country claimed to have relevant expertise.

Luckily, though, Steve had his boss's wise counsel to guide him. Barry's first thought was to try Oxford or Cambridge, on the basis that they always seemed to do very well in the boat race. Having narrowed it to two, he then suggested they visit Cambridge first, on the grounds that they'd clearly been ahead of Oxford in the technology race since the days when the River Cam had had a bridge and the River Ox had still had a ford. Having decided that, he changed his mind and recommended that they should start instead with a certain university more noted for its prowess at swimming, on the rugby field, and at jumping up and down on the spot. Steve was left with the job of making an appointment for the next day.

***

Steve opened the curtains early the next morning to be greeted by a wintry scene that he hadn't expected when he'd agreed to Barry's last-minute plans. A warm westerly air mass and an icy north-easterly one had spent the night fighting for the airspace above his property, with the result that there was now a three inch layer of snow covering everything except for the roof, where the precious escaping heat had kept it at bay. He switched on his mobile phone, with the thought of giving Barry a ring to see whether the trip was still on, but he already had a text message from his boss suggesting that they meet at work half an hour earlier than they'd originally agreed but that he wouldn't be joining them. It would just be Steve, Darren and Lisa. Forgoing any breakfast other than a cold mince pie and a swig of scalding coffee, he grabbed his briefcase plus a thick coat in case he got stuck in the snow, plus a shovel in case he *really* got stuck in the snow. And then he set off to work through the swirling, dancing flakes.

He'd only driven a couple of miles when he realised that the snow was getting much lighter. It was always like that with the extremes of British weather: never extreme enough to be exciting. The rain was never heavy enough; the fog was never foggy enough; and now the blizzard wasn't arctic enough. In fact, by the time he reached the car park at work, he was beginning to feel embarrassed about the shovel and the snow-chains in the boot. Perhaps it was a deliberate response by the weather gods to his provocative over-precautions, but there was only a quarter of an inch of snow on the ground anywhere on the rest of the journey, though the ensuing traffic snarl-ups still cost them an extra hour and a half. Their late arrival didn't matter too much, however, as Professor Smith, the self-proclaimed protective coatings expert, hadn't arrived yet because his car was stuck in a queue that stretched back to Belgium.

Instead they were ushered into a cramped office by a man who introduced himself as Dr Porter, another member of the academic staff in the same research group.

'Why don't we talk over an early lunch?' he suggested as soon as they'd all introduced themselves, a glint in his eye hinting that he knew an opportunity to dine at someone else's expense when he saw one.

The upmarket Italian restaurant that he recommended was very nice, but then Steve hadn't yet seen the prices. Without a good working knowledge of Italian, the menu was well-nigh useless as far as he was concerned. He couldn't even find words that he knew like 'pizza' and 'pasta', which are the Italian words for pizza and pasta. Strangely, when it came to ordering, none of the others had any problems, and they even spoke so fluently and quickly that any attempt to simply copy the noises they made was ruled out. Shamefaced, Steve had to ask the waiter what he recommended.

'The chippy next door,' quipped Dr Porter, in a voice tinged with academic superiority.

The waiter waved the menu at Steve, made a small speech in his mother-tongue, and scribbled something heavily on his pad.

'Now, what's the challenge?' asked Dr Porter, taking a generous sip at the large glass of red wine that had somehow appeared at his elbow.

'Well, we make sensors,' said Steve, a little warily. 'And we're always striving to improve their performance so that they detect ever-smaller quantities of heat, electricity, chemicals, acoustic signals or whatever.'

He looked up, to see what sort of response he was getting so far. It wasn't good; the academic was busy flagging down one of the waiters, who came scurrying over with an equally large glass of white wine.

'Yes, but what's the problem? I'm not interested in all the guff that's going OK. I mean, you don't call the plumber in to look at the bits of pipe that aren't leaking, do you?'

'It's the coating we put on to seal the sensors and protect them from the environment,' said Lisa, sensing that it was time for reinforcements.

'Ah, that mean old devil, the environment,' sighed Dr Porter, taking a swig of the white. 'It's always so unfriendly, so environmentally unfriendly.'

He sat back in his chair, the better his own brilliance to admire. Steve's eyes met Darren's. As funny lines went, it hadn't been very funny. The man was obviously devoid of any real humour. Very much like large chunks of this book in fact.

'We need to find a way to protect our new sensors, without isolating them from what they're trying to measure,' explained Lisa, trying a new tack.

'Well now.' He took another sip of vintage Chianti. 'Let's think big. The sky's our oyster!'

To emphasise the point, he slipped a shellfish into his mouth. For some reason, his starter had been served thirty seconds after he'd ordered it, and forty-five minutes before anybody else's would be. He produced a silver pen with an extravagant flourish, and proceeded to scribble a series of random words on his serviette. When he'd finished, he turned it round for the Sense Less engineers to read while he savoured the rest of his oysters.

'Is that it?' asked Lisa.

'Erm yes, for now. I've run out of buzzwords,' admitted the consultant.

Lisa pushed the serviette towards Steve, and after a quick glance Steve pushed it on towards Darren. It was about as helpful as the passport office and its 24/7 advice line that advises you to phone back during normal office hours[1].

'I know what you're thinking,' said Dr Porter. 'How can anyone with so much experience look so young? Well, actually I'm ninety-three, it's just that I've had ever such an easy life.'

He chuckled slightly, and then hiccupped.

'So what sort of protective coating would you recommend?' asked Steve, who was beginning to get both exasperated and hungry but was determined to try to salvage something from the day.

'Oh, I've no idea. If you want precise, specific information, then Professor Smith's your man. I don't get involved in the trivial little technical details. I like to look at the overall problem holistically.'

'I thought you weren't interested in all the background stuff?' pointed out Steve, now fully exasperated.

Dr Porter frowned and stroked his six inch wide parting thoughtfully.

'This is a single step on a long journey,' he said, his mouth full of smoked salmon.

'You mean, it won't really help us much?' asked Darren.

'Let me go and play with some sensors in the lab,' the consultant volunteered, 'and then we can meet again one lunchtime next week.'

Steve tried again to press him for something that might be more immediately helpful, but keeping the irritating little man's attention off his avocado or his desert wine or his caviar cheesecake proved an impossible task, and eventually Steve gave up and sat quietly waiting for his starter.

---

[1] You might not be surprised to know that I didn't make that one up.

In fact, nothing was gained from the meeting at all, apart from a huge bill, and their escape around two-thirty couldn't come soon enough. Apart from anything else, Steve was keen to get home to finally get something to eat.

The mood in the car on the way back was sombre.

'Fun, fun, fun, till mother takes the teacakes away!' warbled Darren from the rear seat as they joined the motorway.

Sombre I said, Darren.

'Sorry.'

Let's try again. The mood in the car on the way back was sombre.

'What a spectacularly useless waste of time he was,' grumbled Darren.

'Oh go on, don't be shy,' urged Lisa, 'tell us what you really think.'

'Well, honestly! My mother knows more about technology than he does.'

'Putting someone in a lab coat doesn't make them a scientist.'

'No, it doesn't,' agreed Darren, 'although putting someone in a coffin does make them a corpse, if you're willing to wait a bit.'

Lisa turned round to say something to him, but he was leafing through the notes that he'd prepared before the day's meeting.

'Here it is,' he exclaimed in triumph. 'My prediction that we'd get as much out of academia as your average veggiewearian would get from a hog roast.'

'And what would a veggiewearian be?' asked Lisa, justifiably belligerently.

'It's a vegetarian who's very wearing,' said Darren. 'You've got to invent the occasional new word, or it's not literature.'

What absolute mweffle.

***

Barry was predictably unimpressed when Steve and Darren reported back on Monday morning with their stories of consultancy woe, and he directed Steve to find someone who might be able to provide some advice of actual use to them, even if it involved payment. Steve in turn enlisted the help of a trusted colleague – well, actually it was Darren – and following two days of intensive internet research and three and a half more days of filling in ranking and prioritisation matrices, they came up with a shortlist of three consultants. They were all independent freelance operators, highly in demand, and each one had an MBA, much to Darren's undisguised disgust. ('Means bugger all,' he kept muttering.) The one who made it to the very top of the spreadsheet was a Clive Jordan-Brown, and by great good fortune he was available to come in the very next morning. He did insist that a full set of briefing documents be e-mailed to him overnight, so that he could properly tell them what they already knew in the time-honoured tradition of consultants everywhere, but apart from that he sounded OK on the phone. He would have to be: this was getting close to their last chance.

***

'There's a thick hoar about, this morning,' Darren announced loudly and wittily. Several times, to anyone who would listen. As he did every time there was a frost.

As it so happened, no-one was listening. Lisa was over in the factory, Clare was in a secretaries' gossip meeting, and Simon appeared to be in a trance, or asleep. And Steve was running around in a way that would have been the envy of headless chickens everywhere, getting everything set up for the consultant's visit. They would be paying through the nose[1] for him, so they needed to make the most of the meeting. Steve had spent sleepless hours lying worrying about how best to handle the discussions, and now there was a whirlwind of activity and

---

[1] No, you're right, headless chickens don't have noses (though parsons do), but you get the general idea.

inefficiency as he raced around trying to pull everything together in time.

By nine o'clock, when Simon had woken up, there was nothing much left to do before Mr Jordan-Brown arrived, apart from finding the last three sets of engineering drawings, conducting validation and verification of the test methodology, risk analysis sign-off, preparation of a summary of estimated financial returns, and updating the design history file to cover all their efforts of the last three and a half months. Time for a strong, strong coffee.

The meeting was scheduled[1] to start at nine-thirty, and Darren agreed to join Steve, now that the hard work was all done. They had rather hoped that Lisa might have returned by now, but there was still no sign of her, so Steve left a note on her desk to tell her which meeting room they would be pacing the floor of.

Waiting for people to arrive is notoriously stressful, and it's worse if they're late and worse still if you're waiting for them with Darren telling you stories of every meeting he's ever attended that's gone dreadfully wrong. By nine-thirty-one Steve wasn't sure he could take much more of this, and by nine-thirty-two he was sure he couldn't. Finally, at nine-thirty-six there was a knock on the meeting room door to announce the arrival of Mr Jordan-Brown, escorted by one of the geriatric security guards from the gatehouse.

Clive J-B certainly talked a lot for his money. There was clearly nothing he enjoyed more than exploring a subject in all its many aspects via a long and leisurely chat. He didn't seem to much care for getting to the point, or for sticking to it on those rare occasions when he found it by accident. By half past ten, when Clare arrived with biscuits and a gushing, beaming Barry, he had said nothing of any use whatsoever. Every time that Steve had opened his mouth to ask a question or to draw the man's

---

[1] Would you mind pronouncing that the English way, without the American hard c, please?

attention to some aspect of the technical challenges facing them, he'd heard the consultant's voice rather than his own.

Things were going badly, just as the author predicted.

Barry insisted on a new round of introductions as they politely passed the plate of biscuits one way round the table and a pile of business cards the other, Steve noticing that his boss had expanded his own job title again. There was a time when high rank might have impressed Steve. Mind you, there was once a time when double-barrelled names like Jordan-Brown might have impressed him, too, but he had some while ago twigged that double-barrelling now mostly just meant unmarried parents.

Steve's enjoyment of the rest of the meeting wasn't exactly enhanced by the addition of Barry and his penchant for management by numbers. While their new Consultant-in-Chief was expounding at length on the subject of nickel-based contact strips, he was typing figures into calculations of voltages, temperatures, magnetic fields and costs. But mostly costs.

'It's OK. He's only got his spreadsheets set to stun,' whispered Darren to Steve, slightly too loudly.

'The big problem,' said Steve, by way of diversion, 'is that we're playing catch-up with the competition.'

'Leap-frog,' suggested Barry, hopefully. He gave Darren a 'shut up' look.

'Have you tried micro-riveting the sensor's wiring loom into its carcass, so that you can avoid the need for any protective resins or potting lacquers until everything's in its final tensioned position?' asked Mr Jordan-Brown suddenly, just as Darren was about to say something about frogs.

Steve wished that their visitor would use a different word from carcass, which had rather too much of a whiff of death about it for his liking. He was about to suggest 'casing', when he suddenly realised that they had just been given the breakthrough they needed. Even Darren, who was usually three steps ahead of everyone else in his thinking, drat him, hadn't thought of using something other than the lacquered coating approach to hold and protect the clever gubbins inside the sensor until assembly was complete. Here was their answer, so long sought. They would have to change much of the front-end layout, of course, and the hastily redesigned sensor might end up a bit of a camel, figuratively speaking, but with a bit of luck it would at least be a fairly pretty camel. They were back in business.

16

It was early evening, the time when you could stop worrying for another day about the little lad from down the road accidentally putting his football through your windows and could instead start to fret about his big brother deliberately putting a gloved hand through them. On this particular evening, though, that of Tuesday 27th February, the said fifteen year old big brother from Steve's road, his arm still in a sling from injuries sustained whilst trying to land his skateboard on top of a post box, was hanging around on the street corner with a couple of his mates, under-age chain smoking while they tried in vain to impress the posh seventeen year old girl from the big house in the next road. Ah, what it is to be young, free and thick.

Steve, though, didn't have time to observe the interesting social experiment being enacted outside, as he was busy tarting himself up for the big Christmas dinner, a task made more difficult by the fact that he'd stayed at work till after five o'clock to sort out the over-specified test specifications and then had fallen asleep on the bed at home for an hour while attempting a quick power-nap. He now had four minutes before the taxi arrived, to find his shirt, get dressed, and use the nasal hair trimmers that Darren had bought him as a Secret Santa present.

He arrived flustered and a little late at the venue, after Jackie had made him re-iron his shirt following a brief verbal scuffle on the subject, which Steve and the taxi driver had inevitably lost. It wasn't as if he would have been fundamentally opposed to ironing if people were basically flat or cubic or something, but he couldn't see the point when they were rounded and flabby. His mood wasn't exactly helped by the fact that he'd spent the day accumulating a headache, a sore throat, a streaming nose and spots.

Darren and Simon were already propped up guarding the bar when he arrived, Darren quick to point out that it was Steve's round. Two minutes and three glasses of red wine later, Steve was putting his wallet away sixteen pounds the poorer. Sixteen pounds! It wasn't even divisible by three, for goodness sake. Sixteen pounds. And they weren't even particularly big glasses.

They stood for a few minutes, making surreptitious comments about some of their colleagues and their dress sense as they came in. It wasn't especially kind, but it is traditional. A particular highlight was Acrid Annie from the logistics office, who had toyed with the idea of wearing black to hide her bulk, or off-white to hide her dandruff, but who had eventually compromised on scarlet, which hid neither. And then there was Sarah, who would have looked good wearing just about any old thing, which was just as well because she usually wore any old thing. Today she was wearing something that she must have won as a consolation prize in a charity shop raffle.

'I like Lisa's dress, though,' said Darren. 'It brings back so many happy memories from when that colour was in fashion.'

Their male colleagues were left largely unmocked, because they were all dressed in dinner jackets and black ties, except for someone who had already gone home to change after he'd turned up wearing what appeared to be leather pyjamas.

The conversation paused, for Lisa had now come over to join them, and it restarted with Steve attempting to join in with the spirit of the occasion by trying to be witty and amusing. His first attempts achieved about the same effect as if he'd said that he collected string for a hobby. Made more nervous by the lack of response, he tried adding earnestness to wit and amusement, but just then Lisa saw an opportunity for escape and turned to talk to Clare who had just entered the bar, her dress rather too short to conceal all the bites and scratches she'd received at her dog obedience class the previous evening.

'It's OK,' said Darren, 'we needed to talk about important chap stuff anyway.'

Lisa turned back. 'Which? Important, or chap?'

She went into a small micro-huddle with Clare. From the fragments that Steve could hear, their talk was also principally snide remarks about others' outfits. The three men fell silent, for listening in to the women's conversation was strangely but predictably much more interesting than having one of their own. They'd only listened as far as the introductory remarks about the dress that Neena was wearing, though, when Barry came up to them, looking rather dejected. He'd fancied an evening of wine, women and song, but unfortunately he'd remembered that he couldn't sing, that he was driving so that he couldn't drink, and that women tended to get upset if you tried to date them at a rate of more than one at once. That last lesson had been brought home to him particularly forcefully a few days earlier when his wife had somehow guessed that his melodramatic over-the-top confession of marital misadventure had been a double bluff rather than a single one, and he was now sleeping in the motel down the road.

'A double whisky, please,' he said, looking at Steve. He would get a taxi, and come back for his car in the morning. Why he thought that Steve would be buying drinks was uncertain, but he clearly wasn't the first to have that belief and Steve wasn't prepared to get into another argument just yet.

'Which whisky do you want?' he asked, vaguely aware that spirit drinkers could be choosy.

'Oh, any nice single malt will do.'

Why did people always do this to him? He was going to sound silly if he ordered a double single malt, surely? Mind you, at least he wasn't having to ask for a lime top and a little paper umbrella.

'Oh yes, and could I have it with lime and ice and a little umbrella, please?'

'Really?'

'No.'

Along the bar, Lisa wasn't having a great time yet either. Darren had just told her that yes, it did look big in this, and now she'd spied that Debbie Dawson was wearing the same dress. ('But don't worry, it's not absolutely identical,' Darren hastened to reassure her. 'I'm sure hers is a couple of sizes smaller and not quite so tight-fitting.')

Sometimes you have to be cruel to be unkind.

Steve eventually managed to catch the eye of the barman, which was a great achievement, but then caught the eye of Anthony

Archer, the assistant plant manager, which wasn't. Anthony pushed his way over, slapped Steve heartily on the back, spilling most of Barry's Scotch, and placed his own drinks order onto Steve's round.

'You don't have to fight over me, girls. You can share me!' he shouted across the room to two of the women from Accounts Payable, loudly and suddenly enough to make Steve knock Barry's glass over.

He turned to grin at Steve. 'I'm a babe magnet. I've been to see the doctor about it, but there's nothing he can do. Can't be helped, I'm simply a girl lure.'

You're a prat, thought Steve, starting all over again on the process of trying to attract the barman's attention so that he could order a replacement double single whisky for his boss. He finally got served at half past seven, then turned and found himself alone at the bar, as everyone else was making their way through to the room where the meal was to be served.

The tables were filling up quickly as the milling crowd got itself organised, but by good fortune – depending how one looks upon these things – Steve found an empty place between Darren and Barry at a round table for seven in the far corner of the room. Simon and Lisa were round the other side, peering at the residues on the cutlery. For a moment, it looked as if they were going to have two empty, adjacent, spaces, but Chris Tomkinson and Alex Deese came separately wandering over, unable to find places next to anyone they actually liked. As they weren't exactly the best of friends – to put it mildly – it looked like it was going to be a pleasant evening, in a 'not' sort of sense. As fate would have it, they found themselves on a collision course straight away. Literally. Even Steve couldn't work out how two people could bang their heads together quite so hard when all they were doing was trying to sit down, but it was enough to give Chris mild concussion and to send Alex scurrying off to the toilets in search of a cold wet paper towel for a rapidly growing lump on the forehead.

Meanwhile, Anthony had somehow got himself onto a table with Joanne, Becky, Suzanne and Angie from Customer Services.

'Hey, if it isn't the three most beautiful women I know,' he exclaimed enthusiastically. It was a pleasure watching their faces light up at the unexpected flattery, but a greater one to see the subsequent clouds of unease as certain mental calculations took place, rapidly followed by a set of narrowed-eye scowls[1]. Thirty seconds later, he found himself trying to squeeze his chair and place setting between Barry's and Steve's on the corner table.

'Wasn't much room over there,' he muttered, as he sat down, 'so I came to join my old friend.'

He meant Barry, not Steve.

'Shame, though; there were some rather nice single girls over there.'

'I think they all have husbands or long term boyfriends, actually,' said his old friend, who sounded rather like he'd researched such things.

'Not with me they don't – they're single girls when they're with me.'

Steve looked at Darren, and Darren looked at Steve. It was going to be a long night.

'I'm starving!' said Anthony, moving the conversation on from the subject of women. 'This is a bad time for you to look good enough to eat, Lisa.'

She gave him a brief, deliberately exaggerated, fake smile but said nothing.

'Lisa, your outrageous flirting has got to start!'

'I've not had this much fun since I stuck the stick from that motivational lollipop in my eye,' Darren whispered to Steve.

There was a general lull in the conversation.

'Do I need to get any more micro-riveter quotes, do you think?' Steve asked Barry, for want of anything else to say.

'Ah, stop talking shop. Relax and let your hair down, you boring old fart,' commanded his boss.

---

[1] If ever you want to try this amusing little trick yourself, do please first check that none of the intended victims actually have a significant aesthetic deficiency compared with the others.

Coming from a man whose hobbies included waxing his car three times a week, that last bit seemed rather harsh.

'There's no point giving any actions to Steve,' said Anthony. 'He'll write them down and then spend hours and hours prioritizing them, but he'll never actually start doing any of them.'

That was very hurtful, especially as it was largely true, and it left Steve wondering why he was putting himself through this ordeal. Fate can sometimes be kind, though, even to the fated, and just when Steve thought he would have to settle for the displeasure of Anthony's company for at least another two hours, the great Alpha Male spied an empty seat next to some young blonde woman and went off to ruin her evening. His departure was followed a minute or so later by Alex's return from the toilets. Unbelievably[1], Chris was somehow in the way again and there was a second abrupt clash of heads. Under normal circumstances it might have been followed by a serious shouting match, but Fate was in an undoubtedly funny mood right then and instead their eyes met and they each gave an unexpected melting smile. Suddenly Alex looked in need of the other half of the hug that Chris had so desperately wanted for so long, and within twenty seconds all the old animosity had gone for ever and they were groping for one another's buttocks.

***

The evening was an underwhelming, no expense spent, sort of occasion. That wasn't surprising really, as SLSL had only been willing to contribute a fiver a head and had sent everyone a combined invitation and invoice for the rest of the cost. Despite that, everyone who was anyone was there. Except for Andrew Spence and Laura Jones who were off on their honeydoom. And Daniel from Payroll, who had upper limb disorder, or repetitive strain injury as it used to be called. In fact, Steve was pretty sure that it had been called something else again when he was at

---

[1] Even I don't believe it, and I'm the one who wrote it.

school, but it wasn't a phrase he was going to think in mixed company.

Oh, and there was no sign of Abigail, the hypochondriac who worked in the test lab in the brief periods when she didn't have symptoms, presumably because she was confined to bed with something or other. Darren for one was grateful for the absence, as he always tried to avoid people with hypochondria in case he caught it.

A sudden vague thought danced around in the shadows at the corners of Steve's consciousness, paused for a moment, and then hesitantly came forward. 'What happened to Mike Marshall?' he asked.

'He's still in a coma,' said Lisa, and everyone looked respectfully glum.

But Christmas do's are Christmas do's, even in late February, and no-one wanted a dampener put on proceedings, so thirty seconds later they all cheered up and forgot about it again.

And there was good reason to cheer up, because the waitresses were bringing the starters in. Not that anyone could remember what they'd put down on Psycho Pat's form when she'd brought the menus round back in November. Steve didn't even remember eel and beetroot soup being one of the choices, but that was all that was left when all the smoked salmons and prawn and avocado cocktails had been handed out.

'I expect you're all thinking that I'm going to be the master of wit and repartee all evening?' said Darren as he tucked into a large slice of salmon.

'No, not really. We already know you quite well, don't forget.' Lisa flashed him a smile that finished half a second after it started.

Steve ate his soup in stomach-turned silence, and wondered what he'd put down for his main course. He wasn't entirely adventurous in the gastronomic stakes - he didn't believe in eating anything that he hadn't tried by the age of nine – and all he could remember of the menu choices had been a series of dishes with fancy French names like Boeuf Steak Recovère

Mechanique. For some reason, roast turkey and all the trimmings hadn't been on offer.

As it happened, his main course turned out to be gable end of lamb, served with a poultice of vegetables, which wasn't too bad, although it was topped with two hundred little pieces of celery, which Steve didn't much care for. By now, Barry and Darren were having a heated discussion across the front of him about beers, Alex and Chris had gone very lovey-dovey and were gazing fondly into one another's eyes, and Lisa was describing to Simon the sort of sweet little cottage she'd love to own. Seventeenth century, thatched, with low oak beams and with roses around the front door, that sort of thing. Steve sat quietly and made a start on his main course. His lamb was so rare it still had a pulse, and the wine provided on the tables was the fruitiest Shiraz he had ever tasted, which also wouldn't have been his choice. If he'd wanted something that tasted like blackcurrant concentrate, he'd have chosen blackcurrant concentrate. Mind you, it was there and it was free, so he drank it. Quite a lot of it.

By the time he'd finished the bits he could eat and was trying to hide the pieces of celery under his knife and fork, Barry and Darren had moved on to a loud argument about cars, Alex and Chris were looking decidedly pair-shaped, and Lisa was telling Simon how her ideal man would be someone six foot five who could sweep her off her feet; someone clever and kind and muscular and handsome.

Darren paused, mid-way through asking Barry whether he was thinking of swapping his Pompous for the new model where the wheels stayed on when you cornered.

'So,' he asked, turning to Lisa, 'your dream man wouldn't actually be able to fit inside your dream home?'

'Shut up Darren,' said Lisa.

Darren made a funny noise and then chuntered something fairly unfunny.

'I had a nervous twitch in my eye once. It was quite weird,' said Steve, in an effort to restore peace.

No-one was listening. Perhaps Darren had been right that time when he'd said that Steve's typical small talk was as interesting as hearing about the sleeping patterns of someone else's baby.

He was really beginning to regret signing up for this now. Despite it still being early in the evening, he was already finding that the more concentrate he drank, the less concentrate do he could. Especially conversation the on. He made a mental note that he had better switch to soft drinks while he could still find his way to the bar.

The puddings then started to arrive. Although again he couldn't remember what he'd ordered, it seemed that he must have ticked the box that corresponded to an unidentifiable something with the general consistency of breast implant, topped with a piece of flaccid peach. On the positive side, he could count the peach towards his five-a-day. And it wasn't as if things were much better for the vegetarians: from the look of Lisa's small plate of grapes-come-raisins, garnished with a single bruised mint leaf, the chef hadn't been very inspired by the chance to cook for non-carnivores either.

Steve had hardly even started pushing his pudding around with his spoon when there was a sudden five minute hiatus while the paramedics turned up to give a life-saving injection to Bob Freeman, who had experienced a severe reaction to the nuts in his portion of the Shapeless Something. It was nasty, but ultimately it was nobody's fault: how could Psycho Pat have known when she'd collected the special dietary requirements forms that his 'N/A' had meant Nut Allergy rather than Not Applicable?

While that was going on, the waitresses started to bring round the pots of lukewarm coffee and the disc jockey turned the lights down and started the disco. The four women from Customer Services were the first up onto the dance floor, and as is traditional at these sorts of affairs, they were on their own for the first half hour. Darren did his best to encourage Lisa to go up, along with Clare who had joined her for another gossip. At least, his 'Let's see if you can dance half as well as that lot over there with the great legs' was meant to be encouragement.

'Men are pathetic and tedious.' Lisa turned to Clare. 'It's just a chore, dealing with a species that comes back to the same thought every fifteen seconds.'

'Yeah, well it's none too great for us either, you know, having to find something to think about during those long boring fourteen secondses in between,' Darren pointed out.

'Why don't you go and see if you've got any friends at the bar?' asked Lisa.

Darren restrained himself to a single loud 'Pah!'.

'Or you could stay here and join in our conversation about shopping for shoes.'

'I think I'll go and see who's at the bar,' he said, though he didn't make any obvious attempt to move from his seat.

'They had some nice white slingbacks in Ramorski's last week,' started Lisa heavily.

'I don't like to see women in white shoes,' said Darren.

'Well, you're wrong,' snapped Lisa.

Darren rolled his eyes and puffed up his feathers slightly, ready to deliver something starting with that classic lie, 'With all due respect', but unfortunately he was beaten to it by Clare, who pointed left and mouthed the word 'bar', a combination of actions that produced a peal of laughter from Lisa.

'I'd get that laugh fixed, if I were you,' said Darren as he got up to leave. 'Before everybody thinks there's a panicked horse in here.'

'Bar, Darren,' pointed Lisa.

'Have a sugar lump and shut up.'

'You've always got to have the last word, haven't you?'

Darren thought that that was a little unfair, and said so via a two minute rant about bitter and twisted scorned ex-girlfriends.

'Finished?' asked Lisa, when he finally paused for breath.

'Erm, yes, thank you.'

While Darren and Lisa were busy having their very own close encounter of the unkind, Steve slipped quietly away to the bar to get himself a lemonade. He found himself standing next to John Stokes, his boss's boss, which was a little unfortunate as it meant he would have to try to be sociable and intelligent, and sober.

He cleared his throat with a misjudged cough that sent spittle onto the manager's lapel.

'How are Dawn and the little, er, dawnings?'

Not having to remember the names and ages of all your colleagues' children should be a basic human right.

'She's fine, thanks. Still keeping herself busy organising public stonings of bottle-feeding mothers.'

'I think Barry's on the bottled stuff,' Steve said. He gave a nervous laugh, although he hadn't said anything funny. He had just defamed his boss, though, and a combination of that and John's unreceptive frown gave his ears cause to start to turn uncomfortably red.

He was rescued from his discomfort by Anthony coming into the bar with a petite and giggling brunette with eye-lashes so thick it looked like she'd fallen into the mascara jar. Steve had no idea who she was, but he could see at a glance that she'd already had one roast turkey flavoured alcopop too many. She was talking nineteen to the dozen, as if she either didn't get out much or didn't find many people willing to listen. She did, though, have Anthony's full attention on this occasion.

'You know I adore you,' he was saying.

'I think you may have mentioned it, once or twice.'

The girl was wearing a short lime green dress that appeared to have been inspired by (which is a posh way of saying copied from) the bottle that a well-known brand of toilet cleaner came in. There was clearly some sort of a problem with it, though, as she kept putting one hand down the front of it and adjusting her bra, much to her companion's obvious interest ('I promise not to peep, though I don't promise not to stare').

Several other people were also staring, as it happened, John included, and it gave Steve his chance of escape. Such things are all relative, though, and his getaway route led him round to where Barry was leaning on the other end of the bar, one elbow in a puddle of beer and the other arm round the waist of a somewhat embarrassed Sarah from Testing. From the conversation Steve could hear while he was failing once again to get noticed by the bar staff, Barry must have taken the same course in sweet-talking that Anthony had.

'You look gorgeous!' he exclaimed drunkenly, with a hearty leer. 'I could just eat you up, right here and now!'

'Barry!' she protested.

'Well, could I just kiss your lovely little bottom, then?'

'Keep it clean!' she hissed, blushing savagely.

'I hope you do, if I'm going to kiss it.'

'Barry, I wouldn't let you kiss me if you were the last toad in the lily pond of life. Now why don't you go and find someone of your own age to play with!'

'A simple yes would have sufficed,' grumbled Barry. 'Anyway, most people of my age have gone wrinkly. I'm the one exception.'

'Are you?' asked Sarah. 'It's hard to tell under that unfashionable old beard of yours.'

Barry looked shocked. 'I grew it for you! I thought it might tickle your fancy.'

'Well it doesn't.'

'Would you like it to?'

Steve didn't hear Sarah's answer, as he actually got served at that point, although what he'd ordered as lemonade came as whisky and soda and without any change. He went back into the room where the disco was.

Now it might not surprise you to learn that Steve wasn't a big fan of discos. After the mortifying experience of the last one he'd been to with Jackie, about four years ago, he had in fact vowed never to go to another one. Of course, it had partly been his own fault, as she'd reminded him from time to time on the night itself and again the next day on the way to take the stuff back to the fancy dress shop and then for several weeks afterwards. And really, she *was* right. If he'd listened more carefully, he'd have known it was an *over*-seventies disco and he

would have saved them both a lot of unnecessary embarrassment.

Mind you, Steve wasn't great with his resolutions, as his
waistline was beginning to demonstrate, so here he was at a disco
again. Not that he had the slightest intention of dancing, not
even the sort of sequence dancing that Simon was managing
(drink, drink, dance, drink, drink, drink, drink). Instead, he
found an empty table in a quiet corner, and he sat down with a
glass of tap water that he'd poured himself and waited to see if
anyone would come along to talk to him.

After five or ten minutes, Darren wandered over for a chat,
although Steve wasn't quite sure what they were chatting about
because his quiet corner wasn't actually remotely quiet and he
could only hear every fourth or fifth word. He could, though, for
some reason hear every word from the next table, where the
woman from Personnel, or H.R., or whatever they were called
this week, was regaling a couple of friends with a story from the
confidential employee files. She was just getting to the interesting bit when Barry came sauntering in and joined the two men.
Apart from a bottle of imported beer, he was alone: that £1.99
pheromone spray off the market obviously hadn't worked.

'Sarah had to go home to feed her cat,' he explained.

'Oh,' said Steve.

'No staying power.' He took a swig from his bottle.

They sat without talking for a few minutes, Barry draining
his beer while Steve and Darren people-watched. The dance floor
had gradually filled up, and there was a wide range of dancing
styles to observe, from the half-hearted shuffling of Dull Donna,
failing to stand out from the crowd even in her metallic pink
disco wig, through to the stylish high-energy gyrations of Sarah
from Testing.

'Anyone want a drink?' asked Barry, who didn't seem to have
noticed that Sarah's cat had gone unfed for some reason.

Darren shook his head, Steve mouthed the word 'coffee' and
Barry went off to the bar to get himself a pint of the Pretentious
Twoddle. He passed Anthony in the doorway, who was leading

his new-found companion towards the frenzied mass of churning bodies in front of the disc jockey.

'He could drink for Britain,' said Darren, nodding towards where Barry had last been.

Hmm. He couldn't, of course; there was far, far too much competition for that.

While he waited for his coffee and while Darren went off to talk to someone he knew on another table, Steve went back to watching his colleagues let their hair down. Everyone else looked as if they were having fun, so why was it that he felt increasingly weary and morose?

In honesty, not many people from the development labs were dancing, though Lisa was occasionally to be glimpsed somewhere amidst the throng. Meanwhile, over in the far corner, Anthony seemed to have become even more friendly with the brunette in the lime green dress.

Steve's brooding was interrupted by a loud slapping sound, neatly interposed in a gap in the music. Anthony had apparently got a little bit too friendly. This time when he passed Barry in the doorway to the bar, he was without company.

Steve's order for coffee had somehow turned itself into a pint of Utter Twoddle, but he wasn't complaining because he needed something to take him out of himself. In fact, not for the first time, he'd been wondering whether to become an alcoholic. It would be expensive, obviously, but if it meant that he had other things to worry about than his workload and getting the blame for Sling, then it might be worth it. Who knows, given time he might become drinking buddies with Barry.

He looked at his watch, and found to his surprise that it was actually later than he'd realised. A few people had already started to drift away or, in the case of four of the secretaries, march off in battle group formation. Across the other side of the dance floor, Alex Deese and Chris Tomkinson were sharing their first kiss together. And it was quite some kiss. So far, they'd been locked together in a salivary swap-fest for over a quarter of an hour, practically chewing one another's faces off before they went off together for a spot of intimacy. (Insert here a description of romance and/or squealchiness to suit your own taste. I've left both Alex and Chris of undisclosed gender, so you can be as broad-minded as you like, but please don't imagine anything illegal or too immoral, as this is meant to be a nice book. Thank you.)

Steve contemplated his own evening. He must have had a good time. His ears were ringing from the music, his voice was hoarse from trying to talk over it, he was starting to feel a bit sick, and he couldn't remember anything anyone had said. That's a good time in anybody's book, surely.

'Can you keep a little secret?' asked Barry with a slight slur, leaning over to make himself heard.

'Of course.' Of course he could – that's what drinking buddies did.

'We're all going to lose our jobs,' said his boss, taking a hefty gulp at the dark brown liquid in his glass.

Well *that* wasn't the sort of thing that drinking buddies were meant to say to you on a celebratory occasion.

'Massive cutbacks,' added Barry. 'Ssssh.'

He went off in the direction of the bar again, leaving Steve with his mouth hanging open, his heart pounding heavily and his stomach in knots. Things hadn't been great recently, he knew that, but surely they weren't as bad as all that? He certainly hadn't been expecting Barry's secret bombshell.

Steve went off to the toilet, which was something he always tried to put off as long as he could at these events: too many times there was an awkward queue for the urinals or, worse, you tentatively pushed open a half-open cubicle door only to find someone already standing in there. On this occasion it was Barry, who had just been sick in the disabled toilet and was now trying to flush it using the emergency assistance cord.

Steve went into the next cubicle along, and slid the bolt across behind him. He really wasn't feeling too clever now, but then again, he wasn't. He'd devoted half his life to SLSL, and now here he was, a drunken, broken, soon to be unemployed middle aged wretch.

He instantly regretted thinking the word 'wretch', for in truth he had had far too much to drink and his innards were about to get their revenge. Why, oh why, hadn't he stopped after the first three glasses of wine? Why had he carried on tipping alcohol down his throat the whole evening? Fool! Poison.

'Wuh-err.'

The root of all evil.

'Wuh-err.'

Damn and blast it.

'Wuh-err,' yet again.

He stayed leaning heavily forward for a long time, arm extended to prop himself against the back wall of the toilet cubicle while he made his vows. He was never, ever again going to have another drink, as long as he lived.

And for almost three days, his resolve held.

17

Natalie put down her latest Jacqueline Wilson book and sighed. 'Mum,' she said, 'Why can't we be like a normal family? Why can't we live in a bed-sit and only see Dad at weekends?'

Jackie raised one eyebrow.

'Or perhaps he could be an out-of-work drug addick,' Natalie suggested.

'Be careful what you wish for,' warned Jackie, who hadn't yet passed Barry's secret on to the girls. 'The summer before you were born, I wished I could spend more time outdoors, and within a couple of days Dad had broken the key off in the front door and locked us both out for twelve hours.'

As if by magic, Steve popped his head round the door just at that moment.

'OK, I'm going for it. Wish me luck!'

'Good luck Dad,' Natalie dutifully replied, as his head popped back whence it had come.

Now, thrill seeking means different things to different people. Some people have to jump from aeroplanes or swim with sharks or risk dangerous extra-marital liaisons to get their thrills. For Steve, the level was somewhere around changing the light bulb in the spare room, which was where he was going now, after his third check that all the electricity to upstairs was thoroughly turned off at the main fuse box.

Unfortunately, half way up the stairs he tripped over his feet in the semi-darkness and landed fairly heavily on the home for orphaned kittens that Chloe was making out of an old paint tin, in the process giving himself a zigzag cut on his forehead, though not, sadly, any magical powers other than a sudden talent for using words from outside his normal vocabulary.

After he'd tended his wounds and then changed the bulb, Steve's next Saturday morning job was to phone his mother. It was probably at least a week since he'd last spoken to her, and he hadn't been to see her since just after she'd got home following her extended stay at Mrs Collins' over Christmas and the New Year. He'd meant to go, of course, as all sons do, but somehow hadn't quite got round to it. Still, at least she'd appreciate a nice phone call now. Or she might have done, if he hadn't timed it midway through one of the twice-weekly visits from the agency home help sent round to help her clean round her hoard of old tat. Yes, he inadvertently interrupted the vacuum cleaning, but surely she ought to have preferred to talk to him rather than to go straight back to supervising that? It was a little hurtful to know that you came below a compulsive cleaning obsession in your mother's scheme of priorities, though at least there was the one saving grace that it had stopped anybody in the family from dying of dust.

His phone call to his mother having ended after just fourteen seconds, Steve went to see if the rest of his relatives might fancy doing something with him, but they were already engrossed in the task of sorting out Natalie's things for the sleepover she was going to be having that night at Rebecca's. Why the packing took all three of them wasn't clear – perhaps it was a girl thing – but he hoped that adequate body armour for all eventualities was included somewhere in the pile of bags and cases. He well remembered Natalie's one previous sleepover there. When he'd arrived the next morning to collect his daughter, he was met by the sound of shouting and screaming coming from upstairs where the girls had been trying to give Rebecca's cat a makeover. Judging by the state of Snuggles, or rather the state of what little could be seen of his spitting face and arched back on top of the wardrobe, he had been OK with the lipstick and possibly the curlers, but the hair gel had perhaps been a step too far. As it happened, Rebecca now no longer had a cat – he'd left home, for some reason – but there was talk of her trying to persuade her parents to buy her a yeti to help them keep the rhododendrons in their garden under control. Oh hang on, I've already done that one, haven't I? Sorry. Let's make it a goat she'd like, instead.

As his assistance didn't seem to be necessary, or welcome, Steve went downstairs again to make a start on doing some work that he'd brought home a few days before. At least it got him away from the row that might or might not have been Prod's latest single: to be honest, they all sounded the same to him.

Whether there was much point in doing the work, bearing in mind what Barry had told him at the Christmas party, was an interesting question, but Steve thought he'd better do it anyway, in a probably misguided attempt to make a difference. The only slight snag in his plan was himself: he struggled to get his mind properly engaged in it, and instead of getting on and tackling it he got distracted by a series of little displacement activities such as making himself a cup of coffee, reorganising the shelf above the hi-fi system, and rereading Wuthering Heights.

And so the weekend passed.

***

When Steve reached the office on Monday morning he could see that they'd been graced over the weekend by another visit from the work creation fairy. Small memos had been left adorning every computer screen and every desk, each bearing a different instruction or request. The handwriting was coincidentally very like Barry's. For a moment, Steve thought that he'd been missed, but lo and behold, no – there in the very middle of his desk sat a small sticky note bearing the legend 'Please ignore what I told you on Friday – wrong end of stick'. Beneath that was another sticky note saying 'Milk. Washing up liquid. Distemper tablets'.

Obviously keen to learn more - about the top note, not the misplaced shopping list - Steve tried to find Barry. He wasn't answering his telephone, though, and mounting an expedition around the building to track him down also proved fruitless, so in the end he resorted to the old trick of summoning his boss by getting a slightly dodgy website up on his computer.

'You told me on Friday night that things were really bad,' started Steve, switching his screen over as quickly as possible to a picture of some sensors.

'Yes, well, perhaps I was burning our chickens before we'd counted them.' Barry looked a little uneasy.

'But you said we were all losing our jobs!' hissed Steve, trying to keep his voice down enough not to start a panic.

Barry gave a hearty laugh that sounded as if it had been practised. 'Oh, no, no, no.'

'But you said - ,' started Steve again. He wished his voice wasn't becoming quite so shrill.

'Things are fine!' exclaimed his boss. 'In fact, we've just had senior management approval for the full global second-tier launch of Sling in the last week in April.'

'But -,' said Steve, gradually getting less sure of himself.

'And we're having a party to celebrate, two weeks on Friday.'

'But -'

'We thought we'd have it early, because we'll all be too busy to breathe once we get near to Global Launch Day.'

'What sort of party?' asked Darren, who had just entered the room and the conversation. He was walking with a pro-nounced limp, acquired over the weekend during a heated discussion with his two young nieces about who was having which *Monopoly* piece.

'Here.' Barry handed him a photocopied sheet that he'd intended to pin up on the notice board. From what Steve could see over Darren's shoulder, the idea seemed to be to have a meal and disco like the Christmas party but with less sick.

Realising that he was unlikely to be further edified about the on-off redundancy situation, Steve slipped off to his nine o'clock meeting on micro-rivetting machine vendors. Like many of the meetings he had to attend, the majority of the time seemed to be given over to a review of the action points from the previous one. Much to his surprise, on this occasion he turned out to have actually done one of his. It was only by pure random chance, of course, but it still counted. If only it had been something more impressive than to double-check that he really had lost the box of lenses for the new microscope, then he might have been quite proud of himself.

After the meeting he diverted by way of the chocolate machine to get himself one of those rather fragile chocolate bars that you end up wearing, getting back to the office to find Darren waiting to ask him whether he'd heard the new rumours, which obviously he hadn't or I would have told you.

'What new rumours?' asked Steve.

Darren looked around furtively. 'Barry's been misinformed again. The redundancies are back on, after all.'

Steve closed his eyes and took a slow, deep breath. If only he'd followed the old advice and not let them grind him down. There was a part of him that had had enough and just wanted to give up. Instead of always fighting against the current, it would be so easy to concede defeat and go with the flow, face down in the stream.

He tried to keep the metaphor at bay while he went for his Monday lunchtime swim. Unsuccessfully.

***

Thursday. Steve's birthday. So far, the day had got off to a bearable start, and for once no unreasonable tasks had arrived in his e-mail. That wasn't the same thing as thinking he had much cause for celebration, though, especially in view of the very uncertain employment situation. In fact, right at this moment the only thing to which he could think of looking forward was that he wasn't far off starting a new lab notebook.

Thanks to the brilliant, tortured genius of the girl on the switchboard, he'd been fielding enquiries all week from the press and other interested parties about a recent near-fatal fire in the canteen. So when the phone rang at about eleven o'clock, he assumed it was yet another caller wanting to know how the cooking oil had got into the toaster in the first place. Instead, to his surprise the call was from Uncle Dennis, who obviously hadn't forgotten his birthday for once. Unlike Diane and Tony or his mother, who never seemed to remember.

'How's life?' asked the ex-seafarer, over the sound of the ring-pull being pulled on a can of celebratory beer.

'Oh, life's great, thanks,' said Steve in measured tones, 'but not the one I'm having.'

'Oh dear. That's too bad.' There was a loud slurping noise.

And a pause.

'You couldn't lend me a couple of thousand quid, could you, please?'

'What for?'

There was another pause and another slurp. 'Knee operation.'

It was Steve's turn to pause.

'I could lend you a grand,' he said, with all the enthusiasm of worms for blackbirds.

Judging by the noises coming down the line, Dennis was clearly not overwhelmed.

'Oh, I suppose I could manage two, if you pay me back before next Christmas,' agreed Steve. In fairness to Jackie's uncle, he had repaid the previous loan in full, even if it had taken nearly three years to get the last of it back. And he was being rather more frugal this time, as he'd asked for less than before. And he hadn't wasted any of the family money on buying Steve a birthday card.

Nor, come to think of it when Steve put down the phone, had he actually wished Steve happy returns or mentioned the occasion in any way whatsoever.

He didn't have time to dwell on that observation, because just then Darren came stamping into the office, slammed a large folder of papers down on his desk, and promptly launched into a long diatribe about the meeting from which he'd just come. Steve did his best to make enquiring and sympathetic noises but was met with a series of bad-tempered ripostes that left him wondering what the point was of trying to be up-beat if every time he was going to get beat up.

'Beeping bleepers,' said Darren (to paraphrase slightly), as he went out of the door, just managing not to slam it, taking his scowl with him to his next meeting.

'What was *that* all about?' asked Steve.

'He's been doing some scenario planning with Barry,' offered Lisa.

Steve frowned. It seemed a funny thing for him to be quite so cross about: after all, he hadn't reacted so strongly even when he'd heard of Barry's talk of all their jobs going, and he wasn't usually someone who held particularly strong views, depending on how you see things like wishing death upon people who change lane without indicating.

Two minutes later the door opened again, much more slowly, as if whoever was opening it wasn't really sure they could be bothered.

'Where's Darren?' asked two voices in synchronism. It was Sicknote and Workshy, who'd come to see about an urgent modification to the crush strength tester that Darren had requested some months previously.

Lisa answered. 'He's not here. He's gone off to his weekly meeting of Losers for Justice. Can I help?'

'No; we just came to see what he wants that's so urgent.'

You could always rely on Jon and Neil to help you, about once in every six blue moons.

'Have you had a chance to take a look at that microscope that I broke?' asked Steve.

Jon gave a low whistle. 'You're opening a whole new bundle of worms there, mate. We'll have to get back to you on that one.'

'Well, did you at least have an opportunity to read through the notes I left with it?'

'We had the opportunity, but we didn't take it.'

Steve would have rolled his eyes if he'd still had the energy.

'By the way, we're sorry to hear about your jobs,' said Neil, giving a small grin to show how sorry. 'Shame you didn't all try a bit harder.'

And with that, they left Steve to get on with his special day.

Last year, he'd tried to mark his birthday by inviting everyone in the office out to the pub at lunchtime, only to get completely upstaged by the winsome new student in Marketing who was celebrating it being Wednesday with an impromptu alternative 'do' of her own that attracted all but two of Steve's colleagues. This year he determined that he'd get everyone's commitment in advance, and having done so earlier in the week he'd booked a table for ten at the new gastropub on the other side of town. In the event, things were no better than last year, though, and everyone excused themselves apart from Barry and Lisa. Barry did at least offer to drive so that Steve could have a drink, but then suddenly decided that a Mundane was *the* car to be seen in and changed his mind so that he could imbibe. So Steve ended up driving, as he did every year, and then ended up sitting, despite the table having more than plenty of room, crammed in a corner back to back with the regional winner of the most annoying ringtone competition. And there are few things as thoroughly depressing as going out for a quiet birthday meal, only to find yourself sitting next to a large party out celebrating someone else's birthday in lavish raucous style. It's hard to feel very special when you're with two semi-reluctant colleagues and have only a bottle of fairly cheap wine and one glass of lemonade between you, whereas they have twenty loud, rich friends, balloons, ribbons, bunting, party poppers and a seemingly endless supply of champagne.

Not only that, but the surprise birthday cake from Clare that was waiting for him when he got back was a bit of a letdown: presumably out of consideration for his health, the others had left him with the one small remaining piece, plus the cake stand, knife and eight plates to wash up.

***

The evening provided the opportunity for a couple of hours of relief from worrying about his job, as it was Parents' Evening at school and the chance to worry instead about Natalie's academic progress. Steve went directly from work, while Jackie dropped the kids off at Angela's house for the evening and then met him at the school gates. They arrived in plenty of time for their appointment with Mrs Pottlesmirk, as it was a school tradition to put all the children's exercise books out in the dining hall for their parents to browse through before seeing the teacher. Unfortunately, Mrs Pottlesmirk had sorted every book from every child in to one great unstable heap, which gave Steve and Jackie something like two hundred books to search through.

The first of Natalie's exercise books that Steve managed to track down was her science book, which was almost empty. The only piece of work that the class had done since Christmas was a drawing of a wind turbine plonked on top of a local beauty spot, which Mrs Pottlesmirk had made them draw to illustrate how important it was to have wind farms blowing cool air to get rid of global warming. Jackie then found Natalie's geography book, and they were soon able to negotiate a swap that allowed Steve a chance to admire his daughter's drawing of a different local landmark being destroyed by a volcano.

Try as they might, neither of them could find any more of their little treasure's exercise books before it was time for their ten minute slot with the great Mrs P.

The meeting was unhelpful and very confusing. Nine minutes in, Steve realised that she hadn't got a clue which child was which, and that she'd probably been talking about Rebecca, even though she'd kept using the name Bryony. That at least would explain her references to their daughter's supposed obsession with animal euthanasia. It was quite a shame, though, because the teacher had had some really positive things to say about recent progress and latent academic ability.

Jackie went straight home after the appointment, while Steve drove round to pick up Natalie and Chloe from Angela's, consoling himself that his own teachers had never known who he was, either. Not until the day he'd accidentally drained the school swimming bath over the football pitch by clutching at the main drain valve in the boiler room when he fainted while looking for a lost sock.

He got to Angela's house just in time to see them waving Tom off, Chloe almost in tears of disappointment that the air ambulance didn't have a siren and blue flashing lights.

'How do you spell house?' Steve asked his elder daughter above the sniffs of her sister as they drove away.

'H-O-W-S-S of course.'

'No, it's H-O-U-S-E.'

'Really? That's a weird spelling. I prefer mine.'

He'd no doubt she did, but that might somehow be related to why Mrs Pottlesmirk then covered her work with a layer of red ink.

'And why did you draw a leprechaun inside that volcano?'

'That was Satin, having a dance.'

'Satin?'

'The devil.' She rolled her eyes in exasperation at having been dealt such a thick father. 'Satin.'

'Oh.'

Natalie had been learning about some of the world's major religions since the start of term, a process that seemed to involve the creation of lots of artwork featuring bearded men and/or smiting. Steve wasn't entirely sure where it might be leading – he had a small fear that it might make Chloe want to grow a beard – but the pictures certainly covered the remaining bare patches in the hall and at least Natalie might end up with a good understanding of the origins of some of the wars and protests that made up the bits of the news between the abused children, poisoned streams, factory closures and ducks nesting in unusual places.

Ah, what it is to be young and have so many exciting things lying ahead of you still to be discovered.

***

For Steve Oscroft, the week didn't exactly end on a high. Apart from the little matter of the job situation, he had been given the Friday morning task of checking through two hundred invoices to try to find the discrepancy in the lab finances, and he was also still getting occasional invitations (yes, the word does still exist, and no, invite is not a noun) to supply information to the local media about the toaster fire.

Everything felt strangely unreal, in a kind of limbo, with a sombre grey cloud hanging over him, punctuated only by Death Nell's cheerful whistling. It was hard to know what to make of things, and it wasn't reassuring when someone came round mid-morning to confiscate all the office plants to save on fertiliser and annual polishing.

Perhaps, on reflection, Steve wasn't the only one who was getting stressed by all the speculation and uncertainty. Tempers around the office were beginning to fray, and Darren had gone from his usual bickering with Lisa to outright vendetta. He had also got himself into trouble with Recessive Jean, one of the supervisors in the factory, after he accidentally called her an evil inbred cow. It was manifestly a slip of the tongue, but that didn't escape the fact that it was one of those things that you just shouldn't say, almost on a par with the time when he'd taken one look at that four week old child and exclaimed 'What an ugly baby!'. Also to Recessive Jean.

'Lisa postulated that I'd find you here,' said Steve, arriving at the drinks machine after lunch on his own in the canteen.

'Well she would,' said Darren, 'she's a postule.'

'*She's* worried about the future as well, you know.'

'She threw her future away, the day she dumped me.'

'She dumped you because you wouldn't stop having fry-ups and then wiping the fat and remnants of meat out of the pan with her Vegetarian Society tea towels.'

'She shouldn't be telling people the intimate secrets of our relationship,' said Darren in a sniffy tone.

'I think you could have made it work, you know,' Steve said. 'Even then she might have taken you back, if you hadn't started referring to her as the Moaner Lisa.'

'No chance. I have my pride.'

'Pride comes before a fall,' Steve observed quietly - and rather unnecessarily, because it's hardly likely to come just after one, is it?

'Anyway, I stopped calling her that,' Darren pointed out defensively.

'Only when you thought of the expression *Lisa the Leech*.'

'It was her own darned fault,' muttered Darren, not entirely gallantly.

'Couldn't you make up, and at least be friends? I'm sure she'd like to know that it still matters to you.'

'Well, perhaps you'd like to go and enlighten her?' Darren suggested. 'With your boot if you have to.'

Steve took his coffee and walked away with a sad shake of his head that it had all come to this. Barry's crack team was beginning to crack.

18

It was a Friday morning in mid March. The sun was flirting with yet another day in the long history of its third planet, and Steve was trying to avoid the return trip to the Infected Follicle that John Stokes was contemplating for him.

'Wouldn't it be better if Lisa went, instead?'

'No, I need her to work through some calculations for me.'

'Well, Darren then?'

'No, he's asked for a meeting with me, and that's the only time I can make.'

'Couldn't Simon go?'

'No.'

This was starting to become a common theme.

'Well can someone come with me, then, and also give me a hand getting a presentation together for Abbotang?'

'Yeh, that should be OK. You'll get support from the guys in sales.'

'Who?'

John consulted his papers. 'Mike Marshall.'

'Mike Marshall is still in a coma.'

'Well, you might have to manage without him, then, except on the really important bits.'

And so it was that the following Monday Steve ended up back at the *Iffy* for a return visit and overnight stop, some six months since his visit to Abbotang Industries with Ian Firth. The same two locals as before were in the bar, still on the same game of dominoes they'd been playing the previous September, but Steve was encouraged to see that the place had had a makeover, to the extent that the squashed food on the carpet had been changed.

Having learnt the lesson of his previous visit, he had brought sandwiches: after all, the pub wasn't known as the 'Iffy' for nothing. It made no difference, though: he still ended up with stomach ache half the night and a headache the rest. Meanwhile, the people at Abbotang obviously hadn't learnt *their* lesson, as demonstrated by the fact that they'd had him back a second time.

On this occasion they were more non-committal as they came out of the meeting – they didn't laugh in his face and throw his samples in the bin – so he was probably making progress.

He got back to the office late on Tuesday afternoon to be greeted by more stories of threatened redundancies. The rumour was that about five people would have to go. Well, actually, the main rumour of the day was that a nameless somebody in the factory scheduling office (where only two people worked) had run off with someone else unidentified (who also worked in the factory scheduling office). But there was also the second, smaller rumour about the proposed job losses.

'But that's an old story, surely?' Steve protested to Darren. 'I keep asking him, and Barry keeps denying there's any intention of lay-offs.'

'Yes, he does,' admitted his colleague, about to add a further comment but then changing his mind.

'Then why is everyone suddenly talking about it again?' Steve was anxious for some sort of reassurance, even if it had to come from Darren.

'Because people enjoy a good rumour – it helps occupy their tiny little brains. Mind you, did you hear the juicy details about that couple in the scheduling office?'

'Only that strange scuff marks have been found on some of the raw materials order sheets.'

'And that the moans coming from above the suspended ceiling weren't a restless soul in eternal torment, after all?'

'Oh.'

'Anyway, I wouldn't worry about the bleak futility of your career prospects just yet. You've got another little matter to deal with first: John's saying that Sling absolutely has to be launched globally in April.'

'But it's not ready yet. The folks in the factory are still trying to make them properly, and no-one in Marketing can decide how much to over-charge for them.'

'I think they're planning to use dummy devices for the global sales launch, and to lie about the price.'

If he'd had more energy, Steve might have passed comment on their chances of fooling any significant customers, but he was tired after his long drive back and he decided to keep his powder dry on this one.

'If you're still worried, why don't you go and see Barry, so that he can refute the gossip on a one-to-one face-to-face basis?' suggested Darren.

That didn't sound like the best of ideas to Steve, but before he'd had a chance to definitely reject it, Simon came into the office with the unwelcome news that tales were circulating that John had spent the day locked in his office taking a red pen to the organisation chart and that he would be calling them all into an important surprise meeting the next day. Not unpredictably, there was a brief ripple of extra anxiety in the room. 'We're dead,' as Darren so poetically put it.

'I thought there weren't going to be any job losses,' Steve said, apprehensively.

'Well it's changed again.'

Steve groaned. 'It's death by a thousand cuts.'

Simon grimaced, while Darren shuddered at the memory of the time he'd taken the paper shreddings round to Lisa for her hamster. It had been literal that time. Paper cuts all over its poor little body; bit of a mess for all concerned.

'But these stories come and go every day or two. How do you know it's true this time?'

'It's Clare,' said Simon, quietly. 'She's not been asking any questions.'

A sudden light sweat lubricated Steve's palms. It could only mean one thing - that she already knew, but was sworn to secrecy: she was far too inquisitive to sit there and not poke her nose in if she didn't.

'But we don't know for sure?' asked Steve hopefully. 'No news is good news, right?'

Darren scowled. 'Not round here it ever is, no.'

Steve groaned. 'Right. I'd better go and break the news to Jackie.'

Darren nodded. 'Yes.'

'Well, toodle pip, then.' He thought for a moment, 'Whatever that means.'

***

Steve unlocked the front door and let himself in. He put his briefcase down on the one area of hall carpet that didn't have at least one woodlouse crawling across it, and went through into the lounge where his other half was re-watching their wedding video, now newly transferred onto DVD. Steve winced: he had sneezed and snivelled his way through the whole ceremony, eyes red and streaming, due to what he'd thought at the time was severe hayfever but which had later turned out to be an allergy to paper hankies.

'Shhh,' said Jackie, before he spoke. 'It's just coming up to the funny bit.'

Steve hadn't remembered it as being funny at the time.

'We're laying beed off.'

'Pardon?'

'We're being laid off.'

'Who is?'

'We are. All of us, I think.'

'The whole company?'

Blimey. This is going to take for ever.

'Well, at least half the department, if the rumours are right.'

'So it's only a rumour? And, anyway, why would they pick you? It's not as if you're always having days off sick.'

No, thought Steve. He couldn't remember when he'd last laid in bed all day, eating grapes and watching telly. In fact, he'd seemed to have suffered from good health all his working life.

Pausing to brush a dead *Oniscus Asellus* off the sole of his shoe, he sat down in the corner chair so that he wouldn't see the bit where he walked into the pillar on the way out of the church.

'The woman in the baker's has died,' said Jackie.

'Oh.' Steve had no idea who they were suddenly talking about.

'And,' she added, 'Osmarelda's lost an eye.'

'Can't we sew it back on?'

'Lost, I said, not become temporarily detached from.'

'Oh.' It was nice to know that just because John might be telling him tomorrow that he had no future at SLSL, the world still went on. Which was more than could be said for the DVD player, which chose that moment to jam up with a close-up picture of the rip in Steve's wedding trousers frozen on the screen.

Right, let's recap. Steve's probably about to lose his job, Jackie's going out of her mind with grief about the woman in the bakers of whom none of us have heard, Osmarelda has been consigned to a life of partial disability, and now the DVD's on the blink. It's definitely not looking good for a happy ending, I'm afraid.

***

Once upon a long time ago, in days he could no longer really remember or believe, Steve had been relaxed and carefree and had felt that he was going places. Now there was a good chance he was about to become just another footnote on the organisation chart of life. He woke early from a patchy dream about homelessness, made himself a couple of slices of toast, and sat with a mug of strong coffee while he tried to persuade himself that things would be OK and could be worse. After all, he could be the unfortunate insect that the spider in the top corner of the window was systematically dismantling.

He arrived at work very early, disturbing a flock of squawk-gulls that rose up from the empty car park and then circled overhead like vultures.

'Is that a new suit?' Lisa asked, when she came in a few minutes later.

Steve shook his head. He didn't do new clothes; he just occasionally found items at the back of his wardrobe that he didn't think he'd ever seen before.

'Well it's covered in bird mess,' she said.

Steve went off to the toilets to clean his jacket, getting back to the office just as Darren sauntered in.

'Are you dressed for an interview or a funeral?' puzzled his colleague. 'Mind you, it'll probably come to much the same thing in the end.'

Steve gave a token pretence of a smile and went to get himself another coffee. He didn't really want a drink, but the 2p pieces were weighing him down and he needed something warm and comforting to ward off the screaming habdabs.

Why, he wondered tangentially, did they always scream? Why was it never the whispering habdabs?

After he'd burnt his tongue on the coffee, and before he knew it, the appointed hour was upon him. He made a nervous last minute visit to the toilet, and came back to find that all the others had gone in to the meeting room without him. Not only that, but yet again he'd splashed his trouser leg just before something important and would have to blame the wash-basin taps.

Everyone turned to look at him as he sidled into the meeting room and sat down at the back. There was a two minute silence, terminated by Darren growling 'Officer entering the room' as John Stokes came in, with Barry obediently at his heel.

'Right, let's get started,' said John.

'The sooner we finish, the sooner we're all finished,' chipped in Barry, with the suspicious joviality of planned spontaneity. He closed his mouth somewhat abruptly and sat down heavily.

John explained at some length how sales had gone into a sharp downcline recently, due to the lack of new products to sell, and how Senior Management were losing all faith in Barry's group's ability to develop anything successfully.

'You can't push a piece of string,' interjected Barry, so profoundly that it nearly took his own breath away. John gave him a funny look, and continued. About how they'd decided on the need to cut costs, and about how they needed to reduce the workforce, and how up to five jobs had to go in R&D. Steve's stomach started to tie itself into a knot that even the best boy scout would have been proud of. Why was it always R&D that got punished for these things: wasn't some of it to do with company culture? Such as the fact that they were slow to move with the times? If they moved at all, that is: Darren claimed that the Finance Department still used quills to do the accounts, in a racy combination of Latin and Norman French.

'I'll get Clare to fix me individual review meetings with each of you,' finished John. 'I'll try to do half of you tomorrow morning and half in the afternoon.'

There was an immediate clamour to volunteer for the morning session, in case places for survivors were first come, first saved. John, though, didn't have time to stay or to listen, as he had to attend an executive decision-making meeting, with biscuits.

Steve emerged from the meeting room blinking at the daylight, despite the fact that it was now as gloomy outside as it was metaphorically. His worst fears had just been confirmed. Five redundancies in R&D. That was a quarter of everyone.

Or it was all the people in R&D who reported to Barry, he suddenly thought. He didn't bother adding lots of exclamation marks, but he was thinking them.

Darren followed him out of the room, alongside Clare. 'If I'm to be executed, you do all promise to spend the rest of your lives moping about, wringing your hands and weeping, don't you?'

Steve missed Clare's answer, as the awful prospect of all that daytime television swam before his eyes.

'How are you?' Lisa asked him, catching up with him just before the office.

'I've had better lives. I'm hoping to come back as a duck next time. Or perhaps a tree.'

'Yeah,' said Darren, 'and John would probably come back as a waterfowl hunter or a lumberjack.'

None of the others seemed quite as concerned as Steve felt. But then, they didn't have families to support, they just had loud, wild plans about how they would spend their pay-offs and what great new jobs they would walk into. At his desk in the corner, behind all their turned backs, Steve was left to talk amongst himself.

He sat for a long time, looking at his brother's drawing of the young Mediterranean woman. For the first time, he suddenly realised that the object at her feet that he'd always taken to be a lucky horseshoe was in fact the frame of a broken hand mirror. It was strange what you saw when you took the time to look. He wrote himself a little note to remember to take the picture with him if he got marched off site, as it was one of his few tangible reminders of his dead sibling. As he put his pen down, he noticed that he had developed a small twitch in his right cheek to add to all his other stress symptoms. *And* it was now raining heavily.

He picked up his things, muttered to the others that he was going to work from home for the rest of the day, opened his umbrella, and left the building. Outside, he banged his head on the ladder that Jon and Neil had left across the doorway when they'd knocked off halfway through a job. The sound frightened away Sooty, the company cat, who had just been about to cross the path in front of him.

***

That night, a pyjama-clad Steve came into the bedroom from the direction of the bathroom weighing scales.

'I'm getting desperate about my weight,' he confessed. 'I only weigh myself now after I've been to the toilet.'

'No,' said Jackie. 'Desperation would be cutting your toenails first.'

She seemed to have hit a sudden raw nerve, and he slumped down on the edge of the bed, head in his hands.

'It's all too much,' he lamented. 'I'm fed up with being old and fat and stupid and useless.'

His wife squeezed his hand and gave him a soft, supportive smile. 'And bitter,' she added brightly.

***

He got in the next morning to find that Clare had pinned up a list of times for their one-to-one meetings with John-the-hatchet. Ten minutes had been allocated for each one, except for Steve's which was fifteen. Steve really, really hoped that that was a reflection only of the secretary's poor maths. The appointments had been made purely alphabetically, from Cathy Banfield and Ben Downe (yes, really) through to Simon Tennant and Bill Williams. Steve Oscroft's name had one-thirty-five written against it. For some reason, at three o'clock John was scheduled to meet with himself.

It made for a long morning and a lot of trips to the chocolate machine. Steve had long ago given up Lent for chocolate, and today he was making every effort to ensure there wouldn't be any lay-offs in the British confectionary industry. It also gave him a chance to stretch his legs, especially as something kept dragging him the long way round, via the interview room where John was meeting with a string of nervous subordinates and where the large glass window that faced the corridor was defying Steve to resist glancing in each time he went past.

The day went very, very slowly, but eventually one-thirty-three came and he stood up from his desk, stretched, and gave a nervous yawn.

'Right. This is it,' he said, as casually as a volunteer for Russian Roulette.

For the eighth time that day, he made the two minute walk to the interview room, but this time he knocked and entered. There was no-one there, but a small note on the bare table told him that John had only slipped out for a minute. He sat down, and then made the mistake of glancing round at the window behind him, where a line of faces had suddenly appeared in the corridor, pressed against the glass. He shooed them away with a gesture of his arm: their encouraging, sympathetic smiles had got him *really* scared. Everyone further up the alphabet had been behaving nicely towards him all morning, and it wasn't good. He had the horrible feeling that the session might develop into a battle of ideologies: something of the nature of John proposing to get rid of him, and him not wanting to go.

His boss's boss came into the room brandishing a wodge of papers and a vague asymmetrical smile. Then he sat down, and didn't say anything, the smile gradually fading as he read the top sheet of paper. The silence rose to a crescendo, and Steve made an urgent mental note to himself not to have a heart attack in the seconds before John spoke.

'Actually, I'm pleased to say that the situation is starting to turn itself around, thanks to advance interest in Sling, and I've managed to find a way to make the financials start to stack up.'

Oh good. Still wary.

'In fact, we've only got to lose one job now.' He paused slightly, to give Steve the chance to congratulate him.

It's me, isn't it?

'It's you, I'm afraid.'

Well, so much for having bothered to put on his lucky pants. Why was he somehow not surprised? He had already composed himself a little speech for the occasion, something along the lines of 'Well, guess what: I don't give a damn. And guess what also: I've flogged myself to bloody death here, but that's it – I'm not doing any more to help you. I'm going to do naff-all during my notice period, starting right now, and when the others find out, they'll be downing tools too.'

Instead he said 'OK'.

'Do you want to know why I picked you?'

No.

'Well, for a start, there's the little matter of Sling and the fact that it's late and still doesn't work properly. Then there was the SRT, there was your vandalised laptop, that dopey girl you recruited who only lasted one day –'

'You mean Lizzy Knowles?'

'– and the Beauchild business, Oh yes, and could I refer you back to the case of Searston versus Oscroft, 2004?'

Steve groaned. He should have known that his little fight with Darren over who could be first to use the new photocopier would come up again, sooner or later.

'And Randy from Beauchild e-mailed me the other day to say that you were the most uninspiring person he's ever had business dealings with. So I'm afraid I had no option really, you brought it upon yourself. I tried and I tried but I couldn't make a case to save you.'

Oh, I see how this works, thought Steve to himself, catching on faster than MRSA, *you tell me the bad news and then we spend the rest of the time justifying why you shouldn't feel guilty.*

It hurt. It really, truly hurt. At the very least, he'd wanted to be there at the end of the project, to see how it all turned out. He didn't want it to be another experience like The World At War, when he'd sat through over twenty episodes but missed the last one and never found out who'd won.

'I don't want to go anywhere else. I want to stay here, with people who don't hate me. Or at least where I know which ones hate me. Please will you reconsider and give me another chance? Please.'

'Well, there might be an opportunity to work for Anthony Archer, but that's it.'

'Hmm.' That was a second bit-of-a-shock, and Steve was determined to be as non-committal as possible while he thought about it. Work for Anthony Archer? Doing what? Fetching him drinks from the pub across the road? Polishing his ego? Watching him womanise?

'No thanks,' he said dryly, as his determination shattered into a thousand not-very-shiny fragments. He'd made his mind up. He'd take the redundancy and move on to pastures new[1]. If nothing else, it meant that he wouldn't have to see or work with

---

[1] Why is it always pastures new, not new pastures? We're not French, for goodness sake.

Jon and Neil, or Cathy Banfield, ever again. Or Psycho Pat or Acrid Annie or Death Nell.

'OK then,' said John, not pressing the point. 'Now, we don't have much of a budget for your leaving party, so we'll combine it with tomorrow night's global launch party, which will now just be a disco without the meal by the way. Enjoy!'

And with that he ushered Steve out of the room and into the meeting room next door, where most of his colleagues were gathered.

'Steve's leaving us I'm afraid,' said John.

There was a sudden very loud silence, into which Steve happened to notice that nobody inserted the words 'If Steve goes, so do I.'

Nobody said anything very much at all, in fact, although once most of the others had filed out of the door back to their desks Barry made a point of coming over to where Steve was standing in hurt embarrassment.

'I'm really sorry, Steve. On a personal level especially. I mean, you and Jane are like family to me.'

Steve nodded numbly, his mind in a slow whirl. Despite all the rumours and warning signs, this unexpected sudden blow had come as quite a blow, and had been very sudden and, er, unexpected. Everything he'd worked so hard for, over nearly sixteen years, had been suddenly crushed. Now all he had to look forward to were a lonely old age, incontinence and death, which were as it happened the three things that someone had written up as action points for him on the office whiteboard, in Darren's handwriting.

***

All in all, Jackie took the news OK when he got home. She accepted that they would have to scrimp and save and agreed that the girls would only get an ice cream if they could find one on the pavement, that sort of thing.

'We'll cope,' she said, going off to cry.

Breaking the news to his mother on the telephone was less easy, because she just wouldn't listen. In fact to begin with she couldn't listen, because of the all the noise in the background.

'Will you turn that thing off,' she screamed, more down the telephone than to whoever was with her.

The sound of gruff cursing was followed by the sound of quiet.

'She's the worst girl they've sent yet,' moaned his mother.

'Are you sure it's a girl?' asked Steve.

'It's wearing an earring, so it must be a girl,' pronounced Steve's mother, who hadn't entirely moved with the times.

'I've got something to tell you,' Steve began. He hoped her heart was healthy enough to take it.

'Yes, and I've got some things to tell you, too,' said his mother, launching into a list of her aches and pains, the things about Mrs Collins that most annoyed her, the reasons why the TV licence wasn't worth renewing, and the full details of the indignities she'd had to endure during her doctor's last home visit.

'Oh, and he said I have a weak heart,' she added with a triumphant flourish.

'I've been made redundant,' Steve said quietly, when he could get a word in.

There was a three seconds silence, a brief acknowledging 'tut', a few words of wisdom and hackneyed advice, and then a return to the subject of people who made her life insufferable. It was clear that Steve had had all the help and support he was going to get. He didn't know how he was going to cope with the next few weeks, yet apparently it was nothing that a bit of deep breathing wouldn't sort out.

When he'd got his mother off the phone he went to pour himself a large sherry. He didn't normally touch the stuff, but as today surely qualified as momentous, he did feel at least a bit entitled.

He thought back to other memorable days. Like the day he sat the entrance exam for the local private school at the age of eleven and a bit. The exam hadn't seemed too bad, though he irredeemably failed, but he keenly remembered the line of anxious parents waiting to meet them all at the school gates afterwards. Many of them had had bad news that they'd been keeping from their offspring until the exam was over: a grandparent ill here; a pet diagnosed with something terminal there; a divorce in the offing. It had been the afternoon that Steve had learnt within the space of ninety seconds that his grandfather had died the month before, that his father was losing his job, and that Santa Claus didn't exist.

And then there was the day at school that he lost his watch and his first girlfriend within the space of two hours. Or the time that he demolished his father-in-law's gatepost with his car. Or the time he parked on their cat. Or the evening he passed Jackie's mother the wrong medicine. Kink after kink in the twisted old hosepipe of life. All so many years ago, yet as vivid now as then. It's funny what sticks in your mind.

And now here he was, redundant. On the scrap heap, after a career about as successful as a butane-powered fire extinguisher. He sighed the sighiest sigh he had ever sighed. He was just so weary. Weary of having to juggle all the pressures on him. Weary of trying to fit three days' work into every day. Weary of feeling guilty for not being able to get everything done. Weary of not being Superman.

About the only consolation was the fact that he didn't live in Doltburn or Wormhouses.

Still, at least having so much free time would give him a chance to take up some new hobbies and interests, such as keeping warm, eating leftovers, and trying to eke out a daily budget of two pounds thirty six.

***

It's fair to say that Steve's colleagues generally had other things than his redundancy on their minds the next morning, as it was the day of the Sling launch party. Everywhere there was the buzz of excited chatter: they'd not had a big celebration since the Christmas party three weeks ago. Two or three people did ask Steve how he was, but replies starting with 'Not very good actually...' seemed to cause eyes to glaze over with immediate disinterest before he could tell anyone of all his troubles. Most of his day was thus spent alone in morbid contemplation. He'd had some great moments at SLSL over the years, but as he'd been there for the best part of two decades, he calculated that his ratio of great moments to not-so-great moments was less than one part per million, which was rather depressing.

Of course, he would at least be taking a wealth of experience with him from his time there, plus technical knowledge and skills, leadership qualities and personal growth. And then there was the enrichment and enlightenment from myriad training sessions and seminars; mind you, when he thought about it, all he could really remember was the odd joke and the occasional audience-participation humiliation.

Since Darren referred to him all day as being the guest of honour, he reluctantly decided that he'd better attend the evening 'celebrations', at least for an hour or so. Some of the others had gone straight into town to start drinking before the 'do', but Steve went home first to get ready (change his shirt) and to say goodnight to the girls.

'Will Prod be playing the music?' asked Number One daughter.

'I don't think so. No-one at work's ever heard of him; he's a one hit wonder.'

'Seven, actually,' sniffed Natalie.

'Then he's going to be too expensive for us, and anyway, I think it's a disco.'

'Can Osmarelda go with you?' asked Number Two.

'Yes if she's good and stays in the car.'

Osmarelda promised that she would be, and five minutes later Steve and she were setting off for an evening that was to produce a couple of little surprises. It started ordinarily enough, with Steve's journey – and life – almost being terminated at a couple of points by the hot-heads on the road. The world's not short of idiots, especially on Friday and Saturday nights.

The town centre car park was also predictably expensive, and although Steve fed it all of his small change and much of his large change, the ticket machine was still hungrily eating its way through his entire month's pay when Darren strolled up from where he'd just parked.

'Have you heard?' he said, pointing to where it said that charges didn't apply after 6 p.m., 'that there's going to be a new project at work, Sling 2?'

Steve was crestfallen. He should have been leading that, or at least be a valued member of the development team, but it was not to be. It was the final indignity.

They walked in silence to the hotel where the launch party was to take place. Even though the disco shouldn't yet have started, it had. The spotty little DJ – who looked about fifteen – had presumably been too excited to wait. But although it might have started, it was hardly in full swing: all the people there so far were sitting in a different room. That wasn't exactly a surprise, considering that the DJ didn't seem to have anything that wasn't by Prod, but what came next was one of the bigger surprises of Steve's life, or at least his evening.

'Did you know,' whispered Lisa as she passed Steve a diet lemonade at the bar, 'that Darren tried to convince John and Barry not to let you go?'

No, he didn't know.

'He tried over and over again to persuade them to get rid of him, not you.'

Steve was genuinely shocked. Despite working with Darren for years, he would never have expected that of him. Even I'm rather taken aback.

'Why?' asked Steve, trying not to think about the fact that John must clearly have been adamant he had to go.

'He thought he stood much more chance than you of finding something else,' said Lisa. 'And he doesn't have children to support. Or a wife. Or a girlfriend.'

Although bits of that seemed a little pointed, there was no mistaking her admiration for Darren's attempted self-sacrifice.

This was all disconcerting on many levels, and Steve was just trying to decide what to make of Lisa's reference to him struggling to find work when the other bomb-shell struck.

'What do you think of my brother's music?' asked Simon, on his way to the toilets to dispose of his first two pints of lager.

Now Simon's private life had always been a bit of a mystery to Steve, and to be quite honest he didn't remember knowing that he even had a brother, let alone a thin spotty little one with no musical taste.

'It's, er, interesting,' he said, borrowing his wife's Christmas present trick.

'Yeah, one day I'll bring him along in person,' Simon promised.

'What?' said Steve, in inelegant surprise.

'Prod,' said Simon. 'He's my younger brother[1].'

Although this was news to Steve, it clearly wasn't to Lisa, who was giving him a sympathetic smile.

'Yes,' went on Simon, 'I've spent most of my weekends this year travelling round the country, helping at his gigs.'

Steve's mouth was in goldfish mode, so his colleague carried on. 'He's made it really big this year.'

Ah, Steve did know that, because Natalie kept telling him.

'Anyway,' Simon concluded, 'I'll have to bring him along some time.'

Steve grimaced slightly. *He* didn't have any plans to bring *his* brother along some time.

'I wish *I* was famous,' breathed Clare, who had been listening to their conversation. The closest she'd ever come to world acclaim was when she'd once featured in a short article in the SLSL in-house magazine, 'Makes Sense'. True, they'd got her name wrong, made up quotes she'd never said, messed up her job title and been cringingly patronising, but hey, that was fame for you. It was better than being on life's discard pile like Steve was.

---

[1] Oh. Did I forget to mention that?

Grateful that he was stone cold sober so that he could think – but irritated by the thumping beat of '*Wossit and Why?*' from the next room so that he couldn't think straight – Steve tried to re-evaluate everything he knew about Darren and Simon. These revelations would take days to get his head round properly, but there was no time like the present to get started and so it was that he spent the rest of the evening at the quietest corner table that he could find, thinking and introverting. The result, of course, was that he wasn't much in the way of company that evening, guest of honour or not. Which was nothing really new: parties weren't for him, any more than the glory of involvement in Sling 2 would be. No, his was the lot of the man who's fallen off the carousel of consequence and is waiting to be crushed by the juggernaut of worthlessness. Or something like that. It was perhaps all summed up for him at the end of the evening, when he returned to his car to find that even Osmarelda had an indifferent look in her one eye which suggested that she couldn't really care less whether he came back or not.

***

Steve's three month notice period passed in a blur. Partly that was because John Stokes had agreed to reduce it to one month, with the rest as gardening leave, provided that Steve was willing to give his absolute utmost best to selling Sling at a string of meetings and mini trade shows that Marketing had set up for the last week in April. And partly it was because Steve had agreed to take the gardening leave, provided that he didn't actually have to do any gardening. He didn't much fancy spending the beginning of the rest of his life tending his vitamin-deficient roses. Or dealing with that blasted ivy.

His last proper day in the office was Friday 20th of April. No-one made a fuss, no-one made a speech, and no-one gave him a leaving present, except for a scrawled cheque for the modest sum of money raised in a hasty office whip-round.

'You could get something nice for the garden,' suggested Barry as he handed it over just before lunch.

Like a small watering can and a few plant labels, according to Steve's quick calculations.

Lunch was a quiet affair in the canteen with Darren and Simon – a dog's breakfast followed by soggy lemon hydrosponge – and then it was time to go round the site for a series of brief, embarrassed goodbyes. Steve's final afternoon at SLSL was rounded off by a three hour meeting till six o'clock with some members of the Sales and Marketing Departments who were determined that he was suitably briefed for his final week of customer meetings. It was vital that all opportunities were seized to recoup some of the R&D investment and to make the new sensor a success. They would even have attended the trade shows themselves if they hadn't booked themselves on to a week's team-building and golf.

***

Day One of Steve's UK sales tour – Monday – had been set up with two customer meetings in Leeds in the morning and three hours manning a sales stand at a nearby conference on home bread-making in the afternoon. Rather than spending the week wearing out what was left of the Mundane, he'd decided to do the whole thing by train and taxi in an effort to avoid the stress of driving and to instead give himself the stress of updating his CV and composing the first of his many job applications while he travelled. It was a plan that might have worked were it not for Sharon and Louise, the two young women sitting behind him on the first train, who talked on and on, without drawing breath it seemed to Steve, about Maz and how she'd been spending an awful lot of time with Ben ever since that big rock concert last year and about how it had meant that she never had time to go shopping with them at weekends any more which was a pain because now they had to go as a twosome not a threesome and that meant there was no-one to stay outside with the bags when two of them went into the cubicles together to try things on which was probably why finding things to wear on their Saturday nights round town was getting harder and harder which was the real reason that Louise had split that dress the other night when she bent over to snog that guy who looked like he worked out three times a day, and although they weren't talking particularly loudly, several of the intimate details were such that Steve eventually suddenly realised that he'd been staring at the same thing on his laptop screen for the past sixty miles. Which was particularly unfortunate, as he was supposed to be changing trains after fifty.

Despite that, he still reached Leeds more or less on schedule, although there was a slight hiatus when the man at the station wouldn't let him through the barrier because the man on the train had punched a hole through the date on his ticket. As his first meeting was within walking distance of the station, he decided to eschew the taxi rank and instead set off on foot, on a bearing within a hundred and seventy-five degrees of the correct one.

No-one ever asked him for directions at home. Yet within two minutes of being in Leeds, and despite there being several hundred locals around, all of who looked friendly and helpful enough – and not lost - he'd been asked twice. No, he didn't know where, or indeed what, Briggate was. And no, he didn't know how to get to Boar Lane. Oh, except that he was standing in it now, he noticed as he belatedly glanced up at the street name.

His phone rang at that moment, and upon pressing the little green button he had the pleasure of Simon's tele-presence for a few minutes while he walked with quickening pace and heightening concern in the wrong direction and while Simon regaled him with a long tale of recent sensor test results woe and then wished him good luck with the potential customers.

Despite his half hour delay in finding the first set of offices, both meetings went quite well, and Steve was reasonably optimistic that there was real interest and potential sales there. The afternoon session was a waste of time though, the home bread-making industry having a predictable lack of appetite for high performance sensors, although Steve did learn quite a bit about the best way of kneading his leavening agents. By four o'clock he was done, however, and ready for his train journey to the next thoughtfully-planned port of call on his itinerary, Plymouth.

When he got there, he found the hotel that they'd booked him disappointing, frankly. His room was dingy and bare. In fact, it looked as if the previous occupant had helped themselves to the complimentary tea and coffee, complimentary soap, complimentary shampoo, and the complimentary pen and towels and pillows and desk lamp and chair. And the bed and the door. And there was no call for all the laughter behind the reception desk when the juveniles working there realised that he'd been up to room 427, which was being redecorated, when he should have been in 247. What sort of customer service was it to whisper a loud 'senile'?

'I told you he wasn't a twenty-four seven kind of guy,' said their leader while Steve umm'd and ahh'd about whether a request to see the manager would produce somebody older than a school-leaver. When he'd been their age, hotel staff had addressed you as 'Sir', not as 'Mate'. Or 'Grandad'. *And* 247 had been a number, not a lifestyle.

He decided not to fight against unequal odds, and lumbered off to the lift once more. The rest of the week was going to involve some long days and a lot of travelling (Newcastle on Wednesday, London on Thursday and Glasgow on Friday), so he decided to hit the sack and try to get some sleep. He might even have succeeded had he not spent a few minutes peering out at the clear, star-spangled night sky and then a few hours lying awake wondering why stars are spherical instead of star-shaped.

As a result of his greater than usual lack of sleep, most of the next day was a hazy confusion for Steve, and by the time he reached Newcastle he was utterly unable to recall whether the people he'd met in Plymouth had said they were interested in signing contracts or doing further tests or whether they'd just discussed the weather. As he'd not managed to take legible notes, his end of week report to Barry was going to have to gloss over Tuesday.

As it happened, Wednesday and Thursday also sped past in a blur, and before he knew it he found himself on the train north to Glasgow. He'd planned to work further on his CV, but he was running out of plausible things to say, and in any case he'd exhausted his small remaining stocks of energy and enthusiasm.

He went to get himself a copy of the on-board magazine from the end of the carriage, but despite the undoubted fascination of the article that said that nanotechnology was apparently the next big thing, he soon found himself staring into space. The next day was reasonably planned out, and straightforward provided that he could find the name of the trade show venue, but the days beyond were an alarming unknown. With his narrow comfort zones, he'd been known to work himself into an anxiety attack at a change of brand of toothpaste: the idea of having to find a new job was so far off the scale that he couldn't even imagine which symptom to have first. Panic, palpitations, depression, psychosis, feelings of uselessness, insomnia: there were lots to choose from, and he'd run through half a gamut of emotions – missing out all the jolly ones – when he realised that he still had some more work to do on his sales message for the following day. The rest of the way to Scotland was spent in silent practice interspersed with gloomy contemplation.

It was mid-evening when he reached the hotel. Another night, another value-for-money booking: Barry had clearly been determined not to see Steve off in too over-lavish a style. The room offered him a choice of which foot to have flat on the floor, and as usual, although he was trusting them with his clothes, his laptop, and to some extent his life, they didn't even trust him with their coat hangers. The only thing in the minibar was a small packet of potato flavoured crisps, price three pounds. Worst of all, it was clear that the room next door was much nicer, as he could hear from the details that its occupant loudly related on her mobile phone to her husband, for an hour.

Despite the budget surroundings, Steve did get a good night's sleep, once his neighbour had finally finished itemising the contents of her room. The trade show also went well, if a trifle hectically. On a couple of occasions there was even a small queue at SLSL's stand, waiting to talk to him. It almost felt as if he wasn't a failure.

Almost. Reality reasserted itself when he discovered that the blue spot on his badge meant that he was entitled to pay for his own food, and the intense nature of the day only left him ten minutes for a hasty lunch of a couple of living-dangerously crab sandwiches, washed down with the bit of the mineral water that he hadn't spilt.

***

By four o'clock on that Friday afternoon, his final contribution to the technical support of the Sling launch programme was complete, and with it his sixteen or so stressful years of employment at SLSL. All that was left was the train journey home to an uncertain and impoverished future. He made his way back to Central station, boarded a waiting Euston train, and sinking into an empty seat opened his laptop for the last time. Facing him, a few seats away, a smartly dressed businessman was reading one of the free newspapers that Steve had spurned but which was now of sudden fantastic interest. From where he sat, he could see four separate headlines, three of them about gangs of children attacking, robbing or killing law-abiding citizens and one of them about a dog with an A-level in applied psychology. What upset Steve the most, and seemed bitterly unfair, was that when he was a child he'd been afraid of adults, and now that he was grown up he was frightened of the groups of kids who hung around on the street corner. His whole life, he'd been on the losing side. He sometimes wished that he could live in the late fifties or the early sixties, back in the days before civilization had unravelled and society had broken down; when the sun had always shone - albeit mostly in black and white - and people had had manners instead of rights. Pleasures were simpler then, it was true, but so much better for that, he was sure. In all honesty, most things had probably been better then, really, except of course for the toilet paper.

His philosophical musings were interrupted by the discordant row that indicated he'd had a text message on his mobile. It took a bit of deciphering, as it was written in a sub-dialect of gibberish, but it seemed to be reminding him that he had to return his identification pass to the thuggish chief security guard, Timothy Prim. Steve didn't believe in all these 'txt' message desecrations of the English language. His own messages always used proper spellings, grammar and punctuation, complete with capital letters where required and the occasional Latin quotation, et cetera. In fact, he was probably the only person in the country who still maintained proper standards, ending his text messages with 'Yours sincerely' or 'Yours faithfully', as appropriate. Only rarely would he admit to himself that it did take an awfully long time to communicate with anyone.

By now the train was belting through the Scottish lowlands towards the fast-approaching hills, and as the kids would have finished their tea he decided it would be a good time to ring home. Chloe answered it with a cheery burp, and immediately launched into a long story about how having a cute puppy had made her friend Isobel's Dad much less stressed, but just as it was coming to its exciting conclusion she broke off to ask him what animals he'd seen in Squatland. When he couldn't think of any, she started to tell him a story about ants in the bread bin, but he managed to persuade her to curtail it a bit so that he could talk to the others. There was a long silence, followed by Chloe's voice again.

'I'm sorry, Osmarelda doesn't want to talk to you right now.'

'Well could I talk to Natty, please?'

There was another silence, a distant squabble, and the sound of the phone being dropped.

'Hello,' said Natalie.

'Have you had a good day?'

As a matter of fact, she had. She'd (once again) finally chosen what she wanted to do for a living, by deciding that she now wanted to be a cheese lender when she grew up.

'That's good,' nodded Steve vigorously. Anything that didn't involve working for Barry was to be encouraged.

'Who will your customers be?'

'Hello.' It was Jackie; Natalie had already run off to finish a 'Get Well Soon' card for Tom that she'd been working on.

'Yes,' said Steve. 'I mean, hello.' He was surprised to find that unemployment had addled his brain quite so quickly.

'How's freedom?'

Steve thought more carefully before he replied this time. Freedom. Free. Dom. Freedom wasn't too bad. It tasted funny, but he might get to like it. He reassured Jackie that he was ready for a rest and then they chatted about trivia for ten minutes until his battery went flat.

He closed his laptop, untouched. Someone was going to come and collect it on Monday anyway, and his best time at Minesweeper would have to stand. He went to get himself a bacon omelette and a half bottle of wine from the onboard shop a.k.a. buffet, and before he knew it the combination of those and the phone conversation with his loved ones was actually starting to make a difference. It was a beautiful evening of bare trees lit up against a dark sky, and Steve knew deep down inside that there would always be another dawn and, perhaps, new opportunities. Maybe fate had just rescued him from the rut he'd been in, from his treadmill.

He poured some more wine out. He was mixing metaphors faster than a bull in a china teapot.

He poured some of the wine in. When he stopped to think about it, he'd been lucky in all the major things in life, if unlucky in most of the minor ones. Project Sling might not have been his finest hour – OK, it had been a shambles – but he had three fine ladies, which counted for far more.

Calmer than he could remember having been in a long time, he stretched himself out and nursed his drink. Outside, the colours of the evening sky were more beautiful even than before, and the most fantastic light was picking out every fold in the rugged fells around the Lune Gorge. And that, really, is the message of this book. When all's said and done, being amongst the hills when the evening light is on them truly is what life's all about.

Or if it isn't, then the author's wasted a lot of his time trudging slowly up stony paths and across rain-lashed peat bogs.

The End

If you enjoyed reading this book, why not treat yourself and buy another copy?

Or, indeed, several?

Printed in Great Britain
by Amazon